SEVERED RELATIONS

By

REBECCA FORSTER

Severed Relations
Copyright © Rebecca Forster, 2016
All rights reserved

Cover Design: Hadleigh O. Charles

This is a work of fiction. All characters and events are purely the product of the author's imagination. Any license that has been taken is for the tone of the story and the enjoyment of the reader.

For my Brother, Mike Forster

My cheerleader, favorite phone call,
sometimes California cocktail companion

ACKNOWLEDGMENTS

My incredible publishing team:

Jenny Jensen, the most awesome indie editor. Thank you for making me work so hard.

Stef McDaid, a formatting artist who makes my books beautiful.

Hadleigh O. Charles whose artistic talents create covers that capture the essence of my books.

Robin Blakely of Creative Center of America for guiding my career for so many years.

Bruce Raterink whose eyes are probably ready to fall out of his head from reading this book so many times.

Glenn Gallo, my fantastic Twitter friend who waves me on to the finish line with such good humor all the way from Florida.

Nancy Miller, my gorgeous, smart, patient and kind friend with an eagle eye.

My tennis buddies who let me whack a ball around a few hours a week to clear my head.

As always, my wise mom, who knows that hot wings, a Margarita and a good laugh are the best medicine.

Bless you and yours
As well as the cottage you live in.
May the roof overhead be well thatched
And those inside be well matched.

Irish Blessing

All happy families resemble one another,
each unhappy family is unhappy in its own way.

Leo Tolstoy

CHAPTER 1

DAY 1 – MORNING

It was late – or early – depending on one's point of view. Neither Mort, the short redheaded guy, nor the man so unremarkable that Mort had christened him Medium Man, cared about the hour. For them it was just time to go to work.

While they drove, they shot the shit about cars and chicks, the gates, the guard, the price of shoes and booze, and getting into the house. Mort laughed hard and quick and said they would have to quit the business the day they couldn't get in a house. When Medium Man laughed, he huffed and puffed and wiggled like he had to hit the john. Even when he wasn't laughing, Medium Man itched and twitched. But he was reliable and good at his job so Mort didn't mind so much.

They drove the length of Wilshire Boulevard, deserted this time of night, found the side street that would take them to another side street and yet another that would eventually get them where they were going. Mort said getting to this place was like driving through a damn crop circle in the middle of L.A. Medium Man didn't know what that was, and Mort didn't feel like explaining, so

1

they stopped talking until Mort finally pulled over. He parked the car at the curb between two houses. Anyone who looked at it would assume the car belonged to a kid home from college, a maid, or was just the fourth-car-out in the land of three car garages.

Mort and Medium Man walked the wide streets, admiring the houses. Mort put his hands in his pocket and kicked at a pebble. Medium Man yawned. They acted as if they belonged, but if anyone bought that then Mort had a bridge for them. Finally, Mort put his arm out. Medium Man stopped, wiped the back of his hand across his nose, and asked:

"This it?"

"Yep," Mort said and took stock of the property.

One light burned in the back of the impressive Tudor with its peaked roof and leaded windows. In front, the outdoor fixtures were strategically placed for beauty, not safety. The flowerbeds pooled with a soft light that didn't reach the ridiculous sweep of lawn on which they stood. The front door was illuminated but brick arches shadowed the entrance. The houses on either side were set back on lots that were just as big as this one. Between them, beautiful old trees and flowering foliage created a natural sound barrier and screen.

Wordlessly they walked up the driveway, Medium Man cutting off to the side of the house and Mort to the shadows of the entry arches. When Medium Man came around again, Mort tended to the door.

A jab. A touch. A flick. A click and it was done.

Inside, they got the lay of the land. Mort had seen better but not by much. Medium Man, though, stood in the foyer with his mouth hanging open. He looked at the grand staircase, the shiny marble floor in the entry, and the hardwood floors beyond that. He looked at the entry table and all the silver-framed pictures on top of it. Tears welled in his eyes when he saw the picture of a woman caught in a moment of happy surprise. She was so beautiful. Medium Man wished he had a picture of someone like that to put in a frame. He was picking it up, thinking to take it with him, when Mort hissed:

"Don't touch nothin'."

Medium Man wiped the frame clean with his shirt, put it down, and circled back to Mort like a dog returning to the place where the scent was strong. They went up the stairs, Mort first. There wasn't a creak and that impressed Mort. The place was quality all the way.

Upstairs, there were five doors as expected. Three were closed, two ajar. He looked into the first room, stepped back and nodded to Medium Man who reached into his pocket for the gun. It was heavier than the knife he preferred, but Mort said they were there to do a job and not make a statement. Medium Man didn't quite understand that since he never said anything at work. Still, he never argued with Mort so he held the gun and waited for the signal.

When he got it, Medium Man went into the first room and bee-lined for the brass studio bed. A couch by day, the frilly cover was now folded neatly at the foot of the mattress. The woman in it made little sighing sounds while she dreamed. At first Medium Man's heart sank. She looked pretty and that was too bad. He hated hurting pretty things. When he got a little closer, though, he saw that she wasn't all that pretty so it was okay.

His footfall wasn't even a whisper on the plush carpet,

yet as he raised the gun the woman threw back the covers and bolted out of bed. Shorter and stockier than he had imagined her to be, Medium Man was shocked as she lunged for her phone on the night table. He let out a yelp, threw out his arm, and knocked her back. She tumbled to the floor only to roll and push off again. This time, she lowered her head and ran straight for Medium Man. Her skull caught him hard under the ribs.

He doubled over, grunting, the breath pushed out of him. He went down clutching his stomach. The gun dropped out of his hand and fell to the floor. He could feel it against his knee but had no time to grab it up because the woman was everywhere: hands and teeth, arms and knees, hair flying, fighting silently like she was mute, fighting hard like she was an animal. She reached for his face and her nails grazed his cheek. Those nails were short so she didn't draw blood. Her nightdress was long and she tangled in it as she tried to scramble over him. He was mad that she was causing such trouble; he was repulsed by her big breasts, her plump butt, and her woman smell. Still, he was determined not to let her get the best of him so he kept pulling at her. Her foot caught his thigh and she tried to use it for leverage, but she got no traction. In fact, she got nowhere at all because Mort was there.

Yes, there he was, in the room filled with muffled grunts and desperate breathing. He grabbed the woman's arms and twisted her wrists one over the other, flipping her onto her back. Medium Man scampered up at the same time, swiping up the gun just as Mort knelt down hard on the woman's crossed arms.

"I coulda–" Medium Man began, but Mort shot him a

look so he shut up.

The woman was gurgling like she was trying to say something, but her lips weren't working. Medium Man watched Mort, the master, as he looked into the woman's wild, terrified eyes. He put one hand on top of her head, and said:

"Hush now."

The woman trembled and then stopped struggling. That's when Medium Man swooped down, put the muzzle against her temple, and pulled the trigger. In the same instant, Mort moved his hand. The small caliber bullet made a clean exit on the other side of her skull. It brought with it bits of her brain and some bone and a spray of blood.

Mort brushed at the blood spray on his shirt, but it was only a reflex. He knew that you never got all the blood out of anything so it was useless to try to wipe it away. That was too bad since he was especially partial to this shirt. All in all, though, the job went okay. He would have preferred it went perfect, but he blamed himself for not anticipating this woman's reaction and preparing for it.

She was trained to listen for the slightest noise: a call, a moan, a cry in the night. It was her job to protect and she had tried as hard as she could to do it well. Mort admired that in the same way he admired Medium Man for doing his. He would tell that to Medium Man when they were in the car. It wasn't easy to do the kind of work they did. Now they were finished. It was time to go. Yet when he looked at his *compadre* he saw that something was amiss. Medium Man was looking past him, so Mort turned his head to see what had caught the guy's attention. All he saw was a flash of color like you see when someone is running away to hide.

Before he could do anything, Medium Man was out the door, his beloved knife in hand. Mort hung his head for a second and then picked up the gun his partner had dropped. He pocketed the piece and took a second look at the dead woman. If she were alive he would have apologized. He would have told her this wasn't part of the plan. He would have explained that there was no stopping Medium Man once he got the fever.

That was a pity.

Not a crying shame.

Just a pity.

Chapter 2

Murder behind the gates of Fremont Place was unheard of. A triple homicide, two of the victims children, in the home of a wealthy, young attorney was downright bizarre, and it was Finn O'Brien's bad luck that it was his first call since reporting to Wilshire Division. It was the kind of call that would put his heart crossways, as his mother would say. He would have agreed with her except his Irish heart had been crossways for years already – ever since Alexander died – and he had learned to live with it. He doubted what he found in Fremont Place could do more damage.

Finn made a right off Wilshire Boulevard, drove a hundred feet to the guardhouse and stopped at the waste-of-money fancy iron gates stuck into the high stone walls. Inside the shack, a kid barely out of his teens slumped over the desk. He was dressed in an ill-fitting, puke-beige, polyester shirt with an official looking patch on the shoulder.

When the kid realized someone was waiting on him, he swung his head and eyed the dark car and the man wearing a leather jacket and aviator sunglasses. It took a minute, but eventually he figured out who Finn was and dragged himself off his chair. He stood in the doorway of the faux house, arms hanging, his face so long he would have asphalt burns on his chin by the time his shift ended. Finn showed his badge and then started the conversation while he slipped it back in his pocket.

"Been here long, have you?"

"Since midnight."

"Good boy to hang in." Finn swung his head in sympathy. "Tough times. I know how it is. Very rough for you, don't let anyone tell you different."

A little sympathy was all it took for the kid's mouth to run away with him. He stepped down, lowered his voice, and grabbed onto Finn's open window.

"The only people that came through belonged here. I logged every single car and called up to the houses to confirm visitors. I swear I did. Nobody walked through. I would have done something if somebody tried to walk through. I have a good sense for stuff. If somebody tried to come in who shouldn't have been here, I would have known. If they had tried to talk their way in, I wouldn't have let them. I would have called someone... I would have called... I..."

Finn winced as he listened to the boy. He had made those same declarations to anyone who would listen after his brother's death. If he had only known, Finn swore, he would have done heroic things. But he hadn't known because Finn had been seventeen and full of *hisself* as his mother told anyone who would listen. That day he was behind the bleachers, so lost in the deep wet kisses of a cheerleader that he forgot to pick the little boy up from school. The next time Finn saw Alexander he was in a coffin, dressed in a stiff shirt and dark suit bought especially for the occasion of his burial. Still, if he had known what was going to happen, Finn swore that he would have been brave and he would have saved Alexander – or died trying. Finn's father had nodded as if he knew that to be true, his mother had held her oldest son to her and said she believed the same. It was bull but people were kind all those years ago, so Finn was kind now.

"There's no stopping the devil from his rounds. There's nothing you could have done," he said. "And if there had been, I know you would have done it. I can tell you're a brave sort by looking at you."

With that, the young man actually focused on Finn and the detective saw that he had eyes the color of caramel and a heart that was just as soft. He wouldn't have known a liar if he saw one. Finn lifted the edge of his lips and gave him the slightest nod. The boy's chest caved with relief. His relief proved Finn right; the boy didn't know a liar when he saw one.

"We're going to be needing to talk to you, so don't go upsetting yourself when someone calls. It will probably be me; might be my partner. Can't give you a name on that yet, but they'll identify themselves as working with Detective O'Brien. You being in law enforcement yourself, you know how an investigation goes. We'll want to be thorough. You understand?"

The kid nodded, and licked his lips, and nodded some more. He looked like a bobble-head doll.

"Rest up when you get home," Finn went on. "Calm yourself. Don't think too hard about what happened last night. Sometimes you remember more things when you don't think too hard."

"Yeah, okay. Okay." The young man swallowed hard.

Color was coming back to his cheeks, but it wasn't the right color for a healthy person. He straightened up. His voice was more measured when he said:

"The last car came in at one-thirteen. By the book."

"Good man." Finn handed him a card. "Hang on to that log of yours and give it over to your supervisor, not your replacement. If you think of anything call me. If you just find yourself needing someone to talk to, I can manage some time for that too."

If the boy answered, Finn didn't hear him. The detective's eyes were on the gate. The boy with the caramel eyes now knew what was what, and they both had to get on with this terrible day. The kid stepped back, punched whatever button raised the gate, and by the time the arm lowered again he was slumped back in his chair. Now he was holding tight to the card with the name Finn O'Brien, Detective printed neatly under the logo of the LAPD.

As Finn drove on, he took note of his surroundings in the same way a boyo at the pub might admire a beautiful girl who was out of his league. Fremont Place was an impressive enclave: wide streets, big, beautiful houses, set backs the size of small parks, and garages bigger than most people's apartments. These stately homes were built of brick and stucco, leaded windows faced tree-lined streets, and inside the walls were crafted of real lathe and plaster. New money owned them, but old money had built them in the thirties. There were two elite schools and a tennis club within the boundaries.

Just beyond the wall surrounding Fremont Place, the real world was a mash-up. Wilshire high rises, bustling during the day, were deserted after seven. A few blocks over were neighborhoods that had no names where people of color owned houses with bars on the windows. A little further to the east was downtown Los Angeles. Hollywood spread north into the hills. Koreatown, Little Tokyo, and Chinatown were all within spitting distance. Fremont Place was a suburb held hostage in the heart of a big, ugly city and it just got a reminder of that in spades.

When he arrived at his destination, Finn parked his car behind a black and white and two panel vans. There were two more black and whites parked a half a block down. A uniformed officer watched the perimeter of the house while one stood on the porch, eyes forward.

Finn took note of the time and of the well-kept women huddled together in the street. They swayed like tall grass every time a whispered speculation or murmur of disbelief passed from one to the other. When Alexander was killed the women came to Finn's mother, too. They had casseroles and arms to wrap around her while the men lamented the horrible crime over their whiskey. These women would not bring casseroles to whoever was inside and there was no doubt someone was in the house from the looks of the Jaguar in the driveway. The car was bronze-colored, top-of-the-line, and new. The trunk yawned. There was a suitcase still inside and two on the ground. One had burst open, and the contents had spilled over the concrete and brick. A wrought-iron gate stood open in front of the car and past that, deep into the property and hardly visible from where Finn stood, was a large garage. The folks of Fremont Place seemed to be fond of fancy, useless gates.

When Finn got out of his car, it was a lady with red hair who saw him first. She did a double take, touched the woman next to her, and said something. That woman looked at Finn and then another and another. It had been that way since he was thirteen and puberty ambushed his childhood. Overnight he had become a strapping man with a swagger. Of course, that was God's doing and not his. Kicking a soccer ball half his life had made him quick and graceful on the run but the swagger left no doubt he was not meant to fly. He did not regret that he looked like a tough – it was good for the job – but Finn regretted that, at times, the good people feared him because of it.

He went past the gaggle of neighbor ladies, acknowledged no one, and looked for anyone who didn't seem overly curious, stunned, or horrified. That would be the person to talk to. Finn saw no one who fit the bill, so he didn't break his stride. When a news van pulled up Finn O'Brien gave it the evil eye for good measure, picked up the pace, and was past the cop on the porch before the van doors opened and the fools with microphones saw him.

CHAPTER 3

The heels of Finn's black boots made a hollow sound on the veined marble floor of the entryway only to muffle when he hit the intricately woven oriental runner on the staircase. The carpet was delicately colored in shades of ginger, melon, and okra and it was fastened to each riser by polished brass fittings. It did not escape his notice that there was a time when Irish maids polished those fittings. Now it was probably a Spanish-speaking woman who did the same. In fifty years another woman who had not quite melted into America's pot would be doing the polishing in this fine house. On it would go, the women disappearing but the brass always gleaming.

The bottom half of the wall on his right was wainscoted and painted in a whisper of beige. Above the wainscoting, wallpaper with a crosshatch bamboo pattern covered half a football field of stairwell wall. To his left were formal rooms and to Finn's right less formal ones. The house was immaculately kept. Nothing appeared out of place, but Finn jumped to no conclusions about what had gone on here. He looked at the stairs again, keeping his eyes down as he took them one at a time. He paused before stepping around the plastic tent that marked a spot of dried blood on the fourth riser. His eyes flicked further up and he noted two more yellow tents with numbers on them.

When the blood was scraped and the evidence collected, the markers would be gone but stains would remain. He would wager that the lady of the house wouldn't notice those little spots for a very long while. Finn, though, took a look as he passed each one. They were not the result of an attack on the stairs because the drops were perfectly round as if dropped from a weapon or a wound held toward the ground. There was no spatter on the walls or the bannister. Above him, Finn heard the muted sounds of an investigation in full swing and when he looked up he saw that one cop had stopped to watch his progress. The guy was in decent shape, middle aged, and looked none too friendly. Finn put two fingers to his brow.

"Officer Mallard. Good to see you."

"Can't say the same, O'Brien."

Finn tucked his tongue into his cheek, taking a minute before making his way up the stairs to the landing. Once there, he stood beside the man, touched one finger to his shoulder, and inclined his head as if he were about to suggest meeting up for a pint when this dirty business was done. Instead he said:

"There are dead children in this house. Perhaps we could be civil so our bickering won't be the last thing their wee little souls hear as they wing their way to heaven."

Mallard answered:

"Stuff the Irish crap."

Finn's smile faded as he stepped in front of the man. He wanted no mistaking what he was about to say.

"Here's the thing, Officer Mallard, my day has not started well. You see my wife, who had decided we needed time apart because of the awful situation that had befallen us, came to my apartment last night. We made love. I was a happy man, Mallard. This morning my wife tells me that she hadn't intended to make love to me. Instead, she wants a divorce. Do you know why? It is because my fellow officers have made our lives hell during these last many months. Ostracized us. Belittled us. Threatened us. She simply can't take it anymore so she is leaving me.

"Now I have this horrible thing to attend to and that has just made the day a whole lot worse. In fact, all this has made me angry. I find it hard to do my job when I am angry. Since I am in charge, I suggest we make a pact in order to keep me from becoming raging. You will do your job and I will keep my temper. Is that understood?"

"You son o–"

Finn stopped the man with a look. His expression hadn't changed, but the light in his blue, blue eyes became hard and sharp so Mallard shut his mouth. O'Brien had a reputation and he didn't want to be the one to test it – at least not all by himself.

"Fine, then. I'm glad we understand one another." Finn gave the man a pat on the back. "Now, where are the parents?"

Mallard indicated the double doors behind him. "In their bedroom."

"How long have they been in there?"

"About forty-five minutes. It took us awhile to get the wife to stay inside. She wanted to come out and..." Mallard seemed to find his vocabulary lacking. "She

15

wanted to make sure, you know."

"That, I do," Finn muttered.

He reached into his pocket for his notebook but had to search for his pen. A mention of the victims' mother hit his heart. It was hard to see anyone in pain, but a woman who had lost her children was an unsettling thing. Finn knew exactly what had happened as they tried to herd the woman to neutral ground. She would have insisted that it was someone else's children dead in her house. Hysteria. Shock. Denial. Rich people were supposed to be masters of the universe, but they shattered like crystal when the world turned on them. Finn's mother was of a different sort. Her heart broke like pottery. It was picked up, patched together, and put back to use despite the chips and ill-fitting pieces. Finn didn't know which was the right way; he only knew that a woman's sorrow diminished a man's place in the world and Officer Mallard was no exception.

"And the husband?" Finn pulled his pen from the pocket of his jeans.

"He's in bad shape."

"And you?" Finn asked.

"That's rich, O'Brien," Officer Mallard snorted. "Considering the source, if you take my meaning."

The man started for the stairs and then thought again. This time it was his finger on the detective's shoulder. This time Mallard leaned in like he was going to suggest having a pint together. Instead, he said:

"You know, O'Brien, I would like to apologize to your wife for all the misery we caused her." Finn turned, words of thanks on his lips. Those words were never spoken because Mallard came a little closer and said: "Write her number on the wall in the john when you get back to the office, and I'll call her."

Officer Mallard left Finn O'Brien staring at an empty space. A second later the detective turned his head to watch the man go only to find himself making eye contact with the technician who was dusting the front window. The tech was young and homely. Finn gave him a small smile. He smiled back. Finn appreciated the encouragement even though it probably wasn't that at all. It was just the secret handshake of the brotherhood of the shunned.

CHAPTER 4

Finn was back on the landing outside the bedrooms ten minutes later. He clutched his notes in both hands like a prayer book. His usually precise drawings had little shivers of squiggles at intervals too consistent to be a slip of the hand. Alone on the landing, he breathed deeply trying to find his hard core once more, the one that everyone was so sure was impenetrable. Raising his head, settling himself, Finn took some comfort that others in the house were busy doing the things that would ensure a conviction once Finn found the bastard who did this unspeakable thing. But these folks were cops and technicians and that worried him. He had expected a secondary detective on site and there was none. Not only would Finn welcome the assist, selfishly he wanted a witness to everything he did.

Reaching into his jacket, he stashed the notebook in favor of his phone. Before he could punch in the number for Wilshire Division, the door behind him opened. Finn glanced over his shoulder, put his phone away and turned full-face to look into the most beautiful room he had ever seen.

It was cavernous but the furnishings and the light flooding through the tall windows made the room warm and inviting. There was a sitting area with a chaise covered in silk, a brick fireplace tall enough for a boy to stand in, and a king size bed, its four carved posters rising nearly to the ceiling. On the gleaming wood floors were big, deep rugs, the colors of which echoed the one he was standing on. Those rugs were laid at the side of the bed so a bare foot would never touch a cold floor and at the end of the bed so that a body could lie cozy in front of the fire.

On the bed lay a woman. She was weeping, sobbing in such agony that it was hard to believe she was able to lie still. She clutched a large pillow in both arms as if it were the only thing that kept her from drowning in the waves of the yellow brocade duvet. There were more pillows mounded behind her in shades of yellow and gold, blue and crimson. Her knees were pulled up; her feet were shoeless. Judging by the length of her spine and the rise of her hip, she was slim and tall. Her long black hair was splayed out like an oil spill on that ocean of yellow. Even without seeing her face Finn knew she was beautiful, but he noted this dispassionately as a man in his position should. His objectivity was short lived, ending when the woman fell silent. That sudden silence caught him like a bullet in the gut. The man who came out of the room looked like the same bullet had hit him. Since it also appeared as if this man still had some wits about him, Finn took an educated guess and said:

"Doctor?"

"Yes." The man's voice was as flat as the look in his eyes.

"How are they?" Finn asked.

"You're joking, right? You find your kids hacked up

like a side of beef? How would you be? Why don't you answer me that? If you can do that, then you know how in the hell they are."

The doctor exhaled through pursed lips. He had exhausted himself with his tirade. He ran his hands through his hair as he mumbled 'I'm sorry' and 'good Lord' over and over again. Calling on the lord didn't stop the shaking in his voice or put the tears of sadness and horror back behind his eyes. He swiped those away without embarrassment.

"I've never seen anything like this in my life. I mean, blood in an operating room is one thing, but this! I'm a plastic surgeon. A plastic surgeon, for God's sake." He held out his hands as though Finn could understand how little that meant in the face of such a tragedy. "Elizabeth called. She said 'the girls are hurt'. That's what she said. Holy mother. Elizabeth said, 'please come, the girls are hurt'. She said please. Can you imagine? Please."

He fell back against the wall; that pretty wall with the crosshatched pearl-colored paper. He fell so hard that the framed pictures of little girls growing up were knocked askew. The man plucked at the zipper of his sweatshirt and then pushed himself upright again. He pointed down the stairs like he was calling the last play of the big game and knew his team would lose.

"I come rushing over. I run upstairs. Elizabeth grabs me and drags me into that room. 'Put her back together, Donald', she says. 'Alexis. Put her back together.' I couldn't even look at the little one. I wanted to puke, but Elizabeth's got a grip on me like a vice. I never knew a woman could be that strong. She's usually such a reserved soul. She just kept telling me to put Alexis back together while Sam's running around like a crazy man, pumping on their dead little chests, yelling at them to wake up."

The doctor chuckled miserably. Tears rolled down his cheeks freely now. He sniffled and wiped his nose on his sleeve.

"And the nanny. Can you believe something like this happened here? It's a mess, I tell you. It's a mess. I'm not cut out for this. What will I tell my wife? I tried to help, but good grief."

Finn touched him in an effort to stop the incessant movement of the man's hands: hair, wall, zipper, pockets, hair again. If the doctor didn't stop he would be bald or naked before he left the house.

"You came. You stayed," Finn said. "Most wouldn't have done that."

"You do this all the time, do you?" He was oblivious to everything but where his own thoughts were leading. "Let me tell you, no one should have to deal with this. You should quit."

"The suggestion has been made before," Finn said and left it at that.

The doctor pulled in his lower lip and hung his head, probably taking stock of his fine life. It was a sure bet that he and the Barnetts would not be having drinks at the club again in this lifetime, but steering clear of these tragic people wouldn't change anything. The doctor would tell the story of this day for the rest of his life; he would tell it to anyone who would listen. The man might sell his house and move away. He would get religion, or get more if he already had it. In the end, though, the good doctor would be left with a big hole inside him that he would carry to the grave. He took another deep breath.

"Can I go home now? My wife is afraid." Finn nodded. So did the doctor. He was a man and men had to face up to the bad stuff. It was in the rulebook. They both knew that.

"I'll be needing to talk to the parents now," Finn said. The man shrugged.

"You can try, but I don't think you'll get much out of them. I wish they would let me call someone. A minister. A relative. Sam said no. Maybe when they're thinking a little straighter." The doctor was already half way down the stairs when he added: "If they ever do."

Finn barely heard him because the master bedroom door opened again. There was no mistaking who the man coming out of the bedroom was: the husband, the father, the lawyer, Sam Barnett. He moved like a blind man familiar with his surroundings but when he reached for the banister Finn stepped forward and took his hand.

"Don't touch the railing. Not just yet," Finn cautioned.

Before Finn could let go, Sam Barnett's other hand clamped over the detective's wrist. Instinctively, Finn's muscles went tight and his feet repositioned for leverage. He looked the man in the eye, but when a look wasn't enough to back him off Finn took one of Sam Barnett's fingers and bent it back. That should have broken his grip but Barnett was unfazed. He fought Finn as if they were playing some awful game. Instead of pulling backward, Finn stepped in until they were chest to chest.

"Let go, Mr. Barnett." He spoke as if he were talking to a puppy with a slipper. "Let go, man. Deep breath. From the gut."

Sam Barnett quaked and a second later he started to relax: neck, shoulders, arm. When it was time, Finn eased his hands away until they were separated. He stayed close to catch Barnett should he collapse. He didn't. He put one foot in front of the other, hands hanging by his side, feet landing heavily on each step. He had the sense to navigate around the plastic markers.

The doctor plastered himself against the wall to give his neighbor room. Finn moved to the bannister and looked over to make sure Barnett would have an escort. He motioned to Mallard who took the man in hand and led him toward the formal living room that had already been cleared. That was when Finn found himself distracted by a big haired, round-bootied blonde who was standing aside to watch the two men go by. When the blond turned, the first thing Finn saw was her impressive, gravity-defying breasts. He took time to admire them as any man with blood in his veins would. After that he took note of the shit-eating grin on her heart-shaped face and the helmet of big hair that was curled and teased from crown to shoulders.

"Hey, O'Brien." She greeted him with a honeyed voice that should have been singing at the Grand Ole Opry.

"Good day to you, Cori."

CHAPTER 5

"Not a week at Wilshire Division, O'Brien, and you're already drawing attention to yourself. You think you would have learned your lesson."

Cori drawled like a southern belle asking for a refill on her Julep as she came slowly up the stairs. But that wasn't what she was. Her drawl, like her hair, was a remnant of her small Texas town, teenage badass days, when Cori Anderson drank whatever anyone was pouring when time and circumstances allowed.

"I'm a bit of a slow learner, don't you know." Finn met her halfway and then Cori went up one more step to put them on even footing.

"Could have fooled me." Cori took hold of the zipper clasp on his jacket and gave it a little tug. "You can't catch a break. All this drama is getting kind of tiresome, if you ask me."

"You're preaching to the choir, woman." Any hint of a smile was gone. "This is an ugly one, Cori."

"They're all ugly, my friend." Cori let go of the zipper fob and gave that old leather jacket a pat just where it covered his heart.

"You speak the truth, but this falls on the far side of hell."

"Duly noted." She gave him the once over and then gave it to him again as she said: "You look good. I like the shaved head. Makes you look like that movie star guy, Jason something. Turn." She put a finger against his jaw and turned his face just in case he had forgotten how to do it. "Man, those doctors did a good job. You can hardly see the scars."

"I can feel them. Always will, truth be told," he answered.

"Yeah? Well, shit happens. Get over it."

Finn chuckled when she let him go.

"It feels like forever and a Sunday since I've seen you."

"I've been crying in my beer, too," Cori answered, but Finn was not fooled. Her smile had softened and the pat she gave the scar that ran from his ear to his chin was gentle. She had missed him, he was sure of it. Had he asked outright, she never would have admitted it though.

Cori had stayed away from Finn for the last six months as much for her own sake as his and Bev's. The last thing she needed was the kind of trouble Finn had brought down on his head. Her job was just too important. The really last thing she needed was to get involved with a married man, especially one she worked so well with. Partners were a lot harder to come by than lovers. Not that Finn ever once gave any indication he felt that way about her. All she ever heard about was the beautiful Beverly. Cori couldn't blame him; his wife was a looker. Still, when he took her arm and stood her aside as the coroner's attendants went upstairs with their gurneys, there was that thrill. When Finn let go of her arm, they walked down the rest of the way in sync as they always had.

"Just passing through, Cori, or checking to make sure your old partner hasn't been tied to a stone and thrown in the river?" Finn asked.

"Silly you. We're in a drought. There's no water in the river. Besides, they wouldn't go to all that trouble. If they were going to take you out they would have just tossed you off a building and been done with it." Their shoes hit the marble floor at the same time. She pointed left. "Let's talk in here."

Cori opened the dining room's double doors with both hands and went inside. Finn followed in her wake. He should have known it wasn't going to be smooth sailing, but by the time he figured out that she was leading him into a storm it was too late.

Bob Fowler was waiting.

"You should have told me the captain was here, Cori. Or maybe the captain could have just said hello to me himself when he came in."

Finn planted himself near a sideboard that ran half the length of the room. His legs were splayed, and his hands were fisted in his jacket pockets. Bob Fowler had staked out the bay window overlooking the front yard at the foot of the impressive dining room table, and Cori took a neutral position at the head of it. She and Finn exchanged a glance: his was one of reproach and hers one that said 'bite me'. This wasn't an ambush, just an under-the-radar-get-together because the higher ups were nervous. Bottom line, Fowler was going to have this meeting with or without her. It was better with her.

"Three news crews. Two reporters from the Times. TMZ, of course. Harvey Levin himself is out there. It's a media zoo. Have you talked to them yet, O'Brien?"

Fowler unclasped his hands, squared his shoulders, and pivoted so that he could speak to them directly. Finn thought him very Kennedy-esque with his tousled hair and fine suit and photogenic face. He didn't know the captain well enough to dislike him, but he disliked the implication that he, Finn, was a novice.

"I talk when I have something to say, and even then I don't like it much."

"Best you get to like it a little more when it comes to talking to me. You will report directly to me and not hold anything back. I will control the info stream to the media on this one."

"Getting down to their level is an art, if you ask me. I'll be happy to learn it from you, Captain."

Finn's lips twitched. The cut was instantly distasteful and he wished he could take it back. Fowler may not have been welcoming, but he had been fair when Finn arrived at the division. Above that, he was right about the situation and right, in the next instant, to call Finn out.

"You aren't the only one who is licking your wounds, detective. When you killed a cop, every cop in the country took it on the chin so don't get defensive."

"That officer was beating a defenseless man. He beat me. He would have beaten us both to death if I hadn't stopped him."

"And it's over and done. You were acquitted."

"I never should have been charg–"

"That's enough," Fowler ordered.

Fowler might have been waiting for Finn to squirm

but he realized soon enough that wasn't going to happen. He also knew that O'Brien had a right to his anger but this wasn't the time or place to relive recent history.

"I'm not minimizing the impact of what happened to you. What happened to the other officers involved was bad, too. None of it should have gone down but it did, and now is not the time to argue vice or virtue. There are, however, a few things I would like to say.

"A week isn't long enough to know a man, and I don't pretend to know you. Therefore let me tell you something about me, and how I'm feeling about you catching this call. As a private citizen, I'm happy you'll be handling this. You've got something to prove, and that will make you work harder."

He put his hands flat on top of the gleaming table, and held Finn's gaze.

"Speaking as a cop, I'd like to see you screw up and get the hell out of my life."

His chest rose and fell with one deep breath and he righted himself again.

"Speaking as your captain, I want to assure you all the city's resources are at your disposal. Two little girls getting killed in their beds and a nanny executed is worse than our worst nightmare. I want this wrapped up fast, correctly, and professionally. I'm going to do everything I can to help you make that happen."

"Understood, but why bring Detective Anderson here to tell me that?"

"West L.A. agreed to a temporary transfer," Fowler answered. "She's going to partner with you on this one."

Bob Fowler looked her way and so did Finn. She was toying with her mother necklace: a gold chain with a pink glass bead for her daughter and a blue one for her grandson. Finn had never seen Cori without it, and he had never seen her anxious without touching it.

"I thought you were working on the councilman, Cori? The assault with intent? That's a big one. Could put you on the fast track," Finn said.

"Jones is going to wrap it up. It's not that big a deal." She dropped the necklace, put one hand behind her back and took hold of her purse strap with the other. The only thing she didn't do was make eye contact with Finn.

"Bull," Finn snorted. He turned to Fowler. "Schumacher is next up on the rotation."

"Schumacher won't work with you. None of them will," Fowler said.

"So Cori is my test case? If she comes out of this alive everybody will stand down for the Irishman? Is that what you're telling me?" Finn's brogue hung under his question like a safety net ready to catch him should he go too far with his words.

"There's no coercion. I do what I want," Cori said.

It didn't matter how she objected, neither man was listening to her. Fowler moved quickly, going the length of the table and stopping only when he and Finn were eye to eye. It was clear he hadn't been born in a suit; there was still a lot of street cop in him.

"Any other time I'd bust you for a comment like that," he growled. "It is disrespectful to everyone, not the least of whom is Detective Anderson. You will offer her an apology when we are done here. Further down the road, when you've had time to reconsider, I will expect you to apologize to me for implying that I would knowingly put any of my people at risk."

Fowler pivoted and went toward the window. He turned once more and came back. He turned again, talking as he paced.

"The press, your fellow officers, maybe even the victims' relatives will be wondering if you're the right man for the job. You will be under a microscope, O'Brien, and that means Wilshire Division will be, too. I will give you every chance to prove yourself including seeing that you partner up right. Anderson has a track record with you and it has not escaped my notice that it's an excellent one."

Fowler paused and clasped his hands behind his back.

"You know one another, you bring complimentary sensibilities to this investigation. Anderson is a gift that I suggest you accept graciously. If you aren't up to it, let me know now. I want this investigation above-board."

"I appreciate Detective Anderson's willingness to assist, but I respectfully request reassignment myself," Finn said.

"Impossible." Fowler wagged his head as if testing how much room there was between a rock and a hard place. "There was a stringer at the station when this came in. He knew you were on the call. If I pulled you, the press would make it look like a departmental vendetta. There are a lot of people who think you're a hero for what you did out on the street. If you'd been killed, they probably would have petitioned the pope and made you a saint."

Fowler pulled out an upholstered dining room chair and sat down. Cori moved toward Finn. When she was so close that he could smell the scent of her hairspray, he inclined his head and she lowered her voice:

"We don't need anyone else. We never have."

"We're wasting too much time." Fowler rapped his knuckles on the table. "I'm not going to beg for your cooperation or explain myself further, O'Brien. Give the word and you walk, no questions asked. There's nothing I can do to get rid of you unless you screw up or voluntarily take a hike. I hope you don't do the former because I want this investigation clean. I doubt you'll do the latter because then you're out of options with the LAPD. Now, are you going to work with Anderson or what?"

Cori's elbow met Finn's. If she said it was good, then it was. He returned the pressure just before he said:

"Let's do it."

They walked out of the room together. Fowler went outside to meet the press; Cori and Finn went to commune with the dead.

CHAPTER 6

Finn spent twenty minutes giving Cori the guided tour of
the death rooms. They spoke in hushed tones, made
notes, speculated, and traded preliminary strategies. Cori
left her mother self behind, Finn left Alexander to sit
quietly in the corner of his heart, and they focused on the
newly departed because that was their job. The only time
Finn lost that focus was when he looked up to point out
the bruises on the woman's wrist to Cori and looked past
her instead. Elizabeth Barnett was standing in the
doorway; beautiful as he knew she would be, numb, as he
knew she would be. Cori looked over her shoulder.
Neither of them said a word. They just watched Elizabeth
Barnett until she turned toward the stairs and walked on.

Now Finn sat on a velvet-covered, moss colored barrel
chair. His feet were apart and his notebook was in hand.
He felt outsized even in the cavernous room and rough in
the fancy chair, but these feelings were nothing new.
Whether he stood or sat, whether the house was fine or
humble, he was never comfortable in this gut-wrenching
moment. No one knew that but him and Cori, and that
was a testament to how well he did his job. His job was to
play the room, offer a phrase of condolence and a

murmur of disbelief and shock that reflected the survivor's own.

When that was done, Finn changed.

He became a cop, watching for signs that the people in the room might be more than they seemed. The tinge of brogue made his condolences sincere, but his piercing blue eyes and larger-than-life presence made people think twice about lying. Though Finn thought this a sad talent, he embraced it. Yet in this house of unimaginable grief, in front of these two rich and beautiful people who had lost their children, his words of sadness seemed small and unimportant for the first time. Finn felt seventeen again, facing his own parents after Alexander's death. Even for a cop whose job it was to investigate violent crimes there was always an emotional line that, when crossed, made the heart crumble and the gut shiver. For Finn, that time was now.

Behind him, Cori cleared her throat. When he chanced a glance, she raised an eyebrow like it was a flick of a crop to his flank. *Time's awastin'. The first 48 and all that.* Bob Fowler hovered behind her, curious to see how the rabid dog that had been sent to his pound would handle himself. Finn got on with it.

"We know this will be difficult, Mr. and Mrs. Barnett, but you are the only ones who can help us. Are you understanding me?"

Elizabeth Barnett turned her blue eyes on him. If Finn's looked like an icy stream then hers were the color of a warm lagoon. Sam Barnett kept his eyes forward. They were dark but of no particular darkness. The husband didn't look at Finn, but he was the one who spoke.

"Of course. We'll do anything. Naturally. Anything there is for us to do. I mean whatever is done… Should be…naturally…"

He spoke in a flat, quick cadence without shading or emphasis. It was as if the connective tissue of language was missing and, when he could find no sense in his words, he let them trail away. Realizing what had happened, he looked at Finn, his eyes darted to Cori and then they went back to Finn as if he couldn't tell the difference between them. His hand worked his wife's like bread dough. He raised an arm and put it across her shoulders. When she bent beneath its weight, he took it away only to put it around her again a minute later. There was a small tick on the left side of Sam Barnett's mouth. If he could have jumped out of his skin he would have done it and, no doubt, the skin would have carried on while the man ran away to hide. Finn looked at the woman, waiting to hear her voice but when she didn't speak he prodded.

"You have to help us, too, Mrs. Barnett. Do you understand?"

Elizabeth Barnett sat in front of him more beautiful in her pain than any woman decked out in diamonds and fur, but the person of her was below the surface. Her thoughts were of birth and death, and why the latter followed so closely on the heels of the former. She wouldn't cook in her own kitchen without feeling the plunge of the knife into her daughters. She would never look at her husband or her house without imagining screams that, more than likely, had never been. If anything, there would have been whimpers and calls for mama. It was better that she imagined screams.

"Mrs. Barnett? Missus?" Finn said softly, but she didn't hear him.

Her attention had wandered to the entryway. She tilted her head back, stretching the white skin of her throat, her fingertips splaying out against it. Finn scooted in the little chair and followed her gaze. The others in the room did the same. Fowler looked away and Cori's hand went to her mother necklace when they saw what had caught the woman's eye.

The first body was being brought down the stairs; a tiny mummy zipped into a plastic bag and strapped onto a collapsible gurney. Finn looked back at the Barnetts. The woman's bottom lip was caught so tightly between her top teeth Finn expected her to draw blood. She pulled herself erect. She breathed in short puffs, her nostrils flared and her eyes narrowed. Beside her, Sam Barnett moaned and dropped his head into his hands.

On the heels of the first team came a second, the form on the stretcher was smaller still. Elizabeth jerked through the sequence of movements once more. This time Finn touched her hand and she looked at him as if this was an affront. Just as she was about to speak, the man walking backwards down the stairs lost his balance. They all heard his exclamation and the clang of metal against wood. Finn started to rise, Cori and Bob Fowler took a step forward when the body slipped under the straps, but it was Elizabeth Barnett who was on her feet, crossing the marble-floored foyer, before anyone could stop her. She helped the attendant regain his balance, cupping his elbow, putting her other hand on his back. Embarrassed, he mumbled something and hoisted the gurney level. Together with his partner, they eased it down the last few steps before Elizabeth Barnett stopped them again.

She moved to the side of the gurney and looked down at the swell of the body. In the next moment, she grasped either side of the bag and centered it on the stretcher, pulling the straps tight as if tucking the little girl in bed. Her lips moved and though Finn strained to hear what she said, he could not. When she was done, Elizabeth Barnett moved away. The men holding the stretcher looked after her. Bob Fowler seemed to bow his head as she passed. Finn O'Brien and Cori Anderson watched her: Cori with curiosity and Finn with admiration and heartbreak. Only Sam Barnett did not look at his wife. Yet, when she returned to the living room he knew she was there. He stood up and opened his arms. His wife walked into them. He enfolded her, holding her tight until she couldn't bear the embrace and stepped out of it. When she took her seat, Elizabeth Barnett's eyes flickered to Cori only to slide back to Finn as if his gaze was easier to hold.

"Forgive me. I'm afraid I've forgotten where we were."

CHAPTER 7

Could you have made someone angry?

Do you have a disgruntled employee?

Is there someone at your club who hates your guts?

Do you have marital problems?

Money problems?

Is there something else between the two of you?

A meddling mother-in-law? A relative? A teacher? The gardener? A lover? A client? The paperboy?

Phone calls? Letters? Unwanted e-mail? Changes in routine? People hanging around? New people in your life? Old friends you've set aside?

Have you done, said, or thought anything that could make someone crazy enough to do what was done in your home? To your children. To the nanny.

Exhausted mumbles, tearful mutterings, and flashes of lucidity filled the next hour. Through mostly successful attempts to control themselves, the Barnetts answered questions – together and separately -until it was clear nothing was clear to them.

Elizabeth Barnett lasted longer than her husband but only by ten minutes. When they called it a day, Finn was waiting for Cori in the foyer. They left the house together and stood on the steps under the brick archway, surveying the people gathered on the street. School was out long ago. Children had been added to the mix of spectators. Husbands now stood with their wives, home early from work after fielding frantic phone calls.

Cori started down the walk but when Finn cut sharply to the right she did too. When she caught up with him, Finn had hold of an impressive Italian cypress, one of ten that grew against the side of the house like tall, trim soldiers. He pulled on it and the tough old trunk gave a little. He let it go a second later.

"Shoddy work, that. Who puts an alarm in front of the gate? It's not even hooked up to a call center. All the money in the world and no common sense, that's what we have here. They stood on the brick when they cut the alarm. No footprints in the dirt. Easily done."

"They don't close these suckers."

Cori crossed the wide driveway, took hold of one side of the wrought iron gate, and gave it a tug. It didn't move. She pointed to the rust stained hole in the cement where the latch nestled. Finn took hold of the other one and pulled on it, but he had no luck either. He looked back at the side of the house, still curious about the alarm box.

"Whoever cut the wires on that thing didn't have to be taller than a leprechaun or brighter than the village idiot," he said.

Cori ambled back over and pushed between two trees to get a good look. When she pulled her head out, she swiped at her hair to clear away any needles stuck in her do.

"Yeah, but he could have been tall and smart. The alarm is so basic it would have taken seconds to snip it," she said. "Did you see the front door lock?"

"Nothing to see. No sign of forced entry. Anyone worth their salt could have popped it in a jiffy."

"Maybe the nanny opened the door for whoever it was." Cori dug in her purse, found her sunglasses and put them on.

"Then why bother cutting the wires?" Finn asked.

"Because whoever it was had come on some serious business and he wasn't taking any chances," Cori answered. "The nanny just didn't know that when she let him in. Maybe it was someone looking to harm the parents and flipped out when they weren't there. The nanny wouldn't have thought twice about opening the door. Everybody feels safe in a place like this."

Finn shook his head. "I'm not feeling like that's how it went down. And, if that were the case, they would have taken her out in the entry. Why go up to her room?"

Finn walked up the driveway. He looked at the steps and raised porch outside the kitchen door and then at the garage at the end of the driveway. He ran his eyes around the backyard: pool, patio furniture, children's play yard, grass, trees, flowers. This property was a lot to take care of and they would be chasing a bushel of people who had access to it. Since none of them were around at the moment, he rejoined Cori.

"Come on then. We've seen what we can see here."

They walked down the long driveway, watching the neighbors roll back like a retreating tide. Only the reporters remained, stranded on the island of Finn's consciousness. They moved restlessly. Dissatisfied with what Fowler had given them, they pointed cameras at Finn, raised their hands, and pushed their microphones his way. They called out to him and he ignored them. They had burned him at the stake once without so much as asking if he should be standing atop the fagots. They had snuffed out the bonfire months later dubbing him a hero, a saint, a man among men instead of a cop killer but only after a video exonerating him surfaced. As far as Finn was concerned, the members of the press were bottom feeders all and he would have nothing to do with them. Of course, that didn't stop them from trying to reel him in.

"Detective O'Brien." A female reporter from ABC news called out first. "Aren't you just back off of suspension? How are you feeling?"

"Hey, O'Brien, how's the team work in there?" hollered another. "What can you tell us about the kids. Who found them? Is it murder/suicide? Come on O'Brien."

Another voice rose and then someone else's after that. The reporters were salivating, already tasting a sound bite as juicy as a slab of prime rib if Finn O'Brien lost it. Cori stepped close.

"Give them a little something," Cori muttered. "Maybe they'll go away."

"When I need them, Cori, and no sooner." Finn flipped a hand toward the car with its yawning trunk. "We still have work to do."

Cori and Finn looked over the things that had spilled out of the luggage and now littered the driveway. There were souvenirs for the children: tiny t-shirts, a book of French fairytales and two stuffed rabbits wearing berets. Clothes lay on the cement and Finn hunkered down and started putting them back in the suitcase: a skirt, a jacket, a blouse, a sweater. Size four. Pastel colors.

"Look at this." Cori handed him a clear plastic make-up bag. "Everything in its own little compartment. I swear it looks custom made. Me? I toss everything in a Ziploc and be done with it."

Finn took it and looked at all the female treasures: coral blush in a golden compact, lipstick in a tortoiseshell case, fawn colored eye shadow in a clear little box, and mascara in a tube that looked like it was made of obsidian. Birth control pills. Aspirin.

A teddy made of pale blue silk was bunched near the back wheel of the car. Cori retrieved it and held it up. Finn took it from her, only to find himself embarrassed. This was sexier lingerie than he imagined for the likes of Elizabeth Barnett. It bore a label from a Paris shop.

"He wears nice stuff, too." Finn put the lingerie away and looked at the white cotton shirt Cori was holding. It was monogrammed at the breast pocket and the cuff. She gestured with the other to a digital camera and a tablet. "Think we need to look at any of these?"

"Not without a warrant or their permission," Finn said.

Cori put the electronics away and latched the cases. "Where are they putting up tonight?"

Finn indicated the rambling Spanish next door. "The Coulters' house. I don't think they'll want to stay here even when it is clear." Finn pushed himself off the ground, and dusted the knees of his pants. "Mallard talked to them, the neighbors on the other side and those directly across. No one saw anything. We'll want to revisit though…"

Finn looked up at Cori and let his thought trail off

when he saw that Fowler was almost upon them, walking like a man with purpose, tall and proud to be the cop in the suit.

"I'm going to take off," Fowler said when he reached them. He looked at his watch. "Let's plan on meeting in my office in–"

Before he could finish someone on the street cried out and that was followed by a clatter of equipment as the press made ready to record whatever was coming. Finn looked up. Fowler and Cori turned around. Elizabeth Barnett was running toward them, hair flying, arms out as she called:

"Wait! Wait!"

Cori rushed for the intercept and caught Elizabeth on the fly, wrestling with her as the woman chattered frantically and tried to break away. Cori's head tipped from one side to the other in an attempt to catch her eye, but she was having none of it. In the next moment the woman dodged Cori and hurtled toward Finn.

She threw herself at him, grabbing his arms and pulling herself breathlessly close. In the daylight, her almost boyish figure seemed fragile to the point of brittle and her unkempt hair frizzed in a halo around her head. Fiery red rimmed her blue eyes and shot through the whites of them. Her touch was electric. Finn wanted to send Elizabeth Barnett back into the house and away from all those people who hoped she would self-destruct for the sake of a news story or neighborhood gossip. He intended to push her back to Cori, but found himself mesmerized instead.

"Detective O'Brien. They are taking my children's things. Why are they taking my children's things?" She choked on nothing but air and words. She released Finn with one hand and pushed her hair back before latching on again. Her voice lowered to a hoarse whisper and her fingers dug into his arm. "Make them stop. Please."

Finn's eye went to the investigators who were carrying boxes toward the van. He knew what was in those boxes and it wasn't much: bloody bedding, stuffed toys that the girls had been clutching, a blue and red guardrail from the littlest girl's bed from which they were hoping to pull some prints, a plastic bag full of matchbooks they found in the nanny's room even though there were no candles or cigarettes, a broken nail dusted with white powder that they knew was not the nanny's. Rachel Gerber's phone, broken in the struggle, and her encrypted computer. The bloody mattresses were already in the van. The men with the boxes paused, waiting for the go ahead. Finn gave it and Elizabeth's knees buckled. Finn caught her and held her tight to him.

"Stand if you can, Mrs. Barnett," he whispered. "Don't let them see you on your knees."

For a split second, Finn thought that was exactly where she would end up and that she would take him with her. Then her hands tightened on his arms, her knees locked and she found the strength to do as she was told.

"Very good then," Finn said, admiring of her strength.

Fowler made a move to take over, but when Elizabeth Barnett kept her eyes on Finn he backed off. The detective offered a small smile to his captain, a thank you for letting him do the job as he saw fit.

"Mrs. Barnett, we need to see who your nanny has been talking to. We need to analyze the other things for evidence so that we can piece together what happened here."

"I know what happened," Elizabeth whispered as she pulled him closer, so close that he could see the fullness of her lips and the glint of her teeth beneath them. He watched those lips as she confessed: "It was my fault. All of it."

"Mrs. Barnett, don't–"

"It's true. I was going to call before we left for the airport. I knew it was wrong. It just felt wrong. Inside. Do you know what I mean? That feeling? I had the phone in my hand. I dialed. It even rang once. But it was already two in the morning here, and I was in Paris, and…" She shook her head back and forth, trying to put the crackle of guilt and the wash of memory and the turmoil of emotion into some sort of order so she could explain herself. "Sam stopped me. Sam said no one would answer. He told me we would be home soon, but I felt sick. I should have known better. I knew I had to call, but Sam said no and…and…oh my god, I didn't know about the children. I should have felt something about the children."

"You couldn't have known," Finn assured her.

"You're right," Elizabeth's eyes were frantic now. "I couldn't have known about the children. Still, if I had just let it ring longer I'm sure someone would have answered. Rachel wouldn't be dead and neither would my children. Does that make me a bad person that I didn't stop it?"

"No. That is the truth. You must believe me, missus."

Finn took her hand. He shook it once and then again. She blinked and all Finn could think was how painful that must be. She needed to close those red-rimmed eyes and stop those futile thoughts that would rub her mind raw. Finn looked toward the house. Sam Barnett was coming their way and he was walking taller. He was still in shock, still shaken, but at least he was a man coming around to help his wife and Finn was grateful for that.

"Here's your husband. Please, Mrs. Barnett. Go with him to your friends' house."

"No, I'll stay here." She stepped out of Finn's reach just as Sam Barnet came up behind her and took her arm.

"Elizabeth. Come on with me, sweetheart."

Elizabeth Barnett yanked her arm away and stood back from both men.

"I'm staying here and there's nothing anyone can do about it. I want to be where my children are. Don't say I can't."

Everyone's eyes went to Sam Barnett but he only saw his wife. His gaze reflected a pain that seemed chronic. Sam Barnett hung his head. Finn stepped in both to save the man further hurt and to ease the woman's mind.

"Your children aren't in that house," he said. Elizabeth stumbled, off balance as if he had slapped her across the face. Suddenly, her eyes narrowed and she raised her chin.

"You're right. Take anything you want. I only want to see the person who did this. Promise on the heads of your children, detective, that you will bring me the person who did this."

"I have no children, Mrs. Barnett," Finn answered.

"Then we have something in common, don't we?"

In the silence that followed, her husband took her arm again. This time she didn't resist as he guided her away from their tainted house, the bloody rooms, and the bodies.

"Let's get out of here," Finn muttered.

Ignoring the reporters, they went to their respective cars. There was a lot to do and it was up to Finn to sort it out, grease wheels that may not want to turn for him, but first there was Fowler to deal with. Finn belted himself in as Cori took off. Finn pulled away from the curb and then rolled to a stop beside the van that was still on site. The one with the bodies was long gone and the driver of this one was peeling off his jumpsuit. Finn motioned for him.

"Did you hear what Mrs. Barnett said in there? When you brought down the body?"

"She said 'forgive me'. Creepy, huh?"

Finn rolled up his window without answering. What was there to say, after all? He was a cop and everyday was creepy. Some were just creepier than others.

CHAPTER 8

Georgia had been married to Mort for three years, lived with him off and on for six years before that, and had two kids somewhere in between. Bottom line, Georgia knew Mort pretty good. For instance, she knew exactly what was going to happen when he had a hard day at the office – wherever the office was.

First thing, Mort would kick the screen door 'cause it didn't fit just right'. Mort hated that it didn't fit just right, but he never fixed, it and he never called a repair guy to fix it. If Georgia tried to fix it she would break a fingernail or screw it up and that would make both of them mad. So the screen door stayed broke and that was a thorn in Mort's side for sure.

When she heard Mort kick the door, Georgia had two options: stay put and hope he didn't come looking for her or the girls, or go find him, suck a little face, and drink with him 'till he forgot about the bad day at the office, the out of whack door, and life in general. Wait and she was liable to get the back of his hand and the girls the boot. Choose door number two and they would probably end up in the sack whether she wanted to or not.

So Mort was kicking the screen door, making it worse and cursing at it, and Georgia was trying to decide whether it was worth getting naked with him, when she realized the little house had gone all quiet. Mort wasn't coming down the hall making more racket than a little man should. He wasn't hollering for her. She didn't hear the kitchen cabinets slamming or bottles clattering in the fridge while he looked for a beer. The only thing Georgia heard was the little squeak the backdoor made when it opened. Georgia always joked that nobody would get the drop on them because coming or going the house let you know. Mort always said that was the truth, but he said it like it wasn't a joke. He said it like nobody could get the drop on them no how.

Anyway, the back door opened but Georgia didn't hear it close right away which was really weird. Curious, she set aside the polish and blew on her nails hoping they would dry before she had to defend herself or grab Mort for a little nooky to calm his nerves. She stepped over a pile of clothes in the doorway of the bedroom, tottered down the hall, hung a left and peered around the corner into the kitchen.

Mort had been there all right. Georgia could smell him. Redheads had a special smell; musty like an old closet. Not that she had that much experience with redheads, but she imagined her husband wasn't much different than any of them. Now blonds she had experience with and they smelled fine. They smelled like sunshine.

"Honey?" Georgia ventured, but Mort didn't call back. The kitchen wasn't big but the going was slow, hobbled as she was by the cotton balls between her toes, unbalanced because her hands were up and her fingers splayed. She fussed as she inched along. "Baby? Honey?"

Finally, Georgia made it to the back door. She looked through the screen and saw Mort outside standing over the little girls who were huddled at his feet. They weren't afraid – no kid of Georgia's was ever afraid – but they were wary and that was smart. Georgia wondered what he was doing. He must be tired since he didn't leave for the office 'till after midnight and it was almost two in the afternoon now. She pushed her hair aside with the back of her hand and strained to hear what he was saying. To her surprise, Mort was talking all quiet and nice just like a normal person. Georgia leaned on the jamb with her shoulder and blew on her nails. She could have just cried she was so happy right then.

Georgia decided she was having one of those talk show experiences where people shared some amazing thing that happened to them with the whole country. If she, Georgia, knew a talk show person, she would offer to go on TV and tell how they'd been through rough times but still came out okay because her husband was a good man and her kids were brave. Then she would get a great prize. Georgia's huge chest rose and fell as she dreamed about getting a car or a trip to Hawaii just because her and Mort and the girls were such a great family.

Then she got a grip. Her old man would beat her silly if she ever showed her face on one of them programs. He didn't want nobody knowing much about him, not even her. Just as she was thinking how bad things would get if she went on television, the little girls came running into the house to show her what their daddy had brought them. They chattered and jumped and tugged at Georgia's pedal-pusher pants and almost stepped on her freshly painted toenails. But it was kind of nice having them all excited, so Georgia didn't scream at them for making noise. Instead, she looked at the pretty things. Then she started feeling sour and wondered why the little shits rated gifts like that. Then she thought of how a really good mother would act, so Georgia said 'isn't that nice' and sort of air-patted their heads.

When they ran off, she went out to see why Mort hadn't brought her a present. She didn't get further than the porch because she could see right off that something wasn't right. Mort was sitting under the tree on the one part of grass that still looked pretty good. He had a bottle next to him, and he was staring straight off like he saw something important and sad. Georgia looked, too, but all she saw was the fence and the neighbor's Rottweiler throwing itself against the chain link like it would rip Mort's throat out given half a chance. Never having seen her husband looking like that, Georgia was at a loss. Finally, she decided to just leave well enough alone. She hobbled herself back to the bedroom, turned up the sound on the television, and listened to the squeals of her little girls coming through the paper-thin walls. She watched TV and thought about being on a talk show. Then she thought that maybe they better work on the happy family thing some more.

Medium Man had dropped Mort off in good time, thanking him for the business, asking if he had anything else in the pipeline. Mort said no so fast that Medium Man could tell he was still a little pissed about what happened in that house. Well, Medium Man was none too pleased with himself either but what was done was done. He wasn't very good with words, so Medium Man just dropped Mort off where Mort said. He didn't drop him at a house or even an apartment but at the end of a street that had a liquor store on the corner. He bet Mort lived in a real nice place, though. He bet Mort didn't want Medium Man to see where he lived just in case Medium Man got it into his head to hit his place. Not that he would, but Mort was a smart and cautious guy so he got out on the corner near the liquor store.

Then Medium Man forgot all about where Mort lived and drove to the place where he was supposed to leave the car. He wiped down the steering wheel and the seat, locked the doors, pocketed the keys even though he was supposed to ditch them, and walked away, proud that he hadn't made any mistakes. The keys weren't a mistake, really. It would be a few days before anyone noticed the car and had it towed, and Medium Man kind of liked having wheels if he wanted. A day or two of fun wouldn't hurt nothin'. Mort was still so mad, though, that Medium Man didn't want to chance that he might see him driving around just then, so he took the bus to Fairy Tails. He was in need of a drink even though it was only a little after three in the afternoon.

Fairy Tails was crowded considering it was hump day and most people should be at work. Medium Man loved that expression – hump day – but he didn't like crowds. The bartender was busy concocting anything that was ordered and a few things that weren't. *Stand by Your Man* blared from the jukebox. Medium Man hadn't been at Fairy Tails long, but it seemed to him like that was the only song on the darn thing. When it started to play for about the tenth time, one person loudly lamented the passing of Tammy like it was yesterday and some of the guys on the dance floor started to sing along. With all that going on nobody gave the man of medium height, medium build, and medium coloring a second glance.

Just as he reached the bar for another drink a huge guy who was tatted up the wazoo picked up two drinks and backed away. Medium Man moved aside, muscles moved. Medium Man ordered cheap scotch. When he turned around, the first thing he saw was a man even less impressive than himself. Upon closer inspection, Medium Man saw that he was really just a boy. His face was covered with raging acne, infected pimples, and fiery cysts. He had desperate-for-a-friend eyes. He was a runaway for sure. Or maybe he was legal but had been kicked out of a house and his parents had thought good riddance, one less mouth to feed. When the boy looked his way, Medium Man smiled. He didn't expect the boy to see him and that's why he almost fell over when the boy smiled back.

Medium Man's heart beat hard in his chest as he started for the boy. He stopped and winced before he got too far. His ribs hurt where the woman had butted him. That reminded him of what he had done. He felt bad, but not for the nanny. He felt bad for the dark haired lady who, he was sure, had found out about her kids by now. He had wanted to let her know he felt bad, thinking that would make up a little to her for what he had done, but Mort didn't want him leaving a note or nothing. Medium Man promised himself to think of a way to show that he was sorry. Since he couldn't do that right away, he decided to treat the boy nicely.

Dodging a couple of guys who were hitting on each other, he ran into a man's chair accidently causing the man to grumble, and then he was with the boy. The boy didn't run away. He didn't make a face like he wished Medium Man would go away either, so Medium Man leaned down and put his hands on the table between them. He was just about to speak when he realized something was wrong. His pinky finger was naked. The long nail he had so lovingly cultivated was broken off at the quick and that just turned his stomach. That bitch; that nanny bitch. She was the one who did it, fighting like that when she should have just not fought at all.

Medium Man let go of his drink and slipped his hands off the table. He sat down in the chair, weary and disheartened. Wasn't that always the way? You work hard for something and wham, someone screws you out of it. Tammy Wynette wailed, all the conversation in Fairy Tails was just a big blob of sound, and in the middle of the madness the boy waited for Medium Man to speak. When he finally looked at the boy, Medium Man understood the world better than he ever had. They didn't belong there. The boy needed to be taken care of; Medium Man wanted to take care of someone. It was as simple as that.

"Do you want to come home with me?" Medium Man asked.

The boy tipped his head. It was more than he expected, maybe more than he wanted, but it wasn't a bad idea.

A roof was a roof.

A guy was a guy.

He could always leave if he wanted.

CHAPTER 9

In fifth grade, Finn O'Brien learned that bosses were usually no better than the people they bossed.

That lesson was learned when the nuns of Our Mother of Perpetual Peace defied the Vatican and shed their habits. Finn had known all along that there were women hiding under those starched wimples and black habits. He could tell by the hands that would suddenly appear from underneath their scapulars. Those delicate, long fingered hands were definitely those of women but they were not the loving hands one would expect. Those hands were always holding a ruler to whack at a boy who, they all agreed, was too independent for his own good. More often than not, the boy they were whacking was Finn O'Brien. He didn't flinch when they came at him and that displeased the good sisters, but he saw no reason to take exception to the whacking. If the sisters were brides of God, then God must have been whispering in their ears about all the things that made him deserving of their discipline: tying his brother's shoestrings together in a knot, listening at his parents' door in the night to see if he could hear them 'doing it', taking a punch at Aidan Gallagher who called Finn's sister a cow. He deserved a little heavenly wrath if the truth be told and if a rap on the head was okay with God, it was okay with Finn O'Brien.

Yet the day the sisters stood in front of the classroom clad in their new uniforms of blue dresses and sensible shoes, touching their heads as if they might fall off without benefit of a bonnet, Finn figured out that nuns were not only human, they were particularly unimpressive humans. That got him to thinking a little about God's mental state, too. Why, Finn wondered, would God want such a bevy of brides in the first place, plain as they were, timid as they now seemed. He pondered that for many a day and finally he came to a conclusion. Authority had nothing to do with a uniform or a title; real authority had to do with how a body handled himself. Without all the trappings of their high mightiness, the nuns were not handling themselves well. They didn't even whack him much anymore. So, at age eleven, he went about the task of figuring out who was deserving of his respect. His dad and ma made the cut but few others did. Even God didn't fare well under Finn O'Brien's youthful scrutiny and that lack of reverence proved to be his undoing.

God bided his time and then, once the family was well settled in America, God smote Finn down for his arrogance. God's rage was more horrible and humbling than anything a young man could ever imagine. God let Alexander, Finn's littlest and favorite brother, be taken and violated and killed. God let this happen on Finn's watch to make sure that the boy knew the lesson was for him. Finn respected God a whole lot after that terrible smack down, but earthly authority was still suspect and Finn was often at odds with it.

Today, though, he was at war with himself.

Independence of thought and action were being challenged by practicality and caution. On the one hand, Finn wanted to tell Captain Fowler to step aside and stop wasting their time with his micromanaging. On the other hand, Finn was on probation at Wilshire Division and if Bev was truly wanting a divorce he could not afford to be without a job. Not to mention that he could be nothing else in his life but a cop. Given all that, towing the line was the wise decision. So Finn kept his impatience to himself and spent his time admiring Cori's winning ways with the top brass as she gave Fowler exactly what he wanted.

"The Barnetts have been married ten years and moved to Fremont Place...four years ago?" She rewrote that note as she muttered about reading her own handwriting and then picked up where she left off. "They moved four years ago."

"Before that?" Fowler asked.

"Rancho Park. South of Pico. East of Overland. Cheviot Hills adjacent as the realtors like to call it. Mr. Barnett worked out of one unit of their duplex and they lived in the other. It was good real estate but nothing like Fremont Place. That was quite a leap."

"Not if they stretched on the mortgage," Finn suggested. "And a young lawyer's fortunes can change in a blink."

"Except for them it wasn't just a mortgage on their mini estate," Cori reminded him. "It was the whole ball of wax: The Miracle Mile office, the cars, the art, substantial jewelry. Mrs. Barnett says her husband hit pay dirt so fast it made her head spin. They got rich and moved within a year. They've been getting richer ever since."

"Did she give you any idea what the big break was?" Fowler asked.

"The lady is clueless. Me, I'd want to know about every cent that came and went." Cori pulled off her reading glasses and rubbed her eyes with the tip of one finger so she wouldn't mess her blue shadow. "It was a pure division of labor. He worked; she took care of the house and kids. My ex never heard of labor much less division of it."

Finn smiled, until he saw Fowler scowl. He sat up straighter and added his two cents so the captain would know he was engaged.

"Mr. Barnett told me as much, but he made it sound as if he worked his behind off. I'm more inclined to believe him. Sometimes a missus doesn't know the whole story of how hard a man works."

"You're right. What do I know, anyway? I've never actually had a husband," Cori said.

"More's the pity for all of mankind," Finn said.

"Let's keep it professional," Fowler suggested.

He didn't care how the chemistry worked between Cori Anderson and Finn O'Brien, but he sure didn't want the two of them trading pillow talk about this case. He waved at Cori. She gave Finn a little smirk and put her glasses back on.

"We've already requested financials on the Barnetts and Rachel Gerber. Barnett's ex partner is backpacking in the Sierras. We'll grab him the minute he gets home."

"Does Barnett specialize?" Fowler asked.

"He does civil work now. Contracts, some litigation," Finn answered. "But there was a stint with the district attorney's office. It's possible someone's carrying a grudge. If this is about lawyering, I'm betting it's something recent. Civil disputes mean money, and money is always good for blood." Finn flipped a page in his notebook. "He also sits on the stadium commission."

Cori whistled. "There's a lot of people would kill for that appointment."

"Let's hope that's a figure of speech," Fowler muttered. "All we need is for this to turn into some political hot potato. What about his staff?"

"Barnett has had the same secretary for years. He used a freelance paralegal until he moved to Wilshire. Now he's got one full-time. No partners yet. There's a bookkeeper and an accountant. I'll be having Cori meet up with Mr. Barnett's secretary and paralegal tomorrow. According to Barnett, the break-up with his old partner was amicable. Still, it's not unheard of for an ex to be upset down the road when one of them is living large and the other may not be."

"That would be a heck of a grudge if the guy took it out on the kids," Cori muttered.

"Stranger things have happened. Right now all avenues are open. Barnett is also a member of a couple of fancy clubs – tennis and golf. He's straight out of central casting, that one." Finn closed his book and uncrossed his legs, wanting to be out of the small office Fowler had assigned to them. "Their travel checks out. They were at George V in Paris when this went down or they were in transit. We'll know better when we have a time of death."

"Did you ask him about the nanny? Anything personal there that you could tell?" Fowler asked.

"I'm not thinking so." Finn shook his head. "Barnett gave me the basics and there was no sign that he was uncomfortable talking about her. He asked if I thought he should be the one to contact her family or the service that placed her. I told him the placement agency. She had a friend she often saw on the weekends. Checking him out will be priority. The Barnetts didn't have contact information for him. Hopefully, we can get it off the phone or the computer. We'll check out her friends."

"What about the wife? Work? Clubs?" Fowler directed the question to Cori.

"She has a nursing degree." Cori ran her fingertips under the sweep of hair that crossed her forehead. "Lord it's hot in here. Anyway, she quit working when the kids came along. She also thought the nanny was unnecessary since being a mom was her job."

"Then why was the nanny living in the house?" Finn asked.

"Because Mr. Barnett is a poor-kid-makes-real-good and he wanted all the things money could buy," Cori answered. "The wife stopped short of saying he was obsessed, but it was implied. Nothing was too good for Barnett or his family. She did suggest that maybe the nanny took the kids out."

"She was grasping at straws. No way that was a murder/suicide." Fowler dismissed the idea, but Finn was curious about the comment. He asked:

"What was a reason for that thinking?"

"Her theory was that a woman Rachel's age was probably jealous. She tended to other people's children but had none of her own; she had a room in a house that wasn't her own. That kind of thing," Cori said. "But when I pressed her she admitted that Rachel Gerber never expressed those sentiments."

"There seems to be a wee bit of discord between the missus and the nanny," Finn noted. "We'll lock it down."

"What else?" Fowler asked.

"Just the bottom line. Mr. Barnett works like a dog, active in the legal community while Mrs. Barnett volunteers at her kids' schools and at Cedar's hospital three mornings a week at an onsite outpatient clinic for street people, vets, and the elderly with nowhere else to go. According to her, there's never been a problem."

"Looks like you have your hands full," Fowler said. "Are we done?"

"Last thing, we walked the housekeeper through downstairs but she doesn't think anything was taken. Nothing appeared to be moved. She said Mrs. Barnett is very particular about the house. She did tell us that she feels responsible for what happened. It seems the little ones were supposed to be at her house having a sleepover with her grandchildren," Finn said.

Fowler asked: "Was that unusual?"

"Sort of. It was the first time. Mrs. Barnett arranged it before they left. Her girls and the granddaughters had played together before but always at the Barnett house. The housekeeper said that Mrs. Barnett told the girls it was their vacation. All the kids were very excited."

"Then what were they doing in the house?" Fowler asked.

"One of the granddaughters got the flu. The housekeeper called the nanny, and the nanny agreed to stay home with them."

"Did the housekeeper say if the nanny was upset?"

"She said she wasn't happy, but she was good with it," Cori answered.

"Any idea of what the nanny's plans were?" Fowler asked.

Cori said: "The woman couldn't remember if Rachel mentioned specific plans."

"Does the housekeeper have a key?" Fowler asked.

"She does, but she swears it's never been out of her possession," Finn said. "But she has an extended family in East L.A., and I'm thinking some might not be exactly legal. Cori will be paying a visit tomorrow, and we can run the family through for gang affiliation and priors. We'll check with ICE if it's called for."

"Sounds like you're focused. Let's get it down." Fowler stood up and maneuvered his way to the door. He took his jacket off the hook and put it on. "And don't discount a random act. Make checking out the regulars a priority: pool and delivery services, gardeners. They hire day laborers. Those guys are here and gone. Maybe one of them flipped. Let's find the scum bag who did this and get it off the books pronto. I'm counting on you."

Bob Fowler was finished with his pep talk. Finn and Cori had passed muster and for now they were just hugging around the campfire – until the door closed.

"Wastin' his breath, he is." Finn tossed his pen onto the desk. "This was no random act; this was a hit."

"I don't think we should toss the old random-act-guy-gone-berserk scenario out the window, O'Brien. Not unless you've got something solid that makes it a dead end."

"It's Rachel Gerber's boyfriend I'm finding most interesting. Almost every weekend he picked her up, so I think we can assume that's who she canceled when the children had to stay put. The sad part of this tale is that the Barnetts never met him and know nothing about him."

"Well if that just doesn't sour my milk," Cori clucked. "What is wrong with those people?"

"They figured if the placement agency vetted the nanny, then her friends were okay too."

"Are they sure it was a man who picked her up?" Cori asked.

"That's what the husband said."

"Did you get a description?"

"Not of him," Finn answered. "But the car was a four-door sedan. He thinks it was blue and an older model."

"Did he ever see anyone else in the car?" Cori pressed.

"No."

"And there was no picture of him in Rachel's room. Nothing in her wallet. Nothing in her bedside table. Her room was clean as a whistle except for those matches and that picture you found of her. The nanny was either the most boring person in the world or there's something she didn't want the Barnetts to know about." Cori said. "Looks like I'll be adding a trip to the park to find Rachel's best nanny bud in the next few days. If anyone knows about the boyfriend, it will be her."

Cori looked around for her purse, found it, and swung it over her shoulder. It was the same one she had used for years: endearingly unfashionable, terribly worn, and just big enough to keep a few lethal things inside.

"I'll be checking on the phone tomorrow. Hopefully, the lab will get to it fast and we can pull up some numbers." Finn took two steps to the door and held it open for Cori. "Let's the two of us handle as much as we can before Fowler puts his fingers in the porridge."

"Agreed," Cori said.

They walked through the corridors of Wilshire Division, stepping aside for those hurrying home and others coming on for the night. Cori went on about her eighteen-year-old daughter, Amber, who had fled home when the father of her baby took a powder. Finn listened but added nothing to the conversation for two reasons. First, something was niggling at the back of his brain. It was a little Tinker Bell of a brilliant thought that disappeared the minute he tried to split his attention between Cori and the niggle. Second, he did not engage Cori because he had learned long ago that when it came to talk of Amber all she wanted was an appreciative audience. The tune she was singing was made up of notes of resignation, rancor, and relief that she was still needed. Many women sang it, but Finn appreciated Cori's like no other because it always ended up being a love song. He turned to comment on her fine mothering just as they were passing Bob Fowler's office.

Through the open door, Finn saw the man standing by his assistant's desk with the phone to his ear. Finn paused. When Cori realized he wasn't with her, she came back to stand beside him. She looked into the office and when Bob Fowler looked back he pointed at them and said:

"See the woman. Fremont Place."

Chapter 10

Day 1 – Evening

Finn and Cori rang Mercedes Coulter's bell seven minutes after the call came in. She opened the door before the last chime sounded, still wearing her morning clothes: a white sweater with crossed tennis racquets woven over her breasts, a short skirt that hugged her waist and flared at the top of her thighs, white tennis shoes and socks sporting blue pompoms at her Achilles' heel. She looked fresh as a daisy until you looked at her exotic face and saw that the day had taken its toll. She didn't bother with pleasantries.

"Come. Come. Quickly. My husband's outside with Sam."

"Is he all right?" Finn asked.

"My husband?" Mercedes eyes went blank for an instant, and then she understood what Finn was asking. "Oh, no. How could you even think that Sam would hurt him? No, Sam's not dangerous. He's a mess. We just had no idea what to do, so we called you."

She walked sideways, gesturing as she led Finn and Cori through the huge house that was almost as well appointed as the Barnett's. In the kitchen, a light had been turned on over a stove that looked like it belonged in a five star restaurant. Another fixture illuminated a kitchen table that was already set for morning breakfast complete with napkin rings and gold chargers. A bank of French doors opened up onto a manicured backyard that was lilac hued in the early evening dusk. Mercedes pulled out ahead of them. She put her hand against one of the doors and leaned her face close as she peered through the glass.

"We got Elizabeth inside the guesthouse, but Sam wanted to stay here. There were still people outside, and he kept watching them, and we kept watching him and worrying that Elizabeth was alone."

She turned her head as Finn came to her side.

"I made a tray for him to take to Elizabeth – you know, something to distract him – but he forgot to take it when we finally convinced him to get away from the window."

Cori now stood on her left and Mercedes turned her head.

"I closed the drapes because I couldn't stand seeing what was going on. People were walking by and pointing at Elizabeth's house. They were running up to her place and putting their faces against the windows like they were hoping to see something horrible."

Mercedes Coulter shivered. She turned her back to the French doors and hung her head.

"Some of them were our neighbors. It was so ghoulish."

"Take your time," Cori said. Mercedes nodded and collected herself.

"Well, Sam, he went to the guesthouse and we thought

everything was okay. After a while, my husband, Charlie, he went out to tell them goodnight because we were exhausted and were going upstairs. Anyway, he heard them fighting. Sam was screaming and Elizabeth raised her voice. Charlie came back here and after we decided to call you, Charlie went back out. I don't know if they're still arguing or what."

Cori shifted ever so slightly. Her left knee went out, her hand tightened on the strap of her purse. This was her signature tick that flagged it was time to get serious. Finn pulled up a little taller and their eyes met over Mercedes Coulter's head. They had a situation and they could only hope that it would lead to something they could dig their teeth into. Before they said a word, before either of them moved, Mercedes Coulter grabbed their arms and asked an unanswerable question.

"What could they have done to deserve this? What could anyone do to deserve this?"

Dusk slid into home hard and it was dead dark in the Coulter stadium by the time Finn went to see what was what at the guesthouse. He left Cori behind to reassure Mrs. Coulter. The outdoor lights were solar powered and did little to illuminate the huge backyard, but it was enough for Finn to make his way to Charlie Coulter who was hunkered down near a big tree watching the small house nestled beneath a grove of trees. The man looked like a little boy playing hide-'n-seek, worried on one hand that he would be tagged and on the other that he might be left behind in the dark.

"Mr. Coulter?"

When the man made no move to rise, Finn got down

beside him, balanced on the balls of his feet and let his arms rest on his knees.

"I'm sorry to get you out here again." Charlie Coulter spoke quietly even though no one in either the small house in front of them or the big one behind them could hear. He turned his head slightly, but his eyes were glued to the guesthouse.

"You did the right thing," Finn assured him.

"It's been quiet since I came back out," Charlie said.

"How long were you inside with your wife?"

"Five minutes, maybe a little longer." Charlie Coulter sat back on his heels. "I really couldn't make out what they were saying. Elizabeth was yelling a lot and Sam raised his voice and I heard 'stop it' and 'you never' and then just garbled stuff. I think what freaked me out is that I have never heard them raise their voices. Ever. I mean, never since they moved in. Those two just don't fight."

"Grief sounds different on everyone's lips," Finn assured him. "We want to make sure they're safe and then we can figure out what the shouting was about. Do you know if either of them have a weapon, a gun or such?"

Charlie Coulter shook his head and he pulled a hand down his face, eyes to chin.

"I don't think so unless there was one in Sam's suitcase. I don't have one, that's for sure. There is a kitchen in there." Charlie inclined his head toward the small house. "There are knives. You don't think… Oh my God…you think that's why it's quiet in there. You think…"

"I'm not thinking anything, Mr. Coulter. We're grateful you called us and we'll take it from here."

Finn stood up. Charlie did the same, but the man

wasn't ready to let this go. He glanced over his shoulder, looked back at Finn, and then over his shoulder again.

"You don't think one of them had something to do with this, do you? They weren't even in the country." The man dropped his head and shook it, shamed by what he was implying. "No, forget I said anything. I'm not thinking straight. Forget I said anything."

Finn listened to Charlie Coulter argue with himself. While he did that, Finn could feel the ears of the neighborhood pricking as they strained to catch a word or two of what was being said here. They would one-up each other over lunch with a *did you hear...*and *I believe they...*and *I always thought there was something strange...* To speculate was human nature and none of Finn's concern at the moment. Eventually, he and Cori would cut through it all and find the truth. That was what he promised Charlie Coulter as he sent the man back to his wife with a request to send Detective Anderson out to assist him. Charlie delivered the message, closed the doors, and sat with his wife at the kitchen table to wait for the police to do whatever it was they were going to do.

"What have we got?" Cori asked when she reached her partner.

"A lot of quiet after a lot of noise," Finn answered.

"Do tell," Cori drawled. "Want to do this John Wayne or Tarantino?"

"John Wayne always," Finn answered. Guns at the ready were preferable to guns drawn.

Together they walked across the lawn, admiring the little house with its glow of golden light. They couldn't see through the drawn drapes, not even a shadow that would help them determine where the Barnetts might be. Finn knocked at the door.

"Mr. and Mrs. Barnett? It's Detectives O'Brien and Anderson come to see if we can be of assistance."

When there was no answer, Finn put his hand on the doorknob. He and Cori locked eyes. He mouthed a count of three and turned the knob. It wasn't locked so he swung it open. Both detectives stepped inside: Finn to the left and Cori to the right.

"Mr. Barnett! Mrs. Barnett!" Finn called again. "Detective's Anderson and O'Brien."

Cori moved quickly to a half closed door and nudged it open. When nothing happened, she looked in.

"Bedroom," she said. "Sheets are a mess."

The kitchen/living room was empty. The Barnetts' suitcases were in the corner unopened. Finn walked over to Cori and stuck his head in the bedroom.

"No blood. No signs of a struggle."

He walked further in and looked into the small bathroom. It was empty, too. He walked back past Cori who followed him until they stood on the herringboned bricks outside the door.

"The Coulters would have seen them if they went that way." Cori pointed toward the big house, the driveway, and the street beyond.

"Then there's only one other way to go," Finn said.

They headed toward the fence that separated the two houses, their eyes roaming over the trees and bushes, looking for anything that was amiss. They hadn't gone far when they heard Sam Barnett.

CHAPTER 11

Finn saw him first and it was a pitiful sight. His own father had been reduced to this when Alexander died. Sickened by half over what had happened to his child, their father still stood tall while he wept. Sam Barnett was on his knees, his arms wrapped around his middle, hunched over a puddle of his own vomit.

"Mr. Barnett. It is Detectives O'Brien and Anderson. Sir, if you would sit back so we can see your hands."

Finn stood a foot from the prostate man, setting his heavy boots in the soft lawn, his fisted hands by his side, his jacket unzipped so that his weapon was within easy reach. Cori kept one eye on Finn's back and the other looking for any sign of Elizabeth Barnett.

Sam swung his head and cut his swollen eyes toward the detective standing over him. Though it was dark, Finn saw the hatred glinting there, hatred for Finn because he saw that Sam Barnett was not only grief stricken but cowardly. Slowly, very slowly, Sam put his hands flat on the ground. It took more time than Finn liked for him to push himself back. When he did, his hands wilted into his lap. Then he sighed deeply, raised an arm, and ran the sleeve of his expensive jacket across his mouth. He was used up. All the bits of the handsome, successful young lawyer were ground into the dust of the imperfect man. Still, Finn was not fooled. He had seen sadder men cause horrors.

"Is your wife all right?"

"No," Sam said, his voice raw.

"Did you hurt her?"

Sam pulled in a deep, shuddering breath. "Don't be stupid."

Finn swept down and took the man by the shoulders. He needed no flippancy; he needed information because another life might be at stake.

"Answer the question straight, sir. Did you hurt her?"

"Get your hands off me." Sam pulled back, scrambled up, and moved away from the soiled ground. "Elizabeth's just being Elizabeth. She thought she saw someone in our house and she went inside to set things right because that's what she does. She sets things right in the house."

"And you let her go in there alone?" Finn asked, disgusted by this man.

"You can't stop her when she gets some crazy idea in her head. Do you hear what I'm saying? She imagined it."

"She didn't imagine what happened to your children," Cori reminded him, and Sam Barnett shot her a hateful look. He pointed at the trees.

"You can't even see our house from over here, but when I pointed that out she changed her story. She said she 'felt' someone was there." He looked from Cori to Finn and then shook his head. "For God's sake. It's just a fantasy of hers."

"Then why didn't you go with her?" Finn asked.

"Because I couldn't." Sam Barnett became more

agitated the longer the detectives stayed silent. "You want me to say I'm a coward? Is that what you're waiting for? Fine. I'm a coward. I don't want to see those rooms. I don't want to watch my wife running around like a maniac."

Finn thought Sam Barnett said all this proudly, as if he, at least, was rational in the face of the tragedy that had befallen his family. If that were true, then Elizabeth Barnett was not rational and that notion Finn could not abide. Before he could decide how to deal with the man, Cori stepped between them.

"I'll go get her."

Finn turned away from the husband and lowered his voice. "You stay. I don't want to go getting myself written up for knocking some sense into him."

"Then watch your back," Cori said.

"Always," he answered and he was off.

Finn went past the well-tended flowerbeds to the very corner of the lot. Back this far the bushes were arranged in no particular pattern and the bare dirt hadn't been turned in a long while. He smelled tangerine and lemon. The fruit trees and bushes and vines could be hiding any number of things including someone not happy to see him coming. Still, Finn's step was sure and straight because he saw his path clearly; a path that led him to a tall, sturdy fence and a gate almost hidden by the trees and the scrub.

The gate opened smoothly onto the back of the Barnett's property. Here the earth was hard-packed, too, and the air smelled of grass clippings, oiled tools, and manure. It was nearly pitch-black in the narrow space, so Finn used the garage wall as a guide. He reached the end of the structure only to find the yard unlit and looking like an alien landscape with plateaus and craters created by the faint moonlight and the hang of tall trees.

His heart thudded. Finn drew his gun, hating the feel of it in his hand. His stomach went heavy. Unease sharpened the senses; fear, he knew, addled them and that did no one any good. But fear was a bullying sort and sometimes you couldn't sidestep its blows. In the next instant, fear landed a few of those blows on Finn as the yard exploded in white-hot light. His weapon went up, pointing at nothing as he retreated to the safety of the garage wall. He raised his eyes and saw motion detectors on the fixtures. Finn closed his eyes and shook his head. There was sweat on his brow and his hands trembled ever so slightly. He took a deep breath and then another, banishing the flashback of the night when those cops came at him. In that alley, in the spotlight of the liquor store's bare-bulb, Finn saw the pleasure those men took in their vicious attack. He saw his blood mingling with that of the homeless man he was protecting, shimmering bright red in that light. He remembered seeing the blood of the cop he shot.

"Pull up your knickers, O'Brien," he whispered. It was time to attend to this night, not relive a past one.

Clearing his lungs, he peered around the corner of the garage. The lights were still on but dimming. They would brighten again the minute he started to walk across the yard and that meant there would be no hiding from someone who might not have the best of intentions toward the law. Owning that knowledge, Finn stepped into the light. The three garage doors were closed, the Jaguar hadn't been moved, and the gate was still open.

Finn went ahead, across the wide drive and onto the manicured lawn. His eyes were on the backdoor when he caught a flash of movement at eleven o'clock. Dropping low, he raised his weapon but the butt of his gun slipped in his sweating palm. He took hold of it in both hands, hating the thing even as he prepared to use it, unable to deny his love of it either. It had been used to take a life and God would judge him for that. It had also been used to protect another life and God would also mark that down in his book. There was little time to wonder which would weigh heavier on God's scale because there it was again, moving fast, darting toward him.

Nine o'clock now.

Finn's arm swung.

Seven o'clock.

Finn's finger was on the trigger.

Six o'clock.

Suddenly it was on him and just as suddenly it was past him and Finn did not shoot. He could not shoot and he dropped ever lower until he was on both knees, his head bowed, listening to the pounding of his heart, trying to listen to his brain that told him to lower his damn gun and release his finger from the trigger. It was only a cat that he'd been fearing to shoot.

A cat.

He shook his head, and lowered his arms. With one hand he wiped the sweat from his forehead and then ran that hand over his shaved head. He had been six months recovering from his injuries and everyday he wondered what he would do should he need to point a gun and pull a trigger again. He still had no answer and he hoped he never would. To take another life might make him cold as the artic and unable to thaw; or it would leave him frightened as a church mouse, unable to work. He wanted neither, so there was only one thing to do. He would go on his way.

Finn walked past the night-glimmered swimming pool, he crossed the patio where a table waited for a family that would never gather again. There was still a streamer of broken yellow tape attached to the railing on the stoop. Finn ripped it away and dropped it to the ground. But before he took those stairs, he stepped back to take a good look at the house.

The curtains upstairs were drawn, as they had been that morning, but no light shined. The downstairs addition where he knew Mr. Barnett's study to be was dark. Still, Finn wasn't satisfied. Something was different. Something…

Finn looked up at the second floor again and saw what it was. One edge of the curtain in the little girls' room was turned up. Someone had been there and might still be. He hoped it was only one person; he hoped it was only Elizabeth Barnett.

Finn climbed the six steps to the raised porch outside the kitchen door. Small and plain, it was a humble thing on such a grand house and yet great care had been taken to paint it the color of cornflowers. On the crossbar was gold script that read *Beware all ye who enter. This is a happy home.*

It appeared the door had not fully latched, so Finn put a hand out and pushed it open slowly. He hesitated, hanging back the way a man does when he's not sure a woman welcomes his advances but is determined to approach her nonetheless. When all remained quiet, he opened the door further, stepped inside, closed the door behind him and threw the lock as quietly as he could. If there was someone inside who tried to run, that little lock might slow them down long enough for him to control the situation.

Finn stepped lightly, making barely a sound as he made his way through a kitchen larger than his apartment. A granite covered island stood in the center, white lacquer cabinets lined the yellow walls. There were plants in the window and gadgets for cooking on the countertops. On the small desk counter he saw a calendar neatly printed with reminders of things that would now never happen. He noted that each day gone was marked with a red X, drawn with a ruler and painfully precise.

Finn had no trouble imagining Elizabeth Barnett in this heart-of-the-house, making cookies with her daughters, laying the table for dinner when her husband would come home tired from work. It was the husband Finn didn't quite see in this place but that was only because he was not liking a man who could let his wife come here alone on this night.

Sensing there was no situation here, Finn was cautious nonetheless. He moved slowly, trying to imagine the frightening fellow who had come here only hours before. There were so many places to hide and things to take, and yet nothing was taken and no one hid. He had been direct, moving up the stairs, to the nanny's room, killing her cleanly and then…

Then…

The children. Why the children when it would have been shamefully easy to pluck them off the street the way Alexander had been plucked? Why the nanny? Why had that person come to here, on that night, at that hour, to do this thing?

Having no answers, Finn turned out of the kitchen and walked through the dining room. He went through the double doors that Cori had opened to reveal Captain Fowler. Those doors were open as they had been left that morning and the room was empty. In the entry, Finn kept his eye on the staircase and backed toward the front door. He touched the handle. It was locked as it had been locked that afternoon. He looked down the narrow hallway that led to Sam Barnett's study and that room was dark. His eyes rested on the gallery of family pictures that were lined up like good soldiers, each of the same size. When Finn realized he was looking far too long at the one of a smiling Elizabeth Barnett, he turned his eyes away and went upstairs.

CHAPTER 12

Elizabeth Barnett had tucked the edge of the curtain behind the window crank. Enough moonlight seeped through that little triangle of exposed glass to bathe both the room and the woman in a wash of soft yellow. It was not enough to see her clearly, but he could make out the shine of her hair, the curve of her shoulder and the length of her fingers resting on the carpet.

Finn found her sitting on the floor with her back against the bed where her older daughter had died. The mattress was gone, taken to the lab, and only the box spring remained. Finn thought she looked like a saint on the holy cards the good nuns gave out on feast days. He had not been the most pious of fellows in his youth with his hands itching to fist up and his legs wanting to run rather than kneel to take his communion, but he did kneel and raise his eyes to the priest and cross himself. Sister Mary Gertrude rewarded him for his boy-piety by slipping a holy card between his fingers. He always smiled his thanks and she always smiled back thinking that she had managed to touch Finn O'Brien's messy little soul.

Sister Mary Gertrude didn't know that Finn was only happy because the holy cards were treasure. The minute he and his pals were out the church door, they took to trading. Two Saint Christophers for one Michael the Archangel, armor clad, sword raised, coming down from heaven to do battle against the devil himself. Finn, though, traded Saint Michael for Saint Bridget, the pride of Ireland. It was said that Saint Bridget wished for lakes of ale in heaven. Finn vowed that when he went to his reward he would ask Saint Bridget to go to the lake with him and raise a toast. First, though, had to grow up and do the things men did.

He had grown up, done the things of men, but Finn was a bit miffed at how hard God was making his way. Sometimes he joked that his parents should have named him Job, which really was not a joke at all. Still there were good times, too. His marriage, his family, his love of songs that made him weep, a pint at Mick's, an Irish Pub that was owned by a black man from Trinidad named Geoffrey Baptiste. But right then, all Finn could think about was Sister Mary Gertrude and a particular holy card slipped between the fingers of his folded hands.

On the card was the picture of a dark haired martyr pierced through the breast with a dozen arrows. He didn't know the name of the saint in that picture but he remembered that she looked accepting of God's judgment. At the same time, she seemed amazed that He had allowed her to be shot through to the death. Elizabeth Barnett wasn't dead, nor did it seem that she was in God's hands, but Finn thought she looked like that saint.

"I didn't touch anything," she said, her voice weary.

"Fine if you did, missus."

She could have torn the place apart for all he cared now that the house had been vacuumed, fingerprints lifted, bedding bagged and marked. She rolled her head against the box spring, looked up at the ceiling, and then she dropped her chin to her chest.

"I thought I saw someone here, but there's no one. I looked everywhere. There's no one."

Finn walked into the room and crouched down beside the woman.

"Come with me, Mrs. Barnett." He tried to take her hand, but she snatched it away.

"Don't touch me. I don't want anyone to touch me ever again."

"As you say." Finn held his hands up. "But I'll be staying until you're ready to go."

Her lashes fluttered. She cut him a look and raised her chin. "You think I'm crazy, don't you? But I'm not. I did think I saw something here. I had to look."

Finn's knees ached and the scars that cupped his jaw and ran up his neck felt tight. He should have been down at Mick's by now, shooting darts, being joyous before he had to return to his work in the morning. But he wasn't at Mick's. Nor was he lying in his bed thinking to call his mother and inquire after the church social she was proud to be in charge of. He was here, towing this heavy line of sorrow with Mrs. Barnett. It wasn't going to be done quickly, so he set himself down on the carpet that was stiff with dried blood. Keeping a knee up, he draped one arm over it and rested the palm of his other hand on the floor by his hip.

"No, I do not think you're crazy," he assured her even though he now knew that Barnett was right. She could not have seen anything in this house from the Coulter's yard. Still, he knew something the husband did not. "I know how a mother's heart breaks when her child is gone. I do know."

"Did you lose a child? Is that why you said that you had no children?" she asked.

"A brother. He was very young. Murdered like your children."

Finn offered nothing more. She did not need to know about Alexander, or the guilt Finn carried, or how his life had gone on slightly tattered just as his mother's and his father's, his brother's and sister's had. Life, though, had gone on and that's what he wanted Elizabeth Barnett to know.

"Because I understand," he said, "I want to ease your burden sooner than later. Do you believe that?"

Her head moved and he took that as agreement.

"That's fine, then," Finn said. "To do that, I must know everything you know. I must know why you and your husband argued. Perhaps there is something you forgot to tell us. If you've done something to make someone want to harm you, we'll protect you."

"We don't need protection. We disagree about what's next, that's all. I want to see the person who could do this and he doesn't." Elizabeth Barnett sighed, and pounded her head lightly on the box spring. "I want to know why my children had to die."

"This was not about your children, missus," Finn assured her. "It might be about nothing. If that's the case we'll find it out, but something like this usually has a reason. I'm thinking this was about Rachel. We need to know something about her or the man she went with. Did she confide in you about her relationships?"

"Rachel." Elizabeth closed her eyes and went still. "I

don't want to talk about Rachel, not when my babies are gone."

Elizabeth pushed herself off the floor and she seemed another shadow in this shadowy room until she stood near the window. When she did, Finn saw that her face was a mess of dark streaks where her make-up had run, her hair was tangled, and yet her expensive clothes were perfect. Those clothes bothered Finn. He wanted her to take them off because he knew that sackcloth would suit her better.

"Don't tell me things will look better in a few days," she said. "Don't tell me that God is watching over me or that you won't rest until you find the man who did this. Just find him. After that, I don't care what happens to me. Remember I said that, detective. Put it down in your book."

"What about your husband, don't you care what happens to him?"

"My husband? None of this would have happened if it hadn't been for him."

Finn didn't move. He waited for a revelation, but all he heard was a woman looking to lay blame.

"Sam thought things would be perfect in this perfect place, with the perfect wife." She laughed sadly. "And who could forget the nanny? The perfect nanny to take care of the perfect children; the perfect housekeeper to take care of everything else. And the perfect husband. Everyone said how lucky I was. Well, let me tell you, my life wasn't perfect then and it sure isn't perfect now, is it?"

With that, Elizabeth Barnett was done. She now knew what her husband had known all along; there was no one here for her. Finn got to his feet, trying to imagine what

Sister Mary Gertrude would say at a time like this, what blessing she would have, but nothing came to mind. He followed her down the stairs and through the silent house without a word to God. He stayed two paces behind as they retraced their steps across the yard, triggering the motion sensors that switched on the bright lights.

That was when he saw Sam Barnett waiting by the big tree and Cori behind him. Cori caught Finn's eye. He shook his head slightly to tell her that he was coming back empty handed; her shrug indicated that she hadn't fared much better.

Sam Barnett took a step and reached for Elizabeth's hand. She shrank from him but he took it anyway and pulled himself into her, whispering urgently, holding her tight. Elizabeth shook her head once and then again.

"Stop it, Sam."

Elizabeth Barnett wrenched herself away from her husband and walked off, into the dark between the fence and the garage. When Sam Barnett made a move to follow his wife, Cori stepped in front of him and Finn closed ranks.

"What are you doing? I need to go with my wife." Sam's head swung between the two of them until Finn moved around and stood shoulder to shoulder with his partner.

"What did you say to your wife, Mr. Barnett?" Finn demanded.

"Just let me talk to her again. Let me—"

"Are you asking her to cover for you? Is that it?" Cori asked. "Are you the one we should be putting eyes on?"

"How dare you speak to me like that?"

"You've been arguing about something bad enough

that you scared the Coulters into calling us." Finn moved a step closer. "You're still arguing about it. Now, what did you say to your wife?"

Sam Barnett's expression changed and Finn saw the lawyer weighing his words, considering his options. When he spoke there were no more tears and his voice was sure.

"It's someone my wife knows. When I found out she didn't tell you about him, I lost it."

"Her lover?" Finn asked.

"Her patient."

CHAPTER 13

DAY 1 – NIGHT

Finn and Cori left the Coulter house slightly better than they had found it. The Barnetts were settled, Mercedes Coulter had retired, and Charlie Coulter saw them out. Cori spoke first as they walked to the car.

"Do you believe him?"

"I don't know."

Finn opened his door and took the wheel; Cori did the same and rode shotgun. The doors slammed simultaneously. When they were settled, Finn called to assure Fowler all was well. He didn't tell the captain that his assessment of the situation was based purely on the fact that everyone was alive.

"So what part of his story is twitchin' your antennae?" Cori offered him a piece of gum. Finn shook his head as he draped his arms over the steering wheel and stared straight on. He said:

"I believe right enough that he's scared."

"Now there's a revelation." Cori's drawl came on a cloud of spearmint. She unspooled the seat belt. He heard it click and he heard her swear. "Damn these things. Must be some flat-chested chick that designed them. They always feel like they're cutting my boobs in half."

Finn slid his eyes her way. Indeed, there seemed to be no graceful way to harness her in. He chuckled.

"And a shame that would be, Cori."

"You're a gentleman, you know that, O'Brien. Most guys would offer to help settle the girls." She pulled the belt out a little further. "I hope Bev knows what a good things she's got."

Finn took that to be a statement. He no more wanted to talk about his wife than he wanted to discuss Cori's assets. Besides it wasn't a woman on his mind, it was Sam Barnett.

"That man thinks too hard about what he's going to say, Cori. Wasn't that bit of mutton the first thing he should have put on our plate this morning?"

"He didn't know his own name this morning." Cori wiggled under the seat belt and finally settled on angling the strap high on the left. She said: "On top of that, he's a lawyer and lawyers weigh every damn word they say. We're cops. We'd probably give chapter and verse and write the report ourselves if something like this happened to us. That's what we're trained to do."

Finn took hold of his belt and strapped in. He put the key in the ignition. Cori kept her eyes on him.

"What's the matter with you? Why are you ragging on him?" she asked.

"He might as well be crowning his wife with the north star with that confession. I think he doesn't want us looking at him, and he's willing to throw her under the bus to make sure we don't."

"She didn't tell us about this guy either," Cori reminded him. "And the way she cold-shouldered her husband? What was that all about? If we're talking intuition, mine says there's something going on with the wife."

"There's something between them, I can't deny it. But he's the one with the power. He took everything that belonged to her and divided it up between the nanny and the housekeeper. That clinic is the last thing that's hers and she's protecting it. That's why she kept silent." Finn started the car, but Cori wasn't buying it.

"Boo-hoo, poor her being all pampered," she whimpered.

"Cori," Finn warned.

"Don't Cori me," she shot back. "I'm illustrating a point here. The woman has free will. Barnett didn't tie her down and make her take the nanny and the housekeeper. Are you going to argue spousal abuse by virtue of generosity? Give me a friggin' break."

"Point taken," he said, but it was with reluctance.

"Thank you," Cori grumbled and then got back on track. "So either there's nothing to it, she's protecting the guy at the clinic, or Barnett is a jealous husband. Let's prove one and get it over with."

Finn released the emergency brake but before he could drive away, Cori added two more of her cents.

"And you know, what? Maybe you're figuring him for the bad guy because all those lawyers screwed you over. Just sayin' that could be the case; you painting with a broad stroke and all. Think about it my friend."

"Don't be a chancer, Cori," Finn mumbled.

"That better be Irish for brilliant broad, O'Brien."

In answer Finn stepped on the gas, pulling away from the curb so fast he gave that seatbelt of hers a stress test.

It wasn't unheard of for Finn to wish all lawyers a special place in hell, but he was still a good cop. He would give Sam Barnett the benefit of the doubt for a while. Cori stopped him thinking when she said:

"There is one thing we know."

"And that would be?"

"We know the clinic is a good place to start," Cori said. "And we also know there's not much we can do about it tonight. Drop me at my car, it's been a long day and we both should get home. We'll reconnoiter bright and early."

"I'll have a game plan before you wake," Finn promised.

"Don't bust your balls getting out of the gate. You've got a lot riding on this," Cori said as he pulled along side her car at the station. She patted his hand. "It's good to be working with you again. And don't worry, tomorrow will come soon enough."

Finn gave her a smile as she got out of his car and into her own. He watched until she drove away and then turned the car around and headed out. Cori was right about tomorrow.

Then again, there was still tonight.

CHAPTER 14

"Mom! Mom! Mo—"

Amber Anderson hollered for her mother the minute Cori opened the front door. Slim hipped, golden haired, not bright enough for college, and wild enough to get herself knocked up at sixteen, Amber broke into a huge grin as soon as she saw her mother.

"I didn't think you'd ever get home. It's so late."

"Gotta work."

Cori shed her blazer and didn't share news of her day. Amber wouldn't be interested for one thing. For another, Cori was superstitious. She didn't want to talk about dead children with two sleeping under her roof, so she tossed her keys on the table near the door and said:

"How's Tucker? Did you get him to the doctor?"

"Yeah, but I had to wait. I was half an hour late getting him to daycare and an hour late for work. Mr. Anthony is going to dock my pay. I might not be able to make the rent this month. Okay?"

"No, it's not okay," Cori said and she wasn't sorry for it.

It wasn't okay to have an adult daughter and her two-year old living with her while the baby's father was MIA. It wasn't okay that Amber was satisfied being a waitress in a third rate Italian restaurant. It wasn't okay that she didn't worry about Cori being tired and lonely. It wasn't okay that everyone thought Cori was tough and able to take care of herself no matter what came down the pike. It wasn't okay that Cori had managed to raise a daughter who believed everyone should be responsible for Amber except Amber. It sure wasn't okay that Amber chattered on and ignored Cori's objection to the rent lapse.

"Anyway, I made you a cheese sandwich. It's in the fridge. Bread and butter pickles on the side, just the way you like it. Oh. Oh. I bought some brownies at the grocery while I was waiting for Tucker's prescription."

Amber hooked her thumbs on her jeans and smiled gloriously. She looked just like her father. That man had stolen Cori's heart with that same smile, the bastard. He had flashed it again when he walked out on her when she was twenty-four and Amber was six. That was long ago but Cori remembered it like it was yesterday and those memories still ticked her off. The least he could have done would have been to leave her with a completely horrid child so she could hate them both and be done with it. But he didn't. Her ex gave her Amber, and Amber gave her Tucker, and now she had a cheese sandwich and brownies waiting.

"Thanks baby." Cori smiled wearily. Even when so much wasn't okay in her life, a lot was, and she needed to remember that. "Pay me back next month. Come on. Let's have dinner. I could use some company."

"Oh, well, see, the thing is–" Amber began.

"If you've eaten, come sit with me anyway."

Cori took the gun out of her purse and locked it in the breakfront. She looked over her shoulder in time to see Amber tossing her hair, rolling her eyes, getting ready to make Cori's life just a little more insane.

"Actually, I was thinking that maybe you could lend me twenty dollars just until my next paycheck."

The cheese sandwich was explained; it came with strings attached. Cori worked her jaw looking for the right words to tell her daughter that she was at the end of her rope. Instead, Cori headed for the kitchen taking her anger with her. Amber, never one to fully appreciate body language, dogged her mother into the kitchen.

"I swear, I'll work overtime and–"

"I only make loans if it's to help Tucker. That's the deal, remember?" Cori opened the fridge.

"Well, it sort of is to help him." Amber hung on the door. She was a fine talker but when Cori stood up and looked her in the eye she crumbled faster than a teething biscuit on numb gums. "Okay, it's not. I was going to grab something to eat with that guy I told you about."

"The one from the beach? Amber, get a clue," Cori wailed. "A man doesn't hang out at the beach picking up a woman with a baby in the middle of the week unless he's a loser."

"I know it doesn't seem right, but he works for his dad. That's why he was off that day. But just to be sure he's a good guy, I want to go slow. You know, pay my own way so he doesn't think he should expect anything. That's why I need the twenty."

Cori dove back into the fridge, grabbed a can of soda and her food and closed the door with her foot. She went back to the living room with Amber still on her tail and that was when Cori turned on her. If the kid didn't have the sense not to follow a skunk's behind she deserved what she got.

"What about what I expect, Amber? Or what Tucker is going to expect? You're not married. You're a waitress. You're a mother and you're living with your mother. Don't you think you should worry about what you've got going on without bringing some guy into the mix? Your track record with men isn't exactly good."

"And yours is? You didn't marry daddy either," Amber threw up her hands. Tears came to her wide, beautiful eyes. Unfortunately, they weren't tears of regret or shame. They were tears of resentment. "I don't want to just work all the time. I'm not going to dry up holding out for a guy who's already taken like you do with Finn. He's never going to think of you like that. Never. Ever. Even if he did, you'd just be the bimbo on the side until he found someone beautiful or smart or both."

"Hey! Hey!" Cori slammed the plate and the soda on the table and squared off with this beautiful girl who was both Cori's failure and her pride and joy. "Finn is my partner, and I am a professional. If I work all the time it is because I still have to be responsible for you and Tucker. I didn't beg for money when it was just you and me. I didn't pick up men. When you were growing up, I didn't drop you with anyone so I could go out and have a good time."

"You didn't have anyone to drop me with. Grandma lives three thousand miles away and she wouldn't have wanted me anyway."

"Stop it." Cori held up a finger on one hand and planted her other hand on her hip. She took a deep breath and counted to ten. "Seriously. Stop."

Amber was wise enough to hold her tongue while her mother considered her options. There weren't many. Cori rounded the coffee table and sat on the sofa. She couldn't bring herself to look at her daughter, so great was her disappointment in both of them.

"There's money in my purse. You will be home at a reasonable hour. If you're living in my house, you're going to act decently. Midnight, or I swear I put the call out on you and that guy's going to find himself in cuffs in the back of a patrol car."

"I promise. Earlier. Really. Thank you. Thank you."

Cori looked up just as Amber swooped in and kissed her cheek before dancing off. Her blond hair swung down her back, her rear end was tight under her low-slung jeans and Cori knew it wasn't her brain that this guy from the beach found so darn fascinating. She sank back into the couch and flipped on the television. She had half of the sandwich in her hand when her daughter passed the living room on her way out the door.

"Amber?"

"Yeah?"

Those blue eyes were wide, innocent, and so affected. Her jacket was in her hand; her hobo bag was slung over her shoulder. She just wanted to be away, and to be young, and Cori couldn't blame her.

"Did you forget something?" Cori asked.

"I don't think so."

"Tucker?"

"Oh. Yeah. Well, no I didn't forget. He's sleeping. Must be that stuff they gave him for the pain. He'll sleep all night. You know I wouldn't leave if he needed me."

She fussed with her jacket, avoiding her mother's eyes. It was a game they played, telling lies, fooling no one, least of all themselves. Amber left the lie and her baby with Cori and was none the worse for wear because of it.

In the suddenly quiet house, Cori left her half eaten sandwich on the plate, kicked off her shoes, and padded down the hall to the room that Amber and Tucker shared. She went to the crib, touched the baby's soft hair, put her finger against his open hand and felt her big Texas heart swell when his little fist closed around it. Maybe Tucker would fare better than Amber had. Maybe not. Still, Cori would try hard to see that he did. Unable to look at the sleeping baby any longer – knowing he represented too much false hope and too many failures – Cori left the door of the bedroom ajar, went back to the living room, and stopped only long enough to take her notes out of her purse.

The television played in the background and while she read Cori ate the worst cheese sandwich she'd ever had. When she was done with dinner, she clicked off the TV and put her face in her hands. It was time for bed but she was too tired to get off the couch. She was too old to be running around after bad guys and too young to be saddled with a daughter and a grandchild. She wasn't lonely enough to go trolling even if she had the time; but she was so lonely she would have given thought to hooking up with the wrong nice guy just to ease the burden.

Eventually, she dragged herself up, did her dishes, and went to her room. She pulled on the old t-shirt she slept in, sat on the side of the bed, took a minute and then picked up her phone and dialed Finn. He didn't answer and Cori didn't leave a message. Amber was right. Finn wasn't waiting on Cori Anderson to take care of his life; he was probably out somewhere doing it himself. He was probably with Bev making up for lost time.

Turning off the light, Cori got into bed and hugged a pillow tight. She kept one ear tuned to the telephone while the other listened for the baby down the hall, and in her mind she said her bedtime prayer. It was a simple one. Cori Anderson thanked God that she had the troubles she did. She could, after all, be Elizabeth Barnett.

Finn was pleased when he saw the light on in the small office far in the back of the hospital. It had been a long shot thinking someone might be working this late, but since he wasn't going to be packing his things to move back in with Bev that night, and the hospital was on his way to Mick's, Finn decided to check it out. The clinic was housed in a tiny building, outcropped from the main complex. The adjacent parking lot was small and empty except for a minivan. Finn parked, got out and went to the door of the clinic. Surprised to find it wasn't locked, he walked through it and found a woman sitting behind a thick glass partition at a desk that looked like it had been swiped off the street. She took off her glasses and glared at him.

"We're closed. Go through the emergency room, or come back at seven. We open at seven. Do you understand me?"

"That I do, ma'am, but my problem isn't of a medical nature." Knowing he must look a sight if she took him for a man in need, Finn reached for his credential.

"Don't even bother waving a gun around trying to rob

me. I don't have a cent, and this is a free clinic, so just turn around and get your hinny out of here."

"Detective O'Brien. Homicide." Carefully, he reached in the breast pocket of his jacket and withdrew his credential.

The woman pushed her chair back and came close to the window, checking him out – shaved head to booted toes and everything in between. She held her glasses up and looked over his I.D.

"You look like a biker or something. Most detectives I've seen wear a shirt and tie. You should wear a shirt and tie so you look presentable," she clucked. "Well, come on in."

"Yes, ma'am."

Finn put his badge back and thanked her when she opened the door. She led him down a short hall to an office no better than the one they had just left. She took a chair behind the desk.

"I'm Henrietta."

"A fine name." Finn sat across from her, thinking that she had the look of a nun who has left the order.

"How long have you been in the states?" she asked.

"Since I was fifteen."

"Too late to lose the accent or the blarney. Henrietta is a horrid name, no need to pretend it isn't. Etta is better, so feel free to get familiar." Her eyes sparkled and that made her look quite nice.

"I appreciate the invitation."

"So, what brings a good looking guy like you to a hole like this when you should be home having dinner with the little woman?"

"No lass at home." Finn gave her his best woe-is-me

look. "I am here about a woman, though. Do you know Elizabeth Barnett?"

"Elizabeth's dead."

"You aren't surprised."

"Nothing surprises me. I work in a place where people hear voices, eat out of garbage cans, and call a refrigerator box home if they're lucky. Besides you said you were from homicide. You asked about Elizabeth. One plus one." She offered a look that dared him not to answer 'equals two'.

"A reasonable assumption but, no, Mrs. Barnett is still among the living. Her children were murdered," Finn said. "Her children and their nanny."

"Oh, Lord." Etta's chest raised with quick breaths as the woman in her absorbed the shock; the professional didn't miss any more beats. "What can I do?"

"Mrs. Barnett's husband thinks it was someone from this clinic wanting to hurt his wife and getting the children instead."

"Well, that's a gruesome thought. One I'd rather not have since I'm here alone catching up most nights, I might add." Etta pulled at her ear as she thought of ways to help. "Look, I'm the administrator. From what I hear, Elizabeth Barnett is beyond competent, reliable, and very compassionate, but that doesn't mean she's a bleeding heart. At the first sign that one of our clients might be too much for us to handle, we get them off our books as best we can. If any of our volunteers or staff is uncomfortable with a patient, they don't see them again. I'm sure Elizabeth would have said something if she was in that position."

"So you think Mr. Barnett is overreacting?" Finn asked.

"Unless Elizabeth is bringing stories home, I don't see how he would know what was going on here. Did you ask her about it?"

"By the time I heard of it, she was played out," Finn said.

"Understandable, considering."

"All I know is that she was adamant that he was way off base. I guess I wasted a trip."

Finn started to get out of the chair, but Etta stopped him.

"Hold on. I didn't say it was impossible that there was a problem. If you've got the time, I'll try to track down some people who work with Elizabeth. The coffee pot's empty, but I've got a couple of little bottles of bourbon that I took from the plane last time I went on vacation. It should be well aged considering I haven't been on vacation in a while."

"I only drink when I have something to celebrate."

"You must not drink a lot," Etta noted. "Can you give me thirty minutes?"

"I'll give you all night, if you're up for it."

"Best offer I've had in a long time." Etta waved her way out the door. "I'll be back."

"Detective O'Brien? Detective?"

Finn opened his eyes to see Etta beside him. He smiled, not because he was happy to see her but because he had been dreaming of a woman leaning over him just the way she was. His dream woman, though, was not Etta in her too long, shapeless floral dress, but Bev, naked and tall and willing. When Etta touched him, Bev had morphed into Sister Mary Gertrude ready to whack him on his head for entertaining prurient thoughts while Father Michael listed his penance off camera.

Finn pushed himself up in the chair and drew both hands down his face, happy to be awake now that his dream had gone south. He couldn't remember slumping down, crossing his arms over his chest, and splaying his legs in front of him. He couldn't remember falling asleep.

"Sorry. Been a long day."

"No worries. I catch the 'Zs' whenever I can, too." She handed him a manila folder and then perched on the desk. "I got what I could for now."

"You're an amazing woman, Etta. Let's take a look then."

Finn flipped through the folder. Inside were handwritten notations, Xeroxes of two grainy photos, and all the information she could pull together in thirty minutes. Etta plucked one of the pictures out of the file.

"There are two people who showed an inordinate interest in Elizabeth according to Mary Billings, the volunteer coordinator. Her contact info is in the front of the file. She was horrified when I told her what happened, but she thinks you're barking up the wrong tree too."

"It's not our only tree," he assured her. "It's a place to start."

"Alright. Anyway, this is Olive." Etta turned the picture in her hand toward him. "She's about sixty years old as far as we can tell. She's been on the street forever. Olive saw a picture of Elizabeth's children and got very angry when Elizabeth wouldn't bring them in to meet her."

"I should have mentioned we are thinking it is a man Mr. Barnett is worried about. Still, this sounds promising," Finn said.

"Not really. Olive's hands are swollen, her knuckles are gnarled, and her feet are as big and hard as bricks. She can barely get here much less all the way to Fremont Place. Still, she had shown an interest in Elizabeth's children and that's why Mary mentioned her."

Etta tapped the second photo in the file then crossed her arms and knit her brow.

"This guy might be another matter. Stephen Grady. He's bipolar and he won't take his medication from anyone but Elizabeth. Mary heard him say that he loved Elizabeth. When she started taking him to lunch at the food truck, I put a stop to it *post haste*. There are agencies to mainstream these people, and we're not one of them. I don't think Stephen is ever going to be ready for that."

"Nice looking man from what I can tell."

The photo the Xerox was made from was of poor quality, but Finn could see there was something about him. He wasn't better looking than Sam Barnett, but women were funny that way. It wasn't always about who was the most handsome or the richest, but who needed rescuing.

"He doesn't look this good most days. He was quite accomplished before he got sick. Graduate school. Worked as a research scientist. It's a shame. Such a promising young man."

"Did he come in while she was gone?"

"He did, but he was upset when she wasn't here. It was a bad call not to prepare him for her absence. A lot can happen to a person like that if they don't take their medication for ten days."

"Any idea where I can find him?" Finn asked.

"He could be in a flop house or curled up under a freeway. These people have to come to us; we don't go to them."

Finn closed the folder. "This is more than I expected, Etta. I appreciate it greatly."

"Listen, I'll go home and have a hot bath and break open one of those little bottles. Maybe I'll think of something more," she said. "Got a card so I can get a hold of you?"

Finn handed her one and they parted: Etta to her hot bath and Finn to Mick's where he ordered an ale and shot the darts, missing the bulls eye by a bit each time. No matter. He would hit it in good time. With a 'good evening' to Geoffrey Baptiste, The Beanie Man of Trinidad, the fourth owner of Mick's Irish Pub, Finn went home. He took with him more company than he liked: Sam Barnett and his weepy terror and sly eyes, Elizabeth Barnett and her shattered heart that would cut her to shreds from the inside out, Bev relieved that Finn and all his woes were now set aside, and Cori, his firewall against the blaze of hatred he ignited in those at Wilshire Division. As always, sitting solidly in the middle of his brain, were the two people whose deaths he was responsible for: Alexander, his brother, and the cop he, Finn, had killed.

He walked through the back garden that separated his apartment from the main house. His boots were heavy on the wooden stairs that took him to the second floor. Inside his apartment, Finn took off his jacket. He laid his weapon by the bed and the shoulder holster on the dresser. He glanced at the bed; the sheets tangled from the night before when he thought that Bev still loved him.

He left the bedroom in favor of the kitchen where he scrounged around in a nearly empty refrigerator. Finn looked at the file from the clinic, but there wasn't anything in it that he hadn't committed to memory. He thought to call Cori and tell her about Stephen Grady, or maybe even tell her about Bev, but then thought better of it. She would be asleep, or tending to the baby, or wondering where Amber had gotten herself off to. Finn knew too well that the girl caused Cori grief in that way. He also wasn't ready to admit defeat where Bev was concerned.

When he had run out of things to distract him, Finn stood by the window. It was almost midnight and working people were in bed. Streetlights shined but there was no one standing under them. He looked up but saw no stars in the black sky over L.A. There was only one light that drew him. It burned steadily in his landlady's house.

Kimiko was a war bride who followed the man she loved to a strange country where they made their life together. When her heart longed for the land of her birth, her husband built a *sento,* a Japanese bathhouse, complete with a small room for shoes, a shower where one could wash before the bath, a well-tended Japanese garden, and, in another larger room, a deep tub. Her husband was long gone. He left Kimiko with her daughter, a blind *ama,* two blocks of prime Los Angeles real estate, and her beloved *sento* that she shared with a handful of close friends who revered tradition. She also shared her bathhouse with those she felt deserving or in need, never charging for entrance as one might in Japan. Kimiko found Finn deserving because she knew what he had done for the man he saved from the bad policemen. She did not know why he was in need, but she knew he was. He did not take advantage of Kimiko's kindness and that was why, even though it was late, she did not object when he appeared at her door.

"Kimiko-san."

He greeted her with a slight bow, ready to beg the favor of going into the bathhouse so late. He didn't need to beg. Kimiko took one look at him, stepped back and closed her door. When she returned, her night robe was tied tight around her small frame and her outside shoes were on her tiny feet. Gracefully, she stepped onto the stoop. Finn stood back and allowed her to pass.

"*Arigato,*" he whispered.

"*Domo ishi masta,*" she murmured.

They crossed the yard. She opened the door of the building, turned on the low lights, laid out a towel, and made sure that the water was hot. When Kimiko left him, Finn pushed aside the tatami sheet that led to the dressing room adjacent to the Japanese garden. He undressed, soaped his powerful body to wash away whatever stench death had left, took his small towel, and went to the tub. He lowered himself into the hot water and settled in with a sigh. The expression Kimiko had taught him ran like a lazy ticker tape through his mind: *gokuraku, gokuraku.* It meant a good feeling for body and soul, a divine pleasure. Soon, Finn O'Brien stopped thinking at all.

In the silence, immersed in the hot water, his memory was wiped clean for a time. He did not remember the beating he took six months earlier or Bev's exact words as she walked out his door for the last time. He could not conjure up the image of his brother in a coffin, nor that of murdered little girls in their bloody beds. He could not even remember the beautiful tortured eyes of Elizabeth Barnett.

CHAPTER 15

Cori and Finn finished the first day of the investigation late and started the second day early with Finn dividing the labor: him to the case book, recording evidence, processing requests to the lab, getting the tech guys going on Rachel Gerber's locked computer and broken phone, interfacing with the coroner, contacting the Parisian hotel for their records, reconstructing the crime scene, filing photos and writing the initial reports and Cori to follow up with the housekeeper, the agency that placed the nanny, Barnett's office staff and the little girls' teachers.

Now it was day three and they were to meet up at noon to compare notes. Cori had hit the ground running and tracked down a few of the nannies in the park who had known Rachel Gerber. She spent an hour watching them come and go with their charges and was surprised to find only two who knew Rachel. The German, it seemed, was not the friendliest playmate in the sandbox. That done, Cori started in on the neighbors.

By the eighth stop, she thought she might hurl if she had to look through one more fabulous window, onto one more marvelous yard, across one more stunning street, toward one more exceptional home. At some point every antique table, ancient rug, designer sofa, gold-rimmed teacup, and expensive knick-knack had been rendered commonplace. In the last three hours the voices of the rich folks and their servants had morphed into nothing more than white noise: none of them knew anything about anything. Bottom line, Cori Anderson was unimpressed with the entire place and the people in it until she got to the Horace's home. That one was a friggin' bull in the china shop of Fremont Place.

From the outside it was as lovely as any other house in the neighborhood, but inside it was the exception to every rule of good breeding that had ever been written. Hal and Heidi Horace's tastes ran to the eclectic and the erotic. Cori talked to them for forty-five minutes, which was twenty minutes longer than she thought she could manage when she first laid eyes on the twosome.

Heidi opened the door wearing a see-through nightie the color of bubble gum and teetered on matching mules with four-inch, jeweled platforms. Her hair was cotton candy in color and shape. Her nails were candy-apple red and her lips glossed in golden honey. Cori always thought she had it going on, but Heidi Horace was too scrumptious for words. Hal, though, was simply beyond words.

Hal had an old man's body, skinny and wrinkled; the hair on his chest was silver and sparse. He had been sunning by the pool, clad only in a red Speedo, when Cori rang. It was obvious he hadn't been swimming since his comb-over was still in place and the ever-so-discreet make-up he used to try to hide a large mole near his nose was dried and cracking.

The couple was delighted to have company – even a cop's company. Hal threw on a short terry robe, but neglected to tie the darn thing shut. When he sat down in the living room, Cori had a bird's eye view of his truly pathetic private parts. Heidi settled Cori in a chair styled like an upturned hand with the middle finger extended. She was offered coffee in a cup that sported boobs, the nipples of which colored pink when the coffee was hot. Heidi and Hal insisted she nibble some pastry. Cori accepted the seat, the coffee, the pastry and Heidi's compliments on Cori's beautiful hair. Cori returned the compliment with all sincerity. Big hair women were a rarity in Los Angeles, so meeting one of the sisterhood was always a pleasure.

Hal was no less gracious. He told Cori she had an exceptional rack and he could get her work if she ever wanted to make some real money. She would, he warned, have to decide PDQ because those puppies would start to sag sooner than later. Cori thanked him, assured him that she was really happy doing what she was doing, and then she asked about their line of work.

They produced art films, not porn, thank-you-very-much. They paid their taxes. Their distributors were thrilled with their movies. Actors and actresses were beating down their doors because Heidi and Hal's productions were class all the way. Heidi was a producer now but she had been one of the great actresses of her time. She would have been iconic if only she hadn't passed on *Deep Throat*.

"A classic," Hall stated.

Heidi raised her hand, so Cori called on her.

There was one very small, uninteresting matter

pending that was a nuisance. One of their actresses was underage. Just by a few years, Cori had to understand.

"She looked thirty," Hal grumbled. "What's wrong with kids these days?"

The girl's father had complained to the D.A. Hal and Heidi gave Cori the man's name with the assurance that everyone, except this one man, loved them. Even that man actually liked them quite a bit, but most everybody loved Hal and Heidi.

"Love us," Hal agreed.

"That's all you can think of? This one man?" Cori pressed.

Heidi fluttered her lashes and furrowed her brow; Hal's old man lips pulled down or maybe his chin pushed up. No, no, just that one little thing. No one had been fired recently. There were no threats against either of them that they knew of, but they would check with their secretary because maybe she forgot to tell them that someone was ticked off. She could be forgetful; the secretary wasn't as young as she used to be. No, Heidi decided, they couldn't actually be one hundred percent sure that nobody wanted them dead. She made a mental note to ask around.

They had no money problems. They funded their own films from a trust left to Heidi from her first, very-much-older husband.

They liked living in Fremont Place because it was pretty and they were slowing things down. Sadly, it was not a neighborly place but not for lack of trying on their part.

They were horrified by the murders. Heidi was thinking of calling the Barnetts to ask if there was anything she could do. What did Detective Anderson think? Detective Anderson thought that she may want to put that off for a while – like a year or maybe never. Heidi pushed out a voluptuous lower lip and said she would wait. Hal was not so dense. He didn't show Cori to the door, but he thanked her for her honesty. Hal was a stand up guy.

Cori put a little star next to Hal and Heidi's names. She would run them when she got back to the office. Now she was at her last stop before meeting up with Finn and the lady of this house had been less than welcoming.

"I'm sure I couldn't tell you anything more, detective. I really don't know the Barnetts well. They seem quite the successful young couple." Cori turned from the living room window in time to see Rita Stigerson adjust her blouse a bit more impatiently than she would have if Cori had been looking at her all along. "As for the night before last, my husband and I returned from a dinner party about midnight and the streets were quiet, nothing out of the ordinary. We went to bed. Our bedroom is in the back of the house so we wouldn't have heard anything. My husband leaves for work at five in the morning. I was up very early with him and left before anyone knew what happened."

"What about the maid?"

Cori took a couple of steps around the room, her hand coming to rest on a wingback chair as she considered her hostess. Half of Cori's brain was waiting for the answer to her question but the other half was trying to figure out how old Mrs. Stigerson was: fifty-two at best, tops sixty. Cori smiled just to see if she could make Rita Stigerson do the same. Either Mrs. Stigerson literally couldn't return the friendly expression because of the Botox, or Cori wasn't as charming as she imagined. When Mrs. Stigerson sniffed and turned up her nose, Cori figured it was her charm factor that had flatlined.

"With the children gone, there's no need for the extravagance of someone here twenty-four hours a day. Our day lady leaves about four. So you see–" The doorbell interrupted the woman's hollow expression of regret that she had nothing to offer. "Excuse me."

Cori offered a lopsided grin as Mrs. Stigerson went for the door instead of waiting for the day lady to do the honors. She heard the front door open and the sound of well-bred voices greeting one another. Then she heard nothing. Cori imagined kisses on cheeks and whispers as Mrs. Stigerson complained that a detective was in her living room and the visitor commiserated. All this would be said in much the same way the woman might confess to having rats in the attic. When Mrs. Stigerson returned, she was accompanied by a plump, tan woman dressed in a blue Velour sweat suit that had some designer's initials embroidered in gold on the hip.

"Detective," Mrs. Stigerson skimmed over the fact that she had forgotten Cori's last name. "This is Mrs. Mulroon. She lives a few blocks over in that lovely Cape Cod."

Cori smiled politely and calculated the distance a *few* implied. The word *blocks* was plural. The sum of *few* and *blocks* meant that Mrs. Mulroon's house was too far removed from the scene of the crime to do Cori any good. Cori did another calculation. Mrs. Stigerson's arrogance plus Cori's distaste for it added up to time to leave. Unfortunately, getting out of town wasn't going to be easy. Mrs. Mulroon turned a staggeringly wide smile on Cori and moved every time the detective did. Finally, she planted herself. In the interest of good community relations, Cori decided to give her a minute and a half.

"Such a horrible thing. Children. What kind of monster would do that to children?"

Mrs. Mulroon's forehead wrinkled as she attempted to kick-start her imagination. Since Mrs. Mulroon seemed to want to work it out on her own, Cori didn't tell her that in her wildest imagination she wouldn't be able to come up with an answer.

"I'm paying for extra security, I can tell you. You know, I remember lying awake the other night. The night it happened."

Mrs. Mulroon put her hand on Mrs. Stigerson's arm, giving her a look that excluded Cori.

"I was awake in my bed and those poor little things were being killed. It gives me the shivers."

The story around the campfire came back Cori's way, and Mrs. Mulroon's other hand went to the detective's arm as if she was one of the girls again.

"I mean, to be awake and be thinking that all was right with the world and that was happening? So frightening."

"Things like that happen everyday of the week, ma'am," Cori assured her. Mrs. Mulroon, though, wasn't interested in dialogue. She wanted an audience.

"Well, I'll tell you, I can't wait to get the house put back together." The plump lady sighed. She blinked. She thought. She continued on, wanting to share everything with Cori. "I suppose that's why I'm not sleeping well. We're adding on to our home – a lovely rumpus room so the children won't tear up the living room. Of course, we're redoing the bath downstairs at the same time. That's why we've been camping out in the guest room. We feel so exposed with the back of our house wide open. Well, you can see why I'm not sleeping well. Not Tom, he sleeps just fine. Well, he did until this happened."

"Yes, ma'am."

Cori slipped her notebook into her purse and latched it. Mrs. Stigerson smiled, and raised her hand to guide Cori to the door, genuinely happy now that the detective was leaving. They didn't get far. Mrs. Mulroon was not only still talking, she was actually saying something interesting.

"...but it was that car that really bothered me. I mean, hardly anyone ever goes out the back way."

Cori did an about face. "The back way?"

CHAPTER 16

Finn stood so straight that his shoulders and back were flat against the white wall of the examining room. His knees were locked, the toes of his boots pointed forward, and his hands were crossed in front of him. He wore a white coat even though it was unnecessary since he wasn't close enough to the table to get anything on him. Still, wearing it usually made him feel official and that helped him get through situations like this. Unfortunately, the coat wasn't cutting it, so put his fists in the coat's pockets to keep from putting them through the wall. When all that did no good, Finn time-traveled back to his high school biology class and did his recitations.

Large intestine.

Stomach.

Liver.

Little heart.

He catalogued each of the internal organs, following along with Paul Craig, the medical examiner, who was pulling apart the body on the table in the same way most people peel a banana.

"Severe trauma to the chest and abdomen. One incision puncturing the heart. Other wounds well placed, damaging the carotid artery."

Paul paused, grasped a Styrofoam cup and drank deeply of his coffee. Finn had declined a cup when offered. The only thing he wanted once he got outside of this room was to head to Mick's. Today it wouldn't be a pint he ordered, but two shots of the strong stuff.

"Neither the stomach or large intestines appear to..."

Finn zoned out and before he knew it, Paul had finished. The doctor pulled off his rubber gloves with a resounding snap. He flipped off the recorder. His next comments need not be saved for posterity.

"I've got a granddaughter this age. If I were the hysterical type this would send me right to an institution. I don't know whether to be grateful or appalled that I'm not."

He looked at Finn, still rigid against the wall, mute because he had no answer to Paul's dilemma. The doctor smiled and answered Finn's silence instead.

"Right you are! If you haven't got anything to add to a conversation, don't say anything at all." The doctor's usual high spirits returned, but Finn noticed he covered the small body of Alexis Barnett with a bit more care than normal. "So, come out of this meat locker and let's have a chat."

Finn discarded the white coat and paused to let his hand rest on the table as he passed. A blessing, a gesture of comfort, whatever it was it was unnecessary to anyone but him. Paul was already seated behind the desk in his small, glass enclosed office by the time Finn joined him.

"Coffee?" Paul held up a pot. Finn shook his head and sat on a wooden chair that wobbled. Paul didn't have many visitors so the furniture in the office had only to be serviceable. "So, how you doing these days? Settling in down there at Wilshire Division, are you?"

"I haven't unpacked my boxes if that's what you mean."

"There will be time for all that." Paul put a bright spin on Finn's life for him. "Nice jacket. Little hot for leather, isn't it?"

"It's my good luck charm," Finn said. "I've got a different one for when this city is so blazing the devil himself won't walk the streets."

"My wife says I'm too old for a leather jacket. I don't think I am. Then again, I don't think I'm too old for a motorcycle and she won't let me have one of those either. Women." Paul laughed a little, the trill of it fading away while he searched for more small talk to keep from discussing the business at hand. Sadly, business was what they were there for so Finn took over.

"So, Paul. We appreciate the fast track on this," Finn said. "Can you tell me something that will put me to work properly?"

"Most of what I know you know, so I'll tell you what you don't. I have reviewed Doctor Ford's report. He did the nanny. Those bruises on her wrists happened before she died. It looks like someone could have knelt on her or maybe held her down with something round and hard. There was a lot of pressure. She was on her back when the trigger was pulled and they knew exactly what they were doing.

"She died instantly. It would take everything a man had, even if he had bulk behind him, to keep her immobile and still shoot her in that manner. We know she fought because there were bruises and scratches on her legs, too, but the ones on her wrists were deep and deliberate. There were no signs of sexual assault."

"So you're thinking there were two of them?"

"Or more, but two at least. I also don't think the same person would have killed in two different ways. The gunshot and restraint were calculated; the knife was used on the little girls with abandon, almost in a frenzy of sorts. Don't get me wrong. Those attacks were very professional. I mean frenzied like quick, as if he was having fun. There was no hesitation, no regret, and, I hate to say it, all of it was artfully done."

"God help us," Finn muttered.

"We've got one restrained victim, one sleeping girl, and one girl awake and moving. The wounds in the little girl had irregularities probably from her twisting. The weapon/body interaction created a great deal of distortion, but the older girl gave me quite a bit to work with. I was clearly able to measure the long axis, the width and the depth." Paul used his fingers as if pulling along a blade. "The knife had a long, slightly curved blade. Clean edged and sharp. No serration. It made a very distinctive cut, and it was so well honed that it cut like a scalpel. You can get them in any sporting goods store or knife shop. This one was either new or extremely well cared for but it did have a flaw. This person pulled the blade up, straight and fast. Same with the slash wounds: straight and fast." Paul leaned forward with his eyes alight. "Here's the exciting part. There is a chip on the blade at or near the tip. There was tearing at the end of every cut on the older girl. I couldn't ascribe the irregularity to the little one's wounds in a court of law, but on the older girl I could see it clearly. Find the knife and I'll prove it's the right one."

"Sure, isn't that a bit of good news," Finn said. "As

soon as you give me the dimensions on the blade, I'll bulletin all the hospitals and clinics and have them look out for knife wounds. You keep an eye out for anything like it that passes through here."

Paul nodded. "It will be top of the list for all of us."

Finn stood up. He rotated his head; his neck was stiff. "Did you get a fix on whether the killer was left handed or right handed?"

"Right handed for both. No doubt about it."

"Good job."

Paul gave Finn's shoulder a friendly slap. "Come on. I'll see you out."

They walked through the green painted halls, greeting those who came toward them, stepping aside for those who hurried past, ignoring the windows of autopsy rooms when they came upon them. The Los Angeles coroner's office was a busy place, much to Finn's dismay. They chatted about the doctor's upcoming trip to Ireland. Finn admonished him not to stick to the cities. The real Ireland, he said, was in the countryside. Paul promised to bring pictures back to prove he had taken the advice as he held the lobby door for the detective. Finn was turning toward him when he took notice of the woman sitting on the small, worn sofa in the lobby. Her black-stockinged legs were together, knee to knee. Her hands were clasped over a small black purse in her lap. Her dress was black. She looked surprised to see him. He had the feeling he knew her, but it wasn't until they locked eyes – his blue like ice and hers blue like a warm lagoon – that Finn knew who she was.

"Mrs. Barnett." Finn walked toward her.

"Detective O'Brien," she replied as she stood up.

When Finn reached to shake her hand, he realized why he hadn't recognized Elizabeth Barnett immediately.

Her long ebony hair was now the color of gunmetal.

CHAPTER 17

When he took her hand, Finn felt the tremor that ran deep down where muscle met nerve. Her skin was rice paper dry and almost as translucent. They stood looking at one another, hands clasped until Finn let go. He broke the eye contact, and turned toward the medical examiner.

"Paul Craig. Doctor Craig. This is Mrs. Barnett, Paul."

"Elizabeth, please." She held out that cool hand again. Paul took it reluctantly, well aware that his hands had recently probed the bodies of her children.

"Nice to meet you. I'd like to offer my condolences."

"Thank you," she said and when the men had no response, she asked: "Are you finished with my girls, doctor?"

"Yes. Just now. Ms. Gerber, too." He cleared his throat. "Detective O'Brien has all the details. He'll do a fine job."

Elizabeth put her fingertips on the sleeve of Finn's jacket and said: "I know."

"Yes. Well, then." Paul inched toward the door, not quite as comfortable with the living as the dead. "It was nice to meet you, Mrs. Barnett."

Paul executed a graceful one-eighty, but Elizabeth

Barnett caught the open door before he could go through.

"Doctor Craig?" she said. "My girls. They didn't see anything, did they?"

"No, Mrs. Barnett. They died with their dreams and their dreams were of good things. Of you."

Paul Craig, Finn decided, underestimated his bedside manner. His lie was pitch perfect. At least one of the girls had seen something and it terrified her little being to its core. Elizabeth, though, was satisfied. For a second after the door closed, she watched Paul through the window in the door. When she faced Finn she asked:

"Do you have a moment?"

"We can talk outside."

Elizabeth went ahead of him, wraith thin in her black dress. They wandered down the street together, in no hurry, going nowhere. Her hand went to her hair.

"I always thought it was a myth." Elizabeth said.

"What is that?" Finn asked, putting his sunglasses on against the glare of the day.

"Hair turning gray overnight." She laughed a little; she laughed sadly. "I always thought this was something that happened in novels."

Finn watched their feet move. He did not have Paul's constitution and would have welcomed some time alone to put aside what he had seen during the autopsy, but Elizabeth Barnett was oblivious to his unease.

"It's not really important," she was saying. "My hair, I mean. I don't think I'll color it. It will remind me of how I failed."

"There isn't one thing you could have done if you'd been in the house, Mrs. Barnett," Finn assured her, even knowing there were no words on this earth that would make her believe that.

"I could have died with them if it came to that." She answered with a surety that saddened Finn. Elizabeth Barnett would probably fool and torture herself for years, believing that she would have been super human and saved her girls.

"I suppose you could have done that. But then there wouldn't be anyone to carry on in their name." Finn stopped and waited for her to face him. She didn't. Instead, she crossed her arms. The little black purse dangled from her fingertips.

"That sounds like such a wise thing. It isn't, of course, but I know what you're doing. You're trying to make me feel as if there is some good to come of all this."

"Look, missus, I don't wish to be rude. Much as I'd like to help you come to some peace, I'm not your man. All I know is that there's no goodness here, there is only putting one foot in front of the other."

Elizabeth nodded, twining her fingers together and letting them rest at her waist. Finn thought she looked as if she were waiting for a ride to lunch, until he saw that her knuckles were white with the effort of keeping her fingers together and her neck was not elegant, but lengthened because her muscles were corded with tension. Still, she was polite, the kind of woman his mother would have admired. A real lady, his mother would have said.

"Sam and I put you in a difficult position the other night, and now I've done it again. I apologize for being such a problem. I hope you'll forgive me."

"If you're being honest, then there's nothing to forgive."

"Why wouldn't I be honest?" She began to walk again.

"You didn't tell us about Stephen Grady."

"Because he is irrelevant. I made that clear to Sam. Stephen is a sad, brilliant man who the world has discarded," she said. "There's nothing more to it than that."

"But you had a special relationship with him," Finn said.

"Who told you that?" Elizabeth asked only to instantly wave away the question. "Never mind. I know it was Sam. He hated me working at the clinic. He thought it was dangerous for me to be around people with mental problems. My husband doesn't really trust my instincts, but I know a threat when I see one. Stephen was not a threat."

"It sounds as if Mr. Barnett was concerned with your welfare."

She put on her sunglasses and Finn was sorry for it. He preferred to see people's eyes when he was asking about important things and Stephen Grady was important.

"Yes, he always has been. If I were you, though, I would discount anything he has to say about the clinic. He's never been there. He just writes a check when I ask him to."

"It wasn't him that gave me the information. It was Mrs. Billings and Etta. They said that Stephen wouldn't take his medication from anyone but you; they said he once told them he loved you."

"Love means many different things to men," Elizabeth

answered. "A sick man directs his love at the person who speaks kindly to him."

"When was the last time you saw Mr. Grady outside the clinic?" Finn asked.

Though her glasses were large and round, Finn could see her eyebrows rise. She settled herself on a concrete retaining wall and angled her legs gracefully so that her skirt fell over her knees. Her dress skimmed her body instead of hugging it and still Finn couldn't help but wonder if she wore the blue teddy beneath it.

"I'm sure Etta told you that there are strict rules about such things," Elizabeth said, ending the conversation about the clinic in the next minute. "I didn't come here to talk about Stephen Grady. I actually came here to find out when I could claim my girls' bodies. I know I could have called, but I thought if I came here, where they are, that they would come to me one last time." She took a deep breath. "They didn't. I think that's my punishment."

With that, Elizabeth Barnett began to weep. Tears fell from her eyes in sheets. She took off her sunglasses, her body bowed, and her hair waved around her shoulders. If this woman was the cause of her children's deaths either she didn't have a clue why or she was the best actress in the world. Finn touched her shoulder.

"Mrs. Barnett, is your husband here? Is he waiting to drive you home?"

Her head shook back and forth and her words were muffled behind her hands.

"No. He went to work." Elizabeth shuddered and wiped her tears with the fingertips of both hands. She shook back her hair, put her shoulders straight again, and her glasses back on. "It seems odd, doesn't it? For him to go to work."

"I cannot say," Finn answered even though he could have found a few choice words to share if it had been seemly to do so. He wouldn't have left his wife's side for a second if those were his children in the morgue. He wouldn't have left a woman like Elizabeth Barnett no matter what.

"Let's call him then. If he can't come, I'll drive you home and you can collect your car later," Finn offered.

"No, thank you. I got here; I'll get home." Elizabeth's voice dropped a note. "Please don't be too hard on Sam. The truth is, you just never know what you're capable of when things go wrong."

Elizabeth twisted her wedding ring as she spoke. Her voice seemed to drift far away as she thought about choices and consequences. The diamond was a stunning thing. It glinted in the sun and was so big and heavy that it fell to the side of her narrow finger. It seemed to bother her. Then again, the feel of her clothes, the warmth of the sun, the people driving down the street probably bothered her, too.

"It's a shame that you don't have a wife and children, Detective O'Brien. They would be lucky to have you to lean on." She stood up and smoothed her skirt, talking all the while. "And don't be fooled by what Sam may tell you. I'm strong in ways no one knows, not even my husband. I want to be the first to hear everything you find out. If you tell Sam, he will pick and choose what to tell me. I don't want to always wonder what I don't know. You'll do that for me, won't you?"

Elizabeth had come so close that Finn could see

strands of soft, inky black hair beneath the gray. She swayed slightly and touched her forehead as if the sun was too hot. He steadied her and for a second she put her hand over his. Finn pulled back. She smiled as if she knew the affect she had on him.

"I need to get on, or I will never have anything to tell you," Finn said.

"Don't go just yet. There is something I need you to see." She stepped away from him. "Something is missing from our home."

CHAPTER 18

Elizabeth opened her purse and took out a photograph, looked at it briefly, and handed it to Finn.

"I bought those lockets for my children before they were born. I was psychic about their birth, but didn't have a clue about their death. The jeweler who made these was old, and I didn't want him to die and not make something for my children. The jeweler is still alive," she added, and the irony of that was not lost on Finn.

"Are these gold?" he asked.

"Yes." She shook back her hair and moved closer still, standing so that she could look at the picture with him. "There were better pieces in my jewelry box and the safe, but these are each worth about eight hundred dollars. That little glow where the flash went off? That's a diamond. Just over the 'i' in Alexis and just above the tail of the 'a' in Alana."

"The shape is unusual, too. Octagonal. The script isn't standard." Finn mused.

"I took pictures for the insurance company in case the girls lost them."

"Where did you keep them?" he asked.

"In the ballerina box on the bedside table between the girls' beds. They would have been easy to see and easy to take. I remember touching the table and the box. I remember thinking something was out of place and then last night it dawned on me that the box was empty."

"I'll need the name and address of the jeweler so I can get the chain length, size of the lockets, that kind of information."

Finn started to pocket the photo, but Elizabeth took it and turned it over. The information he needed was neatly printed on the back along with the address of the insurance company. He smiled and tucked the photo away.

"I'll get these lockets back to you one of these days," he promised.

"I'm not sure I could touch them now. I'm just glad that they will be of some use." Small lines etched quotation marks at the side of her mouth, her eyes crinkled as if she were about to smile. She never did.

Finn pushed on, knowing he would lose her in the next minute or two. "Was there anything missing from Rachel's room? Has anyone come asking after her?"

"I wouldn't really know if anything of hers was missing," she said. "I never thought it wise to get close to someone who would eventually leave. Perhaps Sam might know. Ask him."

"I know Rachel did not confide in you about her friend, but are you sure it was a man and that he was alone when he came to get her?" Finn asked.

"I suppose there could have been someone else in the car with him. I didn't watch to make sure she got off safely. Rachel was a big girl," Elizabeth Barnett said. A second later she added: "She knew exactly what she was doing."

Finn noted the coolness in the woman's voice, the verbal parsing. "But you did see her picked up at least once. Anything you remember will be helpful."

"The car had four doors. The back door on the passenger side was dented. It was blue, I think. Sam might remember more."

"He doesn't seem to."

"I'm surprised. He seemed to have a soft spot for the help," Elizabeth Barnett said.

Suddenly, Finn did not quite cotton to Mrs. Barnett. She was indeed a lady, but a lady of times gone by who stood above the likes of Rachel Gerber. Finn had never cared for such an attitude but then she smiled and her eyes shined and redeemed herself.

"I'm not being difficult. I simply don't have any information for you about Rachel. She was a very private person, also." Elizabeth opened her bag again. She took out her car keys. "I'll get you the name of the agency that placed her."

"I would appreciate it, missus," Finn said and then she left him.

He watched her go to her car and found himself wondering why she drove such a fancy carriage. An SUV, a station wagon, even a minivan would have been more appropriate for a woman so devoted to her children and their pursuits. He wondered if Sam Barnett gave her a say even in her choice of cars.

That thought was fleeting because just as he turned away Finn O'Brien heard the screech of tires, the slam of brakes and smelled the burn of rubber. He turned in time to see a sedan peel out of the parking garage across the street, narrowly missing the Jaguar as it bolted into traffic and sped off. Elizabeth Barnett slammed on her brakes and stiff-armed the wheel as she was thrown forward. Finn was running before the Jag stopped rocking. He yanked the door open. Elizabeth Barnett's forehead was on the wheel and her hands were still wrapped around it when he pulled her back.

"Are you all right? Are you?"

Finn pushed the hair out of her eyes. He took off her glasses and tossed them aside, looking for blood as he unlatched her seatbelt and helped her out of the car.

Elizabeth Barnett fell against him and he wrapped his arms around her, pulling her close, holding her tight to stop her shaking. Her cheek was against his shoulder but Finn O'Brien still heard her whisper:

"He wanted to kill me, didn't he?"

CHAPTER 19

DAY 3 – AFTERNOON

"Elizabeth! Elizabeth!"

Sam Barnett called for his wife as he threw himself against the door of the Coulter's guesthouse. That door shook and rattled as he turned the handle the wrong way, pulled on it and finally wrenched it open. He flew inside still calling his wife's name, but it was Finn O'Brien he found standing in the small kitchen.

"Where is she? Where's my wife?"

Finn lifted his chin. "In the bedroom. She's fine. She just had a fright."

"It was that man from the clinic, wasn't it?"

Sam Barnett threw back his coat and punched his hips with his fists. He walked a few steps forward, a few back. He eyed Finn. He looked at the tea bag the detective held over a steaming mug of water and waited for answers.

"No, sir. This appeared to be nothing more than a reckless driver," Finn said. "Given what's happened, I think Mrs. Barnett is imagining the worst."

"Nothing new there," Sam muttered.

So as not to show his surprise at the man's aside, Finn lowered the tea bag and watched it bob before the water soaked in and made it heavy enough to sink. Sam Barnett, though, was not fooled. He knew when he was being judged.

"Look, O'Brien, there's something you should know about Elizabeth. She doesn't just have an active imagination; she is paranoid. If she can't control something then it's suspect. The rest of the world is out to get us, every day there's a disaster waiting around the corner – teachers who give our kids a bad shake, my health, financial ruin, plane crashes, car accidents – you name it she's thought about it. That's why we live here, behind a wall, schools within walking distance. When we were first married I thought all this was a charming quirk. It was cute that she thought the world revolved around the two of us; then I found out that she didn't want the world to be anymore than the two of us. No matter how easy I try to make her life, nothing helps. That trip to Paris? Most women would kill to have their husbands take them on a trip like that. It took me three months to convince her to go. You'd think I was torturing her.

"Anyway, I wanted you to know that. About Elizabeth's paranoia, I mean. She hides it well, but it's the real deal with her."

"I wouldn't be so quick to discount your wife's feelings," Finn lifted a brow but kept his eyes on the tea bag. He could hardly see it now as the water colored to bronze.

"I don't think I appreciate your tone, detective."

"I am only thinking that she might have subconsciously picked up on something that led to your troubles." Finn looked up and let his lips rise in an effort to sympathize. "And it is not unreasonable to think either of you might have difficulty distinguishing between an accident and an attack. I'm glad I was able to calm her."

"Yes. About that," Sam said. "Exactly why were you with my wife? Where were you two when all this happened?"

Finn considered the man's polite outrage, his offense at, rather than gratitude for, the detective's help. He tried his damndest to find a soft space in his heart for Sam Barnett, but the only thing that was warming were Finn's hands around the mug.

"I was at the morgue at the same time your wife came to inquire about when your daughters' bodies would be released."

Sam Barnett trembled briefly, the answer pricking at him and then settling into a pain in his gut. He sank onto a chair near a small table. He muttered his wife's name once and he shook his head as if he had just been told his child had cheated on a test.

"When Mrs. Barnett came upon me, she was pleased. I had saved her a trip to the station. She wanted to tell me that two lockets were taken from your daughters' bedroom."

"I didn't know," he said. "And I didn't know that she had gone back to the house again. We've been..." Sam Barnett sat up straighter yet his hands hung between his knees. He was somewhere between defeat and defense. "We haven't actually spoken much."

Finn understood what the man was saying. He and Bev hadn't spoken much in the last six months even though many a word had passed between them.

How do you feel?
Why did you do it?

Did you take your medicine?

You killed a cop.

Do you want me in court with you?

That man you saved was a nobody.

Are you hungry?

I think we should separate.

You ruined our lives for a nobody, Finn.

I want a divorce.

Sam Barnett fell silent. Finn thought of his grandfather and how he would cast a keen eye on him when he went quiet. *Bíonn ciúin ciontach*, he would say. The quiet are guilty. But of what? Of believing his wife incapable when she had already proven herself capable of so much? Was he guilty of needing to prove his own worth by proving his wife worthless? Neither of those things made Sam Barnett a criminal or a sinner; it only made him a sad, small man.

"All right. Well. That is something solid. Something to go on. Yes, that's good." Sam Barnett put his hands on his thighs but made no other move. "And what about the car? Can you identify the driver?"

"No, I cannot." Finn pulled his lips together in what passed for a regretful smile. "The car was an older model. Black. Oxidized paint. Two doors."

"I'm surprised that's all you got. Most cops I know are very observant."

"Sometimes my job is made difficult by circumstances. For instance, I would have appreciated hearing the information about Stephen Grady first thing. Since you were reluctant to share that, I am wondering what else you might be holding back." Finn leaned forward. "Perhaps something personal to you alone. Something your wife knows nothing about. Perhaps you crossed someone and that would explain what has come down upon you."

"If I had pissed someone off, don't you think they would want to hurt me?"

"Perhaps that's what they think they are doing," Finn answered.

"Then mission accomplished. For the record, I haven't pissed anyone off." Sam stood up and headed for the bedroom only to turn around. He held out his hands for the tea. "I assume that is for Elizabeth."

Finn held the mug toward him. Sam Barnett took the tea and didn't try to hide his dislike of everything Finn O'Brien: the way he stood, the fact that he never looked away once he caught your eye, the way his face was cut into planes and his body was mounded with muscle, the disrespect his casual clothing implied.

"I'll have to talk to your captain about this extraordinary kindness of yours. Putting my wife to bed, bringing her tea. Some people might consider that inappropriate behavior but I appreciate it, detective. Seriously, I do."

"Some people might consider going to work so soon after your children are murdered inappropriate."

"You bastard," Sam muttered as he took hold of the mug, but Finn didn't let go.

"I called your office," Finn went on. "Your secretary hadn't seen you today nor did she expect you in."

They squared off, two men as different as night and day with skin in a game neither wanted to play. Sam broke first.

"Okay. Look. I'm sorry if I sound like an ass. It's just

that I've taken care of Elizabeth the last ten years. I know her limitations. There are certain things I do quietly if I think they will upset her," Sam said. "You understand how it is when a man has things to do."

"That I do." Finn let go of the mug but Sam stayed his ground.

"The truth is, I told Elizabeth that I was going to the office hoping she would just stay here and rest. I should have known better. Elizabeth imagines that she is helping when she isn't; she imagines she is bringing something important to the table when there isn't even a table. You understand, right? I mean the morgue thing was out of line. The lockets, she did good on that."

Sam paused but if he were waiting for the detective to agree to Elizabeth Barnett's limitations. When he didn't, Sam Barnett said:

"Okay, look, you don't know either of us really. I'm sorry she interfered with what you were doing, and I'll make sure it doesn't happen again. Let's just leave it at that."

Sam held the mug in one hand. He took Finn's shoulder with the other and gave it a squeeze before dismissing the detective by showing his back. Finn spoke to that.

"Don't underestimate your wife, Mr. Barnett. She is a strong, courageous woman."

Sam looked over his shoulder and Finn thought he saw the man smile just a little.

"I know all about my wife, detective."

"Then why lie to her? Today of all days." Finn pressed on and the button he hit was the right one.

Sam Barnett did an about face. Finn saw the flash of

anger and the determination to keep it under control, but the detective wanted none of that. He wanted Sam Barnett to forget the lawyer in him. Finn stepped forward and met the man halfway, contenders storming into the ring.

"You think I've got some deep, dark secret don't you?" Sam growled. "Well, here's a news flash. The only thing you've found out is just how much I love my wife; how much I want to spare her anymore pain."

"Where were you?" Finn demanded.

"I was seeing about coffins," Sam said. "After what happened today, I suppose I should be glad I don't have to order one more."

CHAPTER 20

At noon, Ariba's Mexican Food Restaurant was a cross between a human beehive and a mosh pit. Everyone tried to be heard over the sounds of the kitchen, the canned mariachi music, waitresses calling out their orders, and customers talking as they tried to wolf down their food before their phones rang. The waitresses were surly, the cooks none too concerned with health regulations, and the chairs and tables held together with gum and glue. Ariba's was, in short, perfect.

Every cop in Wilshire Division ate at Ariba's and when Finn O'Brien walked in each one fell silent. While waitresses called out orders and dishes clattered and recorded Mariachi's sang a song of love, the cops shut their mouths, hunched their backs and bowed over combo plates so they wouldn't have to look at the cop killer in their midst. When Finn took a step, chairs were pushed back, blocking his way. When he turned he found yet another chair in his path and another so that he was forced to walk a maze toward the table where Cori sat perusing a menu at a corner table littered with chips, two water glasses, and three empty bowls of salsa. He pulled out a chair and when he sat down, the hive was buzzing again. Instead of offering him a sweet greeting in the midst of such animosity, Cori said:

"God created phones for a reason, O'Brien."

She closed the menu with a flourish and gave him the stink eye.

"You seem a wee bit upset with me, Cori. Perhaps you've gone to the dark side like the rest of them."

Finn crossed his arms on the table and let his gaze scrape across his fellow officers. Cops ate like the meal in front of them was their last. They did that because the minute they walked out the door their ticket could be punched. Pity, they all thought Finn might be the one punching it.

"Screw them and the horse they rode in on," she said. "But you're over an hour late and you didn't have the courtesy to call me. That made me insane. Everybody hates your guts. Half of these fools want to put a bullet through your head or a bomb under your car. There are also random acts of violence in this city, accidents and my all-time favorite, force majeure. All of that creates a need for partners to communicate appropriately and often so one of them doesn't go out of her friggin' mind with worry."

She put her hands on the table. She was done. It was his turn.

"I'm sorry," he said. "Perhaps you'll be a little kinder when I tell you why I'm late."

Cori twirled a strand of hair around her finger and tucked it behind her ear. Her eyelashes fluttered so he couldn't see how very afraid for him she had been.

"You've got to remember to call so I know you're okay."

She flipped that lacquered strand of hair back over her ear. She was still antsy even though Finn was sitting right in from of her. He couldn't blame her. The last time he'd been missing in action Cori found him in a hospital looking worse than the one-eyed Balor of Celtic myth, his badge gone, and a murder charge on the horizon.

"Okay. I'm done," she said. "Who goes first? What the heck, you go since it seems like whatever you were up to was so newsworthy it drove everything else out of your mind."

"Bev served me with divorce papers this morning," he answered.

"That's a bitch for sure." Cori gave a nod. She pulled her lips together, surprised by the news and determined not to read anything more into it than what it was. "I'm sorry but not everybody can get through tough times, O'Brien."

"Like you did?" Finn smiled at the woman across from him with her big hair and bigger heart. "Do you think I don't know every cop in L.A. had you guilty by association because you were my partner? I never told you how much I appreciated you standing up for me."

"That's what partners do. Whatever you need."

She tended to her napkin because it was hard to look into Finn's eyes and see only gratitude. On a practical note, she didn't want him to see what was in her eyes.

"I love you for it, woman." Finn said that like it was a chuck under the chin.

"Yeah, well, I'm pretty loveable." The moment of wanting to tell Finn the deep dark truth of her feelings passed as it always did. "So, that's where you were? With Bev?"

"No. I just thought you should know now that it's official. I wasn't sure myself until this morning," Finn said. "I was at the autopsy. Elizabeth Barnett showed up."

"The doc didn't let her in, did he?"

Finn shook his head. "She was there to find out about collecting the little ones. She's gray, Cori."

Cori opened her eyes wide and shrugged. Finn put his hand to his head.

"Her hair went gray overnight. I've never seen anything like it."

Cori lifted her gracefully arched brows and that made her eyes look sultry and more than a little sexy.

"So you two talked about her do? That's cozy."

"For just a minute," Finn laughed and then he told her the rest: the locket, the car, and the encounter with Sam Barnett.

"He thinks she has some clinical problems. I don't see it. Did you?"

Cori shook her head. "I'd say she's a tough cookie but everybody has a breaking point. From what little I saw he calls the major shots – where they live, what they do, where they vacation – and her kingdom is home and hearth. Maybe they have a War of the Roses thing going on. You know, territorial stuff. Passive-aggressive."

"I wouldn't have thought she would play games like that," Finn said.

"I think the lady has a lot of layers, so keep an open mind," Cori warned. "I'll write it up for the book, but between yesterday and today I'm starting to color in the lines. She's nice enough but exacting. The housekeeper said there were very strict rules for how the house was cleaned, where she could go and where she couldn't, when she could take a break and what she could eat out of the fridge."

"Was there resentment for the house rules?" Finn asked.

"No. She said it was a good job and paid well. She also said she Mrs. Barnett wasn't mean like some, just exacting. Once she got the hang of the rules, everything was good. She said the little girls were just normal kids and they were happy. Mrs. Barnett made them clean up after themselves but she cut them slack. We're not looking at Mommy Dearest where the kids were concerned."

"Anything else on the housekeeper?" he asked.

"I had Earl do a quick check on two relatives. One of the nephews is a gangbanger, Venice 13. She says he's a good kid when he comes around, but she knows to keep him at arm's length. Her older brother was in Folsom for ten years on armed robbery. He's living up north and the housekeeper hasn't seen him for years. Other than that, I didn't hear anything that worried me."

"How did she get along with Rachel Gerber?"

"Okay. They worked well together. She said Rachel kept the girls in order – homework was always done, they were picked up from school on time, play dates were met. Rachel didn't get personal but she was good to the girls, just a little stand-offish."

"That should have suited the missus," Finn noted and raised his finger to catch the waitress' eye. The waitress ignored him.

"Maybe under different circumstances, but remember it was Mr. Barnett who insisted on the nanny," Cori said. "Scuttlebutt in the park is that the two ladies did not get along. The other nannies thought Mrs. Barnett was intense where Rachel was concerned, but Rachel thought she was a psycho bitch."

"That's not good," Finn said. "Did the ladies give you any reason why?"

"Seems Mrs. Barnett was a fault finder. She accused Rachel of stealing, of not watching the kids closely enough. She used to show up at the park unannounced – that one I could understand since a lot of moms do spot checks on their kids – but what really ticked Rachel off was that she alluded to impropriety with the husband. No direct accusations, just innuendo. Then Mr. Barnett would come home and the wife was perfect. No hint of a problem."

"I doubt Barnett would be interested in the nanny considering the missus is a looker," Finn said.

Cori snorted. "Don't kid yourself. If a woman shows interest in a man you can bet he'll show some back. Besides, Barnett might have made a play for the nanny if Mrs. Barnett is as ridged in the bedroom as she is everywhere else. If he did make a pass, though, he didn't get far. According to her two buddies from the park, Rachel Gerber thought he was a bore. Look, we know Mrs. Barnett wasn't excited about having help, it just sounds like she was trying to make it uncomfortable enough for Rachel to quit. It happens."

"Great. Her husband thinks she's paranoid, the nannies think she's the employer from hell and the ladies at the clinic think she's Mother Theresa," Finn said.

"What do you think?" Cori asked.

"I think that she's extraordinarily clearheaded in this crisis." He took the photo out of his pocket and handed it to Cori. "Those are lockets that were taken from the house. I've already put out a bulletin to the pawnshops. Look at the back. Everything is noted properly."

"Well, if that isn't fine as frog fur." A dazzling smile spread across Cori's face. She considered the picture and then gave it back to Finn.

"One thing's for sure," Cori said.

"What's that?"

"The nanny didn't take them."

Finn laughed, "I cannot argue with that, but wouldn't it be lovely to have just an idea of who has them."

"I might just be able to help out there, my friend." Cori rested her chin in the palm of her hand and gave him a grin. "After the housekeeper and the nannies, I had the pleasure of meeting with some of the fine ladies of Fremont Place."

"And?"

"And," Cori dropped her hand, crossed her arms and leaned over the table to drop her bombshell. "Mrs. Mulroon who lives way, way over on the edge of the development is remodeling. That means she has to sleep downstairs and right around two in the morning she was awakened by the sound of a car–"

"Please tell me she ran out and got a plate?"

"Nope. But she did see a dark colored, four-door sedan heading out the back way," Cori said. "Yes, my friend, there is a back way into Fremont Place where the wall was never finished after construction of the newer area. And what's behind the wall that was never finished?"

"I'll bite," Finn said.

"A dirt field. And what happens at Mrs. Mulroon's

house around 1:30 in the morning? Her sprinklers go off and they make a muddy mess in the field where there is no wall."

"Tell me you have tire tracks."

"Indeed, I do. And only one set, my friend. Nobody has gone that way except the bad guys."

Cori sat back as Finn raised his water glass to her.

"By the work, we'll know the workmen, Cori."

Cori raised her water glass back.

"Whatever, O'Brien."

Chapter 21

Medium Man took the boy home, and for the first day they were both quite pleased with the arrangement. The boy had a roof over his head and food to eat. He told Medium Man that he thought he loved him. That was bull, but the boy didn't want to go back to the streets where there were crazies or to Fairy Tails where there were some rough customers.

The second day they were together, the boy told Medium Man all about how he grew up. The guy actually cried hearing that the boy couldn't remember his mother's face but remembered all too well the back of his father's hand. Medium Man told the boy that he never had a mother to remember and that made him cry all the more. The boy thought that was creepy. Still, he didn't get that hinky-dinky feeling in his privates that told him he had a real weirdo on his hands, so he decided he would stick around until he could trade up. There were some very specific things the boy wanted to trade up to.

First, he wanted a real home with a matching sofa and love seat instead of Medium Man's very old couch, the La-Z-Boy with the ripped upholstery, and the skanky mattress. The boy wanted a lot of windows for light to come through, not just one dirty one like Medium Man had in this place. The boy would like to be with someone he wouldn't forget the minute he went to sleep and would actually remember when he woke up. But the boy wasn't really a self-starter. While his plans to trade up were real, acting on them was something that would happen in a vague future.

Medium Man on the other hand was delighted by the turn of events. No one had ever stayed with him. A few had pretended they wanted to, but they disappeared in the middle of the night having used his body and taken his money and his drugs. They had left Medium Man to wake up afraid, alone, and ticked. He spent countless hours searching the streets of Hollywood looking for the traitors, primed and ready to take back what was his plus a little more. The boy, though, not only woke up with him two days in a row, he made no move to leave, so Medium Man started making some plans of his own.

He would get a picture of the boy and put it in a frame like the picture he had seen in that woman's house. That was a beautiful frame. He also thought she was a beautiful woman, the first woman Medium Man thought he might want. Maybe Medium Man would get two frames and put a picture of himself in one, but that plan was discarded. He didn't like to look at himself in the same way other people didn't like to look at him. The boy looked at him, though. Medium Man felt him looking when he thought Medium Man was asleep. When they made love the boy kept his eyes closed. Medium Man wished it were the other way around.

Medium Man didn't just make plans; overcome with happiness he made changes. He carefully cleaned his knife and put it high on a shelf so that he would not use it against his new lover. Though the boy wasn't beautiful, he was genuine and loyal. Loyalty was important. Mort was loyal and Medium Man was loyal back, and now there was the loyal boy. It was almost like having a family, and a family was what Medium Man wanted more than anything in the world.

"Today is going to be a good day. I think it's going to be a great day. I need you to go to the store and get a newspaper," Medium Man said to the boy when he was done thinking about all the good things that were happening to him.

"I don't want to go."

The boy was sitting in the corner on the mattress that Medium Man called a bed. He was squeezing one of the sores on his face even though Medium Man had told him not to. The boy didn't see Medium Man's brow furrow when he said he didn't want to go. The boy didn't know that Medium Man expected a different answer out of a loving companion. What good was it having a special friend if he didn't want to do anything? He gave the boy another chance.

"Don't you think you should go to the store and get the paper if I ask you? I would like you to go."

The boy looked up. He had very long lashes, just like a girl's. Beneath those lashes his eyes were a watery gray color that Medium Man found sexy.

"That's stupid. What are you going to read? All about the stock market?" The boy guffawed and rubbed his face. "Or the comics. That's what you read, ain't it? Comics."

Because the boy had only been with Medium Man for

a few days, he missed the subtleties of his changing mood that signaled the coming of his fury: the twitch of the older man's wrist, and the tick at the corner of his left eye, and the way his back rounded and his chest caved. The change came on him in a snap when he was surprised or disappointed. Medium Man didn't like that, but he had long ago given up trying to control it.

"Don't call me stupid. Or dumb. I don't like those words," Medium Man warned in a very quiet voice. "I don't like the word crazy, neither."

The boy wasn't listening. He was distracted now that he felt the core of the cyst on his cheek and he was hard at work trying to get rid of it.

"I just don't want to go. I'm tired. You had me up half the night," he whined.

"You loved it," Medium Man said, but there was no affection in his voice. This was the boy's last chance to do right. "I like to read the paper. You should get it because I like the paper."

"If it's so important, you go get it."

The boy heard a pop and when he looked at his dirty fingers he saw that a hard thing had come out of his miserable, sore face. He was about to say something else, something flip, something to let Medium Man know who was going to be calling the shots, when his head was slammed against the wall so hard that he saw stars. His hands clawed at the fingers wound into his long hair, pulling on it as if to rip that hair right out of his head. Medium Man's other hand was around the boy's throat, his thumb on the boy's windpipe. The boy's eyes rolled back in his head, his arms flailed, and the flaming red infections on his face drained to near white. With each desperate move the boy made, Medium Man's grip tightened. He pressed at the boy's throat, pulled and smacked the boy's head against that wall over and over again. But it wasn't just the attack or the gleam in the man's eyes that frightened the boy, it wasn't the way the man's lips had pulled back revealing empty spaces where teeth should have been, it was Medium Man's strength that scared the willies out of him. The sound of Medium Man's whispers into the hollow of his ear made him want to pee.

"I'd like you to go and get the newspaper. I'd like you do that now. Do you understand?"

The boy nodded with his eyelids since he couldn't move his head. Medium Man kept his lips against the boy's ear. The boy hoped he wasn't going to bite it off. Medium Man didn't. Instead he released his hold and snaked his arm around the boy's neck, relaxing until he gently embraced his new friend and slid next to him on the mattress.

"That's good. We have to have rules here if we're going to be happy. You want to be happy together. You want that, right?" Medium Man cooed and nuzzled the side of the boy's head. The boy nodded, and all the while his brain was spinning. "Good. Now, go get me a newspaper."

The boy started to get up but before he could, Medium Man pulled him back.

"Did you forget something?"

The boy feigned a smile and forced himself to kiss Medium Man who, in turn, grinned mightily. The boy slid off the mattress. He would go but he wouldn't get no newspaper; he wouldn't be coming back neither.

"Here, take this. It's enough to get yourself some candy, too."

Medium Man dug in the pocket of his shapeless chinos for the money. He held it out to the boy. The boy took the dollars and the coins. He picked up his pack and opened the door to leave, but Medium Man was on him before he could.

"You won't need that." The man took the backpack that held all the boy's worldly possessions and money. The boy's heart sank. "Remember, a newspaper and some candy. If you don't come back pretty fast, I'll have to come looking for you. I don't want to do that. You understand, don't you?"

Up and down the boy's head went. His Adam's apple bobbed too. He was old enough to understand that he was in bigger trouble than he had ever been in. He was too young to understand that if he really wanted to leave he could because Medium Man wasn't very good at finding people. The only thing Medium Man was good at was following directions, and even then he screwed up sometimes. Like what he did to those kids. That was wrong. He thought about this failing the whole time he was alone, but when the boy came back in record time Medium Man was happy again. The boy sat in the tattered chair and Medium Man sat on the couch reading the paper. He and Mort were still front-page news and he was so proud that he got up, caught the boy in a headlock, and made light with him.

"Yep. That's what I wanted to see," he said, without telling the boy what *that* was.

He let go of the boy when he saw that the paper had fallen open. On the inside page, there was a picture of the dark haired woman, her face resting against the chest of a man who looked like he didn't deserve her. Medium Man picked up the paper again to take a closer look and that's when he saw something important: he saw a chance to make up to the dark haired lady.

"Come on you two! Right now! Get your butts over here."

The young department store photographer watched the trio approach her desk and thanked heaven that she had six months on the job. She would need to be a real professional to deal with the woman with the platinum bouffant walking toward her, giving her two darling little girls what for at the same time. The photographer popped her gum and straightened up; the blonde paused briefly, grabbed the littlest girl by the arm, and gave it a twist.

"I said, get a move on!" she barked.

The little one whimpered and the older girl hovered in the background, smirking at her sister's agony, sticking her tongue out when the little girl looked to her for help. When they were close enough, the photographer put on her sweet face and parked her gum.

"May I be of assistance?"

"I want a picture of these two. Carolyn and Bobbi. That's short for Roberta." The bouffant babe leaned close like they were sharing a secret, but she was really checking to see if the girl was taking all the information down right.

"Those are pretty names." The photographer smiled at the girls and hoped their look of terror would pass so she could get a good shot. "I'll just need your full name and address."

"Stand up straight, Bobbi!" The blonde yanked at her

kid again and then gave the girl behind the counter all the information she wanted. The girl wrote furiously while she tried to figure out what the woman smelled like. She decided it was a mixture of White Shoulders and sausage.

"Will you be in the picture, too?" the girl asked.

"Me? Oh, gawd, no." The woman patted her hair. "I look a mess."

"You look wonderful." The minimum-wage-girl-photographer took great pride in being able to give a compliment like that and not choke on it.

"Thanks, honey, but you should see me when I'm really done up."

Suddenly, the littlest girl yelped and the mom turned on her children like a bulldog.

"What are you doing?"

Another yank, and a slap, and all was well again. The photographer blanched and got on with things. The sooner these people were gone the better. She led them into the room where there were boxes covered with velvet that could be configured for any number of people to sit down. There was also a movie screen thingie.

"I don't want to hear about no packages. I've got this coupon that says four shots for nineteen ninety-five. That includes the twenty-five free wallet size. That's what I want, so don't waste your breath trying to sell me more stuff," the blonde warned.

"Of course." The girl smiled at her and the woman smiled back. Her front tooth was smeared with the same waxy orange color that outlined her lips. The girl wiggled her fingers at the littlest girl. "Come on over here, and we'll get going."

She lifted the little girl and plopped her on the lower

black velvet covered block, but the older girl deliberately made herself heavy and it was impossible to lift her onto the higher block. Mom finally helped with a well-placed hand on the girl's rear and a threat the photographer had no doubt was the real deal. When they were ready, the girl asked:

"Which background did you have in mind?"

"Whatcha got?"

The minimum-wage-girl-photographer pulled on the metal ring attached to the screen and down came a piece of beige seamless.

"Too boring." The blonde dismissed it.

The girl snapped it up and pulled again. A nursery scene.

"No. No."

Snap! Pull! A picture of a den, a fireplace, and one-dimensional snow covered mountains framed by a one-dimensional window. The photographer thought whoever came up with that one should be shot.

"Ooooooh." The woman squealed and clapped her hands. "That one."

"An excellent choice." The photographer set it, walked behind the camera, picked up the squeeze bulb and stood in front of the little girls. "Smile real big. You look so grown up. Smile girls!"

The flash went off four times. The photographer was sure the pictures would be great. They were lovely little girls despite their mother and their kinky red hair.

Chapter 22

Finn stood well back from the graveside, sunglasses on despite being shaded by the narrow limb of a newly planted tree. His expression was solemn, his hands were crossed low, and the only prayer on his lips was to have this thing done so he could be out of the suit Bev had picked out for him to wear to court. The wool was too warm despite its fine hand, the high collar of the shirt chaffed against the scars on his neck and the knot of his tie, he was sure, would render him speechless for the next century if not loosened soon. And then there were the shoes, Italian loafers made of such fine leather that his feet felt naked.

Cori seemed to have no such problems. She was dressed in a suit, too. It was blue, the skirt was short, and the jacket strained over her chest. Now and again her eyes slid his way, silently asking the same question she had asked on the long ride from the church to the cemetery. She wanted to know why they were at the service for the Barnett girls. Finn had no good answer for that other than his gut said he needed to be there. Cori thought it wasn't his gut talking but some lower part of his anatomy. He chided her for that. If any part of his anatomy was in play, it was higher up, around heart level. Finn O'Brien wanted to be there to see that Elizabeth Barnett was still standing at the end of this awful day.

His gaze wandered over the people clustered around the tiny white caskets. The coffins had been placed next to two deep holes in the ground that were ridiculously camouflaged by blankets of Astroturf. Sam Barnett's arm was tight on his wife's shoulders. He stared off into the distance, Elizabeth kept her eyes on the coffins, and Elizabeth's mother held onto her daughter's hand and wept with her eyes closed.

Elizabeth was pale and dry eyed, and it seemed as if her husband's touch was only just bearable. Her shoulders trembled now and again. Her hair was wrapped in a topknot. She looked like a black-clad Geisha come to entertain the Grim Reaper with her elegant sorrow. The minister spoke of heaven and God's love and things that really did nothing to make anyone feel better. To a person, the funeral party was well dressed and solemn except for one. While that woman was impeccably turned out, her attention was split between the ceremony and her little girl. Tiring of the incomprehensible activity, the child pulled at her mother's hand, trying to make the woman play with her. Finally, the girl gave up and began to skate over a grave marker. Finn thought bringing a little girl to this funeral was unthinkably cruel.

Just as the little girl yanked on her mother's hand again, Cori leaned into him. He started to smile, thinking she had been watching the spectacle, too, but she was looking toward a mausoleum at the edge of the cemetery lawn. Finn squinted into the sunshine, trying to see what had caught her interest. It took a minute, but then he saw a man's head bob out from behind the left wall of the stone building. A second later the man pulled back.

Without a word between them Finn and Cori fell back two steps, pivoted, and walked away from the gravesite. When they were well clear of the ceremony, they picked up the pace, hoping the man hadn't made them. Elizabeth Barnett had though. She let go of her mother's hand and started to move away. When Sam saw what she was doing, he tightened his grip. The last person he wanted her following was Finn O'Brien.

When they were far enough away, Finn broke into a run. He flew over the ground, graceful and fast but not without notice. The man he wanted to talk to saw them coming and made a break for a car parked on the wide boulevard that wound through the cemetery.

"Go!" Cori called.

Faster and faster Finn went until he hit a patch of mud around a newly dug grave, slipped and fell hard. He cursed the fancy Italian shoes and their slick soles. Just as Cori reached for him, he took off again, but the distance was too great and precious seconds had been lost. The car was already moving, heading out of the cemetery. Finn sprinted to the middle of the road and kept running until the car disappeared around the bend. Slowing to a trot, then to a walk, Finn finally came to a stop and stood looking down the empty road, phone in hand, calling in what he had. It was fresh, urgent and clear. There was a good chance someone on the street would grab the car fast. Then again, cops were stretched thin and there was just as good a chance that the man would slip through the cracks.

Kicking at the asphalt, scuffing the toe of those fancy shoes, he made his way back to Cori who was resting against the wrought iron door that barred the entrance to the crypt. He paused at a gravestone and let his hand rest on the head of an anguished angel hewn out of rough stone.

"Did you get a good look?" she asked.

"Caucasian. Medium build. Light brown hair. There was a passenger. Darker hair. Smaller."

Finn bit his lip. He wiped the sweat off his brow and pulled at the knot of his tie. He popped the top button of his shirt, and then he smacked the stone angel upside the head.

"Blast, we were close."

"I'm getting too old for this." Cori doubled over and took a very deep breath. When she righted herself, she fussed with the bow on her go-to-a-funeral blouse. "Maybe it was just somebody visiting one of the folks down under. We probably gave them a heart attack. I'd be scared if I saw us coming."

"The devil..."

Finn cursed and he pivoted toward the road, shaking his head in disgust. When he did that he saw something he had overlooked. Finn retraced his steps, stopped at the edge of the grass, and bent down.

"Cori," he called. "I'm needing some tissues."

Cori walked over and handed him two. Finn used one to pick up a greeting card lying in the dirt, and then put it across the tissue that covered the palm of his other hand. Cori put her hands on his back and peered over his shoulder as he opened it.

"That's the ugliest thing I've ever seen."

The white card was made of cheap stock. On the front was a black cross and at the base of the cross was a lamb that looked more like Jack Black with a sheep's rump. Inside was a most interesting message.

Sory abut you kids

"Still think it was an innocent we scared off?" Finn asked.

"No, I do not," Cori whistled.

Finn stood up and wrapped the card carefully, putting it in his breast pocket. He took off his sunglasses, inspected the lenses, and wiped them with his tie. In the distance, people were leaving the Barnett funeral. Elizabeth, Sam Barnett and Elizabeth's mother lingered near the caskets. Finn put his glasses back on and touched the small of Cori's back to usher her to their car.

"That car was a rental," he said. "I saw a Bargain Rent-a-Car sticker on the bumper."

"Excellent. I'll check and see if the lab has identified the tire tracks," Cori said.

"Could be we'll get some prints off this card, too," Finn said.

"Good stuff, O'Brien."

Before they parted to get in their car, he raised a fist that Cori dutifully bumped with hers.

CHAPTER 23

Such a shame. A house isn't a house without children...

Did you sell your place?...can't believe they wouldn't negotiate...

Couldn't bear up as well as Elizabeth. Class all the way...

Red...convertible should be red...besides, there was a waiting list for black...

"Hey. Did you try this?"

Cori poked Finn with her elbow.

"Sorry. What?"

He looked from her to his empty plate. He'd been lost in the bits and pieces of conversation among the people snaking around the gleaming table. It was laden with enough food to feed them all ten times over.

"I asked if you tried the salmon."

Cori flipped the wide silver fork she was holding toward a platter. At one time, there had been a whole fish on it. Now the poor thing's glassy eyes stared at the ceiling as if afraid to look at its cannibalized midsection. When Finn shook his head, Cori dug out a piece and put it on his plate. She added a devilled egg, but before she got to the pastries Finn put his plate aside and walked away. Cori picked it up, shouldered through the people at the buffet, and followed him to a spot in a short hallway by the stairs.

"What's with you? Eat." She shoved the plate at him and he pushed it right back.

"You're not my mother, Cori," he said. "I'll eat when I'm hungry."

Cori lowered her eyes, turned around, and put the small plate in an alcove that at one time probably held the only phone in the house. She checked her anger even though Finn couldn't have wounded her more if he tried with that one. She put her back up against the wall and said:

"What are we waiting for, Finn? Why don't we get out of here?"

"I thought there would be something. Someone," Finn muttered.

Cori turned her shoulder to the wall. "That guy at the cemetery isn't going to saunter into this shindig. I'm telling you, we're done here."

Finn wasn't listening. He was looking into the living room. His attention was on Elizabeth Barnett. Cori didn't have to look to know that.

"Don't hang your wash on someone else's line," she warned. "That woman may have a heap of trouble but she's got folks to help her."

"Did you see the way her husband clamped down on her at the cemetery?" Finn asked this as if he hadn't heard her.

"Good grief. What is she, Rapunzel waiting to let down her hair? Did it ever occur to you that maybe he needed her to stick with him? She's not the only one in a bad way."

"I don't like him."

"Now there's a news flash." Cori's lips turned up in a sad little smile. Finn's dislike for Sam Barnett was almost as obvious as his infatuation with the man's wife. Finn and classy broads; Cori would never get it. She pushed off the wall. "I've got to hit the little girl's room. When I get back we're going."

Finn put his elbow on the banister and watched Cori cut through the crowd. He was thinking about his partner's good heart and good sense when he realized he was looking into Elizabeth Barnett's deep blue eyes. She held his gaze while she offered a word to the people she was talking to. When she walked toward the kitchen, Finn followed because she wanted him to. He was sure of that. The other thing he was sure of was that Cori had been mistaken. There was something for him in this house after all.

"My husband thinks I shouldn't bother you. He says you'll tell us when you have something to say."

Elizabeth started talking as soon as the swinging kitchen door closed behind them. She was about to face him when a caterer's assistant hurried past with a platter full of open-faced sandwiches, the third Finn had seen. Elizabeth moved on, pushing open the screen door and going onto the wide raised landing outside the backdoor. Finn caught the door so it wouldn't slam shut. Outside he noticed things he hadn't seen the night he came in search of Elizabeth Barnett. There was a straw-bristled hedgehog near the door, a smile painted onto its stone face, its back ready to clean shoes dirty from playing outside. Next to the hedgehog was a beach towel. There was a pot of basil nestled in the crotch where the two, old wooden railings met at a right angle. The swing set. A sand box.

"It's so crowded in there." Elizabeth Barnett pulled his attention back to her.

"It's good to have many friends to share your sorrow with," Finn said.

"Don't be fooled. I can count on one hand the number of people who are here to grieve with us: my mother, my friend Mercedes, her husband, and the girls' teachers." Elizabeth put her palms on the railing and pushed down hard, testing it to see if it would hold her weight. "Most everyone else is here because it's like slowing to look at an accident on the freeway. You hope no one was hurt, but the truth is you're just really happy you're not the one lying there dead. They are here because they are curious, horrified, and relieved all at the same time. It's human nature. I can't fault anyone for it."

She narrowed her eyes and Finn saw the macabre glitter in them. Her cynicism, while honest, was disconcerting.

"You're living in this house again, are you?"

"This is my home," she answered. "Besides, you would never know anything happened here. It's strange how some people make their living, isn't it? Can you imagine spending the day wiping blood off walls? What do those people say when they go home and their husband or wife asks how their day was?"

Finn knew the answer but so did she. There was no need to speak it out loud. The people she was talking about said their day was fine. That was the same thing Elizabeth told the people inside her house. *I'm holding up. I'm fine.* Finn had told the same lie when Alexander died and he had gone back to school. But he wasn't fine, he just couldn't stand being home and watching his parents rip themselves apart with sorrow.

"Sam found the idea of Stephen frightening." Elizabeth said this as if their conversation about Stephen Grady days ago had been on going. Then she threw the switch and the train they were on changed tracks again. "Do you have a cigarette?"

Finn shook his head. "I don't smoke."

"I quit when I got pregnant. Guess that was a wasted effort." She laughed a little. "I don't really want one, it's just that I feel like it. Sometimes I feel like I need air even though I'm breathing. The sight of food makes me sick, but I eat anyway."

Her voice trailed away. Then she sighed. Finally, she confessed.

"Stephen came here once."

CHAPTER 24

Elizabeth passed her hand over her forehead as though she found the colors of her make-up constricting, making it hard for her to think. She sighed again. Her fingers worked themselves into a knot.

"I don't usually lie, detective, but Sam, well, he is rigid. He is a good husband. I want you to understand that. I never wanted to cause him worry or give him reason to distrust me, but when I met Stephen I had to do something for him despite Sam's disapproval." Her lashes fluttered. Her fingers went to her lips as she tried to find words to explain herself. "It was such a little thing in the grand scheme of my life, and such a big thing for a man like Stephen. Do you see?"

"No, not really," Finn answered.

She moved just then. One step back, two to the right, one back again: box steps in a dance of agitation. She held onto the old railing and looked into some distance where she was only herself and not a wife and mother.

"Before the schizophrenia, Stephen was a scientist but nobody cares about that. They just care about what he is now. But I cared about who he was. I wanted to do for Stephen what I would want someone to do for me in the same situation. I wanted Stephen to feel useful. I wanted him to feel that someone was truly seeing him. I thought that would make him stronger and the sickness weaker. I think sickness of the mind is the worst of all, don't you?"

Elizabeth didn't wait for an answer. She smiled at Finn as if she pitied him a prejudice because he didn't agree with her.

"Anyway, I brought him here. He cut some bushes. I paid him a little. I drove him back to the clinic. He said thank you. That is all there was to it."

When she looked at Finn, there were tears in her eyes.

"Please don't tell Sam. You saw how angry he gets about this. I don't want to make him angry."

"Are you afraid of your husband, missus?"

She shook her head, "I only want to keep thing calm. He's on edge. We both are. You won't tell him, will you?"

"Not if I don't have to," Finn answered.

"Thank you."

It was clear she had not heard Finn qualify his statement. He would have Cori go back to the housekeeper and the neighbors to find out if anyone had seen Stephen Grady in this house or near this place more than once. He would tell Sam Barnett about Stephen Grady's visit if it meant finding the persons who killed those children.

"I doubt Stephen could find his way back to this house much less get through security. I wanted you to know that. I didn't want you to be hard on him when you speak to him."

"We can't be sure that he couldn't find your home again. Etta said he became very upset while you were gone. If he considered your family a road block to him getting attention from you, he could have lost it."

"I volunteer at an outpatient clinic, not an asylum," Elizabeth said. "If you met Stephen then you would know he's incapable of that kind of rage. He would hurt himself before he hurt anyone else."

"You've never taken him in? Your children never met him?"

Elizabeth shook her head. "No. And that's the truth."

"What else can you tell me about him?" Finn asked, wanting to hear her speak about this man so he could find a rhythm to her truth.

"He has dark wavy hair. Mostly he cuts it very short. When he sits, he entwines his legs and his arms like a child with no friends on the playground." One of Elizabeth's hands moved over the railing as if she was polishing it. "He has brown eyes and he wears jeans. He has a favorite red plaid shirt. I gave him a new one but he wouldn't wear it. His nails are long. He scratches himself with them when he's anxious. You can always tell when he's been off his medication too long. He always has scabs on his arms from scratching himself. I think he's missing a tooth just here."

Elizabeth opened her mouth slightly and pointed as she turned her head for Finn to see. She had small, straight teeth. Her lips were rimmed with the last vestiges of a peach color lipstick. Finn noticed a small mole below her ear and heard how vividly she spoke about Stephen Grady.

"I do wish you could find him. I'd like to know that he's all right," she said.

"We're looking," Finn assured her and that was the truth.

The day before he had searched under the 101 freeway, skid row, and even climbed into the Hollywood Hills to an encampment that someone said was the place the truly hopeless lived. Finn never had much faith in Stephen Grady as a suspect, so he was only tired, not disappointed, when he didn't find him. That man could not have subdued Rachel Gerber much less shot her. The noise made by a terrified little girl would probably have terrified him back. The man's fingerprints weren't found in the Barnett home, and a bipolar male off his meds wouldn't have meticulously cleaned up after himself.

The killers had left little behind other than a few hairs and that fingernail. He and Cori knew one of the people they were looking for had red hair and one had brown, and they knew that whoever lost the nail did coke, they knew that the ginger had kinky hair. Both hair samples were long; a man with a shaved head would have left nothing of use behind. One of the killers used a well-honed knife with a nick in it, the other had a gun and no homeless, insane man was going to have those things much less care for them.

There was matter taken from beneath Rachel Gerber's fingernails waiting for a suspect to match. Finn was sure it wouldn't be Stephen Grady. Still, he would like to have a DNA sample just to be sure. He would also like to see the man who Elizabeth Barnett seemed to have more concern for than she had for her husband.

"Are we all right, now?" Elizabeth's voice startled Finn. He shook his head and gave her a small smile.

"Yes. We're fine. I'm glad you told me."

"I am, too. I don't like secrets and lies. Quite frankly I despise them, but they are necessary at times. You must understand, though, that Stephen is fragile. He doesn't deserve to be caught up in this."

"Still, missus—"

"Elizabeth?" Elizabeth Barnett's mother stuck her head out the door, interrupting Finn. "The Rigolis are leaving now. I thought you'd like to know."

"I'll be right in."

Elizabeth Barnett's mother nodded at Finn, clearly concerned about the porch conference, but she said nothing. When she was gone, Elizabeth asked:

"What happened at the cemetery?"

"Nothing important."

Finn thought about the card he had found that was now in the car in a plastic bag. It would be dusted for fingerprints, they would track down the store it came from, they would analyze the handwriting and, once all that was done, he might tell Elizabeth Barnett about it. Showing it to her now would only cause heartache and horror. When she spoke again, Finn realized it didn't matter about the card. Elizabeth Barnett had lost interest in talking to him.

"Well, then, I suppose I should go. Now that I've been honest about Stephen."

He moved to the door and opened it for her but as she passed the toe of her shoe caught on the flashing of the door. She stumbled and Finn caught her, one hand on her elbow, the other at her waist. It was so narrow that Finn was sure he could have put his hands around her and his fingers would have met in the middle. Elizabeth's head swung toward him. Her eyes were downcast. Her lips parted. When she finally looked at him, her gaze was steady. It seemed that she was going to say something; it seemed as if she might smile. When she didn't, Finn let her go.

Elizabeth Barnett murmured her thanks. Finn caught the kitchen door and followed her inside, but she didn't look back. She glided through the kitchen, past the caterers and into the muted chaos of her home. She went straight to her husband's side. Sam Barnett kissed her grey hair and she wrapped her arm around him. Finn O'Brien saw the couple they were to the outside world. He saw the man and wife who took comfort in one another, loved and respected each other.

What he was seeing was a far cry from what he had been hearing and Finn O'Brien would have to decide what to believe: his eyes, his ears, or his Irish heart.

CHAPTER 25

Hollywood had been left out in the cold a few years back, falling on bad times when the warmth of the spotlight faded and the shakers and movers departed. All that had remained was trash – throw away, non-recyclable, non-refundable trash – human and otherwise.

Hollywood's Chamber of Commerce continued to sell the gold sidewalk stars to actors in the hopes that interest in the city would be revived. The actors paid for their emblems, held a press conference on the Walk of Fame, and scurried back to Pacific Palisades or Brentwood, Malibu or Montana, wherever the streets were clean and the taxes high enough to keep out the riffraff. Recently, though, there had been a turnaround of sorts and the city was off life support. New business was coming in, fine restaurants were opening, and designers were taking a second look at the long-empty storefronts. Still, the sleaze factor remained and you didn't have to look hard to find it. In fact, the sleazy heart of Hollywood was only a short drive from Fremont Place and that's where Cori and Finn headed after they left the Barnett's house.

"Del Shannon is probably turning over in his grave.

They didn't even spell it right. It's supposed to be one word. There's supposed to be an apostrophe. I'm pretty sure about that."

Cori's elbow was cocked on the open window of the car and her chin rested on her fist as she checked out the bar called Run Aways.

"You know, O'Brien, I always thought nannies went to the park and hung out with chimney sweeps when they had the day off."

Finn laughed and got out of the car. Cori did the same and checked out the park job. The rear end of the vehicle was hanging in the red zone but it didn't matter. Cops were like that proverbial eight hundred pound gorilla: they could park it anywhere. Finn joined her on the sidewalk and they took a long look at the place that every cop from Palmdale to San Diego had heard about.

If you wanted to find some kid on the lam from Arkansas or Iowa or a thousand points in between, Run Aways was where you started. Why Rachel Gerber, a woman in her late twenties, a woman with a regular paycheck and long work history, had matchbooks from this place and three other dives on this stretch of Hollywood Boulevard was a mystery Finn and Cori wanted to solve.

"After you."

Finn held the door for Cori but he was on her heels when she walked into the windowless box-of-a-bar. All heads turned their way. Finn counted nine people in the place including the bartender. Four appeared to be under age. All of them looked like they could use a night in jail just so they could get solid food, clean clothes, and a shower.

Finn and Cori looked at them, and they looked back as they ran through the possible grievances the law might have with them. Since each had sinned, it really was only a matter of trying to remember which of their trespasses might interest these two. When it was clear the detectives weren't headed for anyone in particular, the murmurs at the far table resumed, two other patrons set sad eyes on the grimy, mute television hanging from the ceiling, and the rest contemplated whatever vision they saw in the bottom of their glass. The detectives slid onto bar stools and doffed their sunglasses.

Cori swept the place one more time. At the far table, the two men staring into their drinks looked like they couldn't afford one between them much less one for each of them. Their hair was long; one had a beard and the other gray stubble. One wore a sweater over a shirt, over that a torn and dirty jacket; the other wore a hoody that was two sizes too big. Both had pants of no specific color or cut. One wore boots without laces, the other tennis shoes without socks. To Cori's right was a woman whose face was as blank as a check. Her hair was brittle and frizzy, mostly blonde, some gray. There were tracks on her stick-thin arms and Cori knew she was probably a lot younger than she appeared. The kids who were passing the time kept their feet on their worn backpacks and bedrolls. Cori knew all their worldly possessions were inside, and that there wasn't a person in the world who cared about them. It was enough to make her want to run home to Amber and Tucker for a hug and a kiss.

She looked away from the people to the place. Run Aways was bad even by boulevard standards: cracked walls, bare bulbs, sticky wood, and a limited selection of libations. Cori kept her hands on top her purse. There was a ninety-nine percent chance there wouldn't be any action, but she liked to have her gun in easy reach in case this was her one percent day. She also didn't want to touch anything.

"Can I help you?" The bartender had a voice like a helium drinker.

"Hope so," Finn said.

"You don't have to hope, officers. Anything I can do, officers. You name it."

The bartender grinned big, proud that he had tagged them even though a ten year old with half a brain could have done the same thing.

"We're looking for information on a woman name Rachel Gerber. She had a German accent."

Finn took Rachel's photo out of his pocket. They had found it stuck in the back of a drawer in her room. It showed a young woman having a happy day at the beach. She was smiling, holding her hair back because it was windy. They couldn't tell which beach she was at because the picture was just Rachel, the water, and the sand. Finn thought her scanty bikini too small for a big girl, but Cori pointed out that European women had a better body image than Americans. What surprised him was that she had a snapshot when most people her age kept their photos on their phones. Finn held it up for the man to see.

"Look familiar?"

The bartender tipped his head one way and then the other. There was a birthmark behind his ear that crawled up the side of his bald head. Finn thought it looked a little like a *Shillelagh* with the knob knocking on the man's brain to see if anyone was home.

"Naw. Too clean for this joint, know what I mean? Too much meat to be a junky. German, huh? I fought the Germans. Hard people. Women weren't too bad. Know what I mean? Like to be treated rough. Know what I mean?"

"Sure, I know what you mean."

Finn's grip on the photo was unwavering. Suffering fools was part of the job. This man wasn't old enough to have fought the Germans in any war, so Finn concluded he just liked to fight Germans. Finn also doubted he got up close and personal with many ladies much less tough German girls. Finn pushed the photo closer still.

"Look again, friend. The lady had some matchbooks from here. She might have picked them up when she stopped in for a nightcap. She might have been with a man. Average build, five-nine or ten, medium coloring, possibly with wavy hair."

"Who could remember a guy like that? And she could've gotten the matches from any of our loyal customers."

He laughed like a slutty Minnie Mouse as he put an elbow on the bar. The short sleeves on his bowling shirt inched up and exposed an intricate tattoo on his left arm: a woman in the embrace of a dragon. This man thought a lot of himself, Finn decided.

"You've got a lot of loyal customers, do you?" he asked.

"Damn straight. Like one big happy family around here, but I still never saw that one." He shrugged and righted himself. "I'm not on twenty-four hours a day. Why don't you come back at midnight? The night guy's on then, maybe he can help you out."

"Do you work weekends? Sundays? You work Mondays?" Cori asked.

The man turned her way. There were three rolls of extra skin between his skull and shoulders that passed for a neck, and the staff of his mottle-skinned *Shillelagh* went crooked in the folds.

"Sometimes." His good humor faded when he answered Cori.

"In the last week or ten days?" she pressed.

"Naw. Talk to Jimmy. He's on most Sundays and Mondays. I haven't worked a Sunday for a while. The last Monday I was here at night was two months ago. Sorry. Can't help."

The three of them looked at one another, making the points of a nice triangle where they racked their balls on imaginary felt. The guy behind the bar had a big eight on his head, but until Finn and Cori could clear the table he wasn't going down. Finn pocketed the picture and ran his finger over the bar.

"I'm thinking your cleaning lady must be on vacation," he said. "The health department might not like the way you keep this place. It's bad for your customers' well being."

The man giggled. It was a freaky sound coming from a guy with rolls of fat at the base of his skull, a naked woman tattooed on his arm, and a birthmark club whacking his head for all of this lifetime.

"I should be the one to worry. I have to sterilize everything these creeps touch."

He shot a hateful look at the woman three stools down, but continued to smile. The woman didn't notice.

She hadn't touched her drink. Finn and Cori stood up. Finn put a card on the bar.

"If we don't get back tonight, ask Jimmy about Rachel Gerber. I wrote her name on the back there, and you can tell him what she looked like. If he's heard of her, one of you give us a call." He pulled himself to his full height, which wasn't as impressive to the human helium balloon as it should have been. "We would surely appreciate it."

"I'll just do that."

He slid the card off the counter and they heard it fall to the floor. Cori rolled her eyes. People could be so trying. Finn reached into his pocket and drew out another card, wrote the name Rachel Gerber on the back, leaned over the bar and stuffed it into the fat man's breast pocket. That did not make him happy. The pecking order was a bummer if you weren't the one pecking. When that was done, Cori and Finn took off. When they were on the outside, Finn turned his face up to the late afternoon sun.

"'Tis wonderful to breathe again."

He laughed a little but Cori was out of sorts. She had a hand up against the wall of the building and was checking out the sole of her shoe.

"Good thing I'm not wearing sandals. What is this gunk?"

When she couldn't identify it, she opted to let the pavement scrape it away. They walked down the street, Cori's shoe sticking and popping with each step. People coming toward them gave them wide berth; people behind them slowed to match their pace. Everyone on the street knew who the cops were no matter how they were dressed. Cori thought she heard a sigh of pedestrian relief when she and Finn turned into Cholo's, the next bar on Rachel Gerber's matchbook map.

Those who actually turned a profit from their suspect activities satisfied their thirst at Cholo's. They wore clothes that were cheap nods to fashion. Leather was in for the men, but a lot of it looked like it had been ripped straight off the back of a cow in the field. A few of them wore open-necked shirts and knock-off designer Italian cut suits. The women were partial to kohl cat-eyes and maroon colored lips. They showed off their cleavage and abs in T-shirts emblazoned with their resumes: bitch, honey pot, princess. Every belly button sported a jewel; ear lobes were hung with chandelier earrings or hoops big enough for any man to jump through. This razor sharp and semi-prosperous group lived off the foibles of the poor ones who drank at Run Aways.

The bartender at Cholo's was not fat, nor did he make a pretense of happiness. He didn't like his job, his face, or his prospects. Life itself was not something that appeared to thrill him. He was thin and tall and bore acne scars that made him strangely appealing even though he was far from good looking. The one thing he didn't have was a problem with the law. He wiped a glass, filled a drink, listened to and answered Finn and Cori's questions, and checked out the picture of Rachel Gerber that Finn showed him.

"What's she done?" He topped off a mug and sent it down the bar.

"She died," Cori said.

"And not in a good way," Finn added.

The bartender shrugged. His psyche could accept the news of sudden, inexplicable death at the hands of others.

"So," Finn said. "Have you seen her?"

"I have."

He rang up six bucks on the register, took a fifty, and made change for a lovely lady in a Lycra jumpsuit who seemed to have forgotten to zip up past her navel.

"When?" Finn took a seat. Cori stood behind him.

"I don't remember."

"Okay." Finn covered his face with one large hand, a gesture that seemed to indicate his patience, while usually beyond measure, was wearing a wee bit thin. When he dropped his hand, he asked: "Did you see her often then?"

"Often enough." The man flipped a glass over, peered inside to see if there was anything left that shouldn't be. "She'd have a drink, get a little wild, then she'd tone it down. By the end of the night she was quieter than when she first came in. That's kind of opposite of the way it usually goes."

"Did she come in with anyone you know?" Cori asked.

"Some guy," the bartender said. "He never gave me any reason to remember him particularly."

"What did he look like? In general," Finn asked.

"I don't know. What do they all look like?" The man shrugged, his polyester satin shirt fluttered a little. "Like every guy who comes in here who doesn't have a lot of money. Like a wanna-be player. Maybe he was running girls. Not that one in the picture though. He was always hitting on some chick in here, but the German girl helped out."

"How was that?" Cori asked.

"He'd hit up on 'em, then the German got in after a while, bought 'em drinks, and moved them to the end of the bar. She talked to them down there. Those two never left with another girl, they just passed numbers."

"Did you see what kind of car they drove?" Cori asked.

"Does it look like I can see through walls?" The man scowled at Cori. He would have done the same to Finn. "This is L.A. I figure they drive. Maybe they live around here and walk. All I know is that they drink." He turned around and put his skinny butt against the back bar. He crossed his arms. "Any other questions?"

"Did she always stay until closing?" Finn asked.

"They both stayed 'till closing when they were here. They came in late, they drank, they chatted up the girls and had a good time. I still can't give you any names."

"Always the same man?" Cori asked.

"Always," he answered.

"Could you pick him out if we showed you pictures?"

The man shook his head. He lit a cigarette. That was a negative.

"Are any of the girls they talked to here?" Finn asked.

He shook his head again. Finn stood up and did the card trick again. This time it didn't disappear under the bar. The man studied it while Finn gave his instructions.

"I want to know if her friend comes in again. If you see any of the women they were interested in, give us a call."

"They won't talk to you, but I'll call anyway. Hey, there is one more thing. The other reason I remember her?" The bartender shrugged as if to say he knew his information was lame. "She always paid."

They thanked him and went back outside. Cori blinked, put a finger to her eyelids, and then blinked again. She hated dark places on bright days. The sunglasses went on. Like everyone else in California, Cori and Finn didn't feel quite dressed without them.

"It looks like Mary Poppins was cleaning a few sooty chimneys on her day off," Finn said.

Cori laughed, "Bert was the chimney sweep, O'Brien. You should know that."

"Irish are too poor to have chimneys or nannies, so what do I know?" Finn looked at his notebook. "One more to go. Stay Awhile is half a mile down."

"I'm not walking that far in heels," Cori said.

"Ah. You're putting your foot down are you, woman?" Finn deadpanned. Cori rolled her eyes but Finn wouldn't be silenced. He took her arm. "No matter. I'm not wanting to walk down these streets dressed like a mortician anyway."

"When we're done down there, we should call it a day and catch some dinner. It's a shame to waste being all dressed up," Cori suggested as they went on their way.

"No babysitting tonight?"

"Amber's got it covered."

"Let's see how late it is when we finish."

They got into the car and as Finn pulled into traffic food was the last thing on his mind. He was wondering about Rachel Gerber, her encrypted computer, the guy she hung with, the women they hit up on and how strange it was that Mary Poppins was a lush and a kinky one at that.

CHAPTER 26

DAY 5 – MORNING

Elizabeth Barnett was prom queen in her senior year of high school. This surprised her, just as she had been stunned to find herself elected freshman class president, sophomore representative to Government Days, and captain of the debate team in her junior year. She was amazed by her good fortune because in her whole life Elizabeth never quite felt good enough or special enough or smart enough to be noticed.

She grew up in a home in which her mother never made a decision for fear of displeasing her husband; she never made a sound for fear of annoying him. The consequences of this could be swift and brutal. Because of this, Elizabeth learned how to do quiet things. She cooked and cleaned, sewed her own clothes, and smiled at her father. The latter seemed to please him greatly, so Elizabeth smiled a lot. For a long while she was as fearful as her mother, but by the time she graduated from high school, she was worn out from being afraid all the time so she wrapped her fears into one ball, labeled it 'life', and kept smiling.

At college Elizabeth found that the mini-town was

filled with former prom queens and freshman class presidents who wanted to continue their reigns as the best, the brightest, and prettiest. Usually the competition was subtle but at times there was sporadic open warfare so Elizabeth kept her head down, graduated from school and waited for the one thing that would make her feel happy, needed and significant. The day Sam Barnett showed up on her doorstep, the unwilling victim of a blind date, Elizabeth found what she was looking for: a young man of promise who chose her out of all the women in the entire world and would love her forever.

Sam also found what he was looking for – the perfect wife for the perfect man he was determined to become. She seemed a gentle soul that he could treasure, a woman content within her homey kingdom, a beauty who adored him almost to a fault. They married, set up house, worked hard, had babies, became rich and Elizabeth was happy until she wasn't happy anymore.

Now they were still rich, still married, their babies were dead and Elizabeth Barnett was angry. She had been cheated, gyped and taken advantage of by fate. She had been so careful, so proactive, and so protective when it came to her happy family. That should have counted for some cosmic brownie point, some Marvel Comic super-hero shield, but it hadn't. Her family was destroyed and Elizabeth Barnett was dying by inches in her big, silent house so she left it.

Now Elizabeth was sitting in a comfortable yet far-from-comforting office. A dark couch hugged one wall, and a box of Kleenex was conspicuously perched on the back of it. The desk was covered with unimaginative gadgets and leather accessories. A fichus tree thrived near the window and Elizabeth thought that was impressive. It was difficult to get a fichus tree to grow indoors. Elizabeth sat in a gold tweed armchair that wasn't cheap but it was ugly. Behind her the door of the office opened and a woman came in. She was short, plain in middle age. Her hair was sliced off just below her ears, and round tortoiseshell glasses magnifyied her brown eyes.

"Hello, Elizabeth. It's been a long time."

"Fifteen years, Doctor Templeton."

"How is your mother?"

"She's fine. My father is still alive, but he's in a nursing home. We don't see him," Elizabeth said.

Doctor Templeton nodded, but she didn't smile. There was nothing to smile about where Elizabeth's family was concerned. The mother had been suicidal, the father dictatorial and Elizabeth so concerned with keeping everyone happy that she had worked herself into half a dozen phobias by the time Doctor Templeton met her.

Happily she was a quick study – or a gifted actress. After a year of therapy she finished college with honors and announced she would help others by becoming a nurse. Had it been anyone else Doctor Templeton would be pleased, but it was Elizabeth declaring herself healthy and that was worrisome. Doctor Templeton had wanted to continue therapy for at least another year but Elizabeth, having put every duck in her phobic brain in a row, politely said goodbye, thanked the doctor and went off into the world. Doctor Templeton had assumed Elizabeth to be fine until she read the paper and saw what had happened to her children. She was glad to see her back although she would have been happy just to know that Elizabeth was seeking help somewhere. The doctor took her chair behind the desk. Elizabeth had grown into a beauty in spite of the gray hair. Now Doctor Templeton would see how else she had changed – if she had changed at all.

"I am so sorry about your children," the doctor said.

Elizabeth nodded. She smoothed her black pants, her black blouse. She touched her pearls and then her hair.

"I am happy you're here. I want to help in anyway I can," the doctor said. "Where shall we begin?"

Elizabeth shook her head. Back and forth and back. Her long hair rippled across her shoulders and her lips were pulled tight. Any person in her situation would be fighting off hysteria but Doctor Templeton knew what Elizabeth was doing: she was compressing her rage, tamping it down with a shovel honed out of a determination Doctor Templeton had seldom encountered in any human being. Elizabeth was creating a strategy to control herself. Doctor Templeton didn't want to give her a chance to do that because she was after honesty and sometimes it was hard to get that out of Elizabeth.

"Have you cried, Elizabeth?" Dr. Templeton asked.

"Of course. Every day."

The last was a lie. She had cried in shock when she found her children. She had wept a little at the morgue, but she had easily controlled those tears. Still, she thought admitting to tears everyday was what the doctor wanted to hear.

"I see." Doctor Templeton did not believe her because Elizabeth's eyes were bright and clear. "Are you eating? Sleeping?"

"Yes."

Another lie.

"Dreams?"

"No."

The truth.

"But you are angry."

"Yes."

The truth.

"What angers you the most?"

"That my children are dead when they shouldn't be."

"Of course. And the nanny. I understand their nanny also died."

"That doesn't make me angry."

"Then it makes you sad," Doctor Templeton led her.

"No, it doesn't make me sad."

"What does the woman's death make you feel?"

Elizabeth's eyes widened. It was not the question she was expecting.

"It makes me feel nothing. How could I feel anything about her when my children are dead? When they died because of her?"

"Is that what the police say? That the nanny brought someone into the house?"

Elizabeth shook her head. She looked at the middle space over Doctor Templeton's shoulder. "They don't say anything yet and I don't want to talk about Rachel. I don't."

"Then what's next on the list of things that make you angry?"

"That I can't just handle this on my own. I don't want to be here talking to you. My husband doesn't know about you."

Doctor Templeton nodded. "Would he be upset that you're here or would he be happy?"

"Happy," Elizabeth answered. "He has been upset with me for a long while because I liked staying home. He made me go on this trip, you see. We went to Paris. That's when it happened. When we were in Paris. I told him if he made me go something awful would happen. I told him."

"So you're angry at your husband? You blame him for this?"

Elizabeth heard the doctor but her gaze wandered as the woman talked. She looked out the window behind Doctor Templeton, and into the window of an office on the other side of the street, and imagined a window on the other side of the building, looking into another window…

"Yes," she whispered.

"What can he do to make you not angry with him?"

"I want him to show me how sorry he was for changing our lives, for side-lining me. A nanny. A housekeeper. I didn't need that. I didn't want that. And now he excludes me. We can't start rebuilding if he won't include me." Elizabeth plucked at the upholstery on the armchair. Her voice rose but her words were clipped. "He leaves early for work. When he comes home he goes to his study to work."

Elizabeth leaned forward. Her hands were now clasped in her lap. She lowered her voice even though it was only the two of them in the room.

"I've gone into the garden in the dark. I stand behind the bushes so I can see through the windows into his office. He's not working, Doctor Templeton. He just sits there staring."

Elizabeth righted herself. Her hands were on the arms of the chair again.

"He's such a liar. I'm sure he's lied to me before but now is not the time. He just doesn't want to talk to me so he lies and then he runs away to work in the morning."

"So you want him to talk about moving forward even though it's only been a few days since your daughters died. You would like him to stay home with you, is that correct?"

"I want my husband to be a man. Life isn't fun and games anymore. All this time, it's like we were playing a game: making money, having children, making me go places I didn't want to go. What good was any of it? Shouldn't we talk about that?"

"Many men don't know how to do that so they do what they know. They go to work to take care of the family."

"No. No. No." Elizabeth's voice rose as her fists pounded lightly on the arms of the chair. "A real man doesn't just ignore the bad things that happen. Sam is an attorney. He's a rich man. He's a smart man, but he is selfish. He takes no responsibility. He acts like nothing has changed."

"Elizabeth, do you remember how we talked about your mother and father? Do you remember when we made a list of what was good and loving about them and what was not?"

Elizabeth nodded. The list of good things had been very short.

"What was the one thing I asked you to do when we made that list?"

"You asked me to be fair and to see my parents as individuals with strengths and weaknesses."

"That's correct. Now I want you to be fair to both your husband and yourself. Can you do that?"

"Yes," Elizabeth said but it was clear it would be difficult.

"Okay, then. First, let's look at the big picture," Doctor Templeton said. "People, Elizabeth, deal with life events differently. Some are proactive, the way you are being. You long for a resolution and you are ready to assist in finding it. Isn't that true?"

"Yes. Yes. I see something isn't right and I takes steps to rectify the situation," Elizabeth agreed.

"And that is a strength," the doctor said. "Your husband, according to you, wants to hide his head in the sand. He goes to work, he avoids you to keep from facing the reality of your life now. Is that how you perceive his actions?"

"Yes."

"Then I want you to consider that your husband goes to work because it is a familiar place to him. It is a place where he can mourn."

"How selfish." Elizabeth shot out of her chair and stepped behind it. She grasped the back of the chair and dug her nails in. "Don't you see that is selfish? He is not mourning – he's licking his own wounds. He's feeling sorry for himself."

"How can you know that?" Doctor Templeton asked.

"Because I know him. He marginalized me before this, he made us go away from our home, he left our children with that woman. Now he should be home. We should talk about it. That's the only way to move on. I am willing to do whatever it takes. I talk to the police. I make sure I know what is going on with the investigation. He doesn't talk to them at all."

Doctor Templeton smiled. She opened her hands. "There you are, Elizabeth. You are two people mourning in two ways. I imagine that your husband finds your strength, your surety, and your righteousness intimidating. I think he might be afraid of you, Elizabeth. He is afraid to be found lacking."

Elizabeth cocked her head, finally hearing something that made sense. Slowly, she took her seat again and the doctor went on, encouraged by her attention.

"Imagine you and your husband are refugees Elizabeth. Some refugees run from the horrors of war with their belongings on their back. They scratch for food where there is none. They carry their children incredible distances when they, themselves, are almost too weak to stand. They do superhuman things in order to survive. Others run from the same horrors but they don't get far. They give up."

Dr. Templeton picked up a pencil and slid it through her fingers, almost hypnotizing Elizabeth with the fluid movement and the tone of her voice. Like a sleepwalker, Elizabeth came round the chair and sat down, hanging on the doctor's every word.

"You and your husband are refugees on the same road. You both may want to walk it and get to a better place, but you might be the only one with the strength to do so. You can't shame your husband into walking the road with you, but you might be able to give him a reason to do that. Do you understand? He needs a reason, Elizabeth. Your husband perceives that he cannot and did not perform his job as protector. He goes to work to make amends."

"My children were my work," Elizabeth said with great sorrow. "My home was my office. It's empty now and silent and frightening, and yet I can't bear the thought of being anywhere else. I can't stand not knowing the reason this happened. Rachel, I can understand, but my children? They were just children."

Taken aback by Elizabeth Barnett's inability to acknowledge that the nanny's death was a tragedy, Doctor Templeton paused. She would like to explore Elizabeth's detachment, but she would leave that for another day. It had, after all, taken Elizabeth a very long while to even acknowledge her mother was not a disposable human being after watching her father abuse the woman for so many years. The doctor smiled and stayed on point.

"Understood, but your husband has no frame of reference to know what your days are like without your children. He didn't stay home before this happened; it seems illogical to him to stay home now. He goes where he is accepted because the one thing he fears the most is you. He fears your rejection, Elizabeth."

The doctor waited a millisecond.

"Perhaps, Elizabeth, he needs you to just open your arms. Do you think you could stop on your road long enough to embrace him? To pick him up? To show him how to walk with you? Do you think you could do that?

"Elizabeth? Are you listening?

"Could you do that, Elizabeth?"

CHAPTER 27

DAY 5 – AFTERNOON

"Well hi there you two! Drive safe; drive happy! Welcome to Bargain Rent-A-Car. How can I be of assistance today?"

The girl behind the counter was clad head-to-toe in a uniform of neon orange and her greeting was so fierce that a lesser man than Finn might have turned tail and run. As it was, he was simply left speechless, so Cori greeted her and added a flash of her badge.

"Hi there back. I'm Detective Anderson. This is Detective O'Brien." Finn tipped his fingers to his brow. The girl giggled. Cori said: "Is there a supervisor around?"

The girl leaned over to check out Cori's credentials. When she was done she bounced back on the balls of her feet and said:

"Nope. He went out to a late lunch and hasn't come back. I think he has a girlfriend, but I'm not supposed to know." The girl planted her elbows on the counter. "I'm happy to help you, though."

"Okay, Jenny, that would be great." Cori pulled the girl's name smoothly off her nametag.

"Super. It's been slow so it's kind of nice to have

someone to talk to. That's the only thing I don't like about this job. It's a long time between customers mostly."

Finn had no trouble believing that. Most people who lived in this neighborhood didn't have two cents to rub together much less the bucks to rent a car. In fact, it was not the kind of neighborhood Finn would want a daughter of his working in. If boredom were the only thing that befell this pretty teenager before she quit this job she would be lucky.

"We're interested in one car in particular, possibly rented sometime in the last week of March. Blue or dark grey. Four-door. Possibly a late model Ford Contour," Finn said, using the same words he had spoken to the five different salespeople at five different Bargain rental sites. The tire molds were consistent with this model but it was a standard tire so they couldn't be positive the Contour was their car. Still, it was a place to start.

"Oh sure, we've got a ton of those. They're really inexpensive, but they're good cars. We pride ourselves on renting good cars. I can look up the March rentals if you want. I could do it right now. I'd be happy to do it right now, if you want. Do you want me to do that?"

Cori dipped her head and rubbed her nose. She couldn't look at Finn knowing his eyes were probably permanently stuck in the ceiling position. This much girl-energy was hard to take even for another girl.

"That would be super," Cori said.

"The one we're looking for would have been rented either by a man with light brown, wavy hair, medium height or a man with frizzy red hair. They might have come in together," Cori said.

"Oh, those two guys."

The girl gave the detectives a sweeping nod and that was all it took to give Cori and Finn their second wind. Finn moved to the counter and stood shoulder to shoulder with his partner. Cori was nearly vibrating with excitement but her poker face was on.

"You remember them, then?"

"Oh, sure. They didn't talk much. Usually people talk more when they come in here. They tell me why they need a car, and where they're going, and stuff like that." Jenny's right hand punctuated her sentences because she talked so fast it was almost impossible to hear it in her speech.

"Did they say they were from out of town?" Cori pressed.

"No." Neon Jenny shook her head. "I just assume most people are. Those two came in just before I closed on Thursday so they were my last contract. They didn't buy any insurance or anything even though I told them it would be for their own protection and everything. Some people think we're trying to rip them off, but we're not. I swear."

She stood up straighter and laced her hands on the counter.

"Anyway, I remember the one guy because his hair was really, really red. I thought maybe he dyed it at first. I shouldn't have said anything, though. He was pretty mad when I asked him that. He didn't yell or anything, but I knew he was mad. It was kind of scary."

"Can we see the paperwork?" Finn asked, glad that the redhead hadn't left neon-Jenny in the same condition he left the three people in the Barnett house.

"Oh, sure." Jenny was gone and back in a blink. She put a three-page document in front of them. "Here we go. His name was Charles E. Manson."

Finn's gut clenched at the moniker. These were sick bastards, indeed. Thankfully, this girl was too young to remember who Charlie Manson was.

"Which one filled this out?" Cori asked as Finn studied the information. He couldn't swear the printing was the same as on the condolence card found in the cemetery, but it looked darn close.

"You know. I'm not really sure. I think it was the brown haired one. He was very weird. I don't remember what he looked like but he was real fidgety. Kind of like those people with that disease where they shake all the time?"

"Parkinson's?" Cori asked.

"Yes, but not exactly. I don't think he was sick, I think he was just nervous but in a weird way. Anyway, to be honest, I was checking availabilities on the computer and when I got back it was all done, so I don't know which one of them was Charles Manson. I gave them number forty-seven and they left."

"That's just what we were looking for. Think you can make us a copy of this?" Cori asked.

"Sure." Jenny swiped it back and turned around to a copy machine at the same time Cori turned to Finn.

"Don't you just love it when things go right."

"Someone up there is watching over us," Finn muttered and then he raised his voice. "We'll be needing you to put a hold on that car, if you would, miss."

Jenny flipped a smile over her shoulder just as the machine started chugging.

"I can't. It hasn't been returned yet."

Finn shook his head. He turned and put his elbow on the counter as Cori sighed.

"Chutes and ladders, O'Brien," she reminded him.

"I was hoping to stay atop a ladder just a wee bit longer on this one," he said. When he saw Cori's disappointment he added: "No worries. Jenny will be putting a face to the bogus name, which will give us a real name – or at least a string of alias's we can run down – and that's worth its weight."

Cori smiled. She would like to believe it was going to be that easy but there were ten million people in Los Angeles County, a billion ways to get rid of a car and not enough cops to go searching for a Bargain Rent-a-Car. Unless there was a body in the trunk and it started to smell, this was going to be low priority for the boys in uniform. Jenny's I.D. was a long shot. Still, you never did know when the cop Gods would smile on you.

"Here you go."

Jenny was back, handing them paper still warm from the copier. Finn folded it and put it in his pocket, Cori made a date with the girl to stop by the station and look at some photos and they took to the road again, neither under any illusion that they would be talking to Mr. Charles E. Manson any time soon.

They found out pretty quick that no such license existed and the address on the paperwork belonged to a small house nestled off road in the Hollywood Hills. There was a chain link fence around the building and a notice that it was scheduled for demolition. Finn climbed the fence and took a look around. There wasn't a car behind the house or in the garage, which they should have known since the weeds were high and there was no sign that anyone had walked, much less driven, over them.

Finn climbed back the other way, dusted off his hands and got back in the car. Cori had already tracked down the owner of the property who thought it was a crank call when she mentioned Charles E. Manson and hung up on her. The owner's name was Irving Tsao and he lived in Ontario. Ontario was far and their time would be better spent closer to home, so they would probably never have the pleasure of meeting Mr. Tsao. It was going on four o'clock when they got back to Wilshire and a desk laden with paperwork, files and photos.

"I was beginning to think some of our colleagues were draggin' their heels not wanting to help me out," Finn said.

"I think the boys are finally kicking in for you, O'Brien. Let's see what they came up with."

Cori rolled up her sleeves and Finn hung his jacket. Cori picked up a stack of files. She opened the one on top and something fluttered out and onto the floor. Finn bent to pick it up, but Cori was faster, grabbing it, crumpling it, and turning her back on Finn as she chattered some nonsense about bucking broncos and farm work, but Finn wasn't fooled. He took hold of her hand and pried open her fingers as she begged:

"Finn, don't. It's not important. It's really dumb."

"I've had my sticks and stones, Cori. Whatever is on that paper isn't going to do me much harm."

Cori gave up and opened her hand. He plucked it up, smoothed it out, and took a good long look at the picture of a red hair man, naked save for an artful drape of chains crisscrossing his private parts. In the corner was a Post-It on which someone had scrawled a message: *Thought you might want to check this one out yourself, O'Brien.*

"There you go, Cori. Proof positive that my fellow officers are looking out for my welfare."

She stole it back from him and tore it to shreds.

"Men are such pigs," she muttered.

"Maybe it wasn't a man who wrote it." Finn rolled up his sleeves as he sat down.

"No, it was a guy. A woman would have had the courtesy to look you in the eye when she kicked you in the balls."

"Don't I know," Finn said, thinking how lovely Bev's eyes looked as she gazed into his and said goodbye.

"I swear, you're back is slick as ice," Cori muttered.

When he stayed silent, she gave him a glance and saw that she was right about his back, but his hide wasn't as thick as he pretended. She wished she could do something to ease his pain. When she sat down and opened her files, figuring she had done just that. She had, after all, stood with him.

An hour and a half later, just as the rank and file were changing shifts, Finn and Cori's pile of possible suspects was a whole lot smaller than that of the impossible ones.

"Are we looking at women?" Cori yawned through the question, shook it off and snapped the sheet she was looking at. "I've got one here who killed her kid with a knife back in ninety-eight. She weighed over three hundred pounds at booking so she had to be pretty strong."

"But not swift," Finn said. "How old was she when she did it?"

"Forty-seven. Insanity defense. She was in a facility. Never did time behind bars. Released five years ago. Last known address was in Sacramento."

"Too old and Sacramento's too far. We'll work out from L.A. Let's keep it to the valley, over to Riverside and down to the South Bay. The car was rented locally. We may have had one of these two following Mrs. Barnett and that means he has to be within spitting distance."

The phone rang and Finn dropped his feet from the desk to the floor.

"Yes, I'll tell her. Thanks," he said and hung up. "Jenny's here to start looking at the mug shots."

"I'll grab her." Cori closed the file she was looking at and pushed her chair back.

"Bless you. I fear my ears would fall off if I had to listen to that girl's blue streak."

When she was gone, Finn opened a new folder and found bank and phone records for the Barnetts and Rachel Gerber. He picked up a yellow marker just as the phone rang again.

"O'Brien." When the person on the other end started talking, he tossed the marker and grabbed a pen and paper to make notes. "Yeah. Yeah. I got it. Okay. Yeah. Appreciate it."

He cut off the call, and started to dial the medical examiner when he put down the phone and took a closer look at the piece of paper in front of him. He rifled through the other statements that had been sent by the bank and then went back to the first one. Picking up the marker, he highlighted the balance just as Cori came back.

"She's all settled. I think it's going to be a couple hours though. That girl thinks this is all so much fun that she's ready to close down the place tonight." Cori knocked on the desk they shared. "O'Brien? Did you hear me? If she's here later than nine, you're going to have to deal with her. Unless you have something else going on."

"I believe I do, Cori," Finn said. "I'm going to be paying a visit to the Barnetts."

"Well now, what happened in the last ten minutes that I should know about?"

"Stephen Grady is dead." Finn said. "He ran out onto the freeway. A woman on the way to the music center hit him and tossed him into a concrete piling. The officer on the scene says his hair is cut short but not recently. Still it's not long enough to be what they we're looking for. There were scratches on his arms but they were deep and recent. That's consistent with what Mrs. Barnett told us about him. There were none on his face or the back of his hands. We'll get a DNA sample, but I think we can safely assume he isn't the one who attacked Rachel Gerber."

"Nice you want to hold their hands when you break the news. We could call that one in on the way home," Cori said.

"Ah, but there's a bit more to chat about than Mr. Grady." Finn handed her the bank statement that he had found so interesting. Cori took a look and when she handed it back she said:

"I'm going with you."

CHAPTER 28

DAY 5 – EVENING

Elizabeth fussed while she waited for Sam to come home. She pulled the neck of her robe a little lower before closing it back up again. She checked her hair, putting it up and taking it down and finally getting it just the way Sam liked it. She climbed up onto the bed but that made her feel ridiculous, so she climbed down and stood in the most flattering light in the bedroom, just beside the big fireplace.

Finally, she heard him at the front door. Her heart beat fast, only to slow when he didn't come upstairs. Elizabeth ran to the landing and looked over the banister. She didn't see him but she could hear him going to his study.

He slept there now, worn down as he was by her plans, complaints and reproaches. He didn't have to say that's why he didn't come upstairs because she knew what he was thinking. Tonight, though, would have been different. She assumed Sam would have sensed that. He should have at least come up to check on her. If he was so worried about her like he said, he should have –

Elizabeth caught herself before she became too upset. Sam could not read her mind. That's what Doctor Templeton said. Doctor Templeton said that Elizabeth was the strong one – which she had proved already in so many ways – and that she must be stronger now. Elizabeth, Doctor Templeton said, would need to set their lives straight.

Empowered by this knowledge, Elizabeth went to Sam, gliding down the stairs, her satin slippers no more than a whisper over the marble floor below. Sam didn't hear her open the door of his study, he didn't see her come into the room or sense her standing near his desk. But Elizabeth saw him as he was: a broken man, slouched in his leather chair, his head resting on one upturned fist as he stared at the bookshelves. It felt strange to be in the room watching him instead or peering through the window, hiding in the dark. Strange but exhilarating.

"I'm glad you're home," Elizabeth ventured.

"Why?"

His voice was so heavy she was surprised he had managed to lift that one word. Her heart went out to him. She knew that horrible feeling of being of no consequence.

"Because I saw a doctor today. A psychiatrist. I wanted to tell you about it."

Silence.

"I know it's been hard for you to come home."

Nothing.

"Sam?"

Nothing.

"I'm apologizing."

Nothing.

She licked her lips and tried again: "I've been wrong about a lot of things, I see that now."

"Elizabeth, please." Sam's fingers moved, a fluttery gesture of defeat. "I'm just really tired."

She took a few steps so that he could see her. All he really needed to do was look at her and everything would be fine.

"How can you be too tired to listen to an apology? To a confession? I want to confess," Elizabeth insisted.

"Fine. Apology accepted," He interrupted her. "Thank you. Really, I'm just tired and I'd like to be alone. I don't want to talk."

"Please, Sam. You don't have to talk, but I want you to know everything. When you do, you'll see how much I love you. How much—" Elizabeth's voice broke. This was going to be very hard but Elizabeth prided herself on finishing what she started and she would finish this.

She inched closer. The room that at one time seemed so exotic with its dark colors, soft leathers, and the tools of her husband's important trade, now felt old and worn, a caricature of an important man's retreat. She didn't want Sam to stay in this dark place. She moved until she stood between his outstretched legs.

"I know you're feeling the same things. I know you see the girls just like I do. I think I see them run into a room I just came from. I think if I'm fast enough, I'll find them. Then I'll gather them up, and I'll lock the door, and they'll be safe. Rachel would still be..."

Elizabeth paused. Sam hadn't moved an inch. He hadn't twitched. They were on the same page so Elizabeth was emboldened.

"Rachel would still be dead, of course. I don't see her

at all. You don't see her, do you? I can't even remember what she looked like now. Can you?"

Elizabeth whispered the last. It was the two of them in this room, in this house, so it was all right to be brutally honest. She waited a long while for Sam to tell her something truthful back. Instead, he dropped his hand, raised his eyes to hers and said:

"We're moving, Elizabeth. I spoke to a realtor."

"Oh, Sam, no." She moved closer still. "This is our home. There are memories here. We can't leave."

"Good lord, Elizabeth, you are sick." Sam swung his head away from her but not far enough that she couldn't see his expression of disgust. "Do you want to remember what those rooms looked like upstairs? I don't know how you go in them. I can't even think about them."

"But there are good memories, too." Elizabeth cast around for something that would make him understand what this meant to her. If they left, the children would be completely gone, disappeared forever. "Okay. Okay. How about this? We won't ever open those rooms again. I'll move our bedroom down here. I don't know where, but I'll figure it out. Don't make me move. Please. I'll make it better. I'll make it all like it used to be."

Elizabeth untied her robe. Beneath it was the silk teddy he had bought for her in Paris. Her boldness made her lightheaded. She was not a seductress, but Sam wanted that in his life and so she was trying. He just had to try back. Instead, his eyes went slowly up and down her body, comparing her, she was sure, to other women. When she realized she did not measure up, was not even worth his lust, a tear fell down her cheek. It wasn't his lust she wanted anyway. What she wanted was kindness, forgiveness, and a sign that he still loved her. Just when Elizabeth thought all was lost, when she thought of running up to her girls' room to hide, the cool leather of his shoe touched her bare ankle.

Elizabeth closed her eyes. She heard the sigh of leather and the squeak of springs as he leaned forward in his chair and touched her hip. Elizabeth closed her fingers around that hand and held it tight. The fingertips of his free hand grazed her thigh. He put his head to her stomach and slowly rubbed his cheek against the silk as though he could go back in time, so far back that he would be in the womb or at least in a warm bed in Paris.

"I'm so sorry, Elizabeth," he whispered. "Sorry. So sorry."

Elizabeth took his face in her hands and turned it up to hers as she got to her knees. It would all be fine now. This was all she ever wanted. The two of them. Alone. In love. Safe. Happy. The strap of her lingerie slipped from her shoulder. He touched her breast, hesitated and then dropped his hand.

"I can't. I just can't."

Sam stood so quickly that Elizabeth fell back, landing hard on her hip. Sam reached for her, and just as quickly changed his mind and stepped over her. Elizabeth scrambled after him. On one knee, she grabbed for his hands.

"Sam, what happened, what did I do? I'll change. I can be different."

He pulled back only to swoop down once again, take her by the shoulders, and lift her up like a rag doll.

"Elizabeth, for once understand. It's not just about you. This time it's about me and eventually it will be about us if we're lucky." Sam choked on the words. "I don't know if we can get back what we had. I only know it can't be done here. Not in this house."

He kissed her hard and tried to let her go, but Elizabeth threw her arms around his neck. This was the moment; this was the time. If they moved from this place there would be no reminder of mistakes made and those lessons needed to be remembered. If she couldn't rein him in now and tie him to her she had lost, but the moment wasn't hers.

The doorbell was ringing.

CHAPTER 29

Sam closed the front door with one hand on the big, brass knob and the other on the solid, polished wood. He put his forehead against the door. He was shot through with outrage at the insinuations, near accusations, sanctimonious shit that Finn O'Brien and Cori Anderson had brought into his home. Now they were gone, leaving him to deal with Elizabeth; Elizabeth whose righteous indignation was palpable, Elizabeth who was scratching for a fight when he had no strength to defend himself, Elizabeth who embraced innuendo as evidence, and Elizabeth who wanted to believe the worst as she always did.

"Don't start with me, Elizabeth."

Sam turned around and looked at her. As expected, that gorgeous face of hers was twisted into a hateful mask of disgust and loathing. He was not perfect – he would own that – but he was not as imperfect as she believed him to be by a long shot. When she opened her mouth, Sam put up a finger of warning.

"Don't."

"What does that mean, Sam?" Elizabeth would not be put off. "What exactly does 'don't start with me' mean?"

Instead of answering, he headed back to his study, the

almighty kingdom of the almighty breadwinner. But he wasn't there yet, so Elizabeth ran after him and jogged beside him. When he tried to dodge her, she put herself in front of him; when he tried to push through her, she pushed back. She grabbed at his arm and he shook her off. She snatched at his shirt and he knocked at her hand.

"Look at me!" She slapped at his back, demanding his attention but when he turned on her, Elizabeth fell back just out of reach.

"Stop it, Elizabeth. You're acting crazy."

"I am not crazy. I want to know what you mean."

"What I mean is don't you dare accuse me of having an affair with Rachel. She was the nanny for God's sake."

"Oh, like that never happens," Elizabeth scoffed. "Like it doesn't happen every day. Like I didn't know it a long time ago. A long, long time ago. I have eyes and now I have proof. Do you hear me? I knew it!"

Sam turned toward the kitchen. Elizabeth stopped him. He went for his study. She moved in front of him, threw her arms out, hands against the hallway wall.

"I didn't need those detectives to tell me that you were sleeping with her, but I didn't know you were paying for it. Thirty thousand dollars? She had thirty thousand dollars in her checking account. She must have been quite a piece of ass. There was enough of it."

"That's, beneath you," Sam growled.

"I've done a lot of things that are beneath me, but at least I had a good reason. But Rachel? I always wanted to know why, Sam. Wasn't I a good enough wife? Maybe I just wasn't a good enough lay."

Sam shook his head and made to leave, but she grabbed him again.

"Those people just told us Rachel had thirty thousand dollars in her bank account, and I'm supposed to just go upstairs by myself and be quiet? Why would I do that, Sam? Really? Why?"

"Because you heard what I told them," he shot back. "There is nothing more to say."

"Oh-ho, yes there is. There is no way she could have saved that kind of cash in two years unless you gave it to her," Elizabeth shot back. She had saved up words all her life and now she wanted to say them and hear them, but Sam only knew four and he said his words first.

"I. Gave. Her. Nothing." He got in her face, put up a finger, and enunciated each word as though she were hard of hearing. Elizabeth's neck arched, she dragged her fingernails down the delicate skin of her throat until she drew welts.

"You controlled all the money, Sam. You told me I wasn't all that good with money. Well, I sure would have known where thirty thousand dollars went if I was the one writing the checks. I'm smart enough to know that. And you had me thinking I was imagining things between the two of you. Oh, you are so smooth."

Sam grabbed her hands and pulled them away from her throat.

"Stop that, Elizabeth. You're bleeding."

She shook him off and used both hands now to scratch her neck in long, sharp strokes. She put her bloody fingers on his shirt. She purred:

"Did Rachel do everything you told her to? Is that why you paid her so well?"

Sam slapped her hands down but years of fear – imagined or not – kindled her anger; her new grief fanned it to a flame. A lifetime of being a lady, a sweet daughter, a dutiful wife, an admired student and kind human being was undone by her childrens' deaths and torn to shreds by her husband's betrayal. She went at him again.

"Do you realize that makes Rachel a whore? You hired a whore to care for our beautiful little girls. You made me watch her doing it day in and day out. How much did you think I could take? I could kill you for what you brought into this house. Kill you!"

"Oh God, shut up."

He took her hands and yanked her toward him. She fought but he was stronger than she was and he made her be silent. His eyes filled with tears. He thought they were done with this madness. They had been so happy and now here it was again.

"Elizabeth, I love you but this is crazy. Think. Think. When would I have had time to do what you're saying? I slept with you every night, Rachel was with the girls every day."

"Don't patronize me. There are so many ways. You're just like my father. Just like him. Look what he did to my mother and now you're doing it to me. You liar. You cheat."

She yanked on her hands but Sam held her and tried to talk her down. They needed one another. Despite all this, God help him, he needed her.

"Maybe that money was her nest egg, Elizabeth. Maybe she sold her mother's jewelry. I told the cops the truth. I do not know how she got that money."

Sam searched his wife's face, looking for any sign that she believed him. He was done in by her innuendos, her passive/aggressive asides, and now this meltdown.

Elizabeth went limp. Her lips parted and he watched her beautiful mouth form the words that tore him to shreds.

"I don't believe you."

Sam dropped her hands. He nodded and moved away from her. Elizabeth needed more help than he could give her.

"I think that was pretty evident by the way you threw me under the bus when those cops were here," Sam said as he started to walk away. "Forget it. I'm not going to talk about this anymore."

"You threw yourself under the bus," Elizabeth called after him. "You looked like someone punched you when they told you about Rachel's money. You said all the right things but they weren't truthful things. *No, detective, I can't imagine how our nanny would put her hands on that kind of money. No, detective, Rachel never talked to us about her finances.*"

Elizabeth mocked him cruelly and with that Sam stopped. He squared his shoulders and turned around. He put one hand against the door of the kitchen and the other at his hip. He shook his head.

"Don't you ever quit? I mean, really, Elizabeth. We go for months, years, and I think everything is fine and then suddenly you do this. It's like you've been working yourself to a lather inside your head."

"You lied, Sam. I saw Rachel with you in the study just before Christmas. You two were talking about money. When you saw me, you closed the door. And that's not the only—"

"I don't know why I closed the door. I don't even know if I closed the door." He threw up his hands at the futility of the conversation. "Rachel had two grand to invest. That was it. It told her to buy a mutual fund. I wouldn't count that as heavy-duty investment advice or a ton of cash to do it with.

"And instead of snooping around why didn't you just walk in and listen? You would have learned a thing or two. Maybe you would have taken some responsibility for our finances. You just wanted me to make the money so you could spend it on the girls. I think that suited you very nicely."

"Oh, no. Oh, no. That's not right. I never asked for anything except to be able to stay home and be a mother to our children. But you took that away from me," Elizabeth railed. "And we're not talking about me or us, we're talking about Rachel and you and all the dirty things you did with her."

Elizabeth lunged for him again but Sam pushed her away and this time she stumbled and fell against the wall.

"That's it." Sam came at her and pushed her shoulders against the wall to make sure he had her attention. "Rachel is dead. We should be packing her things up. We should be sending condolences to her family. We should tell them that she was so good to our children—"

"And to my husband."

Sam let go of her and raised his arm. Elizabeth threw up her own up in defense, but the blows never came. Sam had clenched his fists and was shaking them at the sky. He grunted. He wheezed and then he lowered his hands.

"I will not talk about this ever again. I will go and see O'Brien's captain. I will have him replaced. It may make you feel better to have him falling all over you like your personal bodyguard, but when he implies I have been unfaithful, that I am somehow responsible for what happened to my children, that's where I draw the line."

"You just got caught, Sam. That's why you're mad."

"You are so naive." Sam shook his head. The fight had gone out of him. "All they want is the case closed, and if they decide to make it look like I am responsible for all this then that's what they'll do. I do the same thing. I point fingers at anyone who is a plausible alternative just so the jury won't look at my client. That's what I do, and that's what the cops do."

Sam leaned against the wall and looked at his wife through sad eyes. Despite the pretty robe and the fancy lingerie, her beautiful body and her elegant face, her suspicions made her ugly. He used to think she was ill, a little off, but now he was beginning to think his wife was selfish and evil. Or maybe she played the lawyer's game better than he did. *Look at someone else. Look at Rachel. Don't look at me because you won't like what you see.*

"They will probably never find out who did this. Even if they do, there is no guarantee those people will ever be convicted. What if we sat through a trial and they got away with it? Could you go through that, Elizabeth? Could you?"

"I would go through hell, Sam."

"We're already there and I am afraid down to my very core." He put a hand over his eyes and sighed. When he looked at her again he asked: "Why aren't you afraid, Elizabeth?"

"Because nothing could happen to us that is worse than this," she answered.

"Oh, there are worse things." He pushed away from the wall. "At least we're straight. We'll just have to see where we end up."

He started for his study. He had heard all this before.

He had loved her despite the crazy ideas that took hold of her at times, but that was when he was strong enough to weather the storm. Now he was injured and sinking fast and his sympathy was gone. He needed quiet and she wouldn't give it to him.

"Is that a threat? Are you threatening to leave me? I won't allow that, Sam."

Sam hesitated. He pulled back his shoulders that seemed to be perpetually slumped these days. He turned, looked at Elizabeth and then walked back to where she sat on the floor. He looked at her bloody neck and fingers. He looked at her clothes. He picked up a strand of her hair. Holding on to it, he pulled her toward him and kissed her forehead. His lips were soft and sweet and he whispered against her skin:

"Dye your hair, Elizabeth."

CHAPTER 30

DAY 5 – NIGHT

"Where are those damn kids?"

Mort burst through the door of the dilapidated house, stomping and slamming and swearing. Georgia responded by flinging a watering can at him.

"What in the hell do you think you're doing?" she screamed. "You're a Goddamn hillbilly, Mort. A no-class hillbilly. What are you thinkin'? Out so late, and then coming in here like that?"

"Shut up, Georgia. Shut up and tell me where those two brats are."

Mort got in his wife's face. She saw a man she barely recognized, but he saw her for what she was: better than he probably should have, and a helluva lot worse than what he dreamed about. The best thing about her was that she was quick.

"Okay, honey. I'm sorry, baby." Georgia hunched her shoulders, and moved back a step like she was bowing to him. Mostly she was just getting ready in case he hit her. Better to whack her bod than get her face rearranged. "Don't get your shorts in a knot."

"Where are they, Georgia?" Mort snarled.

"Bobbi's out back looking for night worms. I don't know where the other one is." Georgia used her little girl voice, but he wasn't buying it. He must be pissed if the little girl voice didn't take the edge off.

"They got on those necklaces?" He was running to the backyard like he already knew the answer.

"I don't know. I don't know. I'll check."

Georgia went after him, holding the squeaky door open more to see that he didn't hurt Bobbi than to offer her assistance. When the little girl wasn't there, he ran into the house again. Georgia followed him to the room the girls shared.

Mort threw open the door and scanned the mess. Hair ribbons, discarded clothes, bed sheets that had been made into tents, all of it littered the floor. Normally this wouldn't have bothered Mort since he actually liked his kids and it was fun to watch them play games. He never played when he was little. Half the time he didn't live in a house when he was little. He knew that his kids wouldn't amount to a hill of beans, but he loved them anyway. Someday they'd get knocked up and have more redheaded little kids. Maybe they'd be happy, maybe they wouldn't. Right that minute, though, Mort didn't give a crap if the girls were happy.

He dove into the room, tossing clothes, throwing toys, kicking at the little princess beds that he had got half price. He knocked his knee on the bedpost and swore. Mort stormed out of the room and slammed through the kitchen again. This time he headed to the playroom that really was just a lean-to a previous owner had knocked together without a permit. He roared as he threw open the door:

"Roberta! Carolyn! Get your butts out here now!"

Georgia hadn't gone further than the porch. She shivered in her peachy-colored K-Mart velour top with the plunging neckline, gave up the chase, and went back to mixing up a facial of honey and egg just like the woman on T.V. had done. She tried to block out Mort's voice and the girls' cries but it was really hard. She had just applied the honey/egg goo to her face when she heard the door of the lean-to slam. A second later it slammed again and this time she heard the girls wailing.

Mort stomped back over the concrete slab they called a patio, threw open the squeaky door again and went through the kitchen. A minute later, the kitchen door slammed open again, and the little girls chased after their father, crying in anguish. Mort was out the front before they could catch him, so the girls ran back to Georgia. They tugged on her peachy velour top and looked up into her egg-and-honey splattered face.

"He took my necklace," Bobbi sobbed.

"Mama, my locket. Daddy took my locket and said I couldn't never have it back," Carolyn cried.

Without missing a beat, Georgia backhanded Carolyn. She was, after all, the older and less favored of the two so it was only right.

"Your dad knows what he's doing," she said even though the egg stuff tightening around her mouth made it hard to talk. "Those damn things didn't even have your right names on 'em. Get to bed."

"It's too early," Carolyn yelled through her sniffles.

"I don't care what time it is, get to bed."

Carolyn, her cheek burning where her mother had hit her, her eyes glittering with rage, stood her ground.

Another year, Georgia knew, and Carolyn would be hitting back. But that was another year. If the kid tried anything now, Georgia was ready for her. She didn't try anything because Bobbi was tugging at her shirt. Finally, Bobbi won out and the girls retreated, but not before Carolyn muttered a few choice words that Georgia didn't quite catch.

Alone in the kitchen, Georgia considered how hard it was to be a woman in this day and age. Good looks weren't nearly enough to get a body by. A woman had to be tough, and knowing that made her feel better about hitting Carolyn. Yep, Georgia decided, she was just helping her girls along best she knew how. They would thank her for it someday.

Pushing aside the egg/honey goo, Georgia grabbed up the warm washcloth and scrubbed the stuff off her face. She tossed the cloth, checked herself out in the toaster, and then sat down and put her head back. Suddenly she felt old and tired. She wished Mort would come back and just put his arm around her, but Mort was halfway down the block, walking fast and thinking hard. In fact, Mort's mind was near bursting with thinking.

It didn't matter that Medium Man had been the one to take out those kids he, Mort, would be blamed because he was the boss. Just like Charlie Manson. That man never lifted a finger, but look where that got him – life in the slammer. And Mort was kicking himself for being fool enough to take those necklaces. Just showed what you got for being nice and thinking about your kids while you were at work. It was lucky he had been at Hussein's Emporium, Pawn Broker to the Stars, passing the time and flipping through the police bulletins just for the fun of it. Old Hussein never even saw the one about the lockets since Mort slipped it into his pocket before he high tailed it home.

Turning the corner, Mort hurried on, walking through puddles of yellow light seeping out of the street lamps. The light made his hair look like it was on fire. A pair of pit bulls kept pace with him behind the junkyard fence. They weren't barking but he knew those dogs were just dying to get at him. He knew that because that's how he was sometimes: quiet, thinking, biding his time. When the time was right – pow!

Three blocks later Mort was at the Los Angeles River that really wasn't a river at all anymore. It was a flood channel, a concrete artery cut through L.A., and it was dry as a bone. Mort always thought it was strange to cover up a river with concrete but then politicians weren't the brightest bulbs. He slid down the steep embankment and landed in the otherworld of Los Angeles.

Graffiti exploded all around him, spray-painted on every inch of the concrete. Mort felt like he was walking through someone's bad trip. No, no. It was worse. It was like God screaming obscenities at him in big, bloated letters colored black and white and green and blue and red. The thought that there might be a God watching him gave Mort even more of the heebie jeebies.

A hundred yards down, he found a drainpipe and poked his head in. It was filled with the dark and creatures gone long without water. He could have hunched over and walked right in, but he didn't bother. Instead, Mort pulled himself back out and looked over his shoulder to make sure he was alone. Not seeing any gang bangers, homeless dudes, or drug peddlers who usually hung down here, he took the lockets from his pocket and threw them in the drainpipe. He heard them clank against the side of the huge, hollow cylinder. When the echoing stopped, Mort kept his eyes on the drainpipe as he slowly backed away; he looked at that thing like he was afraid those lockets might come flying back out at him.

When nothing happened, he sat down and put his back up against the embankment. Mort took the bulletin out of his pocket, looked it over once more, and tore it to shreds. There were probably ten thousand more of these things all around Los Angeles but it wouldn't matter now. The lockets would never be found. Still, Mort was near paralyzed with dread. Since he couldn't think of one thing more to do, he couldn't think how anyone would ever find those necklaces, he dropped his head back, closed his eyes and tried not to think at all.

"Das meh real horse. O'Brien! O'Brien!"

Geoffrey Baptiste, the Beanie Man of Trinidad, the fourth owner of Mick's Irish Pub, called out his Trini hello the minute Finn opened the door. Finn raised a hand in greeting, Geoffrey beamed, and more than a few heads turned. Most of the faces Finn knew because Mick's was that kind of place.

Finn slapped the back of old Sam who was perpetually waiting for his son, young Sam, to come and take him away to his house in Missouri. Since everyone knew there was no son, Finn never asked after him but only said, 'Happy to still see you sittin' here, Sam,' and that made the old man happy enough.

Violet was hanging over the end of the bar. She was a tiny thing with long black hair, beautiful Asian features, and a pedigree from Hawaii. She could pass for twelve until she opened her mouth and then a drunken sailor couldn't match her. She lusted after Geoffrey who already had a wife stashed back in Trinidad. Since that wife was older than he and preferred the company of her children to the Beanie Man's sweet ways, she stayed behind when Geoffrey came to the U.S. to make his fortune. While Geoffrey swore he loved 'dis wife' her existence didn't keep him from dancing a little with the ladies, but Violet was not one of his preferred partners. As he told Finn, if he wanted *basa basa* – a woman to argue with – he might as well go home to his wife. Besides, Violet's *bam bam* was like a little boy's. A woman, Geoffrey said, should have buttocks rounded like two soccer balls. He and Finn had that conversation many times and each time Geoffrey laughed mightily. His gold teeth flashed, his wide smile pushed his ears right up into the knit beanie of the day, and Finn was left feeling fine no matter what had happened during the day.

Finn turned sideways and said his sorries as he moved through a gaggle of fine looking young women, one of whom was wearing a bridal veil with her crop top and jeans. For her, a girl he had seen nearly grow up in Mick's, Finn had a kiss on the cheek. When pressed, Finn offered an Irish blessing for her wedding.

There are 4 things you must never do:
lie, steal, cheat, or drink.
But if you must lie,
lie in the arms of the one you love.
If you must steal, steal away from bad company.
If you must cheat, cheat death.
And if you must drink,
drink in the moments that take your breath away.

The bride and her maids raised their glasses and all kissed Finn before they went back to partying hearty. The young dandy Joseph was there. He had no money because he was a struggling actor. He swore that one day he would put his Academy Award on Geoffrey's bar. Tonight, he shot darts in the corner like he was aiming for the eye of a producer.

Geoffrey was streaming *The Doors* and Finn thought it was apt that the song pounding the place was *People Are Strange*. He slid onto his usual stool and before he could put in his order, his pint was in front of him.

"Harp, mon. Harp lager, O'Brien. New for you all de way from Ireland, don' you know, mon."

Finn smiled and cupped the glass. "I'm a Guinness man, Geoffrey. You know that."

"Yeah, but I try sometin' new. Gotta keep with da time. You tell me how you be likin' it."

Finn took a drink. He smiled and nodded. "It's a good one, Geoffrey. Just don't go tossing out the Guinness."

"No, I won' be doin' dat. Wanna keep de customers happy, specially you, O'Brien. You be my good friend wit' da police. Just wantin' to give you a gift for what you been doin' for dem poor little girls."

"Doing my best, Geoffrey," Finn muttered and stuck his nose back in his glass.

Much as he loved Geoffrey Baptiste, much as he loved Mick's and the crowd of rowdies and working stiffs, he didn't want to share business. At Mick's all Finn wanted was to drink and maybe sing when he had too much to drink, and chat up some folks about politics or listen to war stories from the old guys. Finn wanted to watch Geoffrey work and admire whatever beanie was wrapping up his dreadlocks. Tonight it was a rainbow knit that was pilled and worn. It was his favorite because his mother had made it.

"You gonna be doin' it all, mon. I know. You won' be lettin' down the mooma and faddah. You find da creep who done take dose little girl souls."

"I won't let them down," Finn said, but he wasn't sure that was an actual promise.

Sam Barnett had seemed genuinely surprised by the information about Rachel Gerber. Elizabeth Barnett had barely blinked when they told her about Stephen Grady because she bought into the Rachel scenario faster than the speed of light. Cori agreed she expected more of a rise out of the lawyer. The wife's reaction didn't surprise her at all. Bottom line, if Barnett was messing with the nanny it would give the boyfriend good cause to take her out. The kids might have been collateral damage. What a pity and a waste that would be, but it made sense. The boyfriend would have believed Rachel was alone in the house, a snip of the alarm, she opens the door and God bless her, she's a goner and so are the kids.

Thinking Geoffrey was done with him, Finn lifted his glass intending to mull all this over while he nursed his brew, but Geoffrey had something important to say. The man leaned close over the bar, his dreadlocks swaying, the gold cross around his neck and the gold teeth in his mouth blinking as they caught the light. He lowered his voice as his dark, dark face settled into a somber expression that lengthened it like a marionette's.

"O'Brien. O'Brien." Geoffrey wiggled his long fingers at Finn to underscore the seriousness of what he was about to say.

"I'm all ears, my friend," Finn assured him with due gravity.

"I be wantin' to ask, do ya know if deese dead children be christened? Do you know dat, O'Brien?"

Finn looked straight into Geoffrey Bapitste's dark, slightly blood shot eyes and said:

"From what I know of the family, I would say that I believe they were."

The barman took a huge breath. His hands went to his beanie and his eyes rolled heavenward.

"Tanks be to God. I worried. Oh, I worried, O'Brien, that they be *douens*. If dat were so, it would be bad. Very, very bad for da city; very bad for you, O'Brien."

"And what might that be – a *douen*?" Finn asked, always happy to add to his Trini vocabulary.

"An unchristen child, so I just be tellin' you, O'Brien." It was clear Finn was trying the man's patience. "Dey little feet turn backwards and dey be havin' straw hats like a Chinaman's." Geoffrey made a triangle motion over his head. "Dey wear dem hats to hide their faces because dey got no faces, O'Brien. *Douen* eat baby corn and lure live childrens deep in da forest with sweet songs and games and then poof!" Geoffery's long fingers had come

223

together only to explode open, illustrating his point. "Dey disappear soon as dey be lost in da forest and dose children are gone now too. All dem children gone."

"This is Los Angeles, Geoffrey. We haven't got any forests."

Finn said this kindly because he would never laugh at legend. He, himself, believed in the leprechauns. He didn't exactly buy the pot of gold at the end of the rainbow thing, but Finn knew there was always a kernel of truth in legend that was to be respected. Poor Geoffrey, though, wasn't put at ease.

"It is the expression, O'Brien. O'Brien, you see what I be meaning, mon? If dose little girls be *douen*, dey lure other children because dey be lost souls and be needin' playmates, so dey not be lonely. If dey do that, you be havin' so much work, O'Brien. I am only sayin' for you to check to make sure dey be christened. You don' wanna see more children gone, O'Brien."

"No, Geoffrey. No one wants more children gone. I'll double check on the christening thing for you."

Finn got off his bar stool. He dug into his pocket for money but Geoffrey would have none of it.

"No, mon, first one on da house. On me, O'Brien. I am da house."

Finn smiled but before he could thank Geoffrey, the bridal party cheered as the young woman in the veil clambered atop the bar to dance. That was too much for Geoffrey.

"No! No! No!"

He waved his arms and hurried down to shoo her off. Finn put his money on the bar. Geoffrey's stories and Finn's Trini language lessons were worth more than the price of a beer. He ambled to the back of the bar and picked up another set of darts. Joseph gave him a brilliant smile and Finn figured the guy had about a fifty/fifty chance of making it in Hollywood. Finn bought Joseph a round because he was still way on the wrong side of that fifty/fifty. Then he picked up a set of darts and they took turns at the board.

Joseph made a respectable hit on the second ring with his last dart. Finn stepped up and aligned himself: shoulder, foot, hand. He threw in a practiced sweep, without hesitation, and he missed.

"Bounce out!" Joseph barked, delighted that the master himself had screwed up so royally.

"Up yours." Finn muttered and set himself up again.

Rocking back and forth as was his way, Finn tried to focus on nothing but the board, nothing but the bull's eye, but he was distracted. There was that niggle in the back of his brain again. His little Tinker Bell twinkle was flitting and sparkling. He was missing something important and damned if he could see it through the fairy dust of intuition. Finn threw again; this time it was a flat tire.

"Man, wish I had money on this," Joseph crowed.

Finn took his last dart, rocked on his boots, trying not to think about work, but he did think about it. What, he wondered, was happening at the Barnett house now. Right that very minute was someone confessing, someone apologizing. Was Sam Barnett the bad guy? Was Elizabeth Barnett all right? And why, oh why, did Finn O'Brien still feel like that man, Sam Barnett, was coming to a no-good end?

With that, Finn rocked for the last time, let the dart fly

and hit the absolute center. A double bull. He grinned at Joseph.

"The trick is to come through in the pinch, my friend."

Finn gave him a pat on the shoulder and went back to the bar for a Guinness.

CHAPTER 31

Elizabeth lunched at the Italian cafe on Larchmont. She sat at an outside table so small it was nearly unserviceable. It had taken a long while to get her food and when it came, she spent a longer time moving the fancy lettuce around before pushing the plate aside. She had wrapped her hand around her glass and spent some more time watching the ice melt and the tea turn to the color of pond water.

The day was overcast, warm and muggy and yet Elizabeth sat with the collar of her blazer turned up. Her slacks were wool as was the sweater beneath her jacket. Last night after Sam locked himself in his study, Elizabeth gave up. She sat down on the side of the refugee road. When he left that morning without a word, she knew there would be no one to pick her up.

She spent her morning wandering the shopping street, buying nothing. Elizabeth missed the housekeeper. Even slutty Rachel had at least filled a space in Elizabeth's world that now was so empty.

"Are you done? Lady, are you done?"

A finger poked Elizabeth's shoulder. The girl standing

beside her was dressed in tight jeans and a tighter top. She had tiny, young breasts and a face that looked too old for her body. Elizabeth didn't let go of the glass of ice tea. Opening her hand was too much work. The girl shifted and when Elizabeth lowered her head to dodge her peevishness, she saw the check on the table. The girl wanted her to pay for the food she didn't eat; the restaurant wanted the table. Elizabeth was a refugee and the world wanted her to move on.

"I'm sorry. I'm so sorry."

Elizabeth took out the first bill she found in her wallet – a fifty – and waved the girl with the small breasts away. She stood up, put on her sunglasses, but she didn't move. Her mind drifted as if she didn't have a brain in her head. She laughed a little at that strange image: her brain floating outside her head. Perhaps that was why her body felt heavy and mechanical. There was no brain in her head to tell her body what to do. That was okay, because the waitress was glaring at her; she was telling Elizabeth what to do.

Go.

Leave.

Go.

Elizabeth walked around the wrought iron railing that kept diners and pedestrians at arms length from one another. While she walked, Elizabeth took her keys out of her purse only to drop them. Not a brain in her head and butter fingers, too. There were so many keys for the all the compartments of her life: the house, the cars, the trunk in the attic where her wedding dress was locked away forever, the cabinet where Sam kept his gun that he didn't even know how to use, the safe where she had kept her jewelry.

As she looked at the keys, a man got down almost on one knee and picked them up. When he handed them to her, Elizabeth said thank you and went on her way, unaware that the man followed behind.

He didn't move quickly or he would have been closer when, a few feet from her car, Elizabeth suddenly felt ill. She steadied herself against the window of a shop, overcome by a nauseating dizziness. When she opened her eyes, she was looking through the glass of a children's store, the window decked out for the holiday: Easter dresses, bonnets, coats, lace and poi de soie, satin ribbons. There were glassy eyed stuffed bunnies like the one Alana loved, like the ones Elizabeth had brought back from Paris.

She blinked at the mannequins and was stunned to see that they had her children's faces. She looked past the mannequins and saw a plump young woman helping a customer and it was Rachel. Reflected in the window Elizabeth saw Sam just behind her, reaching for her.

She wanted to thank him for finding her, for forgiving her, for not leaving her. She couldn't bear it if he left her, but then she realized that he was probably there for Rachel and Elizabeth went near blind with rage. Yet, when she put her face against the window and really looked at that plump woman, she saw it wasn't Rachel at all. And if the man reflected in the window were Sam then he was ill. His hair was dull and straight. His skin was sallow, his cheeks sunken. He wore sneakers and baggy pants. His lips moved, but they weren't Sam's lips. When the reflection in the window spoke to her, it wasn't Sam's voice she heard. This voice was quieter than Sam's.

"So sorry about your little ones," the reflection said.

Elizabeth twirled away from the window, threw her hands over her eyes and collapsed screaming in front of the shop window full of pique dresses and pink bunnies.

"Can I come in?"

Elizabeth raised her head. Her hair was electrified from lying on the white butcher paper that covered the examining table in the hospital emergency room. There were dark circles beneath her dull eyes.

"I can't stop you." Elizabeth sat up and hung her legs over the side of the table. She didn't look at Cori Anderson.

"How are you doing?" Cori asked.

"How did you know I was here?" Elizabeth answered a question with a question as she buttoned her sweater up.

"We're on speed dial when it comes to all things Barnett," Cori said. "Especially when whatever happened lands you in the hospital."

"I fainted, that's all. I haven't eaten much lately." Elizabeth slipped off the table, put on her shoes and reached for her jacket. Cori got it before she did and handed it over. "Why didn't Detective O'Brien come?"

"He's got a few things he's running down," Cori answered, not really amused that Elizabeth Barnett thought Finn should be at her beck and call. "I was here anyway. My grandson is in emergency."

Elizabeth's eyelashes fluttered. "I'm sorry. I hope it's nothing serious."

"He's got an ear infection but it's pretty hot. He'll be fine."

Cori picked up Elizabeth's purse and handed it to her. The other woman cut her a look.

"I don't need your help. You can go."

Cori answered. "No skin off my nose as long as you're good. You take care."

"Thank you."

Elizabeth Barnett opened her purse and took out her compact. Cori went to the door, but hesitated and turned back. Elizabeth Barnett looked about as bad as a body could look: skinny as a rail, pale as a parsnip, hair gray as a steel pipe. She was coiled tight as a spring. Cori knew tough times got tougher for a woman when her armor wasn't in place, but the powder that lady was putting on her nose wasn't going to protect her from anything.

"That man was just an old guy who recognized you from the neighborhood. He lives a couple houses down from you and wanted to offer his condolences. He said he was sorry for scaring you," Cori said.

Elizabeth nodded. Finally, when Cori didn't move, Elizabeth snapped her compact shut.

"Is that all?"

"I guess," Cori answered. "Unless you want to get some food."

"You're supposed to bite, chew, and swallow." Cori pointed to the burger in front of Elizabeth.

"You should have let me pay," Elizabeth said as she picked up the burger Cori bought her. There were three bites gone and if half of it disappeared Cori would be satisfied.

"I'll put it on the expense account," Cori said.

"I hope they reimburse you soon." Elizabeth indicated

the coins Cori had been shuffling on the tabletop. "You've been playing with those as if they're your last ones."

"Old habits die hard. I've watched every penny my whole life," Cori said.

"What does your husband do?" Elizabeth asked.

"Never had one."

Elizabeth pushed aside her food. "I'm sorry. I don't think I could have survived if I didn't have my husband."

"Sure you could," Cori answered and moved her coins again: four down and three across. "We all make our own bed and as things go, mine hasn't been all that bad."

She wasn't really lying to this woman. Finding herself alone with a child and no clear road ahead was about as scary as life could get. There were days Cori wasn't even sure where their next meal was going to come from. There were a few months when they lived in her car, a fact she hadn't even shared with Finn. Cori wasn't ashamed of those days; she would just rather focus on what she had accomplished. She made it into the academy and through it. She paid her dues as a street cop. She raised her daughter and if the worst trouble Amber got into was getting pregnant, then Cori counted that a win. The kid didn't do drugs; she wasn't a drunk. Some day Amber would find her road and she'd work hard for her kid because she was Cori's kid. Elizabeth Barnett has to find her road now, and, while Cori didn't have a soft spot for her, she would cut her some slack out of respect for her situation.

"Detective O'Brien talked to your husband's old partner today. Mr. Rivera?"

"We haven't seen Richard since the partnership broke

up. I miss him," Elizabeth said. "How is he?"

"Fine. He's a newlywed."

"Oh." Elizabeth lowered her eyes. "I'm surprised we weren't invited to the wedding."

"I don't think your husband and Mr. Rivera parted as amicably as your husband might have led you to believe," Cori said. "They disagreed about handling a client called Eros Manufacturing. Do you know anything about them? Did your husband discuss his clients with you?"

"I never asked Sam about business."

Cori raised her chin and lowered it, a long, slow nod. A giant O-K of sympathy. This woman's life sucked. Even Cori's ex bent her ear with stories of whatever crappy job he had managed to hold for a week. Cori moved her coins: four down and three across.

"I've been trying to figure this out ever since I saw it in a magazine a while back. The puzzle says there's a way to make it so you have four coins in each row."

"That's been bothering you for a long time?" Elizabeth almost laughed. Cori figured that was a good start down the road.

"Yeah. The answer has got to be something really simple, but you have to buy the next magazine to get the answer and that just puts a burr under my saddle. It's the principal of the thing, you know?"

Cori whipped a nickel from the row of four and fit it onto the other row. That move didn't solve the problem.

"How long are you going to work on it?"

"Until I figure it out. The one thing I've learned is there is always a solution to a problem. Sometimes you have to get creative, but that solution is there," Cori answered. "Besides, it's good training for what I do. Look at the big picture and drill down you might find one small thing that solves the big problem – Ah!" Cori plucked a dime out of the row of four and put it on top of the coin where the two lines intersected. "Damn, I'm good. Four coins are now in each row."

Elizabeth smiled a little but it was obvious that she was sinking fast, her mind wandering, her body seeming to shrink. Unwilling to waste the little progress that had been made Cori said:

"Look, I'm not really a girl's-girl if you know what I mean so take this for what it's worth. It seems like you might need to focus on you and your husband and let us do our job. We are working hard for you; you need to work hard for yourself. It's not too early to start putting your life back together."

"I'd like to do that. I don't think Sam is ready."

"Maybe if he sees you're doing something, he'll get with the program. But it's your life, so pretty much it's got to be your deci..." Cori held up a finger. Her phone was ringing. When she was done, she said: "Sorry. I've got to go. Tucker's ready to come home. Do you want a ride? I can drop you off."

Elizabeth shook her head, "No, thanks. I think I'll stay here a little longer."

Cori stood up and swiped the coins off the table. She looked at them for a minute, jingled them in her hand a second more. She smiled, impressed with her awesomeness when she saw a big picture in that small change.

"You know, Mrs. Barnett, you've got a few bucks to spare so maybe that's the place to start. You know, like a foundation in your girls' names. I don't know how it's done, but your husband's a lawyer. It might be something you can do together. It might help."

"Thank you," Elizabeth said. "You've given me a lot to think about."

"Good. I'm glad you're okay. You just take care now."

Cori dropped the coins in her purse and left Elizabeth Barnett sitting in the hospital cafeteria. Doctors and nurses, relatives of patients all came and went, buying the bland food, grabbing cups of coffee and making just enough noise to cut through the fog in Elizabeth Barnett's brain. The detective had been right. There was something she and Sam could do in the name of their children. It was as simple as putting one coin on top of another; as simple as moving one thing to make it another thing. Elizabeth took out her phone, eager to tell Sam about her plan but he was in court and had a bar event after that and, she knew, after that he would come home and sleep elsewhere.

Elizabeth looked at the clock. It was late and she wouldn't be able to talk to him until tomorrow, but tomorrow seemed an eternity away. Besides, Detective Anderson said it was her life and her decision about how her life would go so Elizabeth made two more phone calls. When she was done Elizabeth was happy, and that, she knew, would make Sam happy. And really, that was all Elizabeth ever wanted: for Sam to be happy with her.

CHAPTER 32

DAY 7 – LATE MORNING

Finn O'Brien followed Bob Fowler's assistant, Tina, down the hall and into her office where she stepped aside and waved him to the inner sanctum where the captain was waiting.

"How are you this morning, Captain," Finn said knowing full well what the answer would be considering the man's glum expression.

"Not so good, O'Brien. Not so good." He motioned toward the door. "Close it and take a seat."

When Finn was settled, Fowler pushed a newspaper across his desk. Finn looked at it and saw nothing of interest above the fold, but when he opened it he saw that Elizabeth Barnett had scored some nice ink below it.

"Did you have anything to do with this?" Fowler asked.

"No, sir. I didn't know the Barnetts were thinking about offering a reward."

"Too bad," Fowler muttered. "I'd like to have someone to blame it on other than the victim's parents."

They sat together for a few seconds and then Bob Fowler tented his fingers.

"I spent yesterday talking to a hundred women at a luncheon. The food sucked and the banquet room was hot. I had to sit through a meeting that included a long discussion about who was going to head up the Christmas boutique committee."

"Condolences, Captain," Finn said, sitting comfortably, knowing Fowler would get to the point on his own time.

"Part of the job," Fowler said. "And it was all a piece of cake until it was my turn to speak. Those women turned into barracudas. They wanted to know exactly what's being done to protect their children from the psycho on the loose. It was pretty weird, all those fancy women staring at me like I'm supposed to rip open my shirt and turn into Superman.

"I assured them that we had things well under control and that it was our firm belief that this was an isolated incident. I told them they didn't have to worry, that their neighborhoods were secure and their children were safe. Now Elizabeth Barnett is on the front page of the Times, giving quotes like, 'We have to find these people before they hurt someone else's children'. Charming."

"Detective Anderson saw her yesterday, but I'm sure Mrs. Barnett didn't say anything about this. You have to admit, she knows how to get attention. That's quite a sum, fifty thousand dollars."

"Don't encourage her," Fowler snapped. "You know as well as I do that we're going to have every nut in the world calling to claim the money. You and Anderson will be chasing your tails and this division's resources will be strained. You'd think she would have the courtesy to at least inform us."

"There's no law against what she did," Finn reminded him.

Fowler puffed out his cheeks, and then let out a long held breath.

"Look, I'm not against it. In fact, I think it could do a lot of good, but it's knee jerk. They printed her number. What will she do next? Invite people to her house to collect the fifty grand? We'll probably have two more murders on our hands then."

Fowler drummed the desk. He looked down then raised his eyes.

"It should have been coordinated. He should have known better. I want you to take those two in hand and then make sure we get those calls routed here. I don't want her or her husband talking to any of these people, understood?"

"Yes, sir. Is that it?"

"Yes. Go," Fowler said and Finn was halfway to the door when the captain shared one more thought. "Get this sucker of a case out of my hair one way or the other and tell the Barnetts your captain isn't pleased. Tell them today."

Finn nodded. He took one last look at the newspaper. Elizabeth Barnett was staring back him defiant, beautiful, and, strangely, alone.

Finn turned the city issue car into Fremont Place, showed his ID to the guard who was older than the one who had greeted him the first time he drove through these gates. He parked in front of the Barnett house and was half way up the brick walk when he heard a car door slam. He went toward the driveway and was pleased to see the wrought iron gate closed and that there was a remote junction box affixed to it. Beyond the gates, Elizabeth Barnett stood by her Jaguar dressed in jeans, a work shirt, and tennis shoes. Her hair was pulled back in a plain rubber band. She had one hand on the roof of the car and she was looking at the things packed in the back seat.

As lovely as the woman was decked out in her high heels and done up hair, dressed as she was now Finn found her truly beautiful. She dropped her hand from the top of the car and stood back. First she looked at the trees separating her home from the Coulter's and then she put her hand up to shade her eyes and looked toward the gate.

"Hello there," she said when she saw him.

Elizabeth Barnett smiled and covered the distance between them in fewer steps than he thought it should take. She curled her fingers around the intricate iron like a prisoner happy for visiting day.

"Are you going somewhere?" Finn asked.

"I'm taking some of the girls' things to the thrift shop." She laughed a little at the look on his face. "Don't worry, it's a good thing. Detective Anderson was right. It's time I did something constructive."

"You'll want to save a few things," Finn said, thinking of the hat and shirt he kept in a small box in his apartment. Alexander's hat and shirt. It was a comfort at times.

"I am: their favorite dresses, some toys, their christening gowns," she said.

Finn dipped his head and rubbed his nose to keep her from seeing the smile. Geoffrey Baptiste would be one happy man to hear this.

"Do you have something for me?" Elizabeth asked. "Has something happened?"

Finn answered, "I've come to talk to you about what is in the newspaper."

"I see," she said as her eyes clouded. "Come around the front."

"Coffee?"

"Black if you will."

Finn pulled out a chair at the breakfast table and checked out the kitchen. With the shutters open, the coffee percolating, Elizabeth Barnett fussing with the china, this room felt as it should: full of life. It amazed him that a home could look like this. He and Bev had shared the chores between them and kept a tidy place, but this house was as near perfect as he had ever seen. Through the glass cabinets he could see all the glasses lined up according to size and shape, not a one any further from the other than its neighbor. On the built in desk the calendar Elizabeth Barnett kept was centered as if the parameters had been measured. The throw rugs were straight, the chairs pushed in without touching the table except for the one he sat upon and the one waiting for Elizabeth. She put his coffee on the table and slid onto the chair cross from him.

"I assume you're on the list of people I've made angry by offering a reward."

"My captain would like me to underscore his displeasure. It seems he recently had cause to speak to a group of neighbor ladies who believe their families are in danger. He didn't think that you offering a reward in the hopes of saving other people's children helped the situation." Finn said. "That being said, I believe it was a gutsy thing, missus."

"It would have been nicer if you said that you approved," she answered.

"I can't do that, and I will assume that you consider your wrists slapped so that my captain will be happy."

"Please tell him that you're too late. My husband did that rather effectively this morning." Elizabeth held up one wrist and Finn could clearly see the bruise on her delicate skin.

Finn took her hand and pushed the sleeve of her blouse up further. "He abused you?"

"He was surprised. He was angry. I hadn't told him I was going to do this." Elizabeth pulled back her hand and pushed her sleeve down. "This wasn't intentional. I want you to know that."

"Was it about the money?"

Finn didn't bother to address her last statement. He had seen abused women apologize for their men for being the cause of their own injuries. Love often took dark turns and, much as Finn O'Brien would like to save this woman from hers, he could do nothing until she asked for help. One way or the other, though, he hoped the lawyer paid for this with hurt of his own.

"He doesn't think we should draw attention to ourselves. Mercedes wasn't happy. She's worried people will come to the neighborhood."

"There is a great possibility of that. Still, that is no reason for him to manhandle–"

"It's nothing," Elizabeth said, and Finn knew that she was not going to be turning on her husband.

"Alright, missus," Finn answered. "We won't be

talking about you and your husband but I have to tell you that he is right. At worst, you put yourselves at risk; at the very least this will muddy the waters for us."

"Is that what Detective Anderson thinks?"

"Detective Anderson is thinking you might have interpreted her words a bit too broadly about putting your money to good use…"

Finn's eyes had wandered past Elizabeth and he found himself looking at the backyard. It took him a moment to realize what was different. When he saw what it was, he felt a tug in his mid-section: the swing set was gone. Elizabeth Barnett propped her chin in her upturned hand and looked at him with such intensity that he tore his eyes away and attended to her.

He said: "You've taken down the swings, missus."

Elizabeth didn't look over her shoulder. She picked up her coffee and before she sipped it she said: "A lot of things are changing. You were saying?"

"I was saying there are protocols for these kind of things so that we make sure information is properly followed up on and recorded. That way any evidence is not tainted and there is no confusion down the road should multiple people believe themselves deserving of the money.

"We'll be having the service reroute the calls to a number that we will monitor. I've already contacted the newspaper and they will publish the new number. Was that your cell number they ran?"

"It's our landline. We only keep it for emergencies. I'll have it shut down," Elizabeth said.

"Our webmaster will set up a dedicated page on our site. We'll post the number there, also. We'll be able to trace calls fairly quickly."

While he was speaking, Elizabeth picked up the saltshaker. It was shaped like a chicken and its pepper counterpart was a rooster. She was thinking about the amazing things that could be done these days. Capturing phone numbers, tracing them, working backward to find the information they wanted.

"Mrs. Barnett?" Finn's voice snapped her out of her reverie. "Have you had calls?"

"I'm sorry," she said but she really wasn't sorry. She was annoyed now that she realized there was something she could have done all along. "Calls. Yes, two hang-ups and one lady whose child was killed. She wanted to talk. I told her no."

Elizabeth put the saltshaker on the table, adjusted it until it was precisely aligned, and then she crossed her arms on the table.

"I'll have access to the phone numbers of anyone who calls, won't I? I want to be able to see…to see if I recognize any numbers or names or that sort of thing."

"No," Finn said. "It could have consequences at a trial and I know you wouldn't want that."

"I have a television interview tomorrow," she said, disappointed by his refusal to share information but not deterred. "I won't sit here and do nothing any longer."

"Then someone from public affairs will call and prep you. If you or your husband have any questions after hours or if someone slips through the cracks looking to talk to you about the money, call me." Finn took his notepad and wrote down two numbers, handing the paper to her. "The first number is Mick's pub. They know me there. Don't be put off by the man who answers. He's very talkative. The second is my home. In the evenings I'll be at one or the other."

Elizabeth got up and went to a small desk. When she came back, she handed him an address. "Sam will be here if you need to talk to him."

"You're moving?" The address was on mid-Wilshire.

"No, Sam is gone. His secretary called me with the address."

"I'm sorry, missus," Finn said, remembering all too well his nights after Bev's leaving.

"He'll come back," she assured him. "Really. Everything will be fine once I get things in order. I just need to get things in order."

Finn nodded. It was no use talking to her. She had in her mind how things would go between her and her man and there would be no dissuading her. It was the same way with Bev, only her mind told her that she would be better off without him. He stood up.

"Are you sure you're fine here alone?"

"I wouldn't want to be anywhere else." She stood up, too, and started leading him out.

"Let me or Detective Anderson know if you're going to be gone for any significant amount of time. And tomorrow when you do that interview, don't talk about the necklaces." Finn instructed her as they walked. At the door he lingered, feeling something tight in the air that needed unraveling before he left Elizabeth Barnett. He asked:

"Do you need any help getting your things to the thrift shop? Can I be moving something in the house for you?"

"No, thank you."

Elizabeth put her hand on the door and hesitated as if

she were about to share something with him. Just as
quickly, she changed her mind and said goodbye. She shut
the door behind him with no smile, no word of hope that
the reward would be effective.

Finn hesitated, half expecting her to open it again,
surprised by her abrupt dismissal. When the door
remained closed, he went to his car only to sit behind the
wheel and watch the house for a while longer. Finally, he
turned the key but before he could pull away from the
curb, his phone rang. Cori didn't bother with a greeting.
She said:

"Pick me up, O'Brien. We've got Rachel Gerber's main
squeeze."

Elizabeth Barnett went upstairs to find what she was
looking for: a phone number that could change
everything. She was amazed she hadn't thought of it
before, then again the initial shock of what had taken
place in her home had been devastating. She could be
forgiven for not thinking straight.

Her step was almost light when she climbed the stairs.
She glanced at the room where Rachel had slept. The
door was closed as the cleaning crew had left it. Elizabeth
made a note to have the furniture disposed of and the
room painted.

The girls' room door was open as it always was, and
Elizabeth paused to look in, still displeased with the
changes she had made. The bed frames and box springs
should probably be removed. When she and Sam had
more children, it would be best for them to have things
they could call their own.

The carpet remained. It had been cleaned but she

could still make out the ghostly outlines of the bloodstains. She would have to talk to the manufacturer. This carpet had a lifetime warranty against stain. Then Elizabeth snorted, wondering if they might not honor that now that two lifetimes were over. She would have the carpet ripped up and put in new. She loved the smell of new carpet and paint. She would have to take the pictures down. It would be a lot of work, but that was all right.

When she spied the curtains, Elizabeth realized that was what displeased her. She didn't like the curtains now that there were no bedspreads or frilly pillows to match. Even though she wanted to get on with her chore, even though she was excited by the possibility of solving so many problems with one phone call, Elizabeth was so bothered by those curtains that she couldn't think without doing something about them.

Muttering to herself, she went across the room and pulled on them. When they wouldn't come down, she dragged Alexis' bed closer to the window, positioned it just so, and climbed on the box spring. She jumped a little and knocked the curtain rod down. It fell with a clatter and Elizabeth was on it, unthreading those damn curtains and then bundling them up.

"Better. That is better. Better," she mumbled and went to her room.

She used to love her bedroom but neither she nor Sam slept there now so it looked forlorn. Dust motes danced in the light streaming in through the tall windows, she could smell the scent of burnt wood from the long unused fireplace.

Unsure of what to do with the curtains now that she

had them, Elizabeth opened the closet door but everything was in its place and it would drive her mad knowing they were tossed in there willy-nilly. She could take them downstairs to the trash. She could burn them. She could cut them to shreds. For now, Elizabeth just didn't want to look at them so she pulled back the satin duvet and stuffed them underneath.

Once that was done, Elizabeth Barnett went round to the bedside table that was hers. In the third drawer, underneath the gardening magazines, was her special diary. She loved its white leather and gold tool work. She sat on the bed and opened it, admiring the entries. She had always been so neat and exacting when she wrote. It was a source of great pride to her as it had been to her father.

Elizabeth flipped back through the pages and found the entries she was looking for. Buried in a long text written six weeks before she and Sam left for Paris was the number she was looking for. She dialed it and no one answered. She hung up and went to the entry the night before they left. This number was different and she dialed that but still no one answered. She dialed and listened. Listened and dialed until she was near tears with frustration. Then she realized the futility of it all. Of course he was gone; she knew that.

"Stupid. Stupid. I'm so stupid."

Elizabeth murmured as she put her special book back under the gardening magazines. She threw herself back on the bed and put one arm over her brow.

"Stupid. Stupid."

Elizabeth was so empty, so exhausted from trying her best, so lonely that she rolled over imagining Sam would be there with his arms out to draw her to him. He would kiss her forehead and hold her tight and tell her there was nothing to worry about because he was there. But when she rolled onto her side, it wasn't Sam she saw but a lump under the yellow satin duvet. A lump that looked like a child cuddled in her bed.

Of course she knew that it was nothing more than a lump of curtains, but still it looked like a little person under the covers. Elizabeth, abandoned and isolated, stripped of all the things that mattered to her in the world, couldn't help herself. She moved across the bed and when she was close enough, she laid her head on a crimson throw pillow, raised her hand and placed it gently on the little child-lump of curtains. People would think her a little mad for imagining that lump was anything more than what it was, but people weren't there. Sam wasn't there, so what did it matter if she wanted to imagine this was Alana safe in bed with her or Alexis playing hide-and-seek.

Yes, even though she knew better, even though she knew she was not really insane, even though Elizabeth Barnett understood that under her yellow satin duvet there was nothing more than a pile of curtains, she put her hand upon the lump and whispered:

"Mommy's here."

CHAPTER 33

DAY 7 – AFTERNOON

"What would you do if we had a lot of money?" Medium Man asked.

"I'd get me some clothes."

The boy flipped a playing card toward a pot he had put on the floor and sighed. Medium Man hadn't been out of the house all week, which meant he hadn't been out either. Now when he wanted a paper or food or something, they went together. The boy was getting worried that he was never going to be left alone long enough to run away.

"No, I mean real money," Medium Man pressed. "Enough that you could do anything you wanted in the whole world."

The boy's hand hovered mid-flip. He had played this game in his own head a million times, so he didn't mind playing it with Medium Man. It was better than just sitting there and having the dude look at him.

"I'd get me a car. A really neat one. A Porsche maybe. Black. And them sheep skin seat covers. Then I'd get me some hot clothes so I'd look sharp. I'd drive out to…"

The boy's eyes flicked toward Medium Man and he

caught himself just in time. He managed a shaky smile and made his voice all sweet.

"I'd drive out to some fancy place and take you to dinner. We'd have a real steak, know what I mean?"

"Yeah?" Medium Man put his hands together, delighted to be included in the fantasy.

"Yeah, that's what we'd do." The boy lied, of course. If he had that kind of money, he wouldn't be caught dead with a creep like Medium Man.

"What else?" Medium Man purred.

"How much money I got?" the boy asked.

"Enough," the other man said, peeved that the boy asked that question.

"Okay." The boy shrugged, he would play along. "I'd go to Las Vegas first. I'd double my money, and then I'd get me on an airplane and go to the Caribbean. I saw a picture of that place once. It's just a bunch of little islands, and you can go to one then the other in these white boats." The boy drifted away on the warm current of his dream. "There's real blue water. I'd lie on the beach and drink and eat all the time. I'd never be hungry or tired or anything." He shook his head, dispelling the fantasy. "Anyway I'd go there 'cause I hear the sun's good for zits. There ain't no good sun in California anymore." He let the ace of spades sail toward the pot. He missed. "Anyway, that's what I'd do."

"That sounds nice."

Medium Man got out of the chair. The boy pulled away from the caress he knew was coming. Medium Man didn't notice. He ran his hand down the boy's arm and back up to his face. His fingers caught the boy's chin and forced his face up. The boy's first instinct was to resist, but he felt the tension in Medium Man when he did that, so he gave in and looked the way he was supposed to. He looked like he was happy.

"Would you like me to go with you to that place?" Medium Man asked.

The boy nodded. He should have been an actor. This fool believed everything he said as long as it was what the guy wanted to hear.

"That's so nice. I appreciate that. I really do." Medium Man released his grip. "I think we should plan on doing something just like that. Maybe we'll skip Vegas and go to all them islands straight off. Maybe we will."

Medium Man pirouetted away from the boy. "I'm going down the hall. Comb your hair and meet me by the phone. We're going shopping when I'm finished."

Medium Man went down the hall, digging in his pocket for the right change because his rooming house still had a pay phone. A real antique, Mort called it. But what the heck. It did the job and he was still flush from payday for taking out that nanny so what were a few coins? Still, there were things that happened that made him question a lot of things lately. The pay phone wasn't one of them.

Mort had docked him some for the kids, but that was okay even though it disappointed him some. Then there was the cemetery. That was a close call. Those cops – for that was who he was sure was chasing him – scared him bad. All that got Medium Man to thinking it was time to lay low, given that he and the boy were a family and all. He could get out of the business with just one more really good score and to do that he needed Mort.

Dropping the coin in the pay phone Medium Man

dialed, leaned against the wall, and waited. It was Georgia who said hello.

"Can I talk to Mort?"

"Who is this?" Georgia demanded.

Medium Man could hear a television in the background. People were laughing. He had disturbed her. At first he thought to apologize, but he didn't because he was a little upset that Georgia didn't recognize him after all this time. When he had lots of money people would remember him and if they didn't, they would be sorry. Right now, though, she didn't remember him so he said:

"It's his friend who works with him? Please, can I talk to Mort?"

"He's not here right now," she said, and then yelled at one of her kids.

"When can I talk to him?" Medium Man raised his voice so she wouldn't forget he was on the phone.

"I guess tomorrow about seven. He's on the night shift, won't be back 'till then."

"Okay, just tell him I called."

Medium Man hung up wondering why Mort hadn't called if he had a job. Georgia looked at the receiver for a minute wondering how she could tell Mort who called when the guy didn't leave a name. She put the phone down and went back to the tube. They were talking about women whose husbands beat them. The broad they were talking to didn't have anything on Georgia. That woman's husband just pulled her hair and screamed at her.

What a lightweight.

By the second commercial Georgia had forgotten all about the call.

CHAPTER 34

Cori and Finn pulled up in front of an apartment building that looked like a thousand apartment buildings in a hundred neighborhoods around Los Angeles.

"2B.We are looking for Todd Webster. He goes by Buster because he busted some heads with another guy five years ago. He did ten days on a ninety-day sentence." Cori sighed. "Gotta love early release. Anyway, there are some outstanding warrants for vehicle violations, but nothing heavier than that in the last few years."

"He's not sounding like a boyo who would take out his lady and a couple of kids." Finn made no move to get out of the car. "What was he driving on the warrants?"

"A red Mustang, but things change. He could have sold it or totaled it. He could have two cars," Cori answered. "Need another look at his mug shot?"

The man's face was already seared in Finn's memory and it was a particularly unattractive image. His nose was big, his eyes small, his hair long in the back and nonexistent on top. He was not the man in the car at the morgue or the one Finn chased at the cemetery, of that he was sure. Still, he looked at the picture again just to make Cori happy. He also gave a little thanks to the tech gods who allowed their lab to crack the Nanny's phone and get the number that led them to this man.

"I'm good," he said and motioned that it was time to get to business.

They got out of the car and took a look around to get their bearings. The quiet street was lined with cars at both curbs and apartment buildings, none of which looked any different than the one Todd Webster called home. There was trash in the gutters, cracks in the sidewalk and potholes in the street. When Finn moved, Cori did too. They went up a concrete path that led to a staircase that would take them to the second floor. They looked for escape routes, children's toys, open windows and doors. A few plants were dying in parched flowerbeds. Windows were covered with bed sheets and curtains. Except for Todd 'Buster' Webster's window. His window was plastered over with tin foil.

"Think we should have called for back-up?" Cori lowered her voice a notch as they approached the apartment door.

"A fellow who doesn't pay for his own drinks doesn't seem a particular challenge," Finn said and then he announced himself with a knock. When no one came to the door, Finn threw another chit into the pot: "Mr. Webster. Detective O'Brien, LAPD. Mr. Webster?"

He knocked again. Again, no one came to the door nor did he or Cori sense any movement inside. Finn took hold of the knob. It was locked. Cori said:

"I'll get the manager."

While she was gone, Finn looked out over the architecturally vague buildings. Behind each window was the final resting place for the painfully marginalized folks of this big city. He counted himself a lucky man not to have ended up like this, or worse, behind bars framed for murder. Bev might be gone, but he had his work and he had Cori who was coming back up the stairs followed by a woman of immense proportions.

"This is Mrs. Feinstein. Mrs. Feinstein, this is Detective O'Brien."

Mrs. Feinstein pulled herself up the last few steps. She managed a nod in greeting. Finn nodded back, feeling the woman's pain. Her eyes were almost obliterated by the rolls of flesh on her face; her chin had been gobbled up by a neck that draped from her bottom lip to her breastbone. She was hooked up to a portable oxygen tank.

"Mrs. Feinstein, we have a warrant to search the premises inhabited by Todd Webster. We would appreciate it if you would open the door to his apartment, ma'am."

"That one told me already. Let me see." She shifted her portable tank and put out a hand the size of a ham. He gave her the warrant. She looked at it and then gave it back to Finn.

"I don't like doing this. Webster seems okay to me," she grumbled.

"Still, we will need you to open the door, missus," Finn said.

Mrs. Feinstein fiddled with a huge bunch of keys, huffing and puffing, pursing her lips to let the air out, pulling them back against her teeth to draw a breath in while the plastic tubing hung from her nose. Her arms were permanently horizontal, held up by a chest that had spread sideways with age, gravity, and caloric intake. Cori was exhausted just watching the woman labor. Finally, the key was found, the door unlocked and Mrs. Feinstein began her arduous journey back down the stairs.

"Mrs. Feinstein, you can come in and watch if you like," Finn offered before she got too far.

"I don't put my nose where it don't belong. Lock the door when you're done."

Cori and Finn peered into the dark apartment. Though he was sure the place was empty, Finn extended an arm and eased Cori behind him. Cori accepted the gesture without objection. She, after all, had Amber and Tucker to worry about; Finn had no one any longer. Still, she was on his heels and when he gave her the thumbs up, she threw the light switch.

"Oh my, my, my," she clucked when she got her first gander at Webster's digs.

Finn went to do a quick check of the other rooms. By the time he came back, Cori had looked behind the kitchen counter and in a small closet to be sure Todd Webster wasn't hiding himself away.

"It looks like good old Todd has given up busting heads," Finn said.

They stood side-by-side looking at the mattress on the living room floor. The sheets thrown over it were red satin and in need of a wash. There was no other furniture in the living room but there were plenty of other things the detectives found interesting: a box of dildos which proved that human hope and imagination knew no bounds, latex toys for girls and boys, a rolling rack of clothes, some light and airy, others dark and studded, all of them crotchless. There were piles of pillows, a cage with a little swing in it, a case of stage make-up, and wigs. There were lights, a camera, and, Finn imagined, plenty of action.

Cori nudged food wrappers tossed into one corner of the room. "Someone has a thing for Twinkies."

"The equipment's solid. These props aren't cheap. Webster knows what he's doing."

"Maybe Rachel was his star," Cori suggested.

"Let's see what we can see," Finn said.

Cori went to the bedroom; Finn went over the living room/dining room/kitchen. He found shooting schedules, headshots and test shots of men on women, women on women, men on men. All were well endowed, not a one was beautiful. Taped on the walls was a gallery of headshots. All adults. No kids, thank God. Bottom line, Rachel and Buster weren't pimping; they were recruiting talent.

"Bingo!" Cori called just before she stuck her head into the living room. "Come on in and take a gander."

Finn went into the hall that was really nothing more than a five foot square from which three rooms radiated. In one room there was a treadmill, to the left was a bathroom, behind the third door was a real bedroom where Cori was dealing pictures onto the bed and making noises like she had a full house.

"Rachel Gerber in the altogether," she said as Finn came to check out the snapshots.

Finn could only shake his head at the pitiful images. Rachel Gerber was an attractive, slightly overweight woman who looked naturally at ease in the beach picture Finn carried of her. What he was looking at was a grotesque caricature of that woman. Sparkling violet shadow colored her eyes top and bottom. Her lips were painted red and slicked over with glitter gloss. Her hair was teased into a mass of tangles that he supposed was meant to make her look sexy but instead made her look like a lunatic. Her chubby arms were crossed and pushed her breasts up so that they looked unnaturally high and flat, in another they hung free, large breasts shaped like torpedoes. She wore a thong. The bikini had been a breach of good taste; the thong was a sin.

"She looks like ten miles of bad road," Cori mused. "Think that's why he killed her?"

"No." Finn strode out of the bedroom, Cori was right behind him.

"Maybe he didn't want her to work for him anymore and she put up a fuss," she insisted.

"She wasn't one of his girls," Finn said. "Buster's got a bunch of snapshots of her. Everybody else has eight by tens. Besides, I doubt he pays real well. Even if he did, Rachel Gerber naked just isn't worth thirty big ones."

Finn stood in the middle of the living room knowing he had missed something. He walked over to a small desk, opened the top drawer and heard a familiar clunk. He tipped the drawer to show his partner.

"A twenty-two," Cori said, delighted with the find. "Anything else?"

Finn opened three drawers. All of them were empty except for a broken pen and a Bruce Springsteen CD.

"He travels light. Nothing other than clothes in the other room and the Bluetooth speakers," Cori added up the inventory.

Finn listened while he took a spin around, nudging the mattress with the toe of his shoe, reopening kitchen drawers. He pulled out a knife or two: they were neither long bladed nor nicked at the tip. He put them back.

"Did you find any drugs?" he asked.

Cori shook her head and said: "So what do we do now?"

"The warrant's specific for the gun so let's bag it," Finn said.

"Then what?"

"Then we wait until Webster comes home."

Cori and Finn ate two-for-ninety-nine-cent burgers and drank Gatorade they got from the gas station a few blocks over. They watched the street and waited for a man who was probably not a killer but might lead them to one. They talked about small things and big things; they made plans for work. The sun sailed across the sky, disappeared behind the bank of buildings and still Todd 'Buster' Webster didn't come home. Cori's head got heavy, her eyes closed, and she went quiet leaving Finn to watch over her. She pushed herself upright twenty minutes later and asked:

"I slept, didn't I?"

"A wee bit," Finn said.

"Sorry. I'm really too old to have a baby in the house."

Finn tipped his lips but made no comment. Babies kept people up at night. Growing up with five brothers and sisters taught him that. He and Bev never got around to finding out first hand but not for lack of trying. At one time that was a huge regret; now it seemed like a blessing. He would want no child of his shuttled between divorced parents, and if he and Bev were together he would want to be home with the family and not in a car waiting for an evil man to show himself.

"What time is it?" Cori ran her tongue over her teeth. She wanted a toothbrush but would settle for gum so she rummaged in her purse for it.

"Nine forty," Finn murmured.

"Anything happen while I was snoozing?"

"Two guys came in around eight. A light went on in the corner unit a little after that. Someone turned on a television."

"Maybe Webster's running." Cori flipped down the visor. The little lights went on and she peered into the mirror, fluffed her bangs, and took out her lipstick.

"No reason he should," Finn said as he glanced at his partner. "And when he shows up, he's not going to be admiring your lipstick, woman."

"Get a clue. Women put on lipstick the way men scratch. It's just—"

Finn stopped her with one hand around her wrist. With the other hand, he flipped the lighted mirror up, plunging them into darkness once again. The headlights on the car coming toward them shined bright in their eyes before the driver made a wide turn into the driveway of the building they were watching. It slowed just long enough for them to see that the driver's hair had a party going on in the back but it wasn't even business on top. The car was an Oldsmobile, '92 to '95. Dented back passenger door. Greyish/green not bluish/grey.

Close enough for government work.

Cori threw her lipstick into her purse.

Todd 'Buster' Webster was home.

CHAPTER 35

Cori and Finn stayed in the car and waited for Todd Webster to show himself. A few minutes later he came around the building. The sound of his hard heels hitting concrete echoed off the stucco jungle. The wind kicked up and he caught that hank of hair hanging down his back like a woman would. He passed by a ground floor apartment with its drapes open and lights on. It was enough for Cori and Finn to get a positive ID.

They got out of the car when he started up the stairs. Someone screamed in a building behind them but it wasn't the kind of scream they needed to attend to, so Cori and Finn stayed to the shadows and took the stairs so deftly that Webster had his key in the door before he realized he wasn't alone. When he looked their way, Finn held up his shield.

"Todd Webster? We'd like to ask you a few questions."

"Sure thing." The man grinned as he turned the key.

That was a disappointment in Finn's book. Nobody wanted for murder with an apartment full of porn, grinned at cops unless there was a plan B. Which there was. Webster shot through the door like a cannon ball, and slammed the door behind him. Finn hit it with his shoulder and sent it crashing back again. The rolling rack of lingerie came at him next, but Finn was quick. He dodged the rack, and it crashed into the wall too.

He hunkered down in a runner's position to get his bearings. The tin foil on the windows made the apartment a dark place, indeed, but not dark enough so that Finn couldn't see Webster crouching beside the desk. In the next second, he heard the sound of the drawer being pulled open and that was all the encouragement Finn needed.

"There's nothing there for you, Webster."

Finn got on his feet and lunged for the man. Webster feigned left and went right. Finn hit the desk and went down. Before he could get up, Webster was on his feet, hauling back and ramming the toe of his boot into Finn's knee.

"Blast," Finn roared as the pain shot all the way to his groin.

Todd Webster jumped over the detective and yanked two of the smaller drawers out, raised them above his head and was ready to bring them down on any part of Finn's body he could connect with, when the room went bright.

"That's enough rough and tumble, boys."

Webster squinted at Cori Anderson. She had one hand on the light switch, her other hand was holding a gun pointed at his gut.

"You may want to drop your drawers there, Buster."

"You doing okay?" Cori asked as Finn limped by her for the third time, walking out the kink the man's boot had left in his knee.

"Passable." He glared at Todd Webster who was sitting pretty as you please on top of those red satin sheets on the mattress where Cori had put him. "Have you got steel tips in those things?"

"Naw, just well made," Todd answered, cordial now that he was caught. "So to what do I owe the pleasure?"

Finn tossed the warrant at his new friend. Todd didn't bother to look at it and tossed it right back.

"I got nothing to hide, and it looks like you already picked up my piece which is all lawful and such, I might add."

"Last I looked, trafficking porn was a big no-no," Cori reminded him.

"No law against taking pictures of your friends. I got a lot of friends."

"Really?"

Finn pulled a picture of a woman out of the stack he had put aside earlier. Her ribs showed through her skin, her arms were turned so that tracks were clearly visible, her eyes were shadowed and it wasn't from make-up. He walked toward Webster and hunkered down so he could see it up close. The man turned his head away more from boredom than defeat. Finn placed his huge hand on Webster's head and turned it back toward the picture slowly, the way he might loosen an especially stubborn bottle cap.

"Nice looking guy like you hangs out with trash like this?" Finn clicked his tongue. "How do you know she hasn't been sharing a needle, Webster? Aren't you afraid you might catch something from a woman like this?"

"I don't sleep with 'em, I just shoot 'em. It's all

business. I'm like a wedding photographer, if you catch my drift? You know, documenting the moment of coupling."

Todd chuckled and snorted. Finn tossed that photo aside and pulled out another one.

"You sleep with this one, don't you? Isn't this your girlfriend?" Todd looked at the picture of Rachel Gerber.

"Hardly," he said.

"You must be close. You've got a lot of pictures of her in the bedroom. They don't look so good, but then the picture they took of her at the morgue doesn't look very good either."

"The morgue? What are you talking about?"

Finn got up. He towered over the man. He asked: "When was the last time you saw her?"

"I don't know, two weeks? Maybe longer. And I don't know anything about her being dead. I swear."

"You were plenty ready to pull a gun on us. Putting a bullet through that woman's head doesn't seem a stretch," Cori pointed out.

"I didn't know you were for real. I got a dozen badges in that box over there. I was protecting myself."

"We're real and Rachel is dead," Cori assured him.

"Why would I shoot her?" Todd cried, twirling toward Cori, twirling back to Finn when he jumped into the conversation.

"Because you got jealous? Because maybe she was thinking of leaving you for her employer," Finn said. "Jealousy is a monstrous thing, especially when the other man is rich and handsome. Detective Anderson, could it be that this scum had one of his many friends shoot Rachel while he carved up those two precious little girls?"

"Little girls? Holy crap, I don't know nothin' about little girls. I never even saw the kids Rachel took care of." Todd started to get up, but Finn pushed him back down again. That didn't keep him from talking. "If they're dead, it's nothing to do with me. I swear on my mother's grave."

"Don't give us that. You never had a mama," Cori said. "We'll just run ballistics on that gun of yours and take a few knives out of your kitchen just to put our minds at rest. But here's the thing, we have witnesses who saw your car and they can put you–"

"Hey! Hey! I ain't done nothin'. I got a gun because my associates can get a little weird. It's for protection. And I wouldn't have hurt Rachel because–"

"Ever get funky with Hal or Heidi Horace? Maybe that's who you were going for in Fremont Place," Cori said. "Could be the Horaces were swiping your talent. Was that it? A little business discussion gone wrong? Did you get high and just sort of miss the mark and hit up Rachel instead? Was that it? Under the influence?"

"I didn't hurt nobody. I didn't do nothing like that. I have alibis. You tell me when it went down with Rachel and I'll give you names. I swear."

Todd Webster was downright agitated now and when he tried to get up this time Finn grabbed him by the scruff and helped him along.

"You assaulted an officer, you're a pornographer, you're scum, and I'm going to prove you're a murderer. Cuff him, Anderson. Let's take this somewhere where I can think straight."

Finn pushed Todd Webster toward Cori even though both of them knew nothing was feeling good about this collar. Still, they'd take it down to the wire, pressure him a little and see what they could find out about the nanny and what went on in the Barnett house.

Cori was exchanging her gun for her cuffs in anticipation of taking custody of Todd Webster and thinking they had wasted a lot of precious time on such a lump of unimpressive humanity, when things went south. In the next second, the man taught Cori and Finn a lesson in good judgment: never underestimate a desperate man.

Finn's grip on the man wasn't as tight as it should have been and their timing of the handoff was a millisecond off. Todd, ever the opportunist, took his moment. He fell back, causing Finn to tighten his grip to steady himself. Todd used the big man to leverage himself, raised his leg and scissor-kicked. He caught Cori in the midsection and she crumbled without a sound, mouth open, her eyes wide.

Surprised, Finn let go of Todd as he reached for his partner. That was when Webster bolted out the door and hauled ass down the stairs. Cori waved Finn away, but by the time he hit the ground there was no sign of Todd Webster. He ran for the street, hoping to catch a glimpse of the man fleeing on foot but he saw no one. He whirled back to where he had come from and saw Cori was hanging over the landing, still gasping for breath, and shaking her head. She did that just before Todd's car came barreling out from behind the building.

Finn was on it, running for his vehicle, throwing himself in and firing up the engine as he kept his eye on the Olds. Webster was turning the corner three blocks down when Finn turned out onto the street and shot ahead. With one hand he steered down the middle of the street; with the other he initiated radio contact.

"1-H-07. In pursuit. 187 suspect last seen turning off Arbor, south on Highland driving grey/green Olds. Damage to right rear passenger door. California license 2-A – Adam, C – Charles, Z – Zebra, 3 5 6. Suspect is Todd Webster. Wanted for assault on an officer. Homicide. Brown hair. Five ten. Blue shirt. Jeans. Boots. Believed to be unarmed, but should be considered dangerous. Code 6-Charles. Request air 3 response. Code 6-Charles!"

Finn listened as the link officer repeated his call for assistance. Three short beeps punctuated the radio static. It should have been seconds before the air response was confirmed and evident. Those seconds ticked into minutes as Finn sped through the streets, he prayed that he would soon see a helicopter crisscrossing the night sky, strafing the ground with its Nightsun. But he didn't see a helicopter, the link officer had gone silent, and Finn heard a message loud and clear: It was O'Brien calling, it was O'Brien in trouble. There would be no air assist; there would be no backup on the ground.

The hell with them.

Finn turned hard left and sped down the street until he turned right and sped down another. He turned and barreled down street after street as he made his way toward the freeway. He needed to find Webster because no one else would. He searched because no one would come to Cori's aid since she was his partner. Finally, his vision blurred by the night, and the street lamps, and the moisture that swam behind his eyes, Finn O'Brien slammed on the brakes. He hit the steering wheel with an open hand, he bellowed a curse, and he trembled with fury. Finn pulled a hand across his eyes and then his lips.

Todd "Buster" Webster was gone.

"1-H-07." The link officer hailed him. "What is your position? 1-H-07?" she said again. "What is your position?"

Finn stared straight ahead and listened to the false concern: too little, too late, spoken only for the record. Finn had no choice but to respond. The record would show that he alone had lost the suspect in a triple homicide.

"This is 1-H-07. Highland and Third. No eyes on suspect." He turned off the radio and added. "You friggin' bastards."

CHAPTER 36

DAY 8 – AFTERNOON

"Sit if you want, Anderson," Fowler said as he paced behind his desk.

"No thank you, Captain."

Cori kept her eyes forward. Her ribs hurt like hell. An inch lower and Todd Webster would have done some major damage to her gut. An inch higher and her ribs would have been broken, not bruised. All in all, her body had fared better than O'Brien's spirits. He stood beside her, his head high, hands behind his back. The only thing he was missing was a blindfold and a cigarette as he waited for the firing squad.

Cori heard Fowler turn and she felt him pause, and he spoke off camera like a director unhappy with the actors who couldn't remember their lines long after opening night.

"I have half a mind to put you both on probation." He reappeared on Cori's horizon. "You have a suspect in a high profile murder case, you don't cuff him during questioning and you leave the door of the apartment open. He kicks – kicks! – a detective and then he drives off into the night pretty as you please. Does that sum it up? Does it?"

Finn's head inched up. Cori wiggled the fingers of her right hand. She was close enough to touch Finn, but he moved away the minute she made contact.

"Yes, sir." Cori answered when Finn didn't.

Fowler was at his desk. He picked up their report.

"You waited over five hours for the man to return to his apartment. Detective O'Brien, did it not occur to you to call for assistance?"

"I felt it would be a waste of manpower given that we didn't know when or if he would be returning. We had taken custody of his weapon. We knew what was in the apartment and I was concerned about escalating the situation unnecessarily."

Fowler fell into his chair, cocked his arm, and put two fingers to his lips. When he had collected himself, he said:

"You were investigating a triple homicide and you didn't want to escalate the situation? If you didn't talk about strategy, why don't you tell me what you did talk about for five hours?"

"Lipstick, sir," Cori offered.

"Don't screw with me, Anderson."

"We talked about Mr. Barnett," Finn said. "We are concerned about a client of his. Eros Manufacturing."

"You're concerned all over the place, O'Brien. Worried about Mr. Barnett, worried about Mrs. Barnett's feelings being hurt because you had to tell her she messed up on the reward, worried about our manpower problems. You just worried yourself up a storm and forgot to follow procedure." Fowler shook his head, hanging it down briefly as though the weight of it was too great to bear.

"At this division we are a team. We do not go off like the Lone Ranger and Tonto. And, if you want to know why your fellow officers are reluctant to partner with you, O'Brien, may I suggest you take a look at the one you have. The one who can hardly stand."

"I called for air support when it was critical." Finn looked directly at his captain because he could not bear to look at Cori. "There was no response, sir, as you can see from my report."

"That miscommunication has been addressed." Fowler spoke too quickly so Finn knew he was ready to protect the many who were so willing to sacrifice the one.

"I have half a mind to take you off this case and put someone on who can really do the job." He turned his attention to Cori. "Webster is as much your fault as O'Brien's, Detective Anderson."

"Yes, sir."

"Letting a possible child killer get away will not make the public happy and the public can be a whole lot pissier than your fellow officers." Fowler started busying himself with stuff on his desk. "You better pray we find Webster fast. Now get out of here."

Cori had already taken a couple of steps when she realized Finn wasn't following her.

"Something else O'Brien?" Fowler asked.

"Sir, I respectfully request that Detective Anderson be reassigned. I don't think she should be caught in the middle of my troubles."

"O'Brien." Cori turned too fast and half of Finn's name was swallowed in a grunt of pain.

"There's nothing to get caught in the middle of, O'Brien, if you do your job." Fowler picked up a pencil.

He was done but Cori wasn't.

"We're good, Captain," she said.

"You're hurt and it's my fault," Finn said quietly.

"I got hurt because I took my eye off the ball," Cori insisted, disgusted that this was the time Finn chose to treat her like a girl.

"Enough." Fowler tired of O'Brien's baggage and Anderson's willingness to carry it. He wanted them gone. "Detective Anderson, you've got no equity here and O'Brien's reputation endears him to no one. I'll do my best to see that your fellow officers do not look the other way again, but I can only do so much. Take two days if you want and think about the position you're in. Next time it might be more than a kick in the ribs."

"No. Thank you, sir," she answered and Fowler gave her a nod.

"There's one more thing, then, since we're laying it all out. Mr. Barnett says you accused him of a relationship with the nanny and that accusation led to estrangement from his wife."

"That's bull." Cori was on top of it before Finn could speak. "We asked him about funds in Rachel Gerber's account. That's it. Whatever interpretation Mrs. Barnett put to that inquiry is hers alone."

"I'm only saying to tread carefully. The last thing we need is a lawsuit. Document everything and get something solid on this. That might calm him down."

With that, they were dismissed. In the hall, Finn reached for Cori's arm to help her. She shook him off, walking slowly, letting her mouth run fast. What she had to say was made harsher, interspersed as it was by sharp intakes of breath and little snipes of pain.

"If you don't start letting me make my own friggin' decisions and treating me like a partner again, O'Brien, the next time you're wrong I won't be around to see it. And, if you ask me, you need all the friends you can get." Her ribs hurt like the dickens. She took two pivots to turn toward him. "Look, I need some time out. You go on to Eros Manufacturing. I'm going to work here."

"Cori, I–"

"Just go. I need you to go."

Cori left him with as much dignity as she could muster. She went down the hall, into the small office she shared with Finn, knocked the door shut with the toe of her shoe and eased herself down in her chair. She wanted to cry, damned if she didn't. Instead, she ran through emails that had come into the division in response to Elizabeth Barnett's offer of a reward. She returned phone calls to the fortune seekers who thought they could score an easy fifty grand with a well-spun story. Three people were ready to take the fall for the killings if they could get the money in cash before they were booked. One man wanted to turn in his son-in-law 'cause he was sure the bastard could have done it. There was an old woman who swore this was all the doing of extraterrestrials and that the girls were in a state of suspended animation when they were found. Of course, the woman added, those girls were dead now because they had been buried so long. It was information, she concluded, and when could she pick up her money?

Cori went through the mug shots of guys that neon-Jenny from Bargain Rent-a-Car said kind of looked like the red haired man who had come into her shop. There was a sketch that improved upon the pictures but it could have been a sketch of a thousand men in Los Angeles. Still, the artist had caught something that did not appear in the photos, it was something about the eyes under the unruly kink of hair that made Cori shiver.

She started going over the records from Sam Barnett's phone, looking for anything that stood out. When she found herself staring at the numbers and not seeing anything, Cori sat back in her chair with a hand on her ribs. She looked at the desk, the phone, the door and then threw in the towel. Fowler was right. She needed to rest, regroup, and rethink whether or not it was worth worrying about Finn O'Brien more than she worried about herself.

In the car, she called Amber but got no answer and that was a shame. She wanted someone to fix her soup and sit on the couch with her and watch an old movie. She wanted to sit down with a friend who wasn't a cop, but she had none. Mostly Cori was ticked at herself for the way she talked to Finn. All cops had pressure and Finn had triple his share. He had been watching out for her by suggesting she be reassigned, but all he did was undermine her position as his partner and a professional in the eyes of the captain at whose will she served.

When she got home, the house was empty so she got into her robe, fixed herself that bowl of soup and watched a movie alone. Finally, any affront she felt dissolved into guilt for treating Finn poorly. She could have insisted on backup. She could have closed the door. She could have been more attentive during the hand-off, but she hadn't been. It took her a good three hours to figure that out, get off the couch, take a shower, and get dressed. She couldn't go to bed until things were square with Finn because if there was one thing she knew, his Irish heart was feeling as bad as her big Texas one.

She dragged herself to his place toting a peace offering that was melting in a grocery bag, mentally mapping out how the rest of the evening would go. Finn would pour her a drink. They would make up over ice cream and whiskey. He would spout some Irish platitude about friendship. He would wrap his arms around her for just a minute and all would be well. That was what Cori was thinking when she rang his bell and when he answered the door she said:

"Hey, O'Brien. Brought you cookie dough ice cream."

She held up the recycled grocery bag, and tried to smile without wincing, but the smile never happened.

Finn O'Brien, it seemed, was entertaining.

CHAPTER 37

DAY 8 – NIGHT

"Not good, O'Brien."

Cori shoved the ice cream into him as she walked by. She smiled and spoke in her nice girl voice.

"Mrs. Barnett, what a surprise to see you here."

"Detective O'Brien was kind enough to spare a few minutes. I was hoping someone had responded to the reward."

"Sure. That's just the kind of discussion you need to have in person. At night. Coming all the way to Detective O'Brien's apartment." Cori chuckled the way women will when another woman has punted and they are left to run with the ball. "I'm surprised he didn't tell you that I was handling the calls. Well, I can tell you a lot of people want your money. I talked to about twenty of them and not a good lead in the bunch."

"I'm sorry you had to waste so much time."

Elizabeth put her drink down. Cori's lips twitched and one of her lovely brows rose when she looked at Finn, shoeless, clad in his favorite jeans and t-shirt. Mrs. Barnett had worn jeans, too. Hers fit her like a glove, her white gauzy shirt was just this side of transparent, and her hair was tousled as if from a breeze – or a roll in the hay.

On second thought, Cori decided, Elizabeth Barnett could probably screw without so much as getting a hair out of place or smudging her lipstick, so maybe she just put the top down on the Jag when she scurried her skinny little butt over to Finn's place right after her husband moved out. Cori knew that was a catty thought but what was a girl to do think when she stumbled on such a cozy scene?

Cori tugged at her sweater, the one she thought made her look scrumptious, but next to Elizabeth Barnett she looked like Finn's maiden aunt. She crossed her arms, but there was no way to hide her overabundance of boobs. She touched her hair and knew that the top of her head looked like a grocery store birthday cake next to Elizabeth Barnett's sleek fall of a refined do.

"So," Cori said. "Who wants ice cream?"

"No, but thank you. I should be going," Elizabeth said, but she made no move to go.

"I'll just put that in the freezer while Detective O'Brien sees you out, Mrs. Barnett."

Cori grabbed the bag from Finn, favoring first one side and then the other because her ribs hurt and there was no good way to get where she was going without walking like a duck. Behind her, she heard Finn reassuring Elizabeth Barnett and Elizabeth Barnett apologizing as he said goodnight. All that polite talk left Cori feeling like an idiot.

She ripped open the freezer and slammed the ice cream inside, but the ice was thick and the compartment small and all she did was crumple the box. She was working on it, muttering curses, damning men and women and big hearts and hormones when Finn came up behind her, reached over her shoulder, took the box, turned it sideways and pushed it in.

"Thank you." Cori ducked under his arm and rested against the counter as he closed the freezer door. When she had his attention, she asked: "What was that, O'Brien?"

"Not what you're thinking, Cori."

"It better not be or you are going to see a lawsuit slapped on you faster than a saddle on a bay at the barrel race." Cori shook her head. "What are you thinking? You're dating a survivor with the investigation open and one complaint already filed? Did those doctors suck your brains out before they closed you up?"

"You know, Cori, I have a lot of people reminding me that I'm not exactly fine and upstanding. I don't need you to do it, too."

Cori turned her head and pulled her lips together. She didn't want to hurt him; she wanted to protect him from himself and that woman. When she looked back, she said:

"You can fool around with a groundhog for all I care, but you haven't come all this way and dealt with all the crap, just to throw it away on her. She's not thinking straight and maybe never will. You've been hit so hard and fast by Bev you're not even on the rebound yet. You've got to know that, don't you?"

"I'm not sleeping with the woman, Cori," Finn insisted. "She found me at Mick's. It wasn't the place to talk, so I brought her here. I did a kindness, that's all."

"No, you didn't. You bucked the system and so did she and that's why you're feeling a kinship," Cori pointed out. "But it's not you and her against the system. You and me are the system. If she goes rogue then she's against us."

"You're right. I'm sorry. You are right, woman." Finn turned and went back to the living room and Cori went with him. He swiped up his drink and motioned toward the open cabinet where the liquor was kept.

"Sure, why not." Cori sat herself down and watched him pour, admiring him as he did so.

He was a real man and not just because he was strong but because he had a brain and a heart. There weren't many like him anymore and if she couldn't have him, she hoped there was another one out there for her. Cori also hoped there was a good woman out there for Finn, but it sure wasn't Elizabeth Barnett.

"When she told me the mister moved out of the house, I gave her the number at Mick's and my cell. We can't trust her security, we don't know that she isn't the focus of all this." Finn handed her a glass with two fingers of bourbon. "She is lonely and afraid."

"Who isn't?" Cori muttered.

Finn raised his glass to that, but Cori just took a slug of her bourbon.

"People wouldn't understand," she said. "Captain Fowler wouldn't understand."

"No one would know. You wouldn't have known if you hadn't come by here," Finn said.

Cori blew out a breath. She put a throw pillow up against her ribs.

"Why are you such a choir boy, O'Brien? Do you think she would give you the same consideration if push came to shove? She would tell the old man about this just to make him sit up and take notice, or she'd tell one of the neighbor ladies, or she'd call Fowler and mention that she was at your place. Get a clue on the woman thing."

"You should have been a nun, Cori." Finn finished off his whiskey. "You give a fine rap on the head."

"Gee, now there's a compliment if I ever heard one," she said, but when he grinned she did the same. Cori could just imagine the little boy he had been. There wasn't a knuckle rapper who could make a dent in Finn O'Brien if his heart said something was right.

"I'm saying I'll own that mistake, and thank you for pointing it out. Now, another drink or ice cream."

They decided on ice cream and some serious talk about business. Finn told her about Eros Manufacturing. It was a small, busy facility. The shipping docks were closed for the day when he got there and the second shift was just coming on. It was a thriving enterprise that turned out a specialty bolt used in aircraft wing assemblies. Eros had no offices in Switzerland or Germany. He had the name of the CEO to follow up with regarding Sam Barnett since no one he spoke to had heard of the man. Eros hardly seemed so lucrative or controversial that it would cause a partnership to break up; Barnett's travel and current client list did not put him anywhere near Germany but he had been in Switzerland twice. The link between him and Rachel, if there was one, had to be personal.

An hour later, the ice cream was gone and Finn walked Cori to her car. The night blooming jasmine perfumed the air between the apartment building and Kimiko's house. The lights in the landlady's place were out and the neighborhood was quiet. They walked slowly because Cori still hurt and because it was a pleasant evening. Cori didn't mean to ruin it, but she couldn't put her head on her pillow unless she was sure she and Finn were on the same page.

"I'm not going to bring it up ever again after this, O'Brien, but I have something to say. I don't trust Elizabeth Barnett. I thought I did, but my hackles don't lie and they are up and squealing like a stuck pig tonight." Cori held up her hand when Finn started to object. "This isn't about the two of you, I swear. I don't give a cow's patootie if it's sexual thing or some deep-seated mother-complex deal with you. Whatever it is shut it down.

"The only gal you better be sniffing after is me. If I'm not number one, then I get taken out. I love you, O'Brien. If things were different, I might not kick you out of bed for eating crackers, but I've got a kid to worry about. In fact, I've got two. Either you're with me when I tell you she makes me nervous or you're not. I need to know now which it is."

"I'm with you, Cori," Finn said. "Always with you."

"Fine, 'cause I don't want to see you confused if it comes down to that lady or me," Cori said. "Now, I apologize for barging in. My bad." Cori tried to take a deep breath. It didn't go far but it was enough. "She's not alone, Finn. Not the way you are. Not the way I am. Just remember that."

"It's all good, Cori. Promise."

She made her way around the car. Finn beat her to it and opened the door. He eased her in and when she had her belt on she said:

"Don't give 'em the rope to hang you with, partner. I don't have the heart to watch you swing."

CHAPTER 38

"I've got to go out for a little while," Medium Man said to the boy.

"How long do you think you'll be?"

The boy forced himself to smile even though his gut was cramping bad. It was getting harder and harder to tell what made this psycho happy, and the boy had the impression he wasn't happy. Then he realized he wasn't looking the dude straight in the eye the way he had been told to, so the boy opened his eyes wider and tried to look all innocent. Medium Man was not fooled. The man's eyes were glinty and sharp like the blade of that knife he liked so much.

"You want me to go, don't you?"

"No," the boy said too quickly. "I just wondered...I thought, that maybe..."

"What? What?"

Medium Man took a step forward and the boy tried not to look at the man's fists clenching or his chest caving as he prepared to strike. The boy tried to sound casual when he said:

"I thought maybe when you come back I could put on all my new clothes and see if you still liked them. You know, like a fashion show kind of."

It took a minute for Medium Man to digest this information and for his face to lose all its edge. When it did, the boy relaxed a little. For his part, Medium Man was ashamed of himself for thinking the boy was only pretending to be grateful for the gifts he had been given.

"That's good that you like your presents," Medium Man said and the boy forced himself to smile a little broader. Medium Man wished that smile was a little brighter, but this was the boy's way. He said: "I don't know when I'll be back. It will be a surprise."

"Sure. That's fun, too."

The boy bounced lightly as if his whole body were nodding yes. And in that spinning mind of his he heard his own admonition not to screw up this opportunity, to take it slow, to get out clean, but get out at all costs.

"When I get back maybe I'll have some special news for you. It will make you happy."

As soon as the door closed the boy muttered 'in your dreams' and then got to business. He ran to the mattress, knelt on it, leaned his elbows on the windowsill, and craned his neck. A few minutes later he saw Medium Man leave the building. Even in the dark there was no doubt in the boy's mind that it was him. The guy walked like he expected the world to stomp on him.

"God damn freak," the boy said to Medium Man's back. Then he yelled, "God damn freak."

That was it. When the boy said the 'F' word the second time Medium Man stopped, turned around, and looked up toward the window where the boy watched from behind the blinds. Medium Man's eyes seemed to bore through those blinds like a wood beetle in an oak tree so the boy fell away. He threw himself onto the mattress but Medium Man's look made a U-turn and pierced him in the gut and the heart and the boy shivered. He was positive that man knew what was in his mind. Medium Man was the devil. Medium Man scared the boy more than anything or anyone he had ever encountered in the whole world.

When the boy ventured toward the window again, Medium Man was gone. At least he seemed to be gone. For all the boy knew the guy was lurking in the dark, waiting for the boy to make his move. A chill started at the end of his tailbone and worked its way up his spine right into his brain. Sweat popped out on the boy's forehead and under his arms, soiling his new shirt. The pimples on his face pulsed and the boy crumpled onto the mattress once more. His chest was heavy with fear and it was hard to breathe. He pounded his fists on the mattress and angry tears came out of the corner of his eyes. If his father couldn't break him, how could this guy? But the boy already knew the answer. Medium Man was not a brute, he was not an animal, he was something worse: he was a psycho.

The boy breathed through his nose. Once. Twice. Three times. He put his hands over his heart and thought about his options. Leave now or wait it out? There might be a better opportunity if he waited. Like, what if they really did get to that island? He could disappear in a nice place. Then he thought again. An island would be the worst. There was nowhere to go on an island and Medium Man would find him.

The boy put an arm over his eyes. The fabric of his new shirt smelled like formaldehyde. There had been a tag in the shirt: inspected by number 482. He wished number 482 were there to help him decide what to do. Since he was alone, the boy agonized for hours. The night would almost be over by the time he made a decision, but once he did the boy was sure it was the only decision he could make.

As soon as Medium Man turned the corner, he forgot about the boy and thought about his plan. He had been so proud of himself for having an idea, but now he was having second thoughts. After all, it was Mort who came up with the ideas and the jobs. It was Mort who gave instructions on how things were to be done and Mort who made sure they got paid. Still, that didn't mean that Medium Man couldn't have a good idea. He just hadn't tried to have one before. Then again, he hadn't had the boy before and some things were worth taking a chance.

Medium Man turned into a seedy little hole-in-the-wall that was actually a step up from Fairy Tails, waved away a smoke cloud hanging mid-air, and spied Mort in a corner booth sucking on a beer.

"Hey."

Mort greeted Medium Man to be polite even though he was miffed that this guy was calling him out at night when he should have been home with his family. But Georgia was dyeing her hair, and the girls were particularly loud, so he guessed it wasn't such a bad time to grab a beer.

"Glad you could make it." Medium Man thought that made him sound like he was the one calling the shots. Sadly, he blew it in the next second when he complained: "Georgia wasn't nice on the phone. I don't think she likes me much."

"She likes you fine."

"Georgia likes me?" Medium Man's eyes lit up.

"Sure. Why not?"

Mort lied easily. Georgia couldn't stand the guy. Even Mort could only take him in small doses. It had taken her awhile to even remember that she talked to him. Bottom line, Georgia had remembered, Mort had called back, the date was made and, since all this was so out of the ordinary, Mort was a little curious about the meeting. When Mort finished his beer, Medium Man asked:

"You want another one? I'll get it for you if you want another beer."

Mort shoved his mug across the table. Medium Man was out of the booth, scurrying toward the bar, excited because it was kind of like Mort had just given him a prize. Mort leaned back and watched. The guy could've been a ghost for all the service he got. Finally, he got the bartender to draw two and he was back.

"Okay. I gotta make this fast. What's up?" Mort asked, but Medium Man was drinking and didn't answer. Then he was wiping his mouth with his jacket sleeve and when it looked like he was going to try to make small talk again Mort got in his face. "What?"

"Well," Medium Man began, nervous now that Mort had shown him his angry face. "Here's the thing. Remember how I told you I like to keep up on things. Especially after a job. I like to read about our jobs in the newspaper. Remember I told you that?"

Mort sighed. Medium Man's confidence waned, but this was too important to let it go so he forged on.

"Anyway, I'm reading the paper 'cause that's how I found out about the funeral for those kids, and I went and checked it out so as I could sort of make up and–"

"Oh damn," Mort muttered. "You went to the friggin' funeral for those kids?"

"I didn't do nothing. They didn't see me." Medium Man whined even though what he said wasn't especially true. People had seen him, and he was almost sure those two had been cops, but he gave them the slip so things were cool. He didn't think Mort would think it was a good thing, and they were getting off topic anyway. "Okay. So, I just want you to know that I read the newspapers and keep up and such. Just to make sure everyone stays dead."

"Shut up," Mort growled and pushed himself up against the table. "Don't you know better than that? This is a public place."

"Sorry. Sorry. Hey, I'm sorry." Medium Man put his fingers to his lips and whispered. This was a chance for him and the boy. "Anyway, that lady with the kids? She's got fifty big ones on the table for information about what we..." Mort's eyes threw daggers and Medium Man lowered his voice even more. "Fifty grand, Mort."

Medium Man's eyes widened, to underscore the importance of his news. But Mort wasn't excited. He didn't even seem interested. Maybe Mort wasn't as smart as Medium Man thought.

"That's a lot of money, Mort. Fifty grand."

"Yeah, a lot of money," Mort answered. "So?"

"So?" Medium Man laughed a little. It was true. Mort wasn't real smart so Medium Man spoke slowly. "So, we can get it."

For a while, Mort didn't move at all. He just stared at Medium Man who assumed Mort was so bowled over by his good idea that he couldn't talk. Then Mort kind of shook his head the littlest bit, lowered his eyes, and put his hand up to his mouth. When he looked again he hoped the guy across from him would have disappeared. No such luck. Mort set aside his beer. It was his turn to talk real slow.

"You are so screwed up. We can't get anything from her."

"Sure we can." Medium Man was excited now that Mort hadn't walked straight out the door. He twitched and scuffled and wiggled in his seat as he laid out his plan. "You're smart, Mort. You're a good talker. You can go to the police. You'll know how to do it."

"You want me to go to the police and tell them I have information on who it was killed those kids and the nanny? And you think after I do that, they're going to hand over fifty grand?"

Medium Man's head bobbed up and down. Mort was so close that Medium Man could smell what he had for dinner. Mort reached over the table and punched the other guy on the shoulder with one finger.

"What're you going to do with fifty grand if you're strapped on the table waitin' for the needle?"

"But I won't be. And neither will you," Medium Man exclaimed, just about jumping out of his skin now. He wished he could talk as fast as he was thinking.

"Yeah? Man, you are nuts. You tell me how you figure that."

"Well." Medium Man whispered now that they had gotten to the hard part, the part he needed help with. "I don't really have it all figured. I thought if you could do the right talking, we'd split it and take off. We could live good Mort. We'd both have a bundle. Look."

Medium Man reached into the pocket of his jacket and pulled out a piece of paper. He shoved it Mort's way. Mort glanced at it. Dumb shit had to cross out the numbers three times before he managed to figure half of fifty was twenty-five. Medium Man kept talking and pushing that pitiful piece of paper across the table.

"We could finger somebody else. You know one of them winos that hang around Susie's place or somethin'. I'd give my knife to plant on him. I think that might be good, even though it would be sad to lose that blade to a wino. Then you tell the cops you know who did it and point to the wino that has the knife. But you might have a better way. I guess you should think up how to do it. What do you say? Huh, what do you think?"

When Mort sat back like he was considering all this, Medium Man smiled. He could already feel that money in his hands. He could feel the sunshine on his face and the boy lying next to him on the beach. But Mort wasn't thinking about Medium Man's plans, he was thinking he was getting old because he hadn't seen something like this coming. When Mort stayed silent for a long time and didn't even drink his beer, Medium Man's smile faded and he curled his fingers around the paper, crumpling it.

"You don't think it would work, do you?" he said, wishing he could take everything back, especially the clothes he had bought the boy now that there wouldn't be extra money to pay for them.

Mort didn't answer right away. First, he looked at a couple walking by the table. The woman kind of looked like Georgia: big tits pushed out of the V-neck of her sweater that was too tight. This woman had no hips to speak of but then again neither did Georgia. He liked Georgia an awful lot. She would love having the kind of money Medium Man was talking about, but he didn't love her enough to get himself killed or caught for the extra dough. They had already been paid well, anyway. At least Mort had been well paid since he saved back a little extra for a finder's fee. He took a long drink of his beer, and then pulled his brows together.

"Can I think on it awhile?" Mort asked. "I mean, that money ain't going nowhere. And if we're going to do this, we gotta do it right. Understand? We gotta make sure they don't think it's us that did it, you see. We gotta find just the right guy to take the fall."

Mort rolled his eyes and snorted a good old boy snort and Medium Man laughed right back at him.

"Yeah, oh yeah. That's it. You're smart, Mort. You're really smart." Medium Man was so relieved that he felt his bladder beginning to give away. "You know, if we work it right I bet that broad would give more than fifty. What do you think? Maybe a lot more."

"Hey, now there's something to think about." Mort took another drink. When he was sure he could look at Medium Man without wanting to smack him, Mort said: "If you have any more ideas, I want to know right away, okay? I'm going to tell Georgia that if you call I want to know about it right away."

"Hey, that's good. And if you come up with an idea you tell me." Medium Man returned the courtesy.

"You betcha," Mort assured him. "Yep, you'll be the first to know when I got it figured out. I can promise you that."

They parted on the street. Medium Man tried not to

grin but he did and that made people coming toward him stare. Once, Medium Man looked over his shoulder to see Mort watching him. Mort gave him a little wave, so Medium Man gave a little wave back. The second time he looked back, Mort was gone. That wasn't a surprise. He was probably in as much of a hurry to get home as Medium Man was.

The boy agonized for almost five hours, and finally figured there were only three things that could be going on.

First, Medium Man was hiding across the street, watching the building, testing the boy's loyalty, and waiting for the boy to do something he shouldn't.

Next, Medium Man had gone somewhere but that somewhere was close and he would be able to see the boy walking down the street after he left the building.

Finally, Medium Man might actually have gone somewhere that a bus had to take him. He had ditched that car real fast after they went to that cemetery. If a bus took him, he would probably be gone a long time.

The first two options scared the boy silly, so he sat around. He thought. He made one decision and then changed his mind. He started to leave, looked out the window, sat down again, and picked at the sores on his face. With every hour lost, his agitation grew. He began to fantasize.

He could have already been gone fifteen minutes…

Half an hour…

An hour…

Almost two if only he had left when he thought he should.

It was just after two in the morning when, more afraid

of staying than of leaving, the boy slung his pack over his shoulder, looked out the window again, and left the apartment. He kept his head down as he shot out of the stairwell, onto the sidewalk, and turned left. Forcing himself to walk fast instead of run, he was almost at the end of the block when he started to breathe easy for the first time in a week.

Georgia was asleep when Mort got home. She had dyed her hair and it looked like a white Brillo pad on the pillow. He looked in on the girls. They were sleeping like angels in the middle of their messy world. He checked the back door. It was locked. He checked the windows. They were closed.

When he was sure his house was secure and his women safe, Mort went into the living room and dialed a number. That number went to another number, and it was the person at that number he wanted to talk to. The man had been sleeping, but Mort knew he was awake enough to understand what he was telling him.

It wasn't that this man needed to know what was going on, but Mort called out of courtesy since he was Mort's bread and butter client. He didn't want him hearing second hand that there was another problem. The guy said it was no skin off his nose. Whatever Mort wanted to do, but the solution to his problem would be on his dime. This man had never seen Mort. If he had ever seen Medium Man, he would never remember. The phone numbers they used during a job weren't traceable since the forwarding number changed all the time and the cells were disposable. It was a class operation all the way and Mort liked being part of it and he was glad to get this off his chest.

Mort said thank you. The man ended the conversation by warning that he expected no more glitches. If there were, he would have to take his business elsewhere. Mort assured him there wouldn't be. They said goodnight, and Mort crawled into bed. Mort slept with Georgia's leg over his skinny hips and his fingers dug into her ample thigh. His household was quiet, and his mind was at rest in this early hour. He fell asleep only to be wakened a while later by a noise. Georgia's leg landed heavily on the mattress as he turned away from her. Mort's hand went under the pillow for the gun he always kept there, but it was only Bobbi standing by their bed. He smiled sleepily thinking how sweet she looked in her girl-power pajamas. Mort let go of the gun and reached out his arms. Bobbi went to him. He lifted her off the floor and pulled her into bed with him.

"I had a bad dream, daddy," Bobbi whispered as Mort arranged the covers under her chin.

"Bad dreams can't hurt you," he mumbled and laced his arms around his little girl. He fell asleep again. He could rest awhile before he had to go to work. It was only three. But, Mort couldn't get back to sleep, so he listened to his little girl breathing softly, and his wife snoring and waited until it would be time to go.

CHAPTER 39

DAY 9 – MORNING

It was four in the morning and light enough that anyone could have seen Medium Man sitting in the alley weeping, but he didn't care. He was inconsolable as he held the boy, and stroked his face, and rocked back and forth. The boy, dead now for some time, looked quite lovely since the blood had drained from his face leaving it all one color. His eyes were closed but his long lashes were still pretty. It was also nice now that his eyes didn't move around the way they had when he was alive, like he was looking for a way out. The boy looked like he was sleeping because there wasn't a mark on the front of him. Sadly, the back of him was kind of a mess. Medium Man had got him good, right between the shoulder blades, pulling down and then pulling up again so that he laid the boy's back open.

Imagining that he was sleeping helped Medium Man stop crying. Realizing that he really had to go helped too. Even in this neighborhood, there were folks who would call the cops on a guy walking around all bloody and all. That would not be fair since what happened was pretty much the boy's fault but they wouldn't know that. As he was thinking of going, the boy's body jerked a little. That surprised Medium Man. He was a little delighted, too, so he petted the boy and cooed and tried to get him to wake up. When he didn't, Medium Man got up.

He stood over the boy for a second and thought about how awesome he had been when he saw the boy hurrying away. He had never moved so fast in his life. Up the stairs. Down again. Knife in hand. Then Bam! Bam! Bam! Into the boy's back. Bam! Wham! The boy didn't even have time to scream, that's how fast and good Medium Man was with his knife.

Before he left, he laid the boy out on the ground nicely and brushed his greasy hair into place. There was trash in the alley that he collected and put over the body. It wasn't a lot but it was better than nothing. He couldn't do anything about the trail of blood that was left after he dragged the boy into the alley, so he didn't try to clean that up. Medium Man walked three blocks to the all night liquor store near his place. That's where he bought himself a bottle. He hadn't looked back when he left the alley. That was the way they did it in the movies when someone wanted to be strong. Medium Man would never know that he should have looked back. If he had, he would have seen the boy's eyes flutter open.

"Come on, Todd. This isn't going to do you any good, and you know it."

Cori sat in the same chair she had taken thirty minutes earlier when she and Finn entered the small, windowless room at Men's Central to interrogate Todd Webster. Finn got the call about the collar at five a.m., Cori at five-oh-five and both of them met up here at six thirty. Finn looked fresh as a daisy, Cori had barely managed to get her hair sprayed into place. It still hurt a little to sit, but it hurt more to stand up. She didn't want Webster to know the damage he'd done so she sat. Not that she held anything against him. Being a prick was his job, and without guys like him she wouldn't be gainfully employed. Still, none of this made for a good mood. The silver lining in Cori's dark cloud was that Todd actually had something to say.

"I never, never killed anybody much less two kids, and sure as hell not Rachel." Todd's head swung from Cori to Finn and back again. "And since it doesn't matter now, and the whole thing is screwed without her anyway, I might as well tell you. Rachel wasn't my girlfriend she was my partner. We made good money. I mean real good money. She's the last person I wanted to see dead."

"No one would pay big money to see that woman naked, Todd," Cori said.

"Tell me something I don't know," he snorted. "Rachel was the distributor, not an actress. We've been working together almost a year. Europe's a big market for the kind of smut we turned out. I wouldn't care who she slept with as long as that pipeline didn't dry up." He scowled and thought for a minute and then added: "How much did she have in the bank again?"

"Thirty big ones. And that's just in the checking account." Cori twirled the little blue plastic stick in what was left of her coffee. She punched the bottom of the cup and felt the Styrofoam give.

"Then she was holding out on me, man." Webster complained. "She told me the exchange rate sucked. I'd make a couple hundred hard copies, we'd sell 'em cheap, and I'd pick up two grand free and clear every time we shipped. The digital stuff we priced way low to get traffic. I just figured it hadn't caught on yet. I should have paid more attention to the business end, but I'm an artist. You know, left brain/right brain?"

"How about no brain," Cori drawled.

He didn't contradict her, he just shook his head and the orange jumpsuit seemed to swallow him up. Then he grinned and Cori shivered thinking about all the Todd Webster's out there just waiting for a single gal like her to hit on; a gal with a regular paycheck.

"I give her credit for scamming the old scammer," he said. "I'll miss her. She really got into the production, you know. She didn't look so good on film, but she had energy. Yep, that woman had energy. Sometimes I used her when the script called for a threesome."

"You had scripts?" Cori asked, but Finn didn't want to get waylaid.

"She fought real hard before she was killed," Finn said. "If you didn't do it then someone you know might have, so we'll be wanting a list of your associates, Todd."

"Aw, come on. That'll put me out of business for sure. There's probably still a domestic market."

"And if one of your associates took out Rachel and you don't cooperate with us, then you are complicit in a triple murder. An accessory after the fact," Cori warned.

Todd's eyes got big, but before he could profess his innocence again, Finn asked:

"How did you meet her?"

"Cholo's. That was her favorite. She was hard to get to know but then she'd tie one on and talk a blue streak. I saw her a couple of times. I told her what I did. I thought

I'd impress her, but she turned the tables. She impressed me. Rachel was a distributor in the homeland until her producer got out of the business and she started looking for something new. The nanny gig was the easiest way to get over here. She started to troll on the weekends and we hooked up. The rest is history."

"Did you ever go into the house where she worked?" Finn asked.

"No, I swear."

"Did she ever talk about the people she worked for?" Cori asked. "Did the man of the house hit on her?"

"If he did, she didn't tell me. And she didn't like the woman much because she had eyes on her all the time. That drove Rachel nuts. Like she'd want any of the crap in that house." Webster looked from Finn to Cori. "Come on, you know I'm not good for the murders. That's really a bad scene. I've had a few scuffles in my time, but I don't kill people. So, are you going to pop me for the porn? If you're not, let me out of here. If you are, I want a lawyer."

Todd flopped back in his chair looking miserable, lost, and alone. He didn't even look up when the door opened and an officer waved some papers at them. Finn collected them and then went back to the table.

"Okay, Todd," Finn said. "We'll be talking to the D.A. about cutting you loose because you've been helping us out. You think of anything else that will help us about Rachel, you call. Are you good with that, my friend?"

"You got it, man." Todd's face lit up. "Absolutely."

"Detective Anderson."

Finn invited her out of the room and that disappointed her a little. If she had her way she would have kept at Todd for days just to get her pound of flesh.

As soon as they were out the door, he handed her the report.

"His gun is clean and the tires on his car don't match the casts found in the back of the neighborhood. The car was a long shot anyway. It's the rental we want."

"Then we are exactly nowhere," Cori sighed.

"Maybe. I have one more question for our friend." Finn opened the door again and Todd Webster jumped ten feet.

"Was Germany the only place Rachel shipped those tapes?"

"Naw. She had clients in other countries."

"Switzerland?" Finn asked.

"Duh. They don't just make cheese over there, ya know."

"You sick?"

Georgia eyed Mort with great suspicion. He hadn't touched the stack of pancakes she had made especially for him.

"Nope."

"You going to work today?"

"Maybe."

"I gotta pay the rent end of the week," Georgia reminded him.

"You'll have the money for the rent. Don't I always get you money for the rent?" he muttered and drank his coffee.

"And the kids need some new clothes. I could use some new items myself," Georgia said, testing the water in case there was any advantage to this strange new mood of his.

"How much?"

"Five hundred?" she ventured.

"Two fifty," he countered.

Georgia met him half way. "Whatever you can spare, honey pie."

"I gotta go. I might be back early, I don't know."

Mort got out of his chair, dug into his pocket, and handed Georgia the cash. For a minute he just looked at her and then he kissed her cheek.

"Thanks for breakfast," he said.

"Sure thing," Georgia answered, more confused than ever. She couldn't remember the last time Mort thanked her for anything.

When the front door slammed, Georgia flipped on the television. Good Morning America faded in. Refilling her coffee, she grabbed the latest People magazine and began to flip through it. Two pages were stuck together with syrup, an inconvenience that didn't bother her in the least. It was a two-page article, and Georgia never read anything longer than one page. She actually preferred the little paragraphs under the pictures. She turned past the stuck together pages. The television babbled on. Finally, she turned off the tube. There wasn't much interesting on it anyway. Just crime and news and politics. No hard luck stories.

That was a bummer.

Medium Man downed a fifth of Jim Beam hoping to sleep but all that happened was that he was thoroughly drunk at seven in the morning. He sat on the mattress under the window listening to the town wake up: trucks and cars, the sidewalk preacher revving up, Mexican ladies going to market. In his lap was his beloved knife and on his mind were his many sorrows.

He was sorry he didn't remember his mother.

He was sorry that he couldn't give the boy a funeral like the one he had seen for those kids.

He was sorry the boy wasn't there because if he didn't have the boy to spend the reward money on, it would mean nothing when Mort got it for them.

As he pondered these things, Medium Man found his addled mind losing the image of the boy and the memory of their sex that he had mistaken for love. Instead, he pulled up thoughts of islands and sun and going away from this place. So maybe he was wrong about one thing. He wouldn't be sorry to have all that money even without the boy. When he had it, he would go to those pretty islands alone. He would find another boy. Maybe not as good as the one he had but that was what he would do.

He raised the bottle to his lips again and then set it down carefully on the floor. He picked up his knife and wiped it once more with an old shirt. When he was done he thought it looked like new. He decided he needed a better hiding place. It was too easy to reach it in the old place when he got upset. Just as he was trying to figure out where a better hiding place would be in a small room like his, just as he reached for the bottle again, there was a knock on his door. That was very confusing since no one had ever knocked on his door before. In fact, it took another few knocks for Medium Man to believe that it was his door being knocked on.

He pushed himself off the mattress, so drunk he didn't even care that his beloved knife had fallen and skidded across the floor. He stumbled toward the door but ran into the old chair and had to right himself. Whoever was knocking wanted in bad, and for a crazy minute he imagined that it was the boy coming back to beg forgiveness. Then he thought maybe the boy was a zombie come to eat his brain, but Medium Man sorted out that it wouldn't be much of a meal. He was stumbling and laughing when he opened the door. When he saw who it was, he swayed with joy.

"Oh," he murmured sweetly.

"How are you, *compadre*?"

Medium Man held the door open for his one and only buddy, a buddy who was better than a hundred boys.

CHAPTER 40

The call came from County USC Medical Center a half an hour after Todd Webster made bail. It came in twenty-eight minutes after Cori and Finn started shooting rubber bands at the wall of the office as they brainstormed their next move. Neither wanted to be the first to admit they were out of ideas. Yet like so many things in life, just when it seems the darkest a light shines.

Now they were cooling their heels in the waiting room of the hospital that dealt with the worst of the worst, County USC. If there was a gunshot victim, this was where they ended up along with every indigent, illegal, gangbanger, and dirt-poor working stiff who had an accident or fell ill.

"Promise you'll never let them put me in here no matter what," Finn said.

"Promise me you'll never get shot," Cori answered.

Finn couldn't make that promise, so he stood up and walked the length of the waiting room, trying not to look at the other people. It wasn't that he was uncomfortable in their presence it was that he and Cori made them nervous.

"Excuse me? Detectives?"

Finn and Cori came to attention for the doctor with the sweet voice and soft handshake.

"I'm Doctor Meyer. You're looking for the young man who was brought in with a knife wound, correct?"

"That would be us. Detective O'Brien," Finn introduced himself before he indicated Cori. "Anderson."

"Nice to meet you both." The doctor's cheeks were rosy, her hair cotton-white. She looked like a storybook grandmother but was a front line physician. "I saw him in emergency. We transferred him to the third floor for surgery. He should be in recovery by now. Take the elevator on the left. I'll call and tell them you're coming."

She kept her promise and on the third floor a young, crisply dressed nurse intercepted them, said the doctor would be with them soon, but could give them no information. She left them in another waiting room and it was exactly twelve minutes before Paul Craig appeared. The Medical Examiner looked out of place in a hospital where people were trying to stay alive. Behind him was Dr. Johnson, a petite young woman. Both were still dressed in surgical greens. She slipped the paper cap off her head. The detectives stood and then everyone sat.

"Sorry you guys. He didn't make it," Paul said.

"The poor kid had simply lost too much blood by the time we got him," Doctor Johnson added. "Everything from the kidney up was ripped like a zipper. Even if we'd been on scene it would have been tough to do anything more for him."

"The good news, if there is any, is this: what killed him was the same weapon used on the Barnett girls," Paul said. "Not that it's going to do you any good to know that."

"We know where he was found. It's a place to start." Cori looked at Doctor Johnson. "Did he say anything at all?"

"If he was going to talk it would have been to the EMTs. You can ask them, but I doubt he could manage anything."

The four people sat in silence. Cori ran the strap of her purse through her fingers and fiddled with her mom necklace while Finn clasped and unclasped hands that dangled between his knees. Paul Craig looked out the window, and Doctor Johnson cradled her head in her hand, catching a wide-awake wink of sleep before she started in again. She dropped her hand, smiled at them.

"Do you need me for anything else?"

"We'll need the death certificate," Cori said. "Paul, can you put him at the head of the line and get us an autopsy report? Distinguishing marks, prior injuries. Fingerprint him. Dental X-rays. Basically everything including anything we didn't think to ask for."

"Sure," Paul said.

Dr. Johnson promised to do the paperwork and have the body ready for Paul's people within the hour. Finn got up as she left and then asked Paul:

"Where are his things?"

"I was kind of counting on him pulling through. I hijacked a bed in an actual room no less."

"You must be Irish, Paul. You're an eternal optimist." Finn clapped him on the back.

It was a double room and in the bed near the window was

a man who looked suspiciously healthy and was puffing on a cigarette while he watched television. He grinned and nodded to them.

"That's illegal." Cori pointed to the cigarette. The man grinned and nodded again.

"He doesn't speak English," Paul said as he spread a plastic sheet on the bed and gave each of them a pair of latex gloves. He opened the cabinet near the empty bed, reached in, and came out with a white plastic drawstring bag. He tossed the bag at Finn.

"Here you go."

"Cori?" The doctor threw her a backpack.

While Cori sifted through the backpack, Finn reached inside the bag and pulled out a pair of bloodied, pleated khaki pants, a white shirt, shoes that were worn down at heel and socks. He dug into the pockets. The clothing was still damp with blood and smelled the worse for it. The pants had been cut off the victim; the shirt had been shredded up the back by the attack and cut up the front and sleeves in emergency. He turned the shoes upside-down and the socks inside out.

Cori emptied the backpack: over-the-counter acne cream, a toothbrush, five dollars, a couple of t-shirts, a pair of jeans, and some underwear. No journal, no matches, no bus ticket, no I.D.

"Sorry," she muttered.

Finn looked at all of it. He fingered the clothes. First the old things: jeans, t-shirts, underwear, and then the khakis and the white shirt. He lingered over the khakis and shirt. They were cheap and the fabric a blend of nothing natural. The clothes were not stylish, but there was something distinctive about them.

"These are brand new," he said. "The pants and shirt were brand, spanking new. His shoes are old, but the socks are new."

Finn turned the collar of the shirt over the back of his hand and saw that the label was intact, but all it told him was that a huge manufacturer had the thing stitched somewhere in India and that it was never to be bleached. The pants, though, were a store brand.

"White Horse. It's on Hollywood and Vine."

"I'll give them a call," Cori said.

"I'll need a description of the victim," Finn said.

"Skinny. Five eight. Really bad skin. Severe cystic acne that was untreated." Paul shook his head. "Dark brown, shoulder length hair that wasn't too clean. Light gray eyes. If anyone remembers him it's going to be because of the acne. It was one of the worst cases I've ever seen. Disfiguring."

Cori listened carefully and repeated the description to the woman on the other end of the phone. The woman was the owner of the store and remembered him well. Cori raised her shoulder, balancing her phone while she dug into her purse for her note pad. When she hung up she held up the pad.

"He came in with another man. The clerk remembers because that guy was always touching the kid and he was kind of jumpy. She can take a look at the clothes and identify them if we want." Cori flicked her notepad with her nail. "And she told us where we can probably find the other guy. He signed the book at the front of the store. You know, the kind you sign when you want to be on the mailing list. We've got an address for John Kramer."

"You don't know how much this means to me, you comin' here just when I was so sorrowful. You didn't even know I was hurting, and here you are. Here you are. My good, good friend."

Medium Man stumbled into Mort's arm. Mort pulled back. Medium Man went with other men. Mort thought that was a sick and terrible thing to do. Unfortunately, Mort wasn't fast enough. Medium Man had his arms around his neck, and his face was against his chest. That felt weirder than weird, so Mort pushed the man and held him away.

"You're in a bad way, buddy," Mort said as Medium Man's knees buckled.

Mort grabbed him under the arms and half dragged him toward the mattress. He was both heavier than Mort would have expected and in better shape. With a grunt, Mort tossed him on the decrepit, dirty mattress. Medium Man dropped and rolled until he was on his back, spread eagle, eyes closed, head lolling from side-to-side.

Mort pushed his hands into the pockets of his jacket and scoped out the little apartment. It was a pathetic place with nary a mark that would claim it as Medium Man's. In his home Mort had hung many things on the walls that were symbols of who he was: posters of fancy cars and fancy women, the mirror he got down at Harry's bar that lit up so the beer bottle was a pretty amber color, a picture of him and Georgia at city hall the day they got married, pictures of his kids that Georgia had taken by real professional photographers since the time they were babies. Mort loved those pictures. He had a favorite chair and had even helped Georgia pick out wallpaper for the bathroom. She didn't do a very good job hanging it, but it was the thought that counted. It was always the thought that counted.

Medium Man, on the other hand, lived as though he had disappeared but didn't know it yet. The furniture that came with his room was worn and ugly. The walls were bare. Old nails were visible where someone had once hung something. Faint outlines of those things still showed on the soiled walls. Hell, the nails were still in the wall. What would it have taken for Medium Man to hang something from those nails? The chair should have a pillow on it. That would make the place look homey. While he was looking around Mort saw the knife sticking out halfway from under the chair. He picked it up. Medium Man was definitely in a bad way if he left his knife on the floor.

"Mort, oh Mort. I want to tell you something." Medium Man rallied. Mort attended to his associate. It was the least he could do, considering.

"Yeah? What is it?"

"I had me a friend I really loved, Mort. Like you love Georgia. I loved him so much."

Mort's knees cracked as he got down close to Medium Man. He wanted to hear all about this since a friend could muck things up plenty. Plus, Mort was curious. He didn't think this guy knew anybody but him.

"Yeah? Why don't you tell me about him?"

"Oh, he was a good kid. I loved him," Medium Man blubbered. "That money? I wanted it for him. I was going to take him to this island. I really loved him, Mort. I really, really loved him."

Tears filled Medium Man's eyes. He threw his arms over his face but he could not console himself. His head whipped from side to side but the rest of him was eerily still as if he were tied down. Mort didn't like it when Medium Man got all strangeoid on him, so he took the man's arms away from over his eyes. He saw the blood on Medium Man's shirt and pants. This was looking worse by the minute.

"So what happened?" Mort asked. "He dump you for someone else?"

Medium Man rolled onto his side so he lay closer to the edge of the mattress; close enough that he could reach out and touch Mort but he didn't. Instead, he pulled up his knees and clasped his hands to his chest like a child.

"I killed him," Medium Man whispered.

"Why'd you do that?"

"He tried to leave me." Medium Man's head pounded into the mattress as he wailed and grieved. "I didn't mean to hurt him, but I saw him running away. I gave him everything, and he was leaving me, and I just got so mad. You understand that dontcha, Mort? I mean, what if Georgia was runnin' away from you?"

Mort thought about that. If she didn't take the kids he wouldn't mind too much. It would be sad, but he sure wouldn't kill her if she did. Mort didn't answer Medium man's question because he had one of his own.

"You sure he's dead?"

"He's so dead. I'm sure he is so dead," Medium Man answered, his eyes half closing as he gave in to grief and booze.

"You tell him anything about us?"

"Oh, no. Not about us. I took him to the funeral, but I didn't let him get out. I didn't say why we were there." Medium Man sighed. "I didn't tell him nothin' about you, or work, or nothin'."

"You friggin' idiot. You shouldn't have even been at the cemetery." Mort's hands came out of his pocket and he slapped the fool right across his head. Medium Man screamed and put his hands over his ears.

"He didn't ask why we were there and he's dead, Mort. He's so dead, and I'm going to be sick."

Mort dropped the knife to the floor and was grabbing Medium Man by the shoulders when a thought hit him like a ton of bricks.

"How did you get there? You took the car, didn't you? Didn't you?"

Mort shook Medium Man but all the man did was blubber, and sob, and roll away and clutch at himself. Now Medium Man was sorry that Mort had come to see him. Mort wasn't being nice. Still, he would be so alone if Mort left and he wouldn't have any work. It had been hard enough hooking up with Mort in the first place. So Medium Man cried and cried thinking about Mort leaving, and his dead boy, and being out of work. Mort sat back on his heels and shook his head. It was a pitiful sound to hear a man cry. It was even more pitiful to hear Medium Man cry. Even though Mort was very tired, he knew he had to rally and take care of things.

"Where'd you do it?" Mort asked.

"A couple of blocks down. In an alley," Medium Man sobbed.

"Okay. Okay." Mort patted the other man's shoulder. Then he took Medium Man's hands in his. He crossed them, wrist over wrist and held them tight. He promised: "I'll find him. You don't worry, okay?"

"Aw, Mort, you'd do that for me? You're like a brother

to me. Just like a brother." Medium Man said, rolling over and showing Mort a tear stained face.

"Yeah, I'm a real prince."

Medium Man smiled at his one, true friend. He looked like a beaten puppy that still stupidly hopes his abuser will pet him. Mort held Medium Man's hands in one of his. He gave them a little shake, looked at his *compadre* and said:

"Hush now."

The apartment building was brick, and there was no doubt it would collapse when the big one hit. Rotting fire escapes zigzagged up the side. Windows were open, catching nothing more than noise and dead air. People driving the freeway could look into the windows, but even at a crawl they would be gone too fast to fully appreciate the unique poverty and epic marginalization of the people who lived in this place. To the right and left of it were similar buildings, some with their windows blown out, some abandoned, some partially inhabited. One or two were under renovation. They were being turned into lofts. Young professionals would buy them in the hopes of staying alive long enough to see the area gentrified so they could turn a profit on their property.

There was a shoe repair shop to the left of the entrance of the building and a liquor store half a block down and across the street. Finn took the liquor store and Cori the shoe repair. When Finn came back Cori said:

"The cobbler hardly spoke English. I got nothing."

"No worries. Our man bought a fifth of Jim Beam. Came in all bloody. He scared the guy in the liquor store half to death, but he said Kramer just pointed, paid and went on his way. He knows he went this way because he watched to make sure he wasn't coming back."

"What time?"

"About five-thirty this morning," Finn said.

"Let's do it, then," Cori said.

Finn needed no more encouragement. He opened the narrow glass door that was scourged with graffiti. At one time there had been a doorknob but now there was only a round hole. Inside, the tiny lobby smelled of pee and smoke and sadness. The linoleum was cracked and peeling. Cori made for the mailboxes. Half of them were rusted shut, the other half hung open. Cori looked at apartment 201 but Kramer hadn't bothered to put his name on the box if he did live there.

They started up the stairs and the climbing was hard. The building was narrow and the builder had created an unnatural rise on the steps. The carpet was ripped, the stairs underneath concrete and the handrail wobbly. Finn was fairly certain that if they fell their heads would be cracked open long before they hit the linoleum.

The second floor was no different than the first. The air was close and hot, the light dim.

"They ought to nuke this place," Cori muttered.

Finn didn't disagree but he wasn't in a chatty frame of mind. They passed a payphone. Cori stuck a finger in the coin slot but it was empty. Finn got a step ahead of her so she caught up with him and took hold of the sleeve of his jacket. He stopped and looked at her.

"Do you want to call for a car?" she said.

"Lot of good it did us last time. You all right with that?"

"Yes."

Finn gave her hand a pat and they made their final approach. Cori moved ahead of Finn and positioned herself to the left of the door. Finn put himself on the right. He unzipped his jacket and retrieved his weapon; Cori strapped her purse across her body, opened it and got her gun. Finn raised his fist to knock but the minute he touched the door it opened an inch. He and Cori made eye contact. Finn put up his chin warning her to wait.

"Mr. Kramer. LAPD. We'd like to have a word with you, sir." Cori looked over her shoulder. The doors pocking the hallway stayed shut. Finn called again: "Mr. Kramer, sir."

When the response again was silence, Finn took a deep and silent breath. He pushed open the door and both of them lay tighter against their respective walls. In the next second when they weren't met with gunfire and no knife was flung at them, when they didn't hear the window being wrenched up as Kramer tried to go down the fire escape, they moved in, split-stepped, and gave the space a cop's once over.

The apartment was dark, the shades drawn. There was a bathroom on the right near Finn but it was small and there was nowhere for anybody to hide. There was a couch, a chair and, on a mattress under the window, a fully clothed man. He was face down, his legs sprawled, his toes touched the floor, and his hands were underneath him. There was an empty bottle of booze on the floor beside the mattress. A shaft of sunlight wove its way through the drawn blinds and landed atop the man's head making him look like he had been scalped.

"Mr. Kramer. LAPD."

Finn locked his right arm to steady his weapon. Sweat

trickled down his back. The gun felt like a stone in his hand. A prone man, a silent man, was no promise of an easily controlled man. He moved to the head of the mattress. Cori kicked at the man's foot.

"Out cold." Cori trained her weapon on him as Finn holstered his. He bent from the waist and took hold of Kramer's shoulder to flip him but the man was damn heavy. He used both hands.

"Mr. Kramer. Come, my friend," he said. "Wake up now and talk to us."

Just then the man went over hard and Finn swore.

"Ah, Mother of God."

Cori's shoulder's slumped. She put her gun back in her purse and stood staring at the blood soaked mattress and the man's wrists that were cut deep and clean. Finn put two fingers to his throat.

"Gone to God, he is," Finn said.

"Least he didn't leave much of a mess," Cori said. "They'll have this place rented by tomorrow."

Cori was right. John Kramer had known where to cut, rolled onto his stomach, and bled into the mattress beneath him. They would toss the mattress and that would be it, the end of Mr. Kramer as the world knew him. Except the world didn't know him. No one, it seemed, knew anything about this guy except for a boy who was lying in the morgue and a person with red hair. Without this man it was going to be hard to find the ginger. As Finn pondered their next step, Finn saw the knife that was wedged between the wall and the top of the mattress. He picked it up, careful to use only the tips of his fingers on the hilt. He held it in the shaft of light coming through the blinds. The blood on the finely honed blade sparkled and Finn O'Brien knew he had been wrong about where this man was headed. The knick at the end of that blade was pointing the way directly to hell.

CHAPTER 41

They had been busy bees, calling for the meat wagon, directing the techs to go over the place with a fine-tooth comb in the hopes of identifying prints that might lead them to the red haired man who had been in the Barnett's house with John Kramer. By the time everyone arrived, Cori and Finn had already done a thorough sweep. There was little enough to see in the place: some clothes, processed food, a few dishes, a comic book, playing cards, and newspapers. Lots of newspapers. It did not escape their notice that the article about the Barnett girls' funeral and the one about the reward were set aside.

When they were done, they headed back to Wilshire to assure Captain Fowler all was not lost and that they would have DNA in a few short days to match against that under the nanny's nails, they would have confirmation on the knife as one of the murder weapons and they would move heaven and hell to get a handle on who John Kramer was, and his known associates. Finn assured their captain that they were closer to a press conference where he could put this matter to rest and the ladies of Fremont Place could be assured that all was right with the world again.

"I'm going to hit the little girl's room," Cori said as they went down the hall. "Then I'll check in with Earl and see if they pulled up anything on Kramer yet."

Finn nodded and went on to their office, wishing they had been assigned space in the bullpen. At times like this it was good to be with your own kind, drawing energy from the work of others. But an office was his home for now and when Finn turned into it he found that it was smaller still because another big man was sitting in his chair.

He was tall and narrow, where Finn was broad of shoulder and solid. This man's eyes were green and startling in his pale, narrow face. They were the only things Finn saw at first because his low brows and short lashes were so light as to be almost nonexistent. His hair was cropped close like a man who had seen service and it was red – not fiery red or even ginger but strawberry. He was conservatively well dressed in a dark suit and red tie. His shoes were spit shined. Finn knew this because those shoes were on his desk, this man's ankles crossed to show them off to their best advantage.

"You're in my chair, friend," Finn said as he took off his jacket and hung it on the hook behind the door.

The man's feet dropped. He apologized even though he looked none too sorry. "Nobody knew when you'd be back so I made myself at home."

"What are you? Internal affairs? I warn you now, I'm not quite feeling it for Internal Affairs just at the moment."

Finn stared down the man until he got the idea that he

was in Finn's way. He stood up, shuffled around Finn to the other side of the desk, and sat in Cori's chair. Finn decided he had no manners and should be invited to go about his business elsewhere. Before Finn could move him on, he said:

"Have you done something Internal Affairs would find interesting?"

"If you have to ask that, then you are not one of them," Finn replied.

The man reached over and put out his hand.

"Taylor. SEC. Security and Exchange Commission."

Finn's eyebrow rose. He took the man's hand and shook it.

"O'Brien–"

"Hey, O'Brien, we've got–" Cori came into the office with her nose buried in a ream of paper but she stopped short and glared at Taylor.

"You're in my chair."

Taylor got up again.

"You people are touchy about your chairs."

"Detective Anderson, this is Taylor. SEC. I was just about to ask to what do we owe the pleasure."

"And I was about to tell you that I came to talk about Eros Manufacturing," he said and then he looked around. "Think I could get a chair?"

"...so we took note of the activity. Your people were searching files on that company and we had it flagged. Then when you visited their offices, we really got interested. We'd like to know what your interest is in Eros?"

"Why didn't you just call and ask?" Finn said.

"I did, but you never returned the call," Taylor shifted in his chair. The only one Cori could find was straight backed and made of wood and she got the feeling Taylor was used to something a little cushier.

"Sorry about that. Sometimes things coming to me get misplaced," Finn said.

"I don't mind getting out of the office now and again to see how the other half lives," Taylor said. "So, what's your interest in Eros?"

Finn swiveled and chanced a glance at Cori. The edge of her lip ticked up. She crossed her legs and her arms, as curious as he was.

"We're investigating a triple murder involving a family: two children and a nanny. We've run down a possible problem with the mother and her work at a mental health clinic. That was a dead end. The nanny was dealing porn overseas, but we're not liking that link. The father is an attorney named Sam Barnett. He and the missus were over in Europe when this happened.

"We are thinking there might be some involvement between the attorney and the nanny so we were running down European connections. We also talked to his former partner who indicated that Eros Manufacturing was the client that broke up the partnership. He wouldn't tell us what the problem was; he would only say there was a difference of opinion about taking them on. I went to the Eros offices hoping to find out what made the place a hot button, but I didn't get anything. The only intersection is that Mr. Barnett has been to Switzerland and the nanny shipped product to Switzerland. We're not into her computer yet so we have nothing to cross-reference with Barnett. Eros doesn't even have a sales rep in those countries. It looks like that's a dead end, too."

Finn opened his hands and bounced a little in his chair.

"I intend to go back to the ex-partner and see if I can get a more satisfactory answer out of him about the beef he and Barnett had over this client. We are getting desperate for a motive. My gut is telling me Barnett is somehow involved. My partner isn't so sure, and that's it."

"I think you are on the right track, but it doesn't have anything to do with porn." Taylor said. "The Swiss connection is solid but it's more complicated than that. PolyGain is a conglomerate headquartered in Zurich and that's where we're looking. It owns a number of other companies that supply parts for airplanes, cars, and buses – pretty much anything that moves. Widgets are big business, but none has a bigger widget business than PolyGain."

"Barnett is an attorney for PolyGain? He's successful, but that puts his practice on another level," Finn noted.

"PolyGain isn't his client, at least they aren't on the books," Taylor answered. "Mr. Barnett and others like him are retained to buy up stock in small companies. Eros isn't Barnett's client, it's his mark. Barnett's clients don't exist except as straw men for PolyGain. He handles all the legalities, stock transfers, etcetera, but what he is really doing is helping PolyGain monopolize the manufacturing market for items that control every form of mass transportation in the world. We are talking about knobs, levers, bolts, nuts, transformers. Barnett is buying up Eros stock for Polygain."

Cori whistled. Finn was impressed, too.

"They could shut down every train, airplane, car, and

bus if they wanted," Finn said.

"And that makes for a heck of a lot of leverage with every government in the world. No wonder hammers cost a grand," Cori said.

"So you see why we wanted to intervene before you went too much further," Taylor said. "I needed to find out what you had."

"Is Barnett going to be indicted?" Finn asked.

"Not yet. We hope to get indictments in home countries simultaneously. We can't touch PolyGain without a few squealers." Taylor lost the half amused tone and got down to brass tacks. "The Barnett murders showed up on my desk three days ago. I didn't think much of it–"

"You're a hard man, Taylor, if it didn't give you more than a pause," Finn noted.

"As a human being I sympathized, as an agent it meant nothing to my investigation," Taylor responded. "So I was curious about what you were thinking when you moved into our territory and that was all. Then this morning something else came across my desk. There was an attorney in Italy who was cooperating. His house blew up killing the entire family. It looks like someone's trying to shut down our investigation the old fashioned way."

"We've got two survivors on our end." Cori picked up the phone and dialed. She listened and then cut the call off.

"Mrs. Barnett isn't answering."

She dialed again and spoke to Barnett's secretary who said he was at home. Cori made one more call and then said:

"Barnett isn't answering either."

"I'll take her." Finn got up and reached for his jacket. "Cori, you get him. You have the mister's new address?"

"I'm on it," she said as she grabbed her jacket and purse.

Taylor was up, too. He stepped in front of the door.

"Hey. Hey. Hold up a minute," he said. "Don't go off half-cocked and compromise my investigation. You can corral them, but you make sure what I told you about PolyGain stays under wraps."

Finn smiled and set him aside. "As I said, a superior human being, Mr. Taylor."

Cori hurried out the door only a step behind Finn. The last thing he and Cori heard was a warning from the SEC agent.

"You don't know who you're dealing with."

Finn almost laughed at that. He had a damn good idea who he was dealing with. A dirty attorney named Sam Barnett.

CHAPTER 42

DAY 9 – EARLY EVENING

There were four gardeners finishing their work when Finn drove up to the Barnett house. He parked behind the truck at the curb, got out, put on his jacket and breathed in the scent of grass clippings. The lawn was as neat as a putting green; the bushes pruned as precisely as a Brazilian wax.

The man with a blower turned it aside while the detective went by. The house was quiet, the curtains drawn. It was a massive thing, too big even for a family. Now it was in danger of becoming Elizabeth Barnett's mausoleum and Finn was glad he was here to take her away. He rang the bell and when the door opened, the words of greeting for the missus were never uttered.

"Mr. Barnett," Finn said.

"What is it?" There was no pretense of civility.

"Detective Anderson is on her way to your apartment."

He stepped onto the porch and half closed the door. "What's going on?"

"We have reason to believe that both of you might be in some danger. We want to get you some place safe until we figure out what's going on. So, if you would collect your wife–"

"Either you tell me the nature of this threat or you get out of here. I've got my hands full with Elizabeth as it is."

Sam Barnett gave Finn no more than thirty-seconds to answer before he stepped back inside and started to close the door. Finn put his hand out and stopped him.

"We know about Eros Manufacturing."

Sam Barnett stopped and the blood drained from his face, but the man's mind was working overtime, putting together the proper response, one that couldn't be used against him in a court of law. Finn didn't want him to have that time.

"I don't give a piss what you're doing on paper, but we're not talking paper now. There might be people who want you dead because of your shenanigans."

"I don't know what –," Sam began.

"Own it, man. In Italy a family was killed because the father was doing exactly what you're doing. Is protecting dirty money worth looking over your shoulder for the rest of your life? Was it worth your daughters' lives?" Finn was begging now. "Please, sir. What will come will come, but now we need both of you to be away from here until this is sorted out."

Sam Barnett looked at Finn's hand on the door and Finn looked at the man's face. What beauty he once had was lost in the dark-rim of his eyes, the sunken cheeks and the pallor of his skin. He wore his fancy clothes, all well cut by a tailor, but those clothes looked like they had been slept in for days.

"Please, Mr. Barnett. Please. I want to save your wife at least."

At the mention of Elizabeth Barnett, the lawyer threw off the detective's hand, stepped back and pushed the door hard. Instinctively, Finn threw out both hands and pushed back.

"You arrogant son of a bitch. Elizabeth is my wife, I will protect her."

"Listen to me," Finn said as he wedged himself between the door and the frame. "Listen, man. I'll not tell the missus about your business. I will not breathe a word to upset her more."

"She wouldn't understand you even if you did. She can't talk to you or anyone."

Sam Barnett's breath was shallow and it was catching on tears but Finn had seen Sam Barnett look this way before. He had seen him look like this the day he found his children murdered. The lawyer knew then that he was responsible for the deaths in his house and he said nothing. It was Barnett's cowardice that angered Finn more than anything.

"Let me by you, or I swear I will go over you."

Sam's eyes darted over his shoulder and that was enough for Finn. He pushed that door with all his might, face-to-face, nose-to-nose with the attorney until with one last, huge effort Finn pushed and the lawyer lost his footing. Finn rushed into the house, calling as he went.

"Mrs. Barnett! Mrs. Barnett!"

Finn's foot was on the first stair when Sam spun him around.

"What do you think you're doing? Stop, you'll make it worse."

Finn looked down on the man. He wanted to hit him, shove him out of this house and gather Elizabeth Barnett up and keep her safe. Instead, he caught the lawyer's wrist.

"I am concerned for the welfare of your wife, Mr. Barnett," Finn said evenly. "I am within my rights as an officer of the law to enter this home whether you like it or not."

"You have no rights here and you know it. " Sam Barnett hissed.

Finn tossed aside the man's arm and turned his back, but before he was half way up the long staircase, Sam Barnett let out a howl of anger and lunged at Finn. The attack, though, was over before it had begun when Sam caught sight of Elizabeth standing on the landing above, watching them. Finn's head snapped around and he pushed Sam aside and went for her.

"Elizabeth? Are you all right?"

"Don't come up here. Don't." Elizabeth put out her hand to stop him.

Sam took advantage of the moment and tried to pass but the detective put out his arm, barring him. Sam fell hard against the railing, breaking one of the spindles as he tried to catch himself to keep from falling. Finn paid him no mind. He only had eyes for the woman.

"Are you alright, missus?" Finn's voice rolled through the big, near empty house.

"Leave her alone," Sam cried, but Finn turned on him and pounded down the stairs. He took Sam Barnett by the collar of his very expensive shirt and pulled him close.

"A normal human being would be appreciative of an officer's concern, so either you're scared or you're responsible for this. Which is it, Mr. Barnett?"

"Get your hands off me," Sam said.

"Detective O'Brien!"

Finn looked over his shoulder, angry to be interrupted. This was no longer about dead children, a nanny cold in her grave, a greedy corporation or a greedy lawyer. It was about this woman and her mother's heart and Finn O'Brien so much wanted to save her from this cowardly man.

"Let go of Sam," she pleaded. "Don't hurt him. Please."

Finn hesitated. He held her gaze – her warm blue eyes looking deep into his icy ones. It was then, seeing how much she wanted this man, that he did as she asked.

To Elizabeth Barnett he said: "Can you come down here, missus. Please."

Elizabeth shook her head and her husband bounded up the stairs and took her in his arms. She put her face against his shoulder as he led her into the little girls' room. Finn hung his head. He had no standing. She was not under duress. She had made her choice. Finn turned around but before he got down the stairs, Sam Barnett called to him.

"O'Brien." Finn raised his eyes. "Look at the walls."

Finn did as Sam directed and saw that all the pictures of the little girls were gone. Some of the furniture in the fine rooms was covered with sheets.

"Is she leaving here, then?" Finn asked.

"No," Sam answered and indicated the girls' room. "Everything is in there; every picture and video of our children. Everything they ever touched. Now leave us alone. I will get her the help she needs, I will make sure no one hurts her and that includes you. Now, get out of my house."

From where he stood atop the stairs, Sam watched through the half moon window above the door. Finn O'Brien appeared in pieces through that window: his head, his wide shoulders, his long legged body. He walked slowly, a gunslinger going off into the sunset. When he got in his car and drove away, Sam ran his hands through his hair as he looked over the house. He made a sound that was part laugh, part sob. The SEC. O'Brien had told him that like he was giving Sam a peek into hell. The SEC was the least of his worries. He went back to girls' room. Elizabeth was sitting on the box springs of Alana's bed surrounded by pictures of the girls, cradling the bundle of curtains.

"Is he gone?"

"Yes, sweetheart. He's gone." Sam was careful to speak slowly and move cautiously.

"I didn't want him to hurt you, Sam," she said.

"I don't want him to hurt you, either, Elizabeth."

"I'm glad you're home, Sam. I don't think I can live without you."

"Oh, Elizabeth."

Sam sat down on the box spring opposite his wife. He was exhausted from his sadness and their passionate, at odds desire for things that could not be: Elizabeth wanting Sam to come home and start again; Sam seeking a way to protect Elizabeth from herself. They didn't talk for the longest time.

Instead, they looked at the little ballerina box their daughters' had loved and the thing lying next to it. That thing was the gun Sam Barnett bought to protect his family, the one Elizabeth kept under lock and key until now. It was the gun she threatened to use if he did not come back and make their home happy again.

CHAPTER 43

DAY 10 – LATE MORNING

"Detective O'Brien?" Tina put her head into Finn's office. "Captain wants to see you. Make it snappy."

He put his hand on Cori's shoulder. She had been hunkered over the computer, going through files, and sending out bulletins on John Kramer and the boy in the morgue.

"Think that means both of us?" Cori asked.

Finn hadn't pulled any punches when he told her about what happened at the Barnett house so he knew full well this was about him.

"No, I do not. You take off when you're done."

Cori nodded and went back to her work. When she looked up again, she was surprised to see a half hour had gone by. Finn was not back so she put on her jacket, took up her purse and headed out, slowing when she saw three people in the hall, heads tipped, as they strained to make sense of the raised voices coming from Fowler's office. Raised voices were never a good thing in a police station but it was really bad when one of them was Finn O'Brien's. She started to walk more quickly, stopping again when a door slammed. Finn stormed out of the captain's office, strode down the hall and paused long enough to say:

"Sam Barnett filed assault charges. I'm suspended."

"The hell you say."

"I say. Fowler says. You keep–"

Cori was past Finn and into Fowler's office before Tina could stop her. The door slammed, she put her butt up against it and opened her mouth. Captain Fowler beat her to the punch.

"I don't want to hear it, Anderson, so get the hell out of my office."

"I've got to say it, Captain, so you might as well listen up." Her great chest heaved but Fowler had a bead on her eyes and his gaze was unwavering. His jaw worked. Finally he said:

"Speak."

"You don't know me from Adam, but I'm telling you I don't make waves unless I'm pretty sure that the boat I'm tippin' deserves it and boy, this one does. We've come as far as we have on this case because of O'Brien."

"Don't give him the power, Anderson," Fowler warned.

"I'm not. I swear." She pushed off the door and put both her hands on his desk. "I know I'm good but he's better, Captain. O'Brien's instincts. His decision-making. His risk taking on behalf of the victims, that's got us where we are. That's what being a cop is about. Right? Right?"

Fowler wasn't buying it so Cori cast about for the right words. She grabbed a chair and sat down, eye to eye with her captain.

"Look, you asked me to come here, and I did because

both of us know that O'Brien is a good cop. The difference between us is that I can say it and you can't. I get it. So see, we're not disagreeing. Are we, Captain?"

Fowler tossed his pen aside and looked away from her. He looked tired but that came with the job so Cori didn't feel bad for him.

"No, we're not, but he's crossed a line. You had sketchy info from the SEC. There was no direct threat, but O'Brien acted like there was. That is not good police work."

"That was his gut."

"I repeat, not good police work," Fowler said. "The only way to satisfy Barnett is O'Brien's head or the heads of the people who killed his kids. Bring me something I can hang my hat on in twenty-four hours or I turn it over to internal affairs."

"That's just plain impossible and you know it," Cori complained.

"Then that's it," Fowler said. "I'll put you with Schumacher until a decision is made about O'Brien."

"You mean the putz that wouldn't work with O'Brien? Don't do me any favors," Cori drawled.

"Then that's it for you, too. Is that what you want after all this?"

"No," Cori answered miserably.

"Look, both of you did a good job. Be proud, but don't put your blinders on. O'Brien brought this on himself." Fowler gave her a nod. "Twenty-four hours is the best I can do, Anderson. Take it or leave it."

"Yes, sir."

As much as Cori wanted to make a brilliant argument for seeing this play out to the end with Finn, she knew she had no words to convince Bob Fowler so she walked her way back: out Fowler's door, past Tina who seemed sad, down the hall and into the office where Finn was packing up. Since he had nothing personal in the office, he was housekeeping the files she would need to move ahead.

"I didn't help much," she said.

"Did you think you would?"

"Yeah, I did." She lifted a shoulder and passed him a grin. "We've got twenty-four hours. If we don't have something big for Barnett you're gone and I'm working with Schumacher."

"Then I shall pray for a miracle for sure," Finn said.

"You do that, O'Brien."

Cori flopped into her chair. She kicked at the leg of the desk and gnawed on her bottom lip, trying to think of something that would make this better. Hoping for a miracle just wasn't going to cut it. She sat forward.

"Shove me the phone."

Finn did. He leaned against the wall and watched Cori dial, and wait, and wait. She sat up fast when it was answered.

"Mr. Barnett?" Cori clamped the phone between shoulder and cheek and slid a pad of paper her way. "Detective Anderson here. I just wanted to let you know how sorry I am that Detective O'Brien's behavior upset you yesterday."

She listened.

"Yes, I do understand that he upset your wife, too. In fact, I'd like to speak to Mrs. Barnett, if I could. I'd just like to apologize personally." Cori fell silent again. "No, of course. I understand now isn't a good time. Maybe I could drop by a little later to introduce my new partner."

Cori listened.

"I could come alone then. I'd like to bring over a picture of the man we believe was in your home. Would that be all right?"

Cori waited.

"No? I see. Yes, of course I understand. Sure. Of course, she should see the doctor tomorrow. Uh-huh. Yep. No problem. I'll check back in. Sure."

She hung up and sat back, pulling her bottom lip under her top teeth.

"What do you think?" Finn asked.

"I think it's time to go home," Cori answered.

She couldn't look at Finn because he would see that she thought he was wrong. Sam Barnett sounded worried not crazy. That meant one of any number of things: Finn had flipped because the idea of dead kids was too much for him, or Elizabeth Barnett hit him where he lived because of what his mother went through. It could be that Finn hit rock bottom because he knew they would never find out who was responsible for this mess in the same way he had never found the person who killed Alexander. Or – and this was the worst – maybe Finn O'Brien was just Irish pissed at everyone and should never have been allowed back at work.

"I'll catch up with you later, Cori."

Finn kissed her atop her head.

"Sooner than later, O'Brien," she answered, unable to look at him.

That sooner or later she had promised him had come a lot sooner than even she thought it would. Two hours after Finn had left the office, Cori was opening her door to him.

"Geoffrey is a bit miffed at you, Cori. I was on my way to running up the biggest tab Mick's has ever seen."

"You're not wasted," she said as she led him into the living room.

"We were just lining them up when you called." Finn dropped into a chair, his long legs splayed. He looked neither tired nor angry, he looked accepting and that was something she had never seen in Finn O'Brien. "Are there no children about?"

"They're watching T.V. in the back."

Cori took the couch, a floral number that was wearing thin at the arms. There was a playpen in the corner and Finn could see a highchair pushed up against the table in the space they called a dining room but which was really nothing more that a space between the living room and kitchen. Cori picked up her mail but before she could speak, Finn opened his hands, raised his eyebrows.

"If you're going to be offering me a drink, now's the time," Finn said.

"I think you're going to need your wits, cowboy." She held out the stack of mail. "Take a look at this."

He fanned the stack but looked at her curiously when he found nothing of interest.

"Third one," she directed. Finn pulled out an oversized postcard and tossed the rest the mail on the coffee table. "Other side."

Finn flipped it and then, it seemed, he stopped breathing.

"I took Amber to that place every year to get her picture taken until she was fourteen. Now I take her and

Tucker. I'm on the mailing list for life. When you sign the contract there's a release to use the pictures for advertising purposes."

Finn heard everything she said, but he had been rendered speechless by the picture on the postcard. Staring back at him, grinning their best Sunday grins, were two little girls, their heads crowned with frizzy red hair, and around their necks, in strange contrast to their cheap, frilly dresses, were two exquisite necklaces. The pendants were shaped like octagons; they were etched, Finn knew, with names that were not theirs. And when the photographer's flash went off, it was reflected back by the two small diamonds placed just above the 'i' in Alexis and the tail of the 'a' in Alana.

CHAPTER 44

DAY 10 – EVENING

They took Finn's car to the home of Georgia Peyton, the woman whose children were on that postcard by default when the intended image disappeared into the printer's computer, never to be seen again. After a bit of wrangling on Cori's part, the store gave up the information they were looking for. Since Finn agreed to Cori's lead, he stepped aside when she called for backup.

Lang was an old timer, burly and near retirement, comfortable in his own skin. Williams was fresh out the academy and kept his hand on the butt of his weapon as if he couldn't believe it belonged to him. Neither of them wanted to shake Finn's hand: Lang clearly knew O'Brien's history and Williams, even if it wasn't as fresh in his mind, followed his partner lead. Finn took no offense but he didn't want this nasty thing coming between the job. He stepped in and took a moment with the big man.

"We're good on this are we not, friend?"

"No beef while we're on the clock," Lang answered. Finn took a look at the young cop, but he didn't have to ask the question because Lang had the answer. "He's good, too."

"Appreciated," Finn answered.

"As I said, not on the clock."

Where the line was drawn was all Finn needed to know. Once he knew that, he could choose to step over it and so could his brothers in blue. Finn gave nod to Cori, who had left her purse and carried her weapon under her jacket at the small of her back.

"Okey-dokey, folks. We're looking at number 4241," Cori said. "I've got Deputy D.A. Palmer working on warrants, so until then we just want to get a look at things. We think there are two little girls, the mother and the man we're looking for in that house. His name is Peyton – don't have a first name. Kinky red hair is all we got at the moment. We've got Earl running Peyton through the system but he doesn't have anything for us yet. We do know that the guy's a pro so stay sharp."

"What are we looking at him for?" Lang asked.

"The Barnett murders. If this man is in the house, and won't talk to us we'll fall back until we get that warrant. But if he bolts, we're on him. Is that understood?" Everyone nodded including Finn. "Okay. Lang and Williams, I want you invisible one on either side of the house. Let's do it."

They moved their cars: the detective's in front of 4241 and the black and white just out of sight line. Lang and Williams took up their stations, Finn and Cori walked up to the front door.

"I start the conversation, O'Brien."

"Sure," Finn answered.

"If you say anything, then you follow my lead," she warned. "I'm not kidding."

"I wouldn't cross you," he said.

"Never lie to a woman with a gun tucked in her britches, O'Brien."

Cori pulled out a step ahead and Finn let her go, but when they stood in front of the door he was by her side. She knocked. When no one answered, Finn pushed the bell and that's when Georgia Peyton presented herself. She gave Finn a smile that was stretched tight like her yellow T-shirt.

"Mrs. Peyton?" Cori said.

"Yeah."

Her black-rimmed eyes narrowed as she looked at Cori and her smile contracted faster than a cheap girdle.

"I'm Detective Anderson, this is Detective O'Brien of the Los Angeles Police Department."

"Yeah." Georgia said again, not particularly impressed by Cori. She was, however, curious about the big, handsome cop. He smiled at her and reached into his pocket. He showed her the postcard.

"Are these your lovely children, Mrs. Peyton?" Finn asked, his brogue like a dollop of honey atop his sweet question.

Georgia's eyes went to the photo. She shifted her weight. A wrinkle of worry snaked between her eyes.

"Is there a law against havin' cute kids?"

"No ma'am. Beautiful, they are," Finn said and when he kept smiling that wrinkle between Georgia Peyton's eyes almost disappeared.

"Have they done something?"

"No. Absolutely not," Cori assured her. "We just wanted to make sure we had the right family. Is your husband home?"

"Yeah." The woman chomped on that word like it was

a piece of gristle. She shifted her weight again.

"Can we talk to him?" Cori asked. "It won't take a minute."

"He's been out all day so he's kinda tired. I take care of the kids anyway, so you can just talk to me about them, except not now 'cause I was just getting dinner. So, I have to go 'cause Mort doesn't like his dinner to be late."

Georgia stepped back and put her hand on the door sure that these people spelled bad news for Mort. Finn, though, needing to see good old Mort, stepped forward and turned the Irish charm up a notch.

"We know it's late, missus. We appreciate that you're a busy mum," he said, his blue eyes tight with hers. " 'Tis amazing how well you look considering you have two little ones to look after, but we only need to ask your husband one wee question about his work. Please, missus, if you would be so kind."

Finn edged ever closer, keeping his hand high on the door to hold it open. Georgia's huge breasts quivered, her eyelashes fluttered, and she licked her lips.

"I guess it's okay," she breathed. "We don't want no trouble. I mean, that's what we're going to get if he don't talk to you, right?"

"Oh, no, missus, no trouble," Finn assured her. "Just a question. A wee minute of his time."

"Yeah. I guess a minute is okay." Georgia thought a second, took one more good, long look at Finn and said: "You wait here, okay?"

Georgia closed the door. Cori and Finn stood at ease, their hands clasped behind their back. They counted off the seconds. Finn had counted to three when he heard Cori say:

"Oh, no, missus. No trouble missus."

Cori mimicked him, brogue and all, and Finn smirked. He counted off one more second and heard her say:

"You are friggin' brilliant."

Georgia leaned against the door and took a minute. She put a hand to her heart that was near beating a hole through her chest. Part of it was because the cop on the stoop was so damn gorgeous, but most of it was because she was so damn dumb. Dumb. Dumb. Dumb. How dumb could she be? Not much more than she already was. Mort wasn't going to be happy that she told them he was home, but there was nothing to be done about it now. She would have to take her lumps 'cause it was a sure bet that they weren't going away until they saw him.

"Jesus Christ All Mighty, Mort," she muttered as she hurried toward the bathroom. "What have you done?"

Georgia threw herself against the door and whisper-hollered at her husband, her hands cupped on the sides of her mouth like a mini-megaphone.

"Mort! Mort, you shit! Mort, get off the can. There's cops at the door and they want to talk to you now."

"What kind?" Mort's voice was muffled and sounded kind of sexy coming through the door.

Georgia breathed a sigh of relief. He didn't sound like he was falling-off-the-john-mad-as-a- hornet so she whisper-hollered back.

"How the hell do I know what kind? Cop cops." She wondered if she sounded sexier talking through the cheap door, too.

"Do they have uniforms?"

The toilette flushed, Georgia opened the door a

342

smidgen, and stuck her head in. Mort was zipping his pants and she could see his face in the mirror over the sink. His pale skin was almost green and his eyes shined bright like he had a fever.

"Baby, you okay? You sick?"

Georgia squeezed in behind him. She reached for the side of his face, her long nails held at an angle so they wouldn't scratch him while she checked for a temperature. He knocked her hand aside, twirled around, and grabbed her by the shoulders. Mort danced her out of the bathroom and around the corner to the bedroom.

"What kind of cops, Georgia?" Mort demanded.

"A guy cop with an accent and a broad in regular clothes. I think there's a guy in a uniform near the neighbor's, but I couldn't be sure," Georgia whispered.

"What did they say? Exactly."

"The ones at the door had that picture of the girls. Remember? I told you I took 'em to have their picture taken at the department store. And, well, they put it on the thing they mail out to people. Sort of like, advertising. It's a real cute picture."

"What picture, Georgia?" Mort pushed her back up against the wall.

"Ow, Mort!" she yelped. He looked at the dresser and then pushed her toward it. The top of it was covered with pictures of the girls. "Which one Georgia?"

She plucked a frame off the top. "This one. This picture."

Mort grabbed it and held it up to the light. His hand fell to his side. He hung his head. He swore, and swore, and swore some more in a really low voice that Georgia had never heard before. Suddenly, he whirled away from

343

her and smashed the frame onto the edge of the dresser. Georgia squealed, glass flew, and Mort seemed to grow ten inches taller before he threw himself on the bed, buried his face in his hands and tried to contain his fury.

"You had their pictures taken with those lockets on? Shit, Georgia. You are the stupidest broad on earth. You had their picture taken!"

"So what?"

She was done with this. Georgia tried to get close to the bed. The broken glass crunched under her feet and shards poked through the thin soles of her slippers, but she moved in on him anyway.

"Did you steal them Mort? If you did, just give them back and the cops'll go away. They're only a couple of necklaces. I mean it, Mort. Just give 'em back."

He sat up straight and pushed her away as he scrambled off the bed. Georgia fell back, almost losing her balance. Mort went to the bedroom window even though he knew he couldn't get out that way. It was barred like every other one in the house. That left the front door or the back. In the back he would have to scale the fence and the wall behind that.

He could try the front, but he wouldn't get very far if there were more cops around that Georgia didn't see. He could try to talk to them. Yeah, he could fake it. He could pretend he didn't know nothing about nothing. What did they have on him? Just a picture. Yeah, that's what he'd say.

And they didn't have a warrant or they would have showed Georgia. They would have him in cuffs by now if they had a warrant. They'd be tearing up the place if they had a warrant. And what were they going to find?

Nothing. No lockets that was for sure. He could say that they borrowed them from someone. He could say he found them. Yeah, borrowed 'em from Hussein's Pawn 'cause good old Hussein hardly ever knew what he had in stock. It was the cops who were at the disadvantage. Not him. Naw, this was his turf.

But there was the gun. If they got that he was screwed for sure. He threw himself on the bed, grabbed his piece, got up and stuck it in his pants and straight-armed his wife.

"Get out of my way, Georgia."

"What are you doing? I gotta tell them something."

Georgia prattled while Mort rummaged through the bureau drawer coming up with fifty bucks. If he worked this right he would be out of the neighborhood before they knew he was gone. He dragged Georgia to the bedroom door, twisted her arm, and yanked her into him.

"Shut up, Georgia, and listen."

He spoke softly, which was scarier than when he talked loud. Georgia turned her head away. She didn't like the way Mort smelled when he sweated.

"I want you to go out there and..." Mort yanked harder to make sure he had her attention. "Listen to me talking."

Georgia's eyes rattled and she nodded hard.

"Good. Go tell them I'll be out in a minute. Go out onto the step and close the door behind you, but not hard so they think something's up. Just kind of natural, so they can't see inside the house. I'm going out the back, but I don't want them to see me. Got that?"

"Yeah, Mort. Sure," Georgia whimpered, positive that he didn't know how hard he was holding onto her. "But, baby, where are you going? When will you be back? What will happen to me?"

"Just do what I say, and do it now." He flung her toward the door. Georgia stumbled, one foot sliding off her high-heeled slippers. She blinked hard and mascara flaked her cheeks. Behind her, Mort was still giving directions. "Do it casual, Georgia. Give me some time."

She nodded, pulled herself up as straight as she could, and then walked back through the house a lot slower than she had walked through it the first time. She looked back once, but Mort waved her on with an upraised fist. Georgia took a deep breath, plastered a smile on her face, opened the door and stepped out.

"It seems I was mistaken," she began as sweetly as she knew how, holding the door half closed behind her the way Mort said she should. "I thought my husband was home, but he must have left without telling me, and–"

While Georgia talked, Finn kept his eye on the ever-diminishing view of the interior of the house. Cori made girl noises, trying to keep the woman's attention as Finn moved to his left. Georgia countered, pulling the door just a little tighter against her rump, her eyes darting between Cori and Finn. It was too little too late. She had blown it.

"Out the back! Blue shirt. Red hair," Finn bellowed.

Finn threw Georgia aside. Cori caught her and put her against the wall, ignoring the woman's screams of outrage as Finn sprinted through the living room and into the kitchen, seconds behind Mort Peyton.

Finn got a bead on everything as he went on: the dishes in the sink, the nail polish bottle on the table, the pictures of kids held to the refrigerator with magnets shaped like food. On the television, Vanna White clapped her hands while someone spun the wheel looking for fortune. The back door was still bouncing.

Finn exploded through it, into a backyard of scrub and trash. To his right, a Rottweiler paced and snapped. To Finn's left, Mort Peyton hung on the chain link fence, legs pumping as he tried to get a toehold and make his escape.

"Stop."

Finn pulled up short at the sound of a voice he didn't recognize. Mort looked over his shoulder, Finn looked toward the dark corridor between the Peyton house and the neighbor's. Williams, the young buck who was still wet behind the ears, appeared with gun in hand.

"Stop. Police."

His voice shook and Finn's heart beat double time but then he saw Cori coming up behind. Williams was in hand, so Finn attended to the man on the fence.

"Mr. Peyton, drop now. To the ground, hands in sight."

Finn advanced with a measured step, stopping when he was close enough to see the bugger in all his glory. He was an insignificant little man, worried about his own worthless rear end, so fearful of what may happen to him. All that would happen would be that he would enjoy the due process of law. Coward. Coward who killed women and children.

"Drop you little turd!" Finn demanded.

The dog was barking like a hound from hell. The red haired man's fingers were slipping and when he saw Finn O'Brien he looked sick. Then Mort Peyton looked away and his skinny butt started gyrating again.

"Damn," Finn muttered, and started for the man on the fence.

Before he took more than one step, Mort Peyton lost his grip and fell to the ground hard, landing with his legs splayed and his arms akimbo. Blood poured down the right side of his face where he scraped it against the rusted chain link. Only his eyes still worked the way he wanted them to. Quick and bright, he checked out the opposition, assessed his chances, got a second wind and went flying for the fence again. That was when everything went to hell.

Finn started to move.

Williams raised his gun.

Cori screamed, "Stop."

And a little girl burst out of the shed on the corner of the property.

"Daddy! Daddy!" she cried as she flew across the yard.

The dog went nuts.

Mort Peyton scrambled on the ground.

Officer Williams panicked and called: "Stop or I'll shoot."

Sadly, Williams forgot the sequence and shot first, pulling the trigger at the exact moment that the little red haired girl threw herself into her father's arms and took the bullet.

Cori took down Williams. Lang rushed around the other side of the house as Finn swooped down and put his hands on the girl. Mort Peyton pulled back, clasping her to him, cradling her head in the crook of his arm.

"My little girl is shot," he wailed. "He shot Bobbi. He shot her."

"Give her up. Give her up," Finn demanded as he

pried the wounded child from him.

The little girl's blood had soaked Mort Peyton's sleeve and, as Finn carried her, it bled into him. He laid her little body on the ground. She was wide-eyed and silent with shock. Georgia Peyton threw herself toward the girl, keening and whimpering and gnashing her teeth. From the shed on the side of the property, another red haired girl peered out at the mayhem, accepting of the bad things happening in her own backyard. Cori slid to a halt next to Finn and put pressure on the girl's wound.

"She's good," Cori said. "The bullet went straight through her shoulder. I've got the paramedics on the way."

"Keep it to yourself," Finn hissed.

Finn stood up and turned on Mort Peyton, towering over the little man, unmoved by his teary eyes, disgusted by his red-splotched face, unsympathetic to the trail of blood from where the fence cut him. Finn O'Brien took the man's shirt collar in his big hands and pulled him up close so that he would not only hear every word Finn O'Brien muttered, but also feel Finn's hot breath and see the deep, cold fury in his eyes.

"You little shit. Look at me! Look at me! I swear, I will let your child die if you don't tell me what I want to know."

"No! No! You can't let my kid die. You're a cop!" Mort dangled and twitched, trying to throw himself to the side to see his daughter. Finn held tighter, near choking the man to get his attention.

"Look at me. Look at me or I'll stuff your tongue down your throat and no one will care if you choke on it. Do you understand me?" Finn threw him against the fence face first, yanking one arm behind him.

"Hey, you can't do this. You gotta read me my rights."

Finn stuffed his hands into the man's pockets. He came up with the money.

"Mort Peyton, I am arresting you for the murder or Alexis and Alana Barnett—"

Finn dug down the front of Mort's pants and came up with the gun.

"Lang!" he called and the cop was on it. Finn handed off the weapon. "Mort Peyton, I am arresting you for the murder of Rachel Gerber."

"I didn't kill no one! I swear—"

"You have the right to remain silent," Finn growled. "Anything you say can and will be used against you in a court of law."

"Bobbi! Is she dead? Oh, God. Oh, God."

The man screamed and cried and Finn pushed him hard into the chain link, talking loud enough for God to hear so there would be no mistaking that he had done everything by the book. He cuffed the man's other hand, perhaps a little more tightly than he should. When that was done, Finn put his lips to Mort's ear.

"That little girl of yours?" Finn whispered. "She is God's payback, man. You take someone's child, God reaches down for yours."

Mort jerked away, but Finn held him tight. He twirled him around and pushed him back up against the fence so it cut into his hands and his back and his head. Finn could only hope that he was pushing hard enough so that the man would be branded by the chain link.

"Ah! Ow! It's cutting me," Mort cried.

"Tell me about the nanny," Finn ordered.

"I want a lawyer."

"I'll let your kid bleed out." Finn's eyes went icy cold as he looked at Mort Peyton and promised: "I will let her die like those poor wee ones you killed. Now, what about the nanny and those children?"

"It was my partner. The kids were a mistake," Mort howled.

"O'Brien," Cori called, but Finn didn't hear her. All he heard was Mort Peyton's voice; all he saw was the killer of Elizabeth Barnett's children.

"Who did the woman?"

"My partner. My partner did it! All of it!" Mort screamed. "I just make sure it goes down."

In the distance, Finn could hear the sirens. He needed to work fast before Mort Peyton's daughter was no longer a bargaining chip.

"Your partner's dead and your kid is fading fast, my man."

Finn took Mort by the scruff of the neck and let him see the child lying on the ground covered in blood. He let him see just long enough to frighten some truth into him. Finn pulled Mort Peyton back and up. They were nose to nose when he said:

"Why did you do it? What did you want?"

"Nothin'. We didn't want nothin'. It was a job," Mort said. "The woman was the mark. That nanny broad."

"And who ordered it? Who?" The sirens were closer now but Peyton wasn't connecting that sound with rescue for his child. Finn pressed his advantage. "I swear, it isn't me who's letting your child die. It's you. You have the power, man. Now who ordered the hit on that woman?"

"Barnett's the name," he screamed. "I don't know

nothin' more than that. My guy gets a gig, he calls me with the place and a date and a name and then I call my partner. The name is insurance. In and out. I don't give a shit why. It was supposed to go down on Sunset but she didn't show so my guy tells us to go to the house 'cause it had to be done that day."

"You're sure it was Barnett who put in the ticket?" Finn insisted.

"Yeah. Yeah," Mort cried. "Now get her help. My kid don't deserve this."

"No, she doesn't," Finn pulled Mort Peyton off the fence and shoved him toward Cori. "Book this bastard, Cori. It was Barnett."

She caught Peyton but handed him off to Lang. She ran after Finn who was dodging the paramedics as they passed one another in the narrow walkway between the houses.

"Don't you go alone, O'Brien. I swear, don't do it," she hollered.

Finn spun around and stormed back to her.

"If I'm needing help, Cori, I'll be the one who asks for it. Don't mess with me on this."

Their eyes locked and for a minute the world went silent. They took no notice of the neighbors standing in the street, red-tinged from the revolving lights of the ambulance. They didn't hear the commotion in Peyton's backyard.

"If you screw this up, you'll be the one behind bars. This time for real, O'Brien."

"I don't care," Finn said. "I want to know why and I want it to be just me and him when I find out."

CHAPTER 45

DAY 10 – NIGHT

Finn climbed the wrought iron gate that was closed across the Barnett's driveway and dropped down. Keeping an eye on the house, he sidestepped to the garage under the hang of the trees, looked through one of the windows that ran across the top of the doors and saw Elizabeth's Jaguar and Sam Barnett's Mercedes.

He pulled his gun and went back the way he came, cutting over at a right angle to the steps that led up to the backdoor, skirting the motion sensors on the outdoor lights. The light over the back door was already on but anyone looking down from upstairs would not be able to see him.

He stayed tight to the wall beside the door that warned him away from the 'happy family' that lived beyond it, and then rolled his head to peer through the window. The nightlight over the stove was on and Finn could see the kitchen was empty. Past that, the dining room was dark.

Finn lay back against the wall again and wrapped the butt of his gun in his t-shirt. Quickly, he stepped in front of the door and tapped the glass. It shattered. He lay back against the wall once more and counted to ten. When the house remained quiet, he stepped in front of the door, put his hand through the broken pane, flipped the lock, and turned the handle.

Easing himself through, he stepped carefully until he was at the foot of the stairs, looking up at the light coming from the girls' room. Finn clasped both hands around his gun, raised his arms and started up the stairs. Every inch of his skin prickled, he heard every beat of his heart and felt the pump of his pulse. He counted to himself as he took each riser:

One.

Two.

Three…

Twelve.

His next step took him to the landing. He inched past the room where Rachel Gerber died and flattened himself against the wall between that door and the one to the girls' room. Finn lowered his weapon but held tight with both hands. He bowed his head, preparing himself to go the next five feet. He was not afraid to face Sam Barnett; he was afraid of what he would do when he did.

Lifting his head, Finn listened to the immense silence in this house of pain. Now he would be the one to inflict more. He would show Elizabeth the man responsible for her children's deaths; he would show her the man she loved and break her heart forever. Then Finn O'Brien stopped thinking as the house filled with the sound of music and the music was coming from the room in front of him. He looked through the crack of the half-opened door and saw a plastic ballerina twirling atop an empty glass box. The sound was so sorrowful that it made Finn want to cry but he was too tired, too done in by the trail of ugly, human failings and frailty he had followed to this point. He did not weep because it would make no difference. The end was near; what was done was done.

Finn pushed the door and let it swing fully open. What he saw made him more sorrowful still. The box springs were still on the bedframe, there were no curtains on the window, but the room was far from empty. The walls were covered with pictures of Alana and Alexis Barnett, Elizabeth and Sam, and pictures of the whole family together. There were pictures taken on vacations, Christmas' celebrated, occasions marked. All were hung helter skelter, willy-nilly, hanging off big nails and small that had been rammed into the walls without care. Little girl clothes hung from the lampshade and the posts of the bed. Stuffed bunnies and bears and lambs sat in rows on the bed where the youngest girl died and, atop the other bed, lay Sam Barnett. Elizabeth stood in the space between.

"Missus," Finn said.

She turned a little and smiled gloriously when she saw him. Elizabeth held a long finger to her beautiful lips.

"Shhh," she warned. "He's not done."

"He can't sleep anymore," Finn said. "I'm needing to talk to him."

"He's not sleeping," she said gently. "He's dying."

When she turned back to look at her husband, Finn saw the gun hanging loosely from her fingers. He moved into the room cautiously and stood at the end of the bed, his eyes on the lawyer but his instinct tuned to Elizabeth.

"I am going to help him now, missus. I'm going to see if we can keep him from doing that." Finn holstered his weapon and inched past Elizabeth, hating to turn his back on her but knowing there was no alternative to it. "Did he do this to himself, missus."

"Oh, yes. Yes, he did," she answered.

"And do you know why?" Finn tried to keep her engaged even as he searched for a sign of a pulse in the lawyer.

"Sam brought terrible things to this house," she sighed. "He never learned, you know. That woman came between us, and then the children died. We could have got past it all. I tried to get him to walk the path with me like the doctor said, but he couldn't do it. He just couldn't live with what he knew."

Finn listened to her, taking in every word as his fingers worked. Finally Finn felt just the faintest sign of life. He saw the bullet hole just above his cheekbone. When he turned the man onto his back he saw that the bullet had exited near the top of his head. There would be no help for him. Even if he were to survive, it was a sure bet he would be a vegetable. Still, Finn had to try. He took hold of the man's shoulders.

"Missus, help me with his feet. We need to get him on the ground. I need him on the—"

Finn stopped talking the minute he felt the muzzle of a gun pushed against his ribs.

"Let him alone." Slowly, Finn let go of the man on the bed and put up his hands as he eased off the box spring. Elizabeth smiled softly. "This is the right thing. I think we should both respect that."

"But I might be able to save him," Finn said.

"Oh, I tried to save him. Many, many times. And this last time. It was a struggle, I mean with the gun and all. It would have been easier if that didn't happen, but it did." Elizabeth shook her head. She looked at her husband and spoke as if she expected him to confirm what she was saying. When he did not move, she sighed. "I loved him so very much. I loved my children. I just couldn't accept what he did. I think you should move away, don't you?"

"You know what he's done?" Finn asked.

"Oh, I know about the money. Richard told me. He said it was a fine line, but he didn't want to take a chance. Sam did. Sam wanted the money and that was beneath him, really. He was smarter than that. And there was Rachel. I know about the bars. I saw pictures of her naked. She was a slut."

"Elizabeth," Finn said. "Give me the gun. Please, missus. Give it to me. You can't let him die no matter what he has done."

"But it's what he wanted. We sat right here and had a long talk and when we finished, when he heard what I had to tell him, Sam said, 'I want to die'. So, I think we should let him."

Even as she said this, Finn saw her hand waver. He stepped forward. He held out his hands: one eased the gun away from her and the other touched her shoulder. When she faltered, he pulled the woman into him. She stood in his arms, rigid and unblinking. He knew what she was feeling because he had felt it himself after the beating. It felt like nothing. It felt as if the world no longer existed, as if the body were something easily discarded because the mind couldn't comprehend what had happened to it in the same way the mind could be discarded when the body was abused.

It took more than a moment but then her arms went

around his waist and her fingers dug into his back. Elizabeth Barnett began to cry.

ONE MONTH LATER

Finn O'Brien and Cori Anderson sat across the desk from one another in their small office as the day wound down. Cori had put him on notice that she was on babysitting duty that night and would leave on the stroke of six. Finn informed her that he intended to be at Mick's by six-thirty so they were even.

They had four new files on their desk – an assault with intent, a cold case with new DNA information, and two murders, one of an old man who ran a bagel shop. They were happy to have them and be back to work. For two weeks they had written reports and been subjected to one interview after another regarding how things went down with Peyton and the Barnetts. The good news was that there was little to be sorted out in the end.

The D.A was moving forward and would prosecute Mort Petyon, the only one in this bloody mess left standing. With any luck, they would find the go-between whose business it was to unleash men like Peyton and Kramer.

The little girl, Roberta, was already home with her mother. Finn couldn't imagine what the future had in store for that family, but he didn't think it was going to be rosy.

Williams had taken the shooting hard. Finn and Cori, if not wholly welcome at Wilshire Division, would be calling it home a while longer.

Cori took up her jacket and had her hand on her purse when Bob Fowler appeared.

"Glad I caught you. This just came in."

"Please don't tell me we're going to be pulling down overtime tonight. I've got to babysit my grandson."

"Not to worry, O'Brien can field it," Fowler said as he handed the paperwork to Cori. "Morning is fine."

"Barnett's autopsy." She passed the paper off to Finn. "Took 'em long enough."

"I'm just glad we got someone to look at him. He wasn't anyone's favorite," Fowler said. "So this will wrap it up. I would have preferred it was a little cleaner, but it is what it is."

Finn set the report on the desk, "Paul's not ruling it a suicide."

"Inconclusive is the best you're going to get considering there was residue on both their hands," Fowler said. "It was impossible for him to shoot himself like that. The man was left handed. But if they struggled the way Mrs. Barnett said, the entry could have looked like that. So let her know she can have someone pick up the body."

"We'll take care of it," Finn answered.

"Want me to do it?" Cori asked, but Finn shook his head.

"I've got it. You go on."

"If I was her, I'd let him rot," Cori said to no one in

particular. "And on that note, I'll be ridin' into the sunset. See you in the a.m."

Fowler took his leave and walked Cori as far as his office. Finn was grateful for a little quiet time. He pulled the jacket on the Barnett case intending to clip the autopsy report inside and be done with it. Instead he fingered the paper work. That little Tinker Bell feeling coming at him again, tiny sparkles in his memory of something he knew he should have caught but didn't.

He pulled out a picture of the Barnett Family in happier times: two beautiful little girls, a handsome blond haired man and a delicately beautiful woman with long black hair who had no idea about the heart ache coming her way. He set aside that photograph. He would take it to Elizabeth when he told her about her husband's body. Perhaps she would be kind to Sam Barnett's memory if she remembered when things were good.

Finn pushed back his chair, put on his jacket and took the Barnett File with him as he went out the door. The desk officer bid him goodnight and Finn O'Brien was pleased. There was at least one man who was willing to speak to him if only to see him off. It was a start.

When he got to Fremont Place, he chatted with the new guard and learned that the wall had been fixed. She was proud to say all was secure and the residents safe. Finn just smiled at that and then drove on, down the wide, tree-lined streets, past the big beautiful houses set back on their carpets of lawn.

He parked in front of the Barnett home and saw there was no car in the driveway and the gates were closed. The house was dark but that did not surprise him. One person living in such a large place needed little light. Finn rang the doorbell but no one came. He ran again, but the house remained quiet.

Finn took the photograph out of his jacket pocket and started to put it in the mail drop, only to change his mind. He wanted to give it to Elizabeth personally. He would come back another day. Finn stepped off the porch just as a car drove in next door. He walked across the lawn and caught Mercedes Coulter before she went into the house.

"Detective O'Brien," she said.

"Missus, how are you?" he asked as they came together.

"We're fine. Thank you so much for asking. I'm glad we've put all that behind us. Charlie and I can't thank you enough for coming that night."

"I'm only sorry it ended as it did."

Mercedes shook her head, "I still can't believe it. I'm usually such a good judge of character. Sam seemed to live and breathe for Elizabeth. It's such a cliché, isn't it? The nanny and all?"

"Yes, ma'am," Finn said. "But I was wondering if you knew when Mrs. Barnett might be home. I have a few things for her that I think will help her through. I didn't want to just drop them in her box."

"She won't be home," Mercedes said. "I assumed she would have told you."

"Told me what?"

"She's gone. She doesn't live here any longer."

"Did she go to live with her mother?"

Mercedes shrugged, "I'm sorry, I really don't know. In fact, the only reason we knew she was gone is because the listing agent came over to let us know they would be having open houses on the weekends soon. I suppose she might know where to find Elizabeth."

"Yes. Yes, I suppose she will. Thank you, missus."

"You're welcome, detective," Mercedes said. She stood watching Finn's back but called to him before he was out of range. "Detective? I know she appreciated what you did."

Finn raised his head, thanking her for the confidence but he said nothing. He got in his car and sat looking at the house as he fiddled with the picture. Finally, he tossed the photo on the seat and headed to Mick's.

"Oh-ho, O'Brien, you be stickin' in de mud tonight."

Geoffrey Baptiste put another pint beside the paper Finn had spread out on the bar. Tonight Geoffrey's beanie was purple and puce. It made Finn cross eyed to look at it.

"I'm busy, my man," Finn said as he swiped up the glass.

"Not too busy for de Guiness."

"Helps me think Geoffrey. Go away. Go talk to Violet."

"Oh, mon, no. She in heat tonight. I be stayin' way away from dat one," Geoffrey said, but still he went off and left Finn alone.

Finn flipped the pages in the Barnett file again, slowly and quickly, hoping one way or the other he would identify something that would stop the niggling in his brain.

He looked at the crime scene diagrams, the statements from the neighbors, the maid, and the gardeners. He looked at the nanny's phone records but saw no incoming call the night of the murders. He rifled through the pages but realized they had not asked for the Barnett's landline records.

Finn turned the page and found himself looking at Sam Barnett's cell record and the notes he had made next to the numbers: Eros Manufacturing, PolyGain's Swiss offices, and other widget manufacturers who he was negotiating with. He turned the page and there were Elizabeth Barnett's phone records. Cori had checked out some of them only to abandon the effort as the investigation closed in on Sam Barnett and Rachel Gerber. Finn ran his finger down the list: hairdresser, a nail salon, the children's schools, the clinic. Finn took another drink and when he looked back again, before he closed the file, he saw something else: three numbers that did not have a local area code nor the area code for San Diego where Elizabeth's mother lived.

Finn drained his glass and took out his phone. He dialed a number called six weeks before the murders and it went nowhere, again two weeks before the murders and another that was made the night before the Barnett's left for Paris. It went were nowhere. Finn cut off the last and set his phone aside.

He went back to the file and ran through, stopping when he found the statement that had come from the Paris Hotel, George V. It had arrived only a week ago. He and Cori had confirmed check-in and check out and nothing more. Finn ran his finger down the first page: spa charges, room charges, taxes, room service. The mister treated his lady like a queen. Finn flipped the page. More of the same. He turned five more pages until he reached the last one and there it was; the call made from France at ten in the morning, the call that rang once, the call that could have stopped everything. It wasn't made to the Barnett home as Finn had assumed, but to a disconnected number that matched the one Elizabeth Barnett had called three times before she left the United States.

Finn threw the file back together and tossed some money on the bar. He pushed through the crowd that had gathered on this Thursday night. Behind him, Geoffrey Baptiste called:

"You be safe der, O'Brien. O'Brien, where do you go so fast? O'Brien?"

Finn parked in front of Run Aways, got out, ignored the people on the street and didn't have a look for the people inside. The man with the helium voice and the *Shillelagh* knocking on his brain was behind the bar. Finn held up the picture of the Barnett family.

"Do you recognize him?"

The big man took one look and shook his head.

"Never saw them before. She's a looker, though."

Finn was out the door a second later, walking down the boulevard looking neither right nor left. Cholo's had a line outside. He pushed through, taking a minute to tell the bouncer to back off for the law when the man tried to stop him. He went in. The bartender was different than the one he had talked to before. He put up the picture.

"Do you know him?" Finn asked.

The man shook his head.

"Her I remember. She was looking for someone to do her a favor. Know what I mean? A big favor."

"You're sure it was her?"

"Considering the way she looked and the kind of

money she was throwing around it would be hard to forget."

Finn slid onto a stool. He put the picture face down on the bar. "Who did you put her in touch with."

The man shook his head. "Nobody. I just got a nice tip for telling her she was in the right place."

"How many times did you see her?"

"Two, maybe three times. She must have found what she was looking for. I haven't seen her for a while. Are we good? I have to work."

Finn nodded. He put his head in his hands and knew Mort Peyton had been right. It was Barnett who hired them, Finn just had the wrong Barnett.

I want to see who killed my children.

The children weren't supposed to be home. Only the nanny.

I didn't have to see them together.

She had imagined an affair between Rachel and her husband.

I know all about my wife. I'll get her the help she needs.

Elizabeth Barnett: smart, passionate, paranoid and dangerous.

After I told him what I'd done, Sam said 'I want to die'.

Elizabeth Barnett who liked things just so in her life, the woman who couldn't bear anything out of place in her kingdom, had killed her husband, the man she blamed for her imagined trials and tribulations.

If only he had listened to the lawyer, if only he had read between the lines when Elizabeth told her half-truths, if only he hadn't been blinded by a mother's pain, Sam Barnett would be alive today.

Three shots later, Finn left Cholo's with the picture of

the Barnett family in his pocket. He walked the two blocks back to his car and got in. For a long while he sat in the dark thinking about what had happened, about where he had gone wrong, about how every mother's heart does not crack like crystal or like pottery because some mothers have hearts of stone that never broke. Finn O'Brien put the key in the ignition and as he pulled away from the curb, he thought about how you can't believe everything you read — not even the golden script painted on a cornflower-colored door.

A happy family never did live in a Tudor mansion in Fremont Place.

Elizabeth pushed her chin into the collar of her coat, lowering her head against the crisp spring air.

To her left, Notre Dame loomed in the gathering darkness. To her right the Seine cut its way through Paris, dark and dirty. Once over the bridge that had led to the Left Bank, she turned into the bookseller, rummaged in her purse for the proper number of Euro and paid for her papers. It would, she decided, be cheaper to learn to read French than pay such prices for the English papers. Not that she couldn't afford it. Sam had been thorough in his planning for the future and she had more money than she could ever use. Not to mention the money left over from selling her jewelry. She had been surprised at the price tag on human life. But what happened to her children taught her a good lesson: a bargain always had unexpected costs.

She stopped for a butter and sugar crepe from a street vendor before heading back to the Hotel De L'Europe. When she reached the Rue St. Severin, she hurried along, shaking her head as she declined a barker's offer to enjoy a feast inside one of the many Greek restaurants that lined the glorified alley. She pulled on the glass door and slipped into the small lobby. The young girl at the desk wished her good evening and gave Elizabeth her room key. Elizabeth thanked her, looked into the small sitting room as she did every time she came into the hotel. She saw no one suspicious, smiled at the girl again and climbed the four flights of narrow steps to her small room.

Elizabeth took off her coat and hung it in the armoire and then sat on the bed and spread out her newspapers. Below her window, music students sang and played their violins in the hopes of picking up a few Euro. Elizabeth would fall asleep to the sound of the music. She loved that about this hotel. So much better than George V where everything was silent as a tomb.

She also liked this room. It was small and she could see into every corner. She slept better when things were close. But the room was too small even for a chair by the window so she sat on the edge of the bed looking out. Sam would not have liked this hotel. He liked grander things.

He could be such a silly man.

Elizabeth remembered his surprise when she raised the gun. He thought she was going to hurt herself when she was simply going to put him out of his misery. That should have come as no surprise. Hadn't he said he wanted to die after he heard what she had done? There was, of course, a little bit of payback for the heartache he had caused her, but killing him was mostly an act of love. He fought well but the outcome was inevitable. If he had survived Sam would have put her in jail or a hospital and

Elizabeth couldn't have that.

Then the moment was over. Sam was fading from her memory. Even the girls were hard to remember. Elizabeth opened the first newspaper wide and took a pen out of her bag. She circled a few ads for available apartments, but found her mind wandering again. Her thoughts went to another man: Finn O'Brien. He would like this hotel, and he had liked her. She knew that from the moment they met. She liked him. They were quite alike; both of them wanting to tie up lose ends, both of them wanting to do the right thing.

Elizabeth thought that one day she would send him the white leather, gold-tooled diary so that he would know exactly what had happened inside her home in Fremont Place. It really would be the right thing to do; it would be like a thank you gift for all his hard work. Yes, Elizabeth wondered about Finn O'Brien. She wondered if he was thinking about her…

Just a little…

Now and again…

Then she pulled the newspaper back onto her lap. Resting one elbow on the windowsill, Elizabeth put her head against her hand. She perused the listings as her fingers toyed with her short blonde hair. While she read, she dreamed of the perfect home she would make for herself. It would have to be big enough to share with the perfect man who she was sure to meet, and with the perfect babies that she was sure to have. And as she circled an ad for an apartment that sounded absolutely perfect for her, Elizabeth Barnett hummed the tune that a plastic ballerina danced to atop the music box she had brought with her to Paris.

WATCH FOR THE NEXT
FINN O'BRIEN/CORI ANDERSON THRILLER

FOREIGN RELATIONS

NEED MORE THRILLS RIGHT NOW?
START READING BOOK #1
OF THE WITNESS SERIES

HOSTILE WITNESS IS **FREE** AT YOUR
FAVORITE ONLINE BOOKSTORE

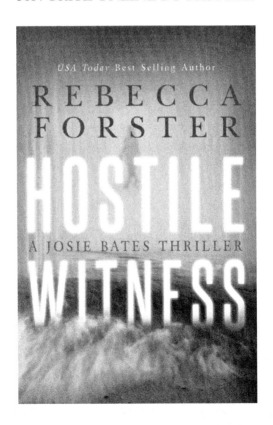

PROLOGUE

Today California buried Supreme Court Justice, Fritz Rayburn. Governor Joe Davidson delivered the eulogy calling the judge a friend, a confidant, and his brother in service to the great state of California. The governor cited Fritz Rayburn as a man of extraordinary integrity who relentlessly pursued justice, continually uplifted those in need and, above all, protected those who were powerless.

It was a week ago today that Judge Rayburn died in a fire that swept through his Pacific Palisades home in the early morning hours.

No formal announcement has been made regarding who will be appointed to fill Justice Rayburn's position, but it is speculated that Governor Davidson will appoint Rayburn's son, Kip, to this pivotal seat on the California Supreme Court.

KABC News at 9 O'clock.

CHAPTER 1

"Strip."

"No."

Hannah kept her eyes forward, trained on two rows of rusted showerheads stuck in facing walls. Sixteen in all. The room was paved with white tile, chipped and discolored by age and use. Ceiling. Floor. Walls. All sluiced with disinfectant. Soiled twice a day by filth and fear. The fluorescent lights cast a yellow shadow over everything. The air was wet. The shower room smelled of mold and misery. It echoed with the cries of lost souls.

Hannah had come in with a bus full of women. She had a name, now she was a number. The others were taking off their clothes. Their bodies were ugly, their faces worn. They flaunted their ugliness as if it were a cruel joke, not on them but on those who watched. Hannah was everything they were not. Beautiful. Young. She wouldn't stand naked in this room with these women. She blinked and wrapped her arms around herself. Her breath came short. A step back and she fooled herself that it was possible to turn and leave. Behind her Hannah thought she heard the guard laugh.

"Take it off, Sheraton, or I'll do it for you."

Hannah tensed, hating to be ordered. She kept her

eyes forward. She had already learned to do that.

"There's a man back there. I saw him," she said.

"We're an equal opportunity employer, sweetie," the woman drawled. "If women can guard male prisoners then men can guard the women. Now, who's it going to be? Me or him?"

The guard touched her. Hannah shrank away. Her head went up and down, the slightest movement, the only way she could control her dread. She counted the number of times her chin went up. *Ten counts.* Her shirt was off. Her chin went down. Ten more counts and she dropped the jeans that had cost a fortune.

"All of it, baby cakes," the guard prodded.

Hannah closed her eyes. *The thong. White lace.* That was the last. Quickly she stepped under a showerhead and closed her eyes. A tear seeped from beneath her lashes only to be washed away by a sudden, hard, stinging spray of water. Her head jerked back as if she'd been slapped then Hannah lost herself in the wet and warm. She turned her face up, kept her arms closed over her breasts, pretended the sheet of water hid her like a cloak. As suddenly as it had been turned on the water went off. She had hidden from nothing. The ugly women were looking back, looking her over. Hannah went from focus to fade, drying off with the small towel, pulling on the too-big jumpsuit. She was drowning in it, tripping over it. Her clothes – her beautiful clothes – were gone. She didn't ask where.

The other women talked and moved as if they had been in this place so often it felt like home. Hannah was cut from the pack and herded down the hall, hurried past big rooms with glass walls and cots lined up military style.

She slid her eyes toward them. Each was occupied. Some women slept under blankets, oblivious to their surroundings. Others were shadows that rose up like specters, propping themselves on an elbow, silently watching Hannah pass.

Clutching her bedding, Hannah put one foot in front of the other, eyes down, counting her steps so she wouldn't be tempted to look at all those women. There were too many steps. Hannah lost track and began again. *One. Two...*

"Here."

A word stopped her. The guard rounded wide to the right as if Hannah was dangerous. That was a joke. She couldn't hurt anyone – not really. The woman pushed open a door. The cock of her head said this was Hannah's place. A room, six by eight. A metal-framed bed and stained mattress. A metal toilet without a lid. A metal sink. No mirror. Hannah hugged her bedding tighter and twirled around just as the woman put her hands on the door to close it.

"Wait! You have to let me call my mom. Take me to a phone right now so I can check on her."

Hannah talked in staccato. A water droplet fell from her hair and hit her chest. It coursed down her bare skin and made her shiver. It was so cold. This was all so cold and so awful. The guard was unmoved.

"Bed down, Sheraton," she said flatly.

Hannah took another step. "I told you I just want to check on her. Just let me check on her. I won't talk long."

"And I told you to bed down." The guard stepped out. The door was closing. Hannah was about to call again when the woman in blue with the thick wooden club on her belt decided to give her a piece of advice. "I wouldn't count on any favors, Sheraton. Judge Rayburn was one of us, if you get my meaning. It won't matter if you're here or anywhere else. Everyone will know who you are. Now make your bed up."

The door closed. Hannah hiccoughed a sob as she spread her sheet on the thin mattress. She tucked it under only to pull it out over and over again. Finally satisfied she put the blanket on, lay down and listened. The sound of slow footsteps echoed through the complex. Someone was crying. Another woman shouted. She shouted again and then she screamed. Hannah stayed quiet, barely breathing. They had taken away her clothes. They had touched her where no one had ever touched her before. They had moved her, stopped her, pointed and ordered her, but at this point Hannah couldn't remember who had done any of those things. Everyone who wasn't dressed in orange was dressed in blue. The blue people had guns and belts filled with bullets and clubs that they caressed as if they were treasured pets. These people seemed at once bored with their duty and thrilled with their power. They hated Hannah and she didn't even know their names.

Hannah wanted her mother. She wanted to be in her room. She wanted to be anywhere but here. Hannah even wished Fritz wouldn't be dead if that would get her home. She was going crazy. Maybe she was there already.

Hannah got up. She looked at the floor and made a plan. She would ask to call her mother again. She would ask politely because the way she said it before didn't get her anything. Hannah went to the door of her – *cell*. A hard enough word to think, she doubted she could ever say it. She went to the door and put her hands against it.

It was cold, too. Metal. There was a window in the center. Flat white light slid through it. Hannah raised her fist and tapped the glass. *Once, twice, three, ten times.* Someone would hear. *Fifteen. Twenty.* Someone would come and she would tell them she didn't just *want* to check on her mother; she would tell them she *needed* to do that. This time she would say please.

Suddenly something hit up against the glass. Hannah fell back. Stumbling over the cot, she landed near the toilet in the corner. This wasn't her room in the Palisades. This was a small, cramped place. Hannah clutched at the rough blanket and pulled it off the bed as she sank to the floor. Her heart beat wildly. Huddled in the dark corner, she could almost feel her eyes glowing like some nocturnal animal. She was transfixed by what she saw. A man was looking in, staring at her as if she were nothing. Oh God, he could see her even in the dark. Hannah pulled her knees up to her chest and peeked from behind them at the man who watched.

His skin was pasty, his eyes plain. A red birthmark spilled across his right temple and half his eyelid until it seeped into the corner of his nose. He raised his stick, black and blunt, and tapped on the glass. He pointed toward the bed. She would do what he wanted. Hannah opened her mouth to scream at him. Instead, she crawled up on to the cot. Her feet were still on the floor. The blanket was pulled over her chest and up into her chin. The guard looked at her – all of her. He didn't see many like this. So young. So pretty. He stared at Hannah as if he owned her. Voices were raised somewhere else. The man didn't seem to notice. He just looked at Hannah until she yelled 'go away' and threw the small, hard pillow at him.

He didn't even laugh at that ridiculous gesture. He just disappeared. When Hannah was sure he was gone she began to pace. Holding her right hand in her left she walked up and down her cell and counted the minutes until her mother would come to get her.

Counting. Counting. Counting again.

Behind the darkened windows of the Lexus, the woman checked her rear view mirror. Damn freeways. It was nine-friggin'-o'clock at night and she still had to slalom around a steady stream of cars. She stepped on the gas – half out of her mind with worry.

One hundred.

Hannah should be with her.

One hundred and ten.

Hannah must be terrified.

The Lexus shimmied under the strain of the speed.

She let up and dropped to ninety five.

They wouldn't even let her see her daughter. She didn't have a chance to tell Hannah not to talk to anyone. But Hannah was smart. She'd wait for help. Wouldn't she be smart? *Oh, God, Hannah. Please, please be smart.*

Ahead a pod of cars pooled as they approached Martin Luther King Boulevard. Crazily she thought they looked like a pin setup at the bowling alley. Not that she visited bowling alleys anymore but she made the connection. It would be so easy to end it all right here – just keep going like a bowling ball and take 'em all down in one fabulous strike. It sure as hell would solve all her problems. Maybe even Hannah would be better off. Then again, the people in those cars might not want to end theirs so definitely.

Never one to like collateral damage if she could avoid it, the woman went for the gutter, swinging onto the shoulder of the freeway, narrowly missing the concrete divider that kept her from veering into oncoming traffic. She was clear again, leaving terror in her wake, flying toward her destination.

The Lexus transitioned to the 105. It was clear sailing all the way to Imperial Highway where the freeway came to an abrupt end, spitting her out onto a wide intersection before she was ready. The tires squealed amid the acrid smell of burning rubber. The Lexus shivered, the rear end fishtailing as she fought for control. Finally, the car came to a stop, angled across two lanes.

The woman breathed hard. She sniffled and blinked and listened to her heartbeat. She hadn't realized how fast she'd been going until just this minute. Her head whipped around. *No traffic.* A dead spot in the maze of LA freeways, surface streets, transitions and exits. Her hands were fused to the steering wheel. *Thank God. No cops.* Cops were the last thing she wanted to see tonight; the last people she ever wanted to see.

Suddenly her phone rang. She jumped and scrambled, forgetting where she had put it. Her purse? The console? The console. She ripped it open and punched the button to stop the happy little song that usually signaled a call from her hairdresser, an invitation to lunch.

"What?"

"This is Lexus Link checking to see if you need assistance."

"What?"

"Are you all right, ma'am? Our tracking service indicated that you had been in an accident."

Her head fell onto the steering wheel; the phone was still at her ear. She almost laughed. Some minimum wage idiot was worried about her.

"No, I'm fine. Everything's fine," she whispered and turned off the phone. Her arm fell to her side. The phone fell to the floor. A few minutes later she sat up and pushed back her hair. She'd been through tough times before. Everything would be fine if she just kept her wits about her and got where she was going. Taking a deep breath she put both hands back on the wheel. She'd damn well finish what she started the way she always did. As long as Hannah was smart they'd all be okay.

Easing her foot off the brake she pulled the Lexus around until she was in the right lane and started to drive. She had the address, now all she had to do was to find friggin' Hermosa Beach.

❧

"For God's sake, Josie, he's a weenie-wagger and that's all there is to it. I don't know why you keep coming in here with the same old crap for a defense. Want some?"

Judge Crawford pushed the pizza box her way. It was almost nine o'clock and they had managed to work out the details on the judge's sponsorship at the Surf Festival, discuss a moot court for which they had volunteered, polish off most of a large pizza, and now Josie was trying to take advantage of the situation by putting in a pitch for leniency for one of her clients.

She passed on the pizza offer. Judge Crawford took another piece. He was a good guy, a casual guy, a local who never strayed from his beach town roots in his thirty-year legal career. His robes were tossed on the couch behind them. His desk served as a workstation and dining table. In the corner was his first surfboard. New attorneys called to chambers endured forty-five minutes of the judge reliving his moments of glory as one of the best long boarders on the coast. Three years ago, when Josie landed in Hermosa Beach, she got the full two-hour treatment but only because she knew a thing or two about surfing from her days in Hawaii. She'd spent the extra hour with Judge Crawford because he knew a thing or two about volleyball.

Josie Baylor-Bates had been big at USC but when she hit the sand circuit she'd become legendary. Everyone wanted to beat the woman who stood six feet if she was an inch, played like a professional, and won like a champion. Few did, but they started trying the minute the summer nets went up. Of course USC and Judge Crawford's surfing days were both more than a few years ago, but still their beach history tied them together, made them friendly colleagues, and gave them license to be a little more informal about certain protocols – including the judge speaking his mind about Josie's current client, Billy Zuni: the surfing-teenage-beach bum with a mischievous smile and penchant for relieving himself in city owned bushes.

"That's a gross term," Josie scoffed as if she'd never heard of a weenie-wagger before. "And it is not appropriate in this instance. I've got documentation from their family doctor that Billy has a physical problem. He's tried to use the bathrooms in the shops off the Strand, but nobody will let him in."

"That's because Billy seems to forget he's supposed to lower his cutoffs *after* he gets into the bathroom, not before," the judge reminded her. "Nope, this time he's got to stay in the pokey. Hey, it's Hermosa Beach's pokey. Five cells and they're all empty. Billy will have the whole place to himself. It's not going to kill him, and it may do him some good. I'm tired of that damn kid's file coming across my desk every three months."

"Your Honor, it's obvious you are prejudiced against my client," Josie objected, pushing aside the pizza box.

"Cool your jets, Josie. What are you going to do, bring me up on charges for name calling?" Judge Crawford laughed heartily. His little belly shook. It was hard to imagine him on a long board or any other kind of board for that matter. "Listen. I understand that kid's got problems. You're in here like clockwork swearing he'll be supervised. I know you check up on him. Everyone at the beach knows that, but you can't do what his own mother can't."

"That's exactly the point. Jail time won't mean a thing. What if I can find someone who'll take him for a week? Will you consider house arrest?"

"With you?" The judge raised a brow.

"Archer," Josie answered without reservation.

Judge Crawford chuckled. "Not a bad idea. Sort of like setting up boot camp in paradise. That would make Billy sit up and take notice. I don't know anybody who wouldn't toe the line just to get Archer off their back."

Josie touched her lips to hide a smile. Judge Crawford steered clear of Archer after a vigorous debate on the unfortunate constitutions of judges facing re-election. As Josie recalled, words such as wimps and sell-outs had been bandied about freely. It wasn't that Archer was wrong, it was just that the opinion was coming from a retired cop who wasn't afraid of anything, who got better looking with age, and could still sit a board while the judge… Well, suffice it to say the judge had been sitting the bench a little too long.

"Archer might do Billy some good," Josie pushed for her plan.

"Or scar him for life." Crawford shook his head and pushed off the desk. "Sorry, Josie. It's going to be forty-eight hours this time and community service. Best I can do."

"I'll appeal. There are a hundred surfers down on the beach changing from their wet suits into dry clothes every morning. Half of them don't even bother to drape a towel over their butts. The only reason you catch Billy is because he's stupid. He thinks everybody ought to just kick back – including the cops."

Crawford stood up, put the rest of the pizza in his little refrigerator, and plucked his windbreaker with the reflective patches off the door hook as he talked.

"That's cute. You still think you're playing with the big boys downtown? Josie, Josie," he chuckled. "What's it been? Three years and you still can't get it through your head that Billy Zuni and his little wooden monkey wouldn't rate the paperwork for an appeal. Let him be. They'll feed him good in Hermosa."

"Okay, so I can't put the fear of God into you." Josie shrugged and got to her feet.

"Only if you're on the other side of volleyball net, Ms.

Bates. Only then." Judge Crawford ushered Josie outside with a quick gesture. She waited on the wooden walkway as he locked up.

The Redondo Courts were made up of low-slung, whitewashed, Cape Cod style buildings with marine blue trim. All the beach cities did business here. It was a far cry from downtown's imposing courthouses and city smells. Redondo Beach Court was perched on the outskirts of King Harbor Pier where the air smelled like salt and sun. Downtown attorneys fought holy wars, and life and death battles, while standing on marble floors inside wood paneled courtrooms. Here, court felt like hitting the town barbershop for a chaw with the mayor. Sometimes Josie missed being a crusader. The thought of one more local problem, and one more local client, made her long for what she once had been: a headline grabber, a tough cookie, a lawyer whose ambition and future knew no bounds. But that was just sometimes. Mostly, Josie Baylor-Bates was grateful that she no longer spoke for anyone who had enough money to pay her fee. She had learned that evil had the fattest wallet and most chaste face of all. Josie could not be seduced by either any more.

"You walking?" Judge Crawford called to her from the end of the walk.

"No." Josie ambled toward him.

"Want me to walk you to your car?" the judge offered.

"Don't worry about it. This isn't exactly a tough town, and if another Billy Zuni is hanging around I'll sign him up as a client."

"Okay. Let me know if you and Faye are in on that sponsorship for the Surf Festival."

"Will do," Josie answered and started to walk toward

the parking lot. The judge stopped her.

"Hey, Josie, I forgot. Congratulations are in order. It's great that you're signing on as Faye's rainmaker."

Josie laughed, "We're going to be partners, Judge. I don't think there's a lot of rain to be made around here."

"Well, glad to hear it anyway. Baxter & Bates has a nice ring, and Faye's a good woman."

"Don't I know it," Josie said.

Faye Baxter was more than friend or peer; she was a champion, a confessor, a sweetheart who partnered with her husband until his death. Josie was honored that now Faye wanted her, and Josie was going to be the best damn partner she could be.

Waving to the judge, Josie crossed the deserted plaza, took the steps down to the lower level parking and tossed her things in the back of the Jeep. She was about to swing in when she caught the scent of cooking crab, the cacophony of arcade noise, the Friday night frantic fun of Redondo's King Harbor Pier and decided to take a minute. Wandering across the covered parking lot she exited onto the lower level of the two-storied pier complex.

The sun had been down for hours but it was still blister-hot. To her right the picnic tables in the open-air restaurants were filled. People whacked crabs with little silver hammers, sucked the meat from the shells, and made monumental messes. On the left, bells and whistles, and screams of laughter from the arcade. Out of nowhere three kids ran past, jabbering in Spanish, giggling in the universal language. Josie stepped forward but not far enough. A beehive of blue cotton candy caught her hip. She brushed it away and walked on, drawn, not to the noise, but to the boats below the pier.

These were working craft that took sightseers into the harbor, pulled up the fish late at night; they had seen better days and were named after women and wishes. The boats were tethered to slips that creaked with the water's whim and bobbed above rocks puckered with barnacles. Josie loved the sense of silence, the feeling that each vessel held secrets, the dignity of even the smallest of them. The ropes that held these boats tight could just as easily break in an unexpected storm. They would drift away like people did if there was nothing to tie them down or hold them steady.

Josie leaned on the weather worn railing and lost her thoughts to the heat and the sounds and the look of that cool, dark water. At peace, she wasn't ready when something kicked up – a breeze, a bump of a hull – something familiar that threw her back in time. Emily Baylor-Bates was suddenly there. A vision in the water. The Lady of the Lake. Yet instead of the sacred sword, the image of Josie's mother held out sharp-edged memories. Josie should have walked away, but she never did when Emily came to call.

Even after all these years she could see her mother's face clearly in that water. Emily's eyes were like Josie's but bluer, wider, and clearer. They shared the square-jaw and high cheekbones, but the whole of Emily's face was breathtakingly beautiful, where her daughter's was strikingly handsome. Her mother's hair was black-brown with streaks of red and gold. Josie's was chestnut. Her expression was determined like Josie's but...but what?

What was her mother determined to do? What had been more important than a husband and a daughter *A good daughter, damn it.* What made her mother – even now after all these years she could barely think the word – *abandon* her? Why would a woman cast off a fourteen year old without a word, or a touch? There one night, gone the next morning.

Suddenly the water was disturbed. Emily Baylor-Bates' face disappeared in the rings of ever widening concentric circles. Startled, Josie stood up straight. Above her a group of teenagers hung over the railing dropping things into the water. They laughed cruelly thinking they had frightened Josie, unaware that she was grateful to them. The water was mesmerizing, the memories as dangerous as an undertow. Emily had been gone for twenty-six years. *Twenty-six years,* Josie reminded herself as she strode to the parking lot, swung into her Jeep, turned the key, and backed out. The wheels squealed on the slick concrete. She knew a hundred years wouldn't make her care less. Time wouldn't dull the pain or keep her from wanting to call her mother back. On her deathbed, Josie would still be wondering where her mother was, why she had gone, whether she was dead, or just didn't give a shit about her daughter. But tonight, in the eleven minutes it took to drive from Redondo Beach to Hermosa Beach, Josie put those questions back into that box deep inside her mind. By the time she tossed her keys on the table and ruffled Max-The-Dog's beautiful old face, that box was locked up tight.

The dog rewarded Josie with a sniff and a lick against her cheek. It took five minutes to finish the routine: working clothes gone, sweats and t-shirt on, and her mail checked. Faye had dropped off the partnership papers before leaving for San Diego and a visit with her new grandson. The tile man had piled a ton of Spanish pavers near the backdoor for Josie to lay at her leisure. The house of her dreams – a California bungalow on the Strand – was being renovated at a snail's pace, but Josie was determined to do the work herself. She would make her own home; a place where no one invited in would ever want to leave.

In the kitchen, Josie checked out a nearly empty fridge as she dialed Archer. It was late, but if he were home it wouldn't take much to convince him that he needed to feed her. Josie was punching the final digits of Archer's number when Max rubbed up against her leg, wuffing and pointing his graying snout toward the front door. Josie looked over her shoulder and patted his head, but Max woofed again. She was just about to murmur her assurances when the house seemed to rock. Snarling, Max fell back on his haunches. Josie let out a shout. Someone had thrown themselves against the front door, and whoever was out there wanted in bad. The new door was solid, the deadbolt impossible to break, but the sound scared the shit out of her. The doorknob jiggled frantically for a second before everything fell quiet – everything except Josie's heart and Max's guttural growl.

Bending down, Josie buried one hand in the fur and folds of his head. With the other she picked up the claw hammer from the tool pile. Standing, she smiled at Max. His eyebrows undulated, silently asking if everything was all right now. For an instant Josie thought it might be, until whoever was out there flew at the door with both fists.

"Damn." Josie jumped. Max fell back again, snapping and barking.

Clutching the hammer, Josie sidestepped to the door. She slipped two fingers under the curtain covering the narrow side-window and pulled the fabric back a half an inch. A woman twirled near the hedge. Her head whipped from side to side as she looked for a way into the house. Her white slacks fit like a second skin, and her chiffon blouse crisscrossed over an impressive chest. A butter colored belt draped over her slim hips. Her come-fuck-me sandals had crepe-thin soles and heels as high as a wedding cake. This wasn't a Hermosa Beach babe and Josie had two choices: call the cops or find out what kind of trouble this woman was in. No contest. Josie flipped the lock and threw open the door.

The woman froze; trembling as if surprised to find someone had actually answered. She started forward and raised her hand, took a misstep and crumpled. Instinctively, Josie reached for her. The hammer fell to the floor as the woman clutched at Josie's arm.

"You're here," she breathed.

Close up now, Josie saw her more clearly. The dark hair was longer than she remembered. The heart-shaped face was still perfect save for the tiny scar on the corner of her wide lips. Those long fingered hands that held Josie were as strong as they'd always been. But it was the high arch of the woman's eyebrows and her small, exquisitely green eyes that did more than prick Josie's memory; they shot an arrow clear through it. It had been almost twenty years since Josie had seen those eyes, and the face that looked like a heroine from some Russian revolutionary epic.

"Linda? Linda Sheraton?"

"Oh, God, Josie, please help me."

MORE BOOKS BY REBECCA FORSTER

USA TODAY & AMAZON
BEST SELLING THRILLERS

THE WITNESS SERIES

Hostile Witness (#1)
Silent Witness (#2)
Privileged Witness (#3)
Expert Witness (#4)
Eyewitness (#5)
Forgotten Witness (#6)
Dark Witness (#7)
The Witness Series Bundle (7 books)

MORE AWARD WINNING THRILLERS

Before Her Eyes
Beyond Malice
Character Witness
The Mentor
Keeping Counsel

Don't miss new release announcements, news about appearances and more. Just send me a note from my website and I'll put you on the list.

RebeccaForster.com

As always, thank you so much for adding my work to your reading list, jotting me a note or writing a review. I truly appreciate it.

ABOUT THE AUTHOR

 Rebecca Forster wrote her first book on a crazy dare and found her passion. Now, with over thirty novels to her name, she is both a USA Today and Amazon best selling thriller author.

Rebecca has taught at UCLA's acclaimed Writers Program. She has been a featured speaker at writing conferences, women's groups and bar associations. Residing in Southern California, she is married to a superior court judge and is the mother of two sons.

CPSIA information can be obtained
at www.ICGtesting.com
Printed in the USA
LVOW13s1427010917
547242LV00020B/582/P